The Last Track

The Last Track

A Mike Brody Novel

by

Sam Hilliard

Buddhapuss Ink   Edison, NJ

Cover Design by Elynn Cohen

Book Design by The Book Team

Author Photo by Charissa Meredith Carroll

Library of Congress Control Number: 2009944195

First Edition

ISBN 978-0-9842035-0-5 (Hardcover)

ISBN 978-0-9842035-1-2 (Paperback)

First Printing February 2010

PUBLISHER'S NOTE

www.buddhapussink.com

For my Mother
and her new birthday,
February 11, 2009

Day One

S ean Jackson counted to four and exhaled. Deep in flight mode, his heart pounded furiously. One thought drove him: he had to make it to the Pine Woods Ranch without being seen.

Because he had been spotted on the main road earlier, he needed an alternate course. Eight miles in the opposite direction was a gas station near the highway on-ramp. Inside were a phone and an attendant. But Sean figured that eight miles could take an hour, which made the filling station hardly an option at all. The ranch, however, was less than a mile out. Even if someone was waiting at the gates for him, heading toward lots of people was much safer than banking on a solitary clerk. And once he explained to his parents what had happened, everything would be fine. They would understand.

Until then, the fewer chances he might be spotted, the better. Facing west, twin mountain caps caught his attention. Their shape was familiar. For the last six days, each time he had seen them from the ranch, he had wished he was back in Brooklyn.

Sean pushed his glasses back up along the bridge of his nose. Usually when he shifted them around, his fingers smudged the lenses. This time they stayed clean.

Committing to his course, he tore through the trees, one eye on the mountains. He stuck tight against the tree line, away from the road. A voice deep inside said not to run full out yet, to save the reserves until he drew closer.

Minutes passed. His inhaler rattled in his pocket. Sean thought he would be near the gates by now. Questioning his chosen route, he hesitated. He stared up at the towering Douglas firs; the pines were so much taller than the maples in Grove Park. Everything about Montana seemed larger.

He glanced behind, mentally retracing his path to this point. In his mind's eye he had moved just as he had planned. He ran again. Swung left, gunned for the road, and burrowed deeper into the woods. But something had gone wrong. He was not where he had expected to be.

Five more minutes elapsed.

Every direction he turned, every step he took, only led to more trees.

07:14:32 PM

Mike Brody inhaled. He was tired from the drive to Montana, too tired for the red and blue lights flashing on the row of police cars. Past the lights and vehicles, a sawhorse blocked the entrance to the Pine Woods Ranch. After a sixteen-hour road trip, this was the last straw. For the sake of his son napping in the back and his ex-wife riding in the passenger seat, Mike checked his displeasure. He kept quiet and rolled up slowly.

An officer with a clipboard hailed them. Since Mike's ex-wife had made the arrangements, the reservations were in her name. The number of people in the truck matched the number of guests listed under Jessica Barrett: three. Jessica, like many women, had never changed her name when she married.

Satisfied there was nothing to worry about, the officer removed the sawhorses and let the truck pass. As they started through the gate, the officer's eyes locked on Mike Brody's side of the truck.

"S&B Outfitters," the officer said, reading the decal on the side of the truck out loud. "You're Mike Brody?" Mike nodded. Facing away from them, the officer called to a plainclothes officer in khakis. "Lisbeth! It's him."

Jessica sighed, leaning toward the driver's-side window.

With a face that put strangers at ease, people often thought they had met Mike Brody before. A feature last month in *News Story* made his face even more recognizable.

"Fantastic. Just who I was looking for." The plainclothes officer offered Mike a card: Lisbeth McCarthy, Detective. She had shoulder-length black hair and the look of someone not afraid to get dirty.

Lisbeth said, "After you check in, let's talk."

"What's this about?" Jessica asked before Mike could. There was just enough tension in her voice for Mike to notice, yet not enough to put off a stranger.

"I just have a few questions for Mike," Lisbeth said. "My cell number is on the back."

The tires scattered dust and stones on the dirt road as he drove away. Mike knew what Jessica was thinking. Was he planning to meet Lisbeth or not? Right now all he cared about was the deadline for check-in, and after that, taking a hot shower. Sixteen hours split across two days was half a lifetime road-tripping with an ex-wife and an eight-year-old.

"Are you going to speak with her?" Jessica asked.

Mike answered by glancing back in the rearview mirror at their son.

At the main lodge, an error in the computer system had morphed their reservation for two rooms with two doubles into a single room with two twins. The mistake—the attendant apologized repeatedly for it—was unfortunate. But because of overbooking, a proper resolution had to wait until the morning. The attendant promised to bring a cot to their room. An hour later, it still hadn't arrived.

On the plus side, the accommodations matched the description in the ads. The lodge itself was a massive ranch-style building. Thick, exposed wood beams supported a vaulted ceiling, giving the rooms a log-cabin feel. Hand-carved furniture—oversized, as if scaled for giants—lined the walls. A bearskin rug covered the floor between the beds. A generous window directly opposite the door offered a stunning view of the landscape, which included a snow-tipped mountain range.

The idea for the trip started right before Mike and Jessica had separated. Both had agreed this was a vacation they wanted. Even as the marriage dissolved, each detail of the trip fell into place effortlessly, as if the vacation was immune to their marital problems. While many things had changed with the divorce—longstanding rituals terminated, assets redistributed—part of their relationship survived. When it came to their son, they avoided conflict and agreed on what made sense for him. So they had kept their promise to Andy and each other. Now they were in Montana at a dude ranch for a week, under the big sky, a twenty-five minute drive from any decent-sized city.

A gray-and-white striped cat slept on a couch near the main entrance of the building. Once they unpacked and settled in, Andy stepped into the lobby to pet it, leaving his parents alone for a moment. The door remained open so they could see him.

"I really like the looks of this place," Jessica said. And then she added more quietly, "Sorry about my tone with Lisbeth before. These obstacles at the last minute get me."

"You and me both," Mike said.

Seated at the edge of the bed, Jessica flipped through pamphlets about the ranch. "There's an article here," she said. "I can see it. Twenty-first century meets cowboy. Wireless Internet access, and lunch from a cast-iron pot over a fire. Modern luxuries and nature's wonders. The best of both worlds." She jotted the last bit in her planner. Anything important to her found its way to the pages, sooner or later. "And I can't wait to ride the horses."

When Andy returned, Mike showered. The hot water relaxed his muscles. Lisbeth's invitation wandered into his thoughts. *After you check in, let's talk,* Lisbeth had said. He had checked in. That left the conversation.

After he dressed, he said, "Think I'll go find out about that cot."

"Is that your cover?" Her question sounded nothing like a question at all. Jessica was good at making questions sound like statements, and statements like questions. The mark of a journalist.

"It's better than sleeping on a hardwood floor," said Mike.

"This missing cot is a bit convenient," said Jessica. She had Mike's number. She always had Mike's number.

Relenting, he said, "I may pop by and chat with Lisbeth."

"Please stay out of this one," Jessica said. "Not for me. For Andy. We're on vacation."

"It'll be fine." He stood in the doorway. "They just want to talk."

"Mike, this is not the first time it's started like this . . ."

08:39:52 PM

Finding the check-in area closed, Mike left the Navajo artifacts and moose head hanging from the stone walls and headed for the main gate. Cool air nipped at his bare arms. Sunset was near. *Only doing this as a courtesy,* he thought. *Besides, Jessica wants the inside story.* He almost laughed aloud at his rationalization. As he reached the front gate, Lisbeth waved him toward her.

"Up for walking a bit?" Lisbeth said. "I move around when I'm problem solving. Helps me think."

"What problems might those be?" Mike said.

"My vacation is coming up. I was thinking about taking an excursion. Figure I have you here, an established sports outfitter, might as well ask a few questions."

Mike played along because he had few questions of his own for her. Although he didn't buy her ruse, sloughing off a potential client out of pride—or other reasons of ego—was risky. He wanted his business to thrive, not go bankrupt. "I can always spare a few minutes," he said.

They headed away from the ranch along a dirt road, with Lisbeth dictating the brisk pace. "A long drive for you," Lisbeth said. "You've got California tags. Where do you live?"

"Maddox. Northeast of San Francisco. My son is very excited about this trip."

"My dad sure wouldn't have made a drive like that when I was Andy's age. You're a good man, Mike. What do you think about this place?"

"It seems like a lot of fun. Can't wait to learn how to be a 'dude.' Andy can't wait either."

"The ranch has always enjoyed an excellent reputation." She paused. "So, S&B Outfitters—the decal on your truck—how long have you been leading tours?"

When asked about his business, he kept the answers short. To Mike, the less market speak, the better. He considered beating his own drum to be arrogant, but, like any small-business owner, sometimes he had to. "Seven years. My partner and I run tours to different countries. Each package is a little different. We go where no one else does. Take the clients just a little bit farther out than the competition would, without pushing them beyond their physical abilities. We cater to the middle-aged man looking to prove he's still got what it takes, and the adventure photographer. All are welcome, however."

"You lead the tours personally?" Lisbeth asked, as if the prospect intrigued her.

"The ones that interest me," Mike said. "I scout out every package beforehand and coordinate safe passage with the local officials. Don't want my customers stumbling into the middle of a coup."

"You mentioned a partner."

Mike nodded. "Erin Sykes. She's the S in S&B Outfitters. Much better with details than I am." A vast understatement. Bookings always increased when he was out of the office. He preferred deals that sold themselves with minimal involvement from him, while Erin worked hard at closing sales.

"You chase the rush and she pays the bills." Lisbeth's lips pursed as if she had uncovered a mystery. "From the sounds of it, your offerings may be a bit too strenuous for me. I'm interested though. Do you have anything for novices? A little less active?"

"If you're looking to sit in a tour bus and gawk at scenery," Mike said, "an S&B Outfitter package is not for you."

"Point taken," Lisbeth said. They reached a fork in the road. The sun had started to set; the trees cast longer shadows. "If you don't mind my saying so, you're not what I expected from the article in *News Story*."

"Wondered how you recognized me." Despite occasional press attention, Mike never considered himself a celebrity. He worked for a living.

"I won't lie," she said. "I'm definitely curious because of the article. You found Senator Hexler's son when no one else could."

"That was a massive search team. I was a tiny part of it." Mike cleared his throat uncomfortably. For Mike, where he had been, what he had seen—was history. He worked hard to keep his past in the past. He did not discuss old cases. Doing so felt like exploitation. "Part of me thinks that story should never have been published." Because of the article, the matter of Bret Hexler's son was his most notorious case.

"Really? Then why did you agree to it?"

"Jessica, my ex-wife, sold the pitch to them, and told me about it after they had accepted it. She had tried breaking into that magazine for a long time."

Regrets aside, he seldom refused Jessica when it came to her career. He felt he owed her that much for the sacrifices she had made for him.

"Blame vanity on the ex, do you?" Lisbeth chuckled. "To be frank, if they wanted to write about me, I wouldn't pass on the chance."

"Might want to be careful who you say that to, Lisbeth. Someday it might come true."

"I'm a gambler but that's a long-odds bet if there ever was one. Here's a bet for you. Six to one you were in the military."

That tidbit wasn't mentioned in the article. "It was a long time ago," he conceded. At thirty-four, his early twenties seemed very distant indeed. He rubbed the half-day stubble on his right cheek.

"It's in your stance," she answered as if the question were asked. "The squareness of your shoulders. Once it's drilled in, life never really smooths it out. That's where you learned to track?"

"Not exactly," Mike said, omitting that when he left the service, he had sworn off tracking for many years.

"Don't like questions about the service, huh? I can imagine there are all kinds of interesting applications for the discipline there. What's it called when you can move around without leaving any traces?"

"That depends on who you ask." Mike had to admit, there was a directness about Lisbeth that appealed to his sensibilities.

"I've heard you can place your hand into a print and see the missing person," Lisbeth said. "Is that true?"

"In some cases," Mike said.

"How does that work?"

"People leave more behind than just marks in the dirt," Mike said. "The tracks capture emotional energy as well."

"So why did you get into the business of finding missing people?"

"Let's be clear about one thing," he said, stopping and looking at Lisbeth, "tracking is not a business to me. I don't charge money for it; I don't teach it; I don't sell it, or anything to do with it; and unless asked, I don't talk about it much. Tracking is something I do. Every once in a while, a call for help comes. Sometimes I can lend a hand." And sometimes . . . it ended differently. He resumed walking again.

"Why do you do it?" Lisbeth pressed, almost repeating herself in spite of his clear message about not wanting to get into it.

Briefly the memory of a desolate field near a supermarket played in his mind. Just a flicker, the images lasted long enough for him to become aware of them. Then he returned to the moment. He wanted to know why Lisbeth really summoned him, but waited. He could hold on a little longer.

"I have my reasons," Mike said.

"Humility. I like that." Her tone packed more sincerity than flattery. "Any idea about what's going on out here tonight?"

"Been wondering about that for the last ten minutes," Mike admitted.

She pressed ahead as if he hadn't responded. "How about the radio? Heard anything through any media channels?"

Mike noticed that Lisbeth closely watched his physical reactions to her questions, instead of focusing on the answers. Interrogation savvy. Skills like that came with experience, not from training exercises or a book.

"No," Mike said. "The only news blurb that comes to mind is the one about an abducted girl in Colorado. Caught an AMBER Alert about her on television at a truck stop."

"I don't believe we're dealing with something quite like that," Lisbeth said. "At least, I hope not."

Although interested, Mike was still a bit guarded, considering the lack of details. He was trained to be cautious.

They reached a group of officers talking at a police line next to the road. "Dagget! My report? Wanted it ten minutes ago." Lisbeth dispatched one of the cops, Dagget, who fidgeted. His face drew long as if he just had his last laugh for the year. "Get going," she added, quelling the leftover chatter. Another officer held up the tape for her and Mike to pass. Ducking beneath the yellow plastic strip, they stepped into the woods, among the pines. "Lucky for us, your name popped up on the guest list, so I asked around about you. Called a friend at the FBI. Ordered a background check, too. You're certainly well regarded in the right circles."

Even as Mike was about to thank her, he sensed a qualification poised on her lips. Lisbeth delivered. "Although, the state troopers in California think you're a fraud."

Far worse allegations had been leveled against Mike over the years. With nothing to prove or lose, words slid right off him. "And what do you think?"

Lisbeth stopped. "I want to show you something." They stood at the threshold of a break in the woods. An empty clearing. The inner perimeter of the Douglas firs formed a broad semicircle.

"What are we looking at?" he asked with his right eyebrow raised.

"And here I was hoping you could tell me." She grinned.

His face flushed, the color more disappointment than anger. *Maybe we're not peers, but a trace of respe ct would be nice,* he thought. "Why does this all feel like a test?"

"Perhaps it is," Lisbeth said.

Mike Brody was in no mood for such things, especially not after that road trip and the heat from Jessica waiting for him. He turned away from the clearing for a second.

"I should get back. This has been an extremely tiring day and my patience is shot. It was nice to meet you. Whatever it is you're searching for, hope you find it." He turned his back on her.

"Mr. Brody," Lisbeth said bluntly.

He had almost decided that Jessica had been right, and he should stay out of this one. Not every situation was the right fit. Besides, it had been a long day and a half in the car. Maybe his judgment had declined along with his energy levels. Then, turning back, he noticed an unusual depression in the soil toward the center of the clearing. The track bothered him.

"Mr. Brody, don't pretend you don't want to know what this is about. Or think for a second that I can't see that."

Looking up from the depression, he faced her again, finding her expression considerably less reserved.

"Let me walk you through some background and you can decide," Lisbeth said. "I got a call today about a possible missing child from the ranch. A fourteen-year-old boy with asthma, from Brooklyn. Only child."

"You want my help with the search?" Mike asked, talking to Lisbeth, his eyes on the clearing.

"I'd like you to take a look at what we have, and give me some scenarios," Lisbeth said. "Abduction, runaway . . . or something else. I want to cover every angle. We'll start here because an officer recovered some personal effects that the parents identified as Sean's. Part of a watchband."

"If I pick up a promising trail, do you want me to track it?"

"Just the scenarios for now." Lisbeth tilted her head to the left, put her hand on the nape of her neck, then smoothed back a few loose strands of hair. "Can I count on you?"

He looked past her, again focusing on the depression. *Something about the clearing looks wrong,* Mike thought. *Definitely need lights for this.* After their short discussion, he doubted what the tracks suggested. Still, there was little choice but to believe them. People lied. Tracks did not.

"Something the matter?" Lisbeth prompted him.

Answering after a long silence, Mike said what he suspected Lisbeth wanted to hear. "I'll be back in a few minutes with my equipment." Then he added, every single word clear and distinct, "We can discuss the murder then."

09:02:27 PM

After Mike Brody set up the portable lighting gear, he searched the scene. He took his time as Lisbeth watched from a spot outside the clearing, silent. In her right hand she held an envelope.

He respected that she avoided pressing too much for details deep in his past, especially subjects where he resisted discussion.

He disliked that she had consulted third parties before asking for his help. But at least she had owned the inquiries, a point in her favor as far as Mike was concerned. In part, her reluctance was understandable. He was an outsider in law-enforcement circles and likely always would be. In their world, he was an observer first, a participant second. He knew the score.

Once the sun set, the temperature dropped rapidly. Enveloped in the work, he ignored a chill in the air. Those few moments when he did notice, the sensation of being cold passed. Survival training taught that coldness was just a mental state, rather than a physical dilemma. Resisting the cold made one colder. Fighting the cold, like fighting pain, prolonged it.

A harvest moon rose. Wide canyons stretched across the surface of the distant sphere. The sky was clear, and packed with stars. The sort of night made for fires and ghost stories and cold beer.

Instead of roasting marshmallows, Mike lay flat on his stomach, staring at impressions in the dirt, rising and dropping again as necessary, depending on which track intrigued him. Points of special interest he tagged with markers, thin sticks with a reflective coating on the tips.

Thirty minutes later, he rose a last time, finished. A narrow strip of cartilage in his right knee cracked loud enough for Lisbeth to hear. He brushed the dirt off his long-sleeved shirt.

"Well, what are your thoughts?" asked Lisbeth, although Mike was still facing away from her. Other officers had gathered and formed a semicircle.

"I'll give you my opinion," Mike said, "but I want to hear a little bit about the murder first. The two are almost certainly connected." Lisbeth was used to setting the agenda and it showed on her face. She hesitated.

"You know a lot more about this than you're telling me," Mike said. "You'd like to know more about the missing boy, and I'd like more details. Way I see it, we both get what we want. Some truth."

At last Lisbeth budged. "We got a call this afternoon from a hunter on a cell phone. Guy's shooting deer out of season. He's wandering. Finds a body."

"And murder doesn't happen often around here?"

"We get more overdoses than anything else," Lisbeth said. "This is a quiet town. So we check the hunter out. He doesn't have any of the necessary permits and he's completely out of line being here. This whole area is posted. To top it off—while he's waiting, the hunter takes some pictures of the victim with his cell phone camera and e-mails them to my office."

"That's odd." Such behavior disturbed Mike. Technology had purposes. E-mailing death pictures was a particularly questionable one. "And a bit twisted. He's not involved?"

"Well, besides the basic reality that hanging around for the police after you report a murder you committed is pathological . . . none of the guns in his possession had been fired recently, and there was no powder on his hands. He's sketchy but clean." She continued. "Now flash ahead. First officer arrives on the scene. Questions the hunter, verifies there is a corpse, and cordons the area. Then he waits for my team with the suspect in his patrol car. Everything by the book."

He glanced again at the soil in the clearing. In his survey, he had recognized more than the signs of a struggle. "Not everything by the book, though. I thought it was common practice to place markers that indicate the arrangement and position of a body." He shook his head. "The only markers here are the ones I placed."

"My team never had a chance to do that." She spoke carefully, each word weighted. "The body is missing." She cleared her throat in such a way that Mike knew she wasn't going to say anything else about it. "Now, what can you tell me about the boy?"

Mike took a breath. "He's a runner. Lanky. Got a real practiced stride, like a cross-country runner. He lands heel first, and rolls forward. Textbook form. And he's scared. Real scared. Something spooked him big time. That piece of watchband you found is where he slammed his wrist into a tree as he fled." Mike stood near the trunk, pointing at a narrow scrape mark. "Matches the edge of the link from the watchband. Also gives us an idea of his height, along with his stride."

"Can you see anything else?"

Something about her inflection made it clear to Mike what she was really pushing for: Lisbeth was looking for an indication he could see more than just the physical evidence. That he knew something about the missing boy that he should have no way of knowing. He hesitated. He usually did at these moments. Once he opened this door there was no going back—she would view him very differently.

Again he bent down, placed his hand in one of the tracks, and closed his eyes. For Mike Brody, the world stopped. Pictures of Sean dashing through the trees raced in his mind. Tapping into the emotional charge people left behind in their tracks was exhausting; he could only manage it for a few seconds at a time. So he let the stream of images continue as long as he needed them to and not a second longer.

When he rose to his feet he was breathing heavily.

"Sean wears glasses," Mike said.

Her next statement told him he was correct. "How can you possibly know that?"

"It's just what I see. What I see isn't always complete."

"That's not something they teach in the military, is it?"

"The training helped." He doubted she would believe him if he told her he had always seen things he couldn't explain.

"Okay, then. So what do you think happened with the body?" asked Lisbeth. She removed a few photographs from the manila envelope and held the picture side toward her. She mentioned nothing about them.

"Any chance the first officer on the scene is here?" asked Mike.

"That would be me." The answer came from Dagget, the same officer Lisbeth had scolded earlier. He wore a squared-off crew cut shaved down to the scalp on the sides: trooper style.

"Is this about where the body was?" Mike asked, pointing to a T-configuration he had marked toward the right half of the clearing.

Dagget shrugged. "It's hard to be certain. The lighting is different now. Might have been."

"Now, any chance he was on the short side, a little stocky? Probably had a paunch, over two hundred pounds. When you found him, he was face down on his stomach, head facing the left, cheek in the dirt. He had a goatee or a beard. Long red hair, tied up in a ponytail. Right arm wedged under his chest, left arm out at his side." Mike fired the details off like a grocery list, emotionless yet severe.

Dagget's startled expression told Mike he was near the mark, far closer than the officer had expected. "Possibly. I really didn't spend a lot of time with the corpse," said Dagget.

Mike believed Dagget, though he doubted the sentiment was mutual.

"What else do you see, Mike?" asked Lisbeth. With an eye on Mike, she studied the photographs—the pictures from the hunter's cell phone.

"The killer took the shell casings and left. Your corpse wasn't dragged away by a mountain lion or coyotes. No traces of either animal here, no scat, no prints. It was moved by humans. Same ones who sprayed down all the blood with ammonia."

"The killer came back afterward?" asked Lisbeth.

"Almost," said Mike. "I believe two different people moved the body."

"So one killed the man, the other moved . . ."

"No," Mike said. "I mean two different people besides the killer, as in addition."

"Three?" Her eyebrows shot up, and she shook her head in doubt.

"There are enough differences among the various tracks to indicate three different individuals. Your gunman, and then two more who moved the body shortly afterward."

Lisbeth spoke. "Okay, we'll keep that in mind. Is there anything else you can tell me?"

"Yes," Mike said. "You suspect Dagget is involved somehow."

Dagget grunted. "Who the hell does this guy think he is, accusing me?" Dagget said with a snarl. He spewed his petulance like an explosion.

"Mike," Lisbeth spoke over Dagget. "Please finish."

"Dagget is not one of the two men who moved the body," Mike said.

The other police officers glanced at one another. Mike thought that their expressions could have indicated anything. Maybe they disliked him. From a political standpoint, he probably said the wrong things. Mike would never know for certain. He could not. What he suspected: they planned to discuss the matter further and they wanted him gone.

He collected his lighting gear and excused himself.

"If you plan to leave the ranch," Lisbeth said, "check with me first."

09:45:41 PM

For Crotty, one of the big drawbacks of firearms was residue. Pulling the trigger was definitely easier than watching a life disappear at the other end—each time it took a little more gin afterward to bury that memory.

But firing a gun spewed black powder on everything. On the barrel, slide and trigger, inside the chamber, into the air and onto the shooter's body and clothes—the umbrella of discharge covered a far larger area than simply the target. And a single granule bound the shooter to the crime. So dealing with that residue was a task no professional approached lightly. He tackled the problem with both calculation and experience. He never took shortcuts.

After carrying out David St. John's grisly, yet unavoidable execution in the woods, Crotty drove home in his late-model gray sedan. Other than a squeak in the front disk brakes, the vehicle was unremarkable, forgotten by pedestrians and motorists alike in moments. Just as he intended.

The car reflected a deeper purpose. First, it was reliable. Modest, economical, and while not cheap, no enthusiast lusted for this ride. He rejected flashy cars because the Partner craved them so. The Partner wanted everything bigger, louder, greater than it was. Meanwhile, Crotty worked behind the scenes and got things done, however ugly. Things like David's termination were certainly ugly. At least that part was over. Back at home, Crotty focused on the cleanup; it was better than thinking about what happened in the woods.

Stripping, he stood on the linoleum-tiled floor in the laundry room, and piled clothes on the machine. The windows were frosted, the flooring warm. He set the wash to extra hot, then dumped in a mixture of scented detergent and bleach. The dial crackled like the gears on a carnival ride. Letting the water rise halfway, he then arranged the clothes around the agitator evenly and shut the door.

After rinsing his hands and forearms three times in lemon juice, he slid on a pair of surgeon-grade latex gloves. While the laundry churned, he disassembled the Glock 17 on a pile of week-old newspapers spread across a card table. He cleaned the weapon with a bore cleaner and solvent, scrubbing the slide and chamber. With a dowel wrapped in emery cloth, he scraped inside the barrel, then dunked the metal cylinder in solvent. He allowed the cleaning solution to dry on the barrel. He wrapped it in plastic, ditched the gloves, and washed his hands in lemon juice again. His eyes returned to the Glock 17. He worked a different barrel into the frame, a well-used one that had seen a few thousand rounds at the firing range. For each gun in his collection, he kept a half dozen extra barrels around to frustrate ballistics analysis.

The science hinged on matching defects in the barrel with recovered bullets and shell casings from a crime scene. He always pocketed the casings, which left the barrel.

By creating his own set of defects, even if the barrel and the casings were recovered, the link between them was broken.

Crotty finished reassembling the weapon and felt an odd comfort following the sounds of the parts dropping into place. Loading a fresh magazine with a different brand of 9mm ammunition, he racked a round into the chamber. He dropped the magazine, added another 124-grain bullet, and jammed the fully loaded magazine back home. Seventeen, plus one in the pipe, made eighteen. Round numbers. The only way to carry.

He folded and bound the newspapers with twine for recycling.

The washer buzzed. Crotty ran the laundry again, this time heavier on the detergent than the bleach, and turned to matters of personal hygiene.

Steam from the shower fogged over the bathroom. A narrow

band of it vented through the open window. The sill was moldy from years of condensation.

He washed his entire body with lemon juice, including his hair, face, and neck. Then he scraped every inch with a pumice stone, soaped, and shampooed. The mixture of chemicals burned his already irritated skin.

After the shower he tossed the clothes in the dryer, dialing the temperature to maximum. He crimped the metal coupling on the exhaust valve, which forced more heat back into the machine.

The washer chugged one final round, loaded with bleach and warm water. He sprayed an aerosol-based agent on the card table, and laid out clean clothes on the bed.

His daily attire merged street clothes with business casual: blue jeans, polo shirt, black socks, boots with a shaft that covered the ankle, and a dive watch. Dressed, he slumped on the couch and watched the news for a half hour. There was no mention of David on the television, even on cable. Not entirely unexpected.

The dryer buzzed.

The second helping of bleach had etched white streaks into the fabric. The stains were acceptable. Crotty folded, smoothed, and formed tight corners. He placed the garments in a shopping bag with handles.

After dinner he ditched the evidence. Goodwill was the first stop. He stuffed the shopping bag in the donation container near the supermarket. The bound newspapers he tossed from the car onto a stranger's lawn for recycling. He wedged the barrel under the seat of a car scheduled for demolition at the local junkyard. Last, he tossed the two shell casings down two different sewer systems.

Back home Crotty paged through a file and nodded at his handiwork. All the wire-transfer records implicating his business partner fit in a small box. Reviewing them gave him pleasure so he did this twice weekly. He returned the records to their hiding place, and then wrote in his journal, making a few notes on how he wanted to grow the company. Crotty had big plans for growing the company, and the extra money expanding it would bring. He really needed the money. Well, his girlfriend wanted the money, anyway;

she made that point clear enough. He just wanted enough cash to get out of the business and go away with her. For now, he wrote.

His pen moved carefully across the page and formed orderly rows of tight neat letters.

The phone rang, interrupting his writing.

"It's Joan Berman from the New Hope Orphanage. Just wanted to thank you for your most recent gift. The children are so excited about the new playground equipment. If you could just see the smiles on their little faces."

"I'm sure it's quite something."

"And as you requested, all your contributions will remain completely confidential."

"That's fine," Crotty said. "I'm really sorry to cut this short, Joan, but I had a rough day at work."

"Of course," Joan said. "Perhaps someday we can meet in person. It would be nice to put a face to the name on the check . . . "

"I'm afraid that's not possible. I'm really busy with my work."

Crotty hung up and reflected on David's murder that morning.

The timing was deliberate. He had long contemplated dismissing David—planning the execution carefully over many months, and settling on the exact place after great deliberation. David had become a liability. David had known too much about Crotty's plans for too long. And if David leaked the details, the Partner would figure out what Crotty had been scheming. So he killed David. Crotty's men had already moved the body to a safe place for disposal; nature would handle the rest. As it had with the others.

He anticipated the typical response when he would speak with the Partner: an interminably long conversation that had nothing to do with the situation and everything to do with the rift between them. Then once the bickering settled down, they would have to deal with the new threat.

The boy who saw too much.

Day Two

A stranger loomed in the doorway of the main lodge, staring at Mike. Through the window, the sun crested over the horizon. Mist rose off the grass. A kaleidoscope of beams danced on the walls, light refracting off a stained-glass ornament dangling from the frame. The large room had a pitched ceiling, and rose forty feet from floor to peak. Black-and-white photographs of various cowboys coated the walls. Decades old, the ceiling beams had the look of fresh-cut lumber.

The cot the clerk had promised never materialized, so Jessica and Andy each had taken a bed, with Mike on the floor. He had no trouble getting comfortable. Falling asleep was seldom his issue, getting real rest was. Like most nights recently, last night he had not dreamed. His mind, unwilling to relax, had resisted a chance to discharge emotional energy.

At the first light of morning he woke, wanting and needing strong coffee. That was an imperative. What Mike got instead was a strange man staring at him.

The man pushed an aluminum cart on rubber wheels. He was tall, broad in the chest, a little less so in the shoulders. His presence filled the doorway. The stranger spoke first. "Good morning, Mike. Hope I didn't wake you."

"I was already up," Mike said, his voice rasping like gravel beneath a rake. *Great, this guy knows my name, too,* he thought.

"I'm very sorry about what happened last night."

Briefly Mike wondered if he meant the search or the cot. He didn't like a second stranger in two days knowing who he was.

"Erich Reynard. I own the Pine Woods Ranch." Here Erich offered his hand. They shook; Erich matched Mike's strong grip. "Apparently the reservation system needs an overhaul. I'm sorry our incompetence left you in the lurch."

"Apology accepted," Mike said.

"Right after breakfast we'll move you into a room. Plus, I want to make up for this mistake." Erich snapped his fingers excitedly, then pointed his first finger and thumb at Mike. "I'll take ten percent off the price of your visit."

"That's great." Mike sensed Erich wanted to say more, and perhaps that Erich needed to say more.

"Wait! No, I've got it!" Erich said. "There's a Cessna flight over the lake. Usually the fee is a hundred dollars a head per hour. For you and your family—free. A two-hour flight work for you?"

The offer was appealing, but Jessica hated flying. That was the reason they drove to Montana. Getting her aboard a small passenger plane would be a tough sell. Still, he appreciated Erich's apology. "That's very generous," Mike said. "But I have to talk to my family and see if they're interested."

"You sure know how to beat a guy up on price," Erich said.

"I'm not trying to. This seems like an honest mistake." A sincere apology was enough for Mike. He knew what deception sounded like.

"There are no mistakes—only chances for improvement," Erich said.

Sensing a compromise that he hoped worked for everyone, Mike moved quickly. "Tell you what, my ex-wife is a journalist. Jessica is planning an article about the experience. She'd love an insider's perspective on the daily operations."

"Fantastic! Free publicity," Erich said. "My business partner will appreciate that. I'll definitely find Jessica." He paused. "Excuse me, but I have to go. Stop by the front desk any time after breakfast for your key. And let me know about the plane ride. The seats fill up fast."

"Absolutely," Mike said. From the decanters on the tray, a most welcome scent wafted through the air. "That smells like the good stuff." For emphasis, Mike gestured toward the tray.

"Fresh-ground Jamaica Blue Mountain," Erich said with pride. "The water is triple-filtered and stored at room temperature. The whole beans are packed in airtight containers, then refrigerated. We grind seconds before brewing."

Mike nodded his approval. He would fill his cup as soon as the drip finished. While there were many preparation techniques for coffee, to Mike this was the best he had ever heard. Especially the bit about refrigerating the beans. Coffee lovers often froze whole beans to make them last longer—an unfortunate decision. Subzero temperatures degraded the natural oils, tainting the flavor.

Alone, Mike enjoyed the serenity of the early morning. The quiet offered a chance to appreciate the landscape, and take a moment for himself. In the background, a set of twin mountain caps, peaks frosted with snow, thrust high above the horizon. Last night, lost in the check-in process, he had overlooked them. Now he appreciated their magnificence.

Barely a sip into Mike's third cup, a man stormed through the living area in the lodge. A woman chased behind, pleading for him to wait. Muttering, the man ignored her, ramming the door back into the frame.

The woman stopped on the porch, watching her husband thunder across the parking lot. He stormed the main gate.

She hesitated on the porch as if unsure whether to pursue, wait, or break down. She looked like a substitute teacher—very nice, very accommodating, yet forever in transition.

Mike witnessed the exchange from a bench on the front porch. An unsettling contrast against such a peaceful backdrop. With a well-practiced pivot, the woman faced the bench. Hours of sobbing had puffed up the skin under her eyes. That was Mike's guess.

"Oh, just great," she said. "I didn't think anyone was up to see us like this."

Mike Brody wasn't sure if she was talking to him. "I didn't see anything," Mike said.

"You're a terrible liar." A spot-on assessment Mike concurred with silently. She added, "I apologize for my husband. We have a family emergency."

"I'm sorry to hear that."

"You remind me of someone." She brushed off a tear.

"I'm sure it's just a coincidence," Mike said.

"Let's go!" yelled the burly man.

She tore off as if any further conversation was forbidden.

08:12:22 AM

Orientation began inside a building next to the main lodge. A narrow red carpet separated rows of padded seats, the same number of chairs on each side. A state-of-the-art sound system pumped loud rock music with a driving beat. Behind an empty stage, a digital video projector mounted to the ceiling ran a montage of action-based shots. Pictures of families riding horseback, pictures of guests eating meals, pictures of people gathered around campfires at the Pine Woods Ranch. Images advanced, changing in time with the songs.

Forty guests watched from their chairs, enthralled.

The screen went black. Massive red and white letters scrolled in from the sides, one line at a time.

Pine Woods Ranch!
Here for YOU
Because that's what we do!

The music reached a crescendo, and then faded. Digits replaced the text on the screen. A countdown, complete with the sound effects of a rocket launch. *10 ... 9 ... 8 ... 7 ...* metal rumbled ... *6 ... 5 ... 4 ...* a tone beeped ... *3 ... 2 ...* images flashed ... *1.* At liftoff the rockets fired and a husky female voice said: "Ladies and gentlemen, the owner of the Pine Woods Ranch, Mr. Erich Reynard."

Erich raced up the carpet from the back of the room, waving at the guests with one hand.

The music hit one final apex.

Mike rolled his eyes at the grand production of it all. He gave Erich credit. The man knew how to put on a show. Despite his caffeine rush, several times Mike fought back a yawn. If he broke down, Andy would follow, then his ex-wife. And Jessica had an infectious style about her, a peculiar ability that drew others into her physical state. If she yawned, a tidal wave would roll through the room.

Erich Reynard took the podium. He spoke with authority.

Within seconds, the crowd jerked awake.

"Welcome! Welcome! Welcome!" he said, each welcome more exuberant than the last. "I'm Erich, the owner of the Pine Woods Ranch. Everyone is going to have a great time this week. Why? Because the staff is here for you—and that is WHAT WE DO!" He shook his fist for punctuation. This was a man who could fill a cavern with a solitary gesture, Mike bet.

Jessica straightened up, and pushed her shoulders back. Mike grinned as Andy rolled his eyes, modeling his father. Jessica glared at Mike as if he had interrupted a religious ceremony.

Erich continued. "Now before I introduce the best staff in the world . . ." He paused. The attendant who had helped Mike at check-in was there holding a sheet of light blue paper folded in quarters.

She walked to the edge of the stage and whispered something to Erich, who nodded. From there she walked to the front row, where Jessica and Mike sat, Andy between them. She handed Mike a folded note:

> *Mike,*
> *Nice work last night. I have a more interesting proposal.*
> *Det. Lisbeth McCarthy*

Mike pocketed the message before Jessica could read it.

Erich paused at the podium. The two men's eyes met for a moment. Mike gave Erich the all-clear sign. Erich smiled and continued the presentation. As soon as the orientation wrapped and everyone went to the dining hall for breakfast, Mike broke away from the crowd and called Lisbeth.

"All right," Mike said. "What's this about?"

"Bottom line, I don't know how you did what you did last night. You not only figured out where the body was in the clearing, but you had the arrangement right. And the hair color. I triple-checked against the pictures. Never seen anything like it. And you were dead-on about the ammonia. Our blood samples are worthless."

"What is it you're asking me? Do you want help finding the body?"

"Forget the body for now," Lisbeth said. "I've got a bigger problem. The boy is still missing."

"You know where to start," Mike said. "That's the most important thing."

Lisbeth disagreed. "This is a quiet town with a shortage of resources. Finding someone missing in this terrain takes people and equipment. I have neither."

"Did you call up the chain and get some help?"

"Same old story," Lisbeth said. "Oh, the missing kid is over eleven? Call us back in another day. But we don't have a day. Sean's mom thinks he carried enough meds for thirty-six to forty-eight hours. After that . . ." He imagined her raising her palms as she spoke, shrugging with her hands.

"What about search volunteers? There's a whole ranch full of people."

"Sure, forty people who don't know the first thing about this terrain. Tourists. Last week there was a mountain lion a mile outside this very building. Plus I've got a murderer and some co-conspirators at large. Losing more people to exhaustion and inexperience and who knows what else is not an acceptable risk. Every spare officer is on this. The local search and rescue squad is en route, and they're trying to round up a helicopter." She paused. "Are you everything they say you are?"

"Lisbeth, what are you asking me?" Mike asked.

She relented. "I'd like it if you took another look at what we have. See if there's any possibility someone is involved with Sean's disappearance. If there is foul play, show it to us, and I can get whatever help we need."

"Do you want me to track Sean?" he asked.

"Not at this time," Lisbeth said.

Second time she's said that, thought Mike. A tough decision confronted him. On the one hand, he sensed there was more about Sean and the business of the missing body than had been disclosed. He understood. During a crisis, people often left out details more from stress than by design. Intentional or not, the net effect was the same. He couldn't know everything beforehand. There were always gaps and he allowed for them.

On the side of helping, there was one issue that bothered him:

the hours wasted on bureaucracy and procedures. Mike now understood the police had bet Sean had wandered off and would return. More than nine times out of ten with teenagers, reasoning like that panned out. Kids his age came back, exhausted but unharmed.

To Mike, Lisbeth seemed an honest person with the best of intentions, as tough as she was fair. He decided he trusted her enough. "I'll help you," he said. "But I have to take care of something first."

09:23:35 AM

A ndy took the news much better than Mike expected. His son had been a force behind the dude-ranch trip from the start, so Mike had anticipated lots of resistance. Instead Andy turned to the television. "We have a week, Dad. Hurry back."

Relieved, Mike tousled Andy's hair. At times, Andy was patient and logical far beyond his years, superior to either parent. Mike believed Andy inherited this disposition from Jessica's father, though he had never dared voice that sentiment.

"I will, champ," Mike said. "Before I leave, we should pick a new code phrase."

Years ago, Mike had developed a code-phrase system with Andy. If an adult approached Andy and claimed he was sent by Andy's parents, and he should come with them, Andy simply asked for the code phrase and waited.

If the person did not provide the proper phrase, Andy was to run, scream "child molester," and never look back. Both parents drilled this habit into Andy as soon as he could speak in complete sentences, and they role-played scenarios with him until the routine became a reflex. They recruited trusted associates to test Andy, friends who drove near the sidewalk as the boy played in the yard and invited him into their car. After the thorough battery of tests Andy passed, Mike was confident Andy could handle a real-world situation.

Neither Mike nor Jessica ever revealed the actual phrase outside of their home.

"That's a good idea." Jessica already had her planner open to record Lisbeth's cell number. "You want to pick it this time, Andy?"

The boy thought for a moment, scrunching his face in contemplation. "The Velveteen Rabbit wears a brown skirt."

"Got it," Mike said. "I'll see you soon."

Both parents knew the routine when Mike left on a case. Jessica recorded the phrase for safekeeping in her planner. Mike programmed additional contact numbers for the ranch into his cell phone: the nurse's station, proprietor, front desk, and others which he might need if he had trouble contacting Jessica directly. When they finished, she followed Mike into the hallway and shut the door behind her, leaving Andy in the room. Unlike their son, Jessica voiced her complaints. "So much for just talking with Lisbeth, huh?"

"I think I can help on this one."

"Can I remind you that you're on vacation?"

Arguing was pointless; he left.

09:31:16 AM

Whatever his family's reaction, Mike Brody respected their feelings, but tracking was his decision. For Mike, the matter of Sean Jackson had chosen him just as he had chosen it.

His truck started on the first crank, as it had for each of the last two hundred thousand miles.

At the main gate, the man with the crew cut, one half of the couple from earlier that morning in the lodge, screamed with fury. The man was possessed; his face flushed red. He spared no one, especially not the cop he was yelling at.

Has to be Sean's dad, thought Mike, driving past the two men. It was common for parents to express frustration with the progress of a search, particularly if they were not allowed to be involved.

The mother was nowhere in sight. Mike parked the truck where Lisbeth had requested, on the shoulder of the dirt road, near the taped-off trail that led to the clearing. She was waiting for him.

"What's with the Buddha?" Lisbeth pointed to a four-inch ceramic statue on the dashboard of Mike's truck. Years ago, Jessica had affixed the avatar with epoxy, without his consent or knowledge. It was one of her less subtle attempts to change him. Like the deity it represented, the statue refused to budge. To Mike, that said a lot about Jessica.

"Gift from the ex-wife," he said.

"I begin to see why you divorced," said Lisbeth, eyes fixed on the ceramic statue.

"There's a bit of Buddha in all of us. Perhaps that's the part that wants you to quit smoking."

"How did you know that?" Lisbeth asked, recoiling like she had stepped from a hot shower onto a cold floor.

From the reaction, Mike could tell smoking was a vice she kept under wraps. "You pat a bulge in the right pocket of your slacks a lot. A bulge shaped and sized exactly like a cigarette pack," Mike said. "Checking to make sure your smokes and lighter are safe?"

Lisbeth slid her hand away from the pocket with a casual ease. She smiled at Mike, who spied her maneuver anyway. "So . . . you need anything else from me?" she said.

"If you have a recent picture of Sean and an old pair of his shoes," he said.

"The ranch takes family pictures the first day," Lisbeth said, "so we have one. Mom and I can have a chat about footwear." She looked at him for a moment. "I'll leave you to it."

At the clearing, he started where he had left off the previous night, studying the knee-sized depressions next to the tree trunk. These tracks differed from the others. They were from someone younger and lighter, definitely not yet an adult. Something else was off about the scene, too. None of the reflective markers he placed in the soil the night before remained. He wondered why, and made a note to ask Lisbeth. Dropping down beside the tracks, he recalled the many times he had done this before.

More than technical details, what he remembered most clearly about cases afterward were the faces of the people involved. Where situations turned ugly, he wrestled with the memories, especially while awake. He remembered cases with pleasant resolutions best. These were the right match for his skills. Where he helped. Where the loved ones drove home happy. A sliver of him shared in their exuberance. The faces of loved ones carried him a few nights, maybe a little more. Then the night terrors returned. They always returned.

What are the odds these are from Sean? he thought. If so, the first track—the second most important one in any case—had presented itself.

From there, Sean sprinted off into the woods, toward the road, pushing off on his toes. Swaying leftward several times, he had considered glancing backward, then had changed his mind mid-stride.

Reversing course, Mike returned to the murder scene. He wanted verification the boy had not entered the clearing, or even breached the perimeter. Although he was almost positive Sean had nothing to do with either the murder or the removal of the body, Mike wanted to be certain. He found nothing implicating the boy of either.

Unless he wanted to follow a particular set of tracks out of the clearing, there was little else there for Mike, so he left the scene. Back at the road, Dagget blocked his way. "I'm not buying it," Dagget said. "This whole business of yours is crap. You're a lucky guesser is all."

"I won't add your name to the newsletter then," Mike said. Many times before he had dealt with officers like Dagget. Though Dagget's opposition was more rabid than most, there were always critics. Arguing with them was reckless. Ignoring them when they were in his face was worse.

He had never been concerned about his image, though Jessica long had lobbied for him to consider how his actions appeared to others. *Results aren't everything,* she had said. *Sometimes even when you win, you lose, because results aren't enough.* On a gut level, he knew she was right. But in practice, when the hammer dropped, and there was a missing person, results were the only thing that mattered. Mike did what he had to and held his ground. The fallout landed where it must.

"I need to go that way," Mike said, pointing toward the road.

Eventually Dagget yielded, stepping aside with a scowl. Mouthing the word *faker,* he also muttered a few expletives.

Unfazed, Mike found Lisbeth at the road. "Here's your picture," she said.

It was a color photograph of a boy like most any other fourteen-year-old on vacation with his parents—an awkward kid that yearned to be anywhere else. The first detail that leaped out was Sean's glasses. The plastic frames were aviator style and too large for his thin face.

"Anything on the footwear?" Mike asked.

"Sean brought one pair of shoes," Lisbeth said, "and he's wearing them. Did you find anything?"

"If Sean's path crossed with anyone else's, it happened elsewhere, away from here."

"Had a feeling that's what you'd tell me." She exhaled slowly, clearly pondering a half-formed idea. "Now what do we do about that?"

Enough with the "guess what I'm thinking" game, Mike thought. He cleared his throat. "I could track Sean." His mouth stayed opened very slightly when he finished his offer, waiting for her response.

"Okay," she agreed finally. "But you're not going into the wild without a buddy."

09:40:51 AM

The hardest part of tracking for Mike was right before he started. Once in motion, the momentum snowballed, and one discovery fed on another. Before that point he was almost paralyzed with excess energy and ideas, waiting for the go-ahead.

Near the group of officers, he gathered the following gear: a Global Positioning System device with a special attachment to improve accuracy, a cloth canteen, a small pair of high-powered binoculars, iodine tablets, a knife, a bag of reflective markers, and a microsized butane torch. Some of the more hard-core survival experts dismissed modern equipment as cheating; it made the challenge too easy. A stable and predictable flame and access to worldwide navigation information were not needs Mike Brody questioned. There were times for proving one could start a fire without a match, or navigate by landmarks, a compass, or the stars.

But with a life on the line, bravado could wait. Besides, everything fit securely in the pockets of his cargo pants and kept his hands free.

Focused on the main problem, he worked over some initial impressions about Sean, and reviewed the short profile about the boy that Lisbeth had provided.

As far as negotiating the woods, Sean Jackson had a few advantages. Only children often had independent streaks. That could serve him well in unfamiliar or uncomfortable settings. Used to being alone, the solitude might not have such a dramatic impact. Also, Sean was innately curious. He walked toward the crime scene prior to the murder willingly. The mere fact that he wandered far off the road and away from a marked trail also proved that Sean was an explorer of sorts. Another check in the plus column.

On the minus side, Sean previously had only minimal exposure to the deep woods. The cement streets of Brooklyn were very different from the wilderness of Montana, especially once the sun set. There was food and water for the taking, but Mike doubted Sean would know where to look. As for what sort of choices Sean might make under duress, Mike wanted to speculate, but he needed more information.

It was imperative that he have more than just the tracks. Physical evidence only took one so far.

One of the more gnawing details Detective Lisbeth McCarthy had not shared: why the boy left the ranch. Exactly where Sean found the time was puzzling. The daily schedule was packed with activities from breakfast through lights-out. Mike needed an answer. That meant dealing with the parents.

Sean's father had cooled considerably from earlier, and shifted from yelling to pacing and grumbling. Ignoring his rants, the police asked that Mr. Jackson remain behind the sawhorse and stay calm. Still, he was in better shape than Sean's mother, the woman from the porch who had dashed off after her husband earlier, who looked ragged from concern. On her arm just above the wrist was a bruise.

The marks matched a large pair of hands. Mike had a good guess whose hands had clamped down on her forearm.

Mike introduced himself to the Jacksons. Clearly, Sean's father, Gerald, was unimpressed. "You don't look like no cop," Gerald said. "Why are you here?"

"I help find missing people," Mike said. The wife, Faith, kept avoiding eye contact.

"Oh, neat." Gerald wore sarcasm badly. "I sure would like to help. *Somebody* doesn't want my help." All the emphasis was on *somebody*. So much emphasis the man practically spat the words.

"I've helped the police in similar situations before," Mike said. "And every time, it rips a hole in my heart to see parents suffering like this. No one has definite answers, and all you want is some kind of assurance that everything is going to work out. I have a son, a little younger than Sean, and I'd be devastated in your position."

Gerald fell silent.

"Was there any reason Sean was out this way?" asked Mike.

"He's always wandering off," said Gerald, shrugging. "Boys do that. Usually he comes right back."

"But this time he didn't," Mike said, remaining calm, hoping to inspire trust. "I'm asking why. And I ask because we want the same thing. To see Sean home again as soon as possible. There are a million things happening all around us, but what matters is Sean. If you can help me understand why he left, I may be able to help find him. Did anything unusual happen that morning?"

"He's lost is what happened," said Gerald. "That's all I know."

Already Mike doubted Gerald would help, but these answers were paramount, so he forged ahead and hoped for the best. "In order to help, I need to understand his mental state. The more I know about what he might have been thinking or feeling, the better."

Faith Jackson stepped up and put her hand lightly on Mike's arm. "Sean was a little upset when he left yesterday."

"Who asked you?" Gerald strained his vocal cords barking the words.

Mike faced Sean's mother. "What might have upset him?"

Averting his gaze, she stared mostly at the road. "I didn't say this to the police. Yesterday was our last day and Sean really wanted to stop somewhere on the way to the airport, and . . . "

"How this matters is beyond me," said Gerald gruffly.

"I ask these questions because they're important." With a glance toward Faith, Mike said, "There was a difference of opinion over the stop?"

"Yes," Faith said, finally meeting his eye.

"What kind of disagreement?" Mike asked.

"Normal sort," Faith said, like the memory of it had drained her energy. Based on Gerald's stance, it was clear that he felt she had shared too much already.

"Tell me about how he left," Mike said. "Did he sneak off or was it more in the open? Might he have been a little confrontational about it?"

"He just . . . just . . ." Faith sobbed.

Again Mike recognized he had nailed a raw nerve ending. By not admitting anything specific, Faith betrayed quite a lot. Mike suspected she avoided looking at both men for different reasons. Certainly Mike's questions intimidated the suffering woman. But if Mike's questions bothered Faith, it seemed Gerald's presence positively terrified her.

He could tell there was nothing more Faith would share with him. At least in this setting.

"I'm sorry that you're in limbo right now," Mike said. "I hope there's some good news for you very shortly."

"Yeah, well," Gerald said, "unless you got some, you're no better than the rest of them."

09:49:16 AM

Mike had an image of Sean now, the genesis of a profile. But even with a clearer idea about Sean through, or perhaps in spite of, his parents, Mike was still unsure about what made the boy tick. Typically he received a more thorough briefing about his subject. Here his impressions rested largely upon a short string of adjectives: only child, scared, city dweller, independent, lanky, asthmatic. The tracks would have to fill in the blanks.

He directed his energies to the equipment.

He checked, then double-checked his water supply. The canteen was full, the iodine tablets intact.

Catching his racing thoughts, he inhaled twice and redirected his focus. Lisbeth had mentioned a search buddy. The idea had merit.

There were tremendous advantages to multiple sets of eyes, especially ones familiar with the terrain. Besides the advantage of local area expertise, it greatly expanded their reach. If fatigue became a factor, a partner would help ease the mental burden.

Often police recruited him several days or weeks after a person vanished. Sean Jackson was an exception, since this call had arrived early. That was a plus. Not necessarily a trump card, but very helpful. So far the tracks were fresh and intact, the weather clear, the ground dry. The last storm was three nights back, leaving the soil firm and highly responsive. With highs in the low sixties and hours of light before dusk, the odds were definitely in a searcher's favor.

He had missed breakfast so he scarfed down a protein bar, swallowed some lukewarm coffee from his thermos, and longed for just one more swig. But Lisbeth's appearance meant the wait had ended.

"You look tense," she said as she came over, looking a bit tense herself.

"I found the first track," Mike said. "The second most-important, and where I start. Waiting for the go-ahead. So who's my partner?"

Lisbeth was all business. "No word on the helicopters," she said. "Scent dogs are coming. They're newbies. First time out. It's a bit disturbing."

"A lot comes down to the handler." *Nice of her to dodge the question,* Mike thought.

"He's green, too." She sounded like someone fishing for reassurance.

"Gotta work with what you have, right?"

Lisbeth sighed. "What's your basic strategy today?"

"That depends somewhat on you. First off, I'd like to see where the tracks in the clearing lead. That's a promising area. If the searchers find something you'd like me to check out, I'll do that. But, I'd like to begin with a known track from Sean."

"How far do you think Sean wandered?"

"Too early to tell," Mike said. "He might be a mile away, he might be five. Right now he might even be within shouting distance."

Lisbeth considered the prospect with interest. "You'll check in every three hours."

"I can do that."

"That wasn't a question, Mike. We got you some long-range walkie-talkies. Secure encrypted transmissions and they're a direct line to me. Whenever you check in, communicate your coordinates as precisely as you can manage. I expect you to make use of your GPS."

Something told Mike she was not worried about him getting lost. To this point instincts had served Mike well with Lisbeth. She was sharp; he liked her. "I'll watch the time."

Lisbeth continued, glancing around. "Your counterpart was given identical instructions." She paused for a moment. "In as much as we don't have a large number of searchers right now, we do have quality talent, which includes you. Much thought was given to what expertise might jell best with yours. There's not much point in sending you out there with a shadow."

"I agree entirely. If you're going to do something . . ."

". . . do it right." She finished the sentence. "That was my mother's favorite saying by the way. So let's do this right."

"Absolutely." Mike nodded. Her voice, her plan, it all made perfect sense.

"Great then, let's get these introductions done." She appeared increasingly perplexed. "Excuse me. He seems to have slipped away." She scanned the road, then motioned toward a lone figure who faced away from them. A low hanging branch at the tree line obscured the man's face. She summoned the officer with a single command. As the figure approached, Mike recognized the trooper-style haircut before remembering the name. Disbelief showed on the tracker's face. Either Lisbeth did not notice, or she pretended not to.

Choosing a police officer was reasonable, but her particular selection was shocking. The last person he had expected, the one who had given him grief on two separate occasions, Officer Dagget, was now standing before him.

09:51:22 AM

After orientation, Jessica retreated to her room with Andy. Had anyone asked why, she would have lied. She had been here before; the role of single parent was nothing new for her.

Even if Mike had golden intentions, Jessica resented his bolting. For any reason. They had agreed this was a work-free vacation, a time-out. A chance for Andy to visit both parents at the same time. Such events happened so rarely, even before the divorce. Once again, Mike had left behind a mess of open issues that needed attention.

At least she had a temporary distraction. The digital SLR camera was the latest and most expensive brand on the commercial market. Though just within her economic means, this one was borrowed. It belonged to the editor of *Pacific Coast Reader*, Jack Graber. Graber was a former boss and a longtime freelance contact.

The tough-talking editor, who chewed cigars down to stubs but never once lit them up, had offered her a deal. Jessica could use the camera in exchange for a sneak peek at any promising story before she shopped the piece elsewhere. Many times Graber had said he depended on her to honor the bargain.

Jessica uncovered the stories with big themes that caught a reader's attention. Reporting assignments had led her through the belly of prisons, crack houses, and police actions. She covered civil unrest and violent, bloody riots. Once, she even tempted fate and exposed links between organized crime and high-ranking state politicians.

Months after a story ran, she would review a piece and remember what really happened. The feelings were often overwhelming. She had no choice. She operated this way because doing otherwise risked her sanity and health. Because she dealt with the best, and worst, parts of humanity.

Many buckled under the stress of chaos, slithering for the nearest exit. They numbed the pain with alcohol or drugs. Something they could ingest to dull the edges, to escape the pressure. Jessica Barrett worked differently. She thrived on instability. The backdrop fit her like a book she wanted to disappear in, over and over. Journalism offered a perfect marriage of ability and ambition. The work was its own reward.

Throughout the regional and national press corps she was known for gripping real-world accounts. Unsure how this reputation started, she reveled in its benefits. Like the camera.

She missed the classic 35mm single lens reflex terribly, but a high-capacity device that spared her the task of finding a photo lab was a great asset. Documenting a story could mean taking a tremendous number of pictures; she never knew how many in advance. That feature alone saved her, and the paper, money.

Testing the sound levels on the mini cassette recorder, Jessica played back a few recent observations. Nothing important so far, just a joke about a gas station attendant they passed in Nevada. Jessica hit *stop*, satisfied the instrument worked perfectly.

Wherever she went, she carried a recording device and a package of blank tapes. Stories might break at any time, with little warning. The slender cassette recorder was solid enough for capturing raw ideas in the field. Later she would transcribe the audio notes to a laptop.

She set the mini recorder on her planner and looked for the essential spare batteries. Backups, especially data backups, were critical. Once a magnetic business card wiped her PDA clean. Since then she used paper for appointments and contact information.

Andy screamed, bounding off the mattress as if ejected by booster rockets. On the windowsill—a praying mantis. It was a perfect specimen, four inches in length, with large pocketknife forelegs. Beneath the legs, the serrations appeared like spiky teeth.

"Go away!" Andy hollered at the insect.

Outside, a hand rapped the door twice.

With practiced ease, Jessica opened the window, cupped the insect between her hands, and released it into the wild. Her maneuver was the quickest solution, if not the most helpful from a developmental perspective. One day soon, she hoped Andy would confront this childish fear. She knew the struggle; she had nursed quite a few into her teen years. The boy could not be rushed through the growth process. For now she sympathized and understood why he was scared of them. She guided the window along the runners, locking the frame shut.

Jessica opened the door, revealing Erich Reynard. In his left hand he held a basket sealed in plastic wrap. Beneath the clear wrap: snacks, bottled water, scented soaps, and chocolate.

"Is everything okay?" Erich asked.

"Yes. Sorry about that," Jessica said. She glanced at Andy, who breathed heavily, still crouched in the space between the second bed and the wall.

His fingers gripped the comforter tight enough that his knuckles whitened. Even with the window locked and the insect gone, Andy seemed unsettled.

She added, "It's nothing."

Erich offered the basket to Jessica. "Just a few things to make your stay a little more comfortable."

"Thank you so much," Jessica said. "That's very thoughtful of you." Unlike many hospitality baskets, often loaded with junk, this one looked useful. Stepping away from Erich, Jessica placed the basket on the bureau before returning.

Erich continued. "I spoke with Mike earlier about the mix-up, and asked him to stop by the front desk after breakfast. His room is ready. So far he hasn't come for his key."

"He probably won't," Jessica said. "Not for a while anyway."

"Is everything okay?" Erich asked, again.

"Andy and I are fine."

"Does that mean you're up for a plane ride?" Quickly Erich relayed the same offer he made Mike.

"That's very kind of you," Jessica said. "Unfortunately, I'm not a big fan of airplanes." Fifteen Septembers before, a small plane had crashed into a field behind her parent's house. At the time she was at school. Jessica never forgot the sight of the burnt wreckage. Since then she had only flown for business, and only when she had to.

"The Cessna is barely a year old," Erich said. "And the pilot is highly skilled."

"I don't know." And she meant just that. Her vague response baffled her. Being concise about what she wanted was rarely a problem for Jessica.

At the word *airplane,* Andy had leaped up from his hiding spot. Jessica knew he'd always wanted to fly. "Come on, Mom!" said Andy. "It'll be awesome."

"Jessica, I'd love to fly with you and Andy. Reconsider, please. There is nothing like autumn at three thousand feet." Erich had a likable smile that struck her as genuine. "And every view is great from *Destiny.*"

"I'll think about it." Her first offer of a private plane ride. Jessica wondered why she had not said no immediately, when the idea seemed so preposterous. She did not fly for fun. That was final.

"Can't ask for more than that," Erich said. "I heard you were researching an article about my ranch. I'd like to help."

"An interview for a plane ride. Is that your proposition?" Irked that Mike had leaked her plans, she hid her resentment as best she could. Ideally, the longer it stayed quiet she was a journalist, the easier that the writing would go. Once word spread she was a reporter, wild tales would come to her from every corner. People loved being written about as much as they liked talking about themselves.

"I do like a good conversation." Erich held up the room key. "About Mike, how do I get this to him?"

"I'll take it for now." She reached outward for the silver key. Erich cupped his hand around hers. The gesture surprised Jessica.

More surprising to her was how long she hesitated in the doorway.

09:52:53 AM

Dagget lingered near enough for a conversation, yet far enough away that it was clear he preferred talking with anyone other than Mike.

"This is not what we discussed when I agreed to go in," Dagget said, his voice strained.

"You're critical here, Dagget," Lisbeth said. "You and Mike."

Dagget grunted loudly and harshly, almost as if expectorating something he could not purge from his throat fast enough. "I think it would be best if I helped with the search in another way."

Lisbeth gave both men a glance. "Concern noted. I'm not going to sell you on this arrangement or convince you of the merits. There are a lot of complementary skills between you. Dagget, you know this area extremely well, and you're one of the few officers with advanced search-and-rescue training. Plus, you've always demonstrated a tremendous enthusiasm for assignments like this in the past. Mike, between your references and my hunch, I'm certain this pairing will work well for you, too. Trust my judgment. That's all I ask."

"With all due respect, Detective . . . ," Dagget said.

Lisbeth cut his protest short. "The choice has been made. You're working with Mike. Your first report is due in three hours. Now go see Shad Hammer. He's got some gear for you."

Mike considered her reasoning curious, but the decision was hers. Dagget and Mike stared at each other for a long and awkward moment. Irony wore badly on Dagget; the officer was obviously uncomfortable. When it was clear to Mike that Dagget would never make the first move, he broke the silence and put out his hand. "The name's Mike."

"I know who you are." Dagget folded his hands under his arms, declining the handshake. He glared past the tracker. A disparity in their heights—Mike was easily six inches taller—blunted the effect.

"Dagget, right?" Mike asked. He wasn't crazy about the arrangement. He wasn't sure he really trusted Dagget, either. Still, he wanted to help with the search. He had to.

"That's Officer Dagget, pal."

• • •

Shad Hammer was the sort of tech who preferred handling gear over dealing with people; that was Mike's impression. The tech probably had learned to appreciate the equipment because it was a crutch during conversations and a ready-made excuse for tinkering. As Dagget and Mike approached the van, Shad was reading the movie section of the local newspaper, his back propped against the vehicle. From behind his pages, Shad hummed the *Mission Impossible* theme.

"You need gear, you need the Shad," he said, smirking at the cleverness of his own introduction. Ditching the paper, Shad opened the rear door of the white van. Inside were neat, ordered rows of firearms, ammunition, and various electronic devices. Unzipping a black tactical bag with shoulder straps, Shad rattled off its contents: "Two walkie-talkies, encrypted transmissions. First aid kit, water filter, flashlights, batteries, maps. Protein bars, Gatorade mix and assorted freeze-dried provisions, and two syringes of epinephrine for the kid's asthma."

Besides the weight factor—food was heavy—to Mike the gear made sense. Except one item. "Why syringes?" Mike asked. "Auto-injectors are more portable and sturdy."

Shad nodded. "They would have been a better choice, yes. Unfortunately, this is what we had on hand." He continued. "A flare gun and three flares if we have radio trouble and need to locate you. And here's a special GPS, already calibrated for the terrain and preloaded with more than two dozen local maps . . ."

With a shake of his head, Mike said, "I've got my own, thanks."

Shad countered. "At least take it as a backup device."

"Definitely appreciated, but I only trust my own navigation gear," Mike said.

"Okay," Shad said. "Last—weapons. That USP is not going to cut it for you, Dagget."

"I know what I want," said Dagget, pointing toward a rifle with a high-capacity magazine and shoulder straps. "Gimme the AR with the scope."

Shad reached for the firearm.

"You don't want that," said Mike in such a way that Shad stopped reaching.

"And why not?" Dagget asked, snorting.

"It's heavy," Mike said. "Carry that for a few hours, it'll tire you out." He knew a few things about hauling heavy weaponry all day, even when he was exhausted.

"Pretending you even know what you're talking about, what do I want?" Dagget asked.

Mike pointed to a Marlin 444. It was a big bore rifle, designed for backwoods hunting and just over seven pounds loaded.

"I'd have to agree with him," said Shad, who nodded at Mike.

"Looks like a cap gun," Dagget said dismissively, his jaw clenched.

"That . . . ahem . . . cap gun can drop a grizzly bear. Forty-four pounds of recoil," Shad said. "Not for the meek. What about you, Mike? You want something?"

Mike shook his head no. He rarely carried anymore, and hunted even less. Weapons had their time and place.

Dagget stared at the rifle, hesitating.

"Listen," Shad said to Dagget. "It's what I would pack in this situation."

The last bit sold Dagget on the Marlin. He relented, reached for the rifle, and conceded. "It is pretty light."

"Let me get you a shoulder sling and some shells." Shad reached for the appropriate ammo box while Dagget checked the chamber, pointing the rifle at the ground. Shad grabbed the correct box without checking the label; the dimensions and weight told him all he needed to know. The shells rattled in the package.

Dagget found that the chamber was clear. Presenting two boxes of twenty rounds, each shell three hundred grains, Shad asked, "That enough?"

"If it takes more, we've got real problems," said Dagget, checking his watch. "I'll be back in a minute."

Shad laid the weapon against the bumper. The barrel pointed upward. "I'm impressed, Mike. Most cops grab a machine gun."

"We're not trying to clear a room," Mike said.

"No, you're not," Shad agreed. "Looks like Dagget is giving you a hard time."

"I don't take it personally," Mike said.

"Good." Shad paused. "Man, I'd swear our paths have crossed before. Were you ever in Fort Benning, Georgia?"

"A long time ago," Mike said, wistful for the past and at the same time, hesitant about looking back right now.

Shad yanked up his sleeve and revealed the Ranger scroll tattooed across the toned shoulder. Mike recognized a brother in his midst and smiled. When the sleeve fell back over the ink, they shook hands.

"What brings you out this way?" Mike said.

"Same thing that always held me back in the Army," Shad said. "I'm better with gear than getting promoted." He scrawled a cell number on his business card and tucked it in the gear bag. "If you need support out there, give me a shout. Technical or otherwise."

"I really appreciate that." *Never shall I fail my comrades.* Part of the Ranger creed.

"You'd do the same for me," Shad said. "And don't sweat Dagget. He just acts like he hates everyone."

10:00:42 AM

A public telephone at the corner of West End and 66th rang twice. The old phone booth had rusty hinges and glass covered with fingerprint smudges. Nicked and battered, the handset was slippery in his gloved hand. On the first ring of the fourth attempt, Crotty answered, and he shuttered the booth door. The barrier did little to deflect the noises of the morning commute. Horns beeped. Pedestrians shouted. And sweat beaded across his brow. Not from nerves, but rather from the heat outside.

"About time," a voice said to Crotty in a flat tone. This was the Partner speaking. "I've been trying to reach you since last night. Why did you do it?"

"I'm sorry, but it just wasn't working," Crotty said. Dealing with the Partner angered him enough, but having to justify his decisions over the phone was intolerable. His distaste surged through his voice. "You knew this was coming. Think of it like an early retirement." For his part, Crotty preferred thinking of it that way. He almost had to. And now David's body had to stay missing until it was safe for someone to find it.

"But he was with us from the beginning," the Partner said. "He was important."

"And had his efforts remained consistent," Crotty said, "he would still be with us. But he was slipping. Quality was down, complaints were up. I acted like an executive and made a decision. Try it sometime."

"You have no sense of loyalty."

"Look who's talking," Crotty said. "You make Dr. Jekyll look sane. One minute you're cracking skulls, the next you're preaching peace. It's not like you can't pull a trigger. Just spare me, okay? Maybe we can send some flowers anonymously."

"Flowers? Do you realize his mother is dying of cancer? That she's half blind? What sort of flowers would do in that situation?" The Partner continued, gathering steam. "You would understand these things if you actually talked to our employees once in a while."

"Who do you actually talk to? You talk to me and learn about issues through my status reports." Beyond the primary structure of the company was an elite group Crotty handpicked and trained, who answered only to him. Those men prepared reports he could trust. Those men he valued. Everyone else was a line item on the expense ledger. That included the Partner.

"Your bad judgment has placed me in an incredibly awkward position. You could not have picked a worse place for this. I hope you know that." Yet another token of resistance from the Partner.

"Life is about risks. Some pay off." He waited until that sunk in. Then Crotty added, "You mentioned a background check."

The Partner sighed, yielding. This argument was over. As usual, the Partner lost against Crotty's logic, because twisted as it seemed, Crotty delivered fiscal results. And there was no bringing back David St. John now. "Standard battery. Driving records, education, employment, medical. If you can find it, I want it."

"Give me the name," said Crotty. He read and spelled it back to the Partner, recording it correctly the first time. Beads of sweat smeared the ink into his palms. "Anything in particular I'm looking for?"

"Everything you can find." The Partner paused. "Now what about the boy?"

The boy who saw too much. The boy who saw the murder. That *was* a substantial wrinkle. Crotty had some regrets about the job. Most of all he regretted that the boy had wandered into company business. The scene ran over and over in his mind, refusing to disengage, like a videotape with the *play* button jammed. His own little Frankenstein—a mess he created and lost control of.

After killing David St. John, Crotty had driven along the dusty road toward the highway, wondering how many glasses of Tanqueray it would take to blot out what had just happened. More than a few, for certain.

While he was calculating, the boy lurched across the road, waving furiously, hailing Crotty like a cab ride out of a rough neighborhood after last call. Crotty had stopped and unrolled the window.

Panic had broken out on the boy's face, and he flat-out refused a ride back to the ranch, backing away from the sedan like Crotty's words were toxic. Noting the grass and mud stains on the boy's jeans, Crotty had made the connection: the boy had seen the murder. Before Crotty could give chase, the boy had dashed for the trees, disappearing among the greenery.

The only course then was to leave and dispatch his men, and break the news to the Partner. So Crotty fled. And now the morning after, the Partner wanted answers about the boy; the Partner wanted the problem fixed.

A pretty girl in a convertible and a tank top glanced at the phone booth, waiting for the stoplight on West End, jarring Crotty back into the present. He had a particular weakness for strawberry blond hair. The red tint accented the golden strands like a halo. He smiled at her.

The light changed and the car crept past the upscale shops that lined West End. When she was gone, his face morphed back into the face of a businessman who could kill, as if a fader on a light switch controlled his disposition.

With the phone held between his shoulder and chin, he removed a chain of rosary beads from his pocket. Crotty rubbed the two largest beads together. The smaller plastic spheres clicked as they slipped around in his hand. Some of his best ideas came when he did this.

"Every problem has a solution," Crotty snarled back at the Partner. "You just might not have the stomach for it."

Truth be told, Crotty wasn't convinced he had the stomach for it either.

Still, he knew what had to be done.

10:01:46 AM

The tactical bag topped out at more than twenty-five pounds. Between the shells and the rifle, the entire load breached the forty-pound mark. Though brimming with niceties, the excess mass was an awkward burden, and limited their flexibility. Constraints like these they did not need, given Dagget's physical condition.

Perhaps Dagget was in sound aerobic shape, a point he hammered again and again, but Mike was concerned. An hour a day on the treadmill, as Dagget claimed, was not the same as hiking in the open, toting a lead anchor for an unknown period of time. Mike appreciated the difference. Despite assurances from Dagget that the extra weight was a nonissue, the tracker held firm. Locked in a stalemate, yet another cell call arrived for Dagget, who ditched Mike to answer.

While the officer was out of earshot, Mike repacked the bag. First, he added back the walkie-talkies and maps. From the first aid kit—a dozen penicillins, surgical tape, a short tube of antibiotic cream, and the syringes and two vials of epinephrine. Despite the redundancy, he tucked an additional four penicillins in his pocket in a watertight container. There were also two thermal blankets, sealed in the original plastic. He added fifty feet of nylon rope. Gone were the three packs of batteries, the flashlights, and most of the food packets. This left them enough food for a day, maybe even forty-eight hours with careful rationing—nothing more. Beyond that, eating would take improvisation. In less than five minutes, Mike halved the load. His instincts said this was sufficient. He trusted his instincts.

Shad accepted the returned equipment with a wink and a nod. Nothing more needed to be said; Shad knew Dagget's ways.

When Dagget returned, Mike asked, "All set?"

"If we must," Dagget said, his tone disparaging.

"I'm curious," Mike said, facing Dagget squarely. "What is the source of this latent hostility?"

"Let's just get this done," Dagget said.

"No. We won't just get this done." Mike held the bag, just as before, his tone flat. "We can play this game a thousand ways, Dagget. I'm not here to be a shock absorber and I'm sure as hell not here to argue. I could be riding horses with my son. I could be patching things up with my ex-wife. There are bigger things going on here than our petty problems. Are you willing to live with the possibility that if Sean isn't found it was because two grown men couldn't be civil? I'm not."

Dagget leaned forward. "Don't you lay that crap on me. I didn't want this assignment." He stared at Mike intensely, the veins in his neck swelling. His chest heaved. He leaned closer to Mike, hands gnarled in tight fists.

Lowering the bag to the ground carefully, Mike said, "Well, you got the assignment. Now what?"

The last question touched off a crack in Dagget's armor like a pick spiked into a bed of ice. "Everyone gets what they deserve. . . ."

Ignoring the threat, Mike drove the conversation forward. "Lisbeth said you know the terrain. Let's talk about that."

"That's from years back," Dagget said. "Nobody really knows much of this area outside the ranch anymore. The tourist part wasn't always here. It used to be a purely commercial ranch. I worked on it as a teenager for a few summers. Thousands of acres, nearly all undeveloped. You could wander for days and not see anyone."

"Is the water safe?"

"Near the ranch?" Dagget asked. "Safe enough, or at least it was back then. Never hunted much. Always heard there's plenty of game and fish."

Polluted with one or more bacterial contaminants, nearly every open stream in North America required treatment before drinking,

Mike mused. Most filtration techniques took time and equipment. The best choice for hikers on the move were iodine tablets. The pills were messy, fouled the water, and usually stained one's hands and clothes, but they worked. Penicillin picked up where iodine fell short. Sean had neither option; he would have to drink from whatever water source was available. If Sean was lucky, diarrhea was the worst consequence he faced.

"What about that mountain lion sighting?" asked Mike.

"It wasn't that far from here. Personally, I've never been up close to one and I hope I never am. Had an attack about six years ago. Big cat ripped a college student right off a mountain bike. Wasn't much left to find."

Dagget's aversion to mountain lions resonated with Mike. Mike loved domesticated cats, and had owned a few, and still never wanted to encounter their larger brothers. Aggressive hunters, mountain lions attacked without provocation. "How's your shot with the handgun?" Mike asked.

"Good," Dagget said.

Mike pressed further. "What kind of groupings?"

"Two inches at a hundred yards," Dagget said. "Roughly."

"Closer to two or closer to three?" A huge difference between those numbers, Mike knew better than to blindly accept self-appraisals. A very fine line separated asset from liability. Before a crisis, it was best to know which he had.

"I said two," Dagget said, irritated.

"Can I see the Marlin for a second?" Mike asked.

"Why?"

"I might need to fire it. What if a mountain lion eats you?"

Begrudgingly, Dagget handed the rifle to Mike. The maneuver was fluid enough, though Mike noticed something else: Dagget's hands shook as he draped the big caliber weapon across Mike's palm.

His hands shake a bit, Mike thought. *Not good.* "Let's split the carrying duties—one guy the pack, the other the rifle. We'll swap based on fatigue."

"Hell, I don't expect to get tired," said Dagget.

Mike slung the rifle over his shoulder.

Heading west from the road to the dude ranch, they crossed a field of burnt-out grass, then plunged into a thicket of Douglas fir. The canopy dampened the morning light, and cut the temperature by five degrees. Cooler air from the south wicked away the moisture beading on their foreheads and necks.

Beech trees, sprinkled among the pines, formed a green and silver tapestry. Unlike beech trees in more traveled areas, these trunks were spared the initials, hearts, and other etchings. So many hikers carved messages in beeches, the trees earned the nickname 'American Graffiti' trees. Though the hikers hoped the missives scraped into the trunks lasted lifetimes, the engravings actually weakened and killed countless specimens each year. But the ones bordering the ranch were flawless and unspoiled.

Soon the two men moved beyond the sight of the other searchers. Periodically, the voices of officers calling for Sean reached them. The trees muted their voices.

Mike breathed through his nose, the air passing through the sinus cavity almost silently. This reflected his fitness level. For Mike there was no more inhumane form of self-punishment than aerobics. He disliked cardiovascular exertion like a child loathed vegetables. Dr. Stoler, his knee surgeon, had prescribed a rigorous rehabilitation plan that included bike, elliptical, and stair work. Mike balked, yet followed the regime.

Not only was Dagget not in such good shape, he had, as Mike suspected on many other points, greatly exaggerated his capabilities. Now there was no doubt who led this expedition.

The tracker set the frenetic pace.

Mike moved like a coyote, nimble and sure of himself, ready to change course at any time. Technique came with practice, with time in the woods and dirt, out among the elements. Every tracker developed a distinctive stalking style based on his gait and personality.

Crossing among the pines, Mike halted and threw his arm out without warning, blocking the officer across the chest. The maneuver was unexpected and unappreciated. Dagget complained loudly between gasps.

Leaves shredded by exposure to the elements concealed the edges of a narrow trail. The dirt was loose, highly responsive to touch.

Crouching where the trail met the tree line, Mike cast circles with his first and second finger around several indents in the ground. As he bent down, his knee cracked. Though it happened often, he rarely noticed the popping, the way someone who lives near a highway no longer hears the drone of traffic. Busted knees; sciatica; broken backs, arms and necks—all these maladies plagued former smoke jumpers. A torn meniscus had been the price of smoke jumping for Mike—his token and burden.

When Dagget righted his breathing, the officer was furious. "What the hell was that for?"

With his fingertips hovering over the print's center, Mike placed his hand inside the track. His hand remained still. Dagget, the woods, and everything else became irrelevant. He waited through the moment and the images came to him, even with his eyes open and hostility in the air. Ready or not, the pictures flooded his head.

For an instant he was acutely aware of Sean; Mike *was* that fourteen-year-old boy running from a murder scene, instead of a thirty-four-year-old man on vacation.

Animals left behind more than smudges in the soil or broken branches. They left fragments of their emotional state; the tracks temporarily preserved that energy. The intersection of the trail and the tree line marked a substantial shift in the boy's emotions. Sean was more than frightened crossing the trail. He was confused. The boy had turned around several times and wandered, almost skirted, sideways. His steps were stilted, his gait shorter than normal. Less thrusting off from the toe, more on the heel. All that suggested uncertainty and caution.

Sean thaought that the ranch was this way. He only realized the truth at the trail. He had aimed for a landmark in the distance. Intuition had failed him, and he knew he was lost.

Mike rose and turned away from Dagget.

"Quitting already?" Dagget asked.

"I'll be back in a few minutes. Wait here for me."

"What are you looking for now?"

"I'll know it when I see it," said Mike, stranding Dagget with nothing more than a voice and the pack. He wanted to find the landmark that Sean had been running toward. If Sean had locked on a visual cue in the midst of panic, it likely was striking. And it had to be dramatic, because a frightened child would notice nothing less. Mike worked backward over the last hundred yards. Nothing appeared impressive enough to captivate a kid from Brooklyn.

Ten minutes passed; it was time to move forward. Lisbeth's status report loomed. Mike filed the question for later, certain the answer would reveal itself in time.

Returning to the trail, Mike saw that Dagget and the backpack were gone.

11:17:45 AM

Gathering the background report the Partner had requested was fraught with complications. Not that the work was beyond his capabilities. Crotty certainly had the necessary access levels. He knew the computer systems and the right people to ask. No, what he lacked was an explanation. A reason that cloaked the request in such insignificance that questions about why he wanted the information would be unnecessary.

He faced the usual constraints at his day job at the Department of Homeland Security. Even though a National Security Letter opened all the doors and brought instant cooperation from any number of corporations and government agencies, an administrator had to sign off on the request, and that meant a paper trail. Documentation could be deadly; words on a page might boomerang and return later at the worst of moments. Exactly the reason all communication between himself and the Partner was conducted via pay phones, or in person. He refused to give anyone the proof to hang him with later. Crotty knew that when dealing with the bosses, what he said mattered far less than what someone could prove he had said. So he was cautious about what he committed to paper.

Once he had trusted people at DHS. Well, now he knew better.

Crotty thanked Rosen—a former Section Chief with his own motives—for that lesson. Rosen taught him how to make the job work for him, rather than work the job for the check.

Under Rosen, Crotty's autonomy far exceeded his stated title: Senior Case Agent. Practically a license to kill, in fact. Technically only Directors could authorize discretionary lethal force—albeit unofficially—and though Rosen had not yet become a Director, rumors said the job was his. Until then, Rosen was building bridges in anticipation of the promotion. He promised Crotty a fast track to the top alongside him. In exchange, Rosen wanted Crotty to penetrate M2.

For years, the M2 crime syndicate had funneled stolen intellectual property out of the United States and Western Europe to the former Soviet Republics and Asia in exchange for heavy and small arms. The arms were resold and used to bankroll legitimate businesses. Crotty's direction was simple: figure out who was in M2. Not periphery characters, either. Rosen coveted figureheads; he wanted everything. Convictions, not red tape, he said. Getting results meant getting creative because the organization was so clever.

A convoluted, almost cell-like structure, it eluded any serious investigation for ages. Year after year, M2 and its subsidiaries prospered, circumventing federal and state authorities as if an invisible hand guided the organization past the reaches of prosecution. Before Crotty, no law enforcement agency had breached M2 any deeper than the first tier.

Armed with his mandate, the complicated tangle of relationships and laundering fronts slowly unfurled. After eighteen months of night-and-day maneuvers—many of dubious legality—Crotty amassed enough evidence and sources for a substantial sting. He worked to put the bad guys away. He worked for the promotion. He worked like a loyal dog who believed in its master. His findings implicated one high-level M2 member and scores of mid-level operatives dead to rights. Success was so close.

Then Rosen spiked the operation. Every trace of the M2 case files, photographs, voice recordings, and digital archives were "refiled," reclassified as "Top Secret." Rosen barred Crotty legally from reading his own investigation materials. Three days later, a fire in Crotty's apartment destroyed all of his personal copies of the case files.

When Crotty pressed for an explanation, Rosen claimed that due to budget overruns there was no longer sufficient funding. So Crotty protested. He had good reason to.

There was a fortune in seized assets available for agency use. On one M2 buy, Crotty employed a three million dollar flashroll—real money "flashed" ahead of a buy to show M2 suppliers he was a legitimate buyer and could be trusted to deliver the entire amount when the time came. Rosen had pushed back from the desk and explained the scope of the investigation had changed course. Discussion closed.

Crotty got the point. And just in case Crotty misunderstood, Rosen also mentioned his concern about Crotty's recent investigative tactics. What a shame it might be if those allegations found substantiation, Rosen had said.

No charges were filed, no case ever was presented for prosecution. Six months later Rosen retired, Maui-bound. Turned out a rich uncle willed Rosen a generous stock portfolio. Yeah, Crotty knew better. And despite his frustration with the outcome, Crotty marveled at how well Rosen had played him. Rosen got valuable information worth a fortune if it was kept in the shadows, with no risk to his safety—right at his front door. He blackmailed M2 and made the investigation go away.

From that moment Crotty opened himself to the possibilities. He knew the investigation pipeline. He knew the protocol. He knew the evidence, which team had it and how much and what they had. He knew what cases lacked merit, and what might stick.

Most importantly, he knew what confidential information about underworld figures was worth. He kept the day job, and freelanced at night. Nearly all customers were welcome. Personal or professional affiliation was seldom a basis for discrimination. Call it bribery or treason, he preferred the term competitive intelligence.

One of the most valuable things Crotty could offer the underworld were names and places. Who was working undercover.

When were they most likely alone and least suspecting retribution. Absolute gold to someone unaware he was an investigation target.

Initially the duplicity had tugged at his sense of ethics. Selling out the first name was rough. He had hesitated. He tortured himself endlessly, second-guessing the consequences, missing sleep and meals as he considered what his decision really meant. Then he got a postcard from Rosen in Maui. A blank card, except for the phrase:

Life is good. —R

Crotty had taken one look around his tiny apartment and decided life could be good for him, too. Just not on his salary. And then there was the girlfriend and her needs. He made the call.

Shortly after revealing the identity of an agent to the leader of a gang he was investigating, the compromised agent disappeared. Maybe the outed agent had quit or was convinced to resign. Maybe he had double-crossed the wrong person. Maybe the thug who bought the profile had liquidated the poor bastard. Maybe it was a coincidence. Crotty always wondered, but he never asked.

On occasion, the day job called him away from business. Brief diversions, usually. Lately though, the Suits rode roughshod, and harped about quotas. Undercover work defied traditional metrics; it wasn't like setting up a speed trap and writing tickets. Building cases, working sources of information—these activities took time. Success at them meant knowing the street. The only time some Suits saw the streets was through a limousine window.

Unfortunately, there were far more new managers than there was logic and experience. Younger, unseasoned, and far less accommodating, green managers seemed bent on some hidden agenda. Many case agents suspected housecleaning, a deliberate process of cycling out older agents for younger models. The net effect: neither the new guard nor the experienced agents trusted each other, and both sides wished the other would fail.

And today Crotty needed information and his sympathetic cohorts were on assignment. Approaching the division head was out of the question, because claiming that the target was a source of information meant opening a file. Right back to that paper trail.

This was the chore he pondered over a cup of decaffeinated tea.

He stirred the beverage, steeped precisely for four minutes. Steam floated off the surface of the dark brown liquid. He sipped and thought, neglecting the pending case report next to the keyboard. An agent passed by his desk. The reflection of the passing man displaced the text and blinking cursor on his screen.

Crotty smiled at the sheer elegance of a solution that had presented itself. Reaching into the drawer for a USB flash drive and a pad of paper, he knew exactly what to do.

First he pulled up the contents of the file from the disk drive on the screen. He kept the file on the drive, because once it was on the local machine, a compliance program logged details about the file.

Deleting the logs created another entry far beyond his reach. Traffic to the network printer from any terminal was monitored. Details about every print job—including the author and the raw data—were archived indefinitely. Only at the shell prompt at the machine was the action untraceable. Writing text to the pad, he respected both case and spelling.

The program was simple, only a few lines of code. Now he needed to push the program where it served him best. That meant the Internet. Street agents had Web access for research; however, the Network Operations Center tracked all browsing activity. State-of-the-art equipment recorded and logged phone calls on hard drives in a remote data center. While his cell phone had Web access, the building was a dead zone and no signal could penetrate the walls.

Not a problem for Crotty. One machine—available to all staff—lay outside the firewall and the reach of the NOC. Instead of a commercial trunk line connection, the phone company listed the line as a residential DSL customer, registered under a false name and billed to a private mailbox. The kiosk had no physical connection to the network and existed for one purpose: a mechanism for browsing in complete anonymity. A slow connection; the lack of a USB port, floppy drive, or printer; and no local file storage, ensured data remained on the screen. Since the kiosk was in the center of the office, visible to nearly everyone, illicit uses were impossible. Any deed, evil or otherwise, required time and risked being observed.

The dilemma: find a mechanism to unleash the code. He drafted a message. A brief note, it requested someone's presence immediately at the usual place, at the usual time, without mentioning details. For the recipient, he chose a Suit.

Saving the code as an attachment inside the e-mail, he submitted the form. An e-mail anonymizer service did the rest, bouncing the message across the globe between participating remailers. Each hop altered another message header until the forged message resembled a legitimate e-mail from the sender.

Merely viewing the message executed the code inside the attachment, which retrieved a program from another server and installed it on the local machine. All this happened automatically, and without the recipient's knowledge. Although Network Operations warned management about the risk of Internet mail, Suits ignored techs. Janitors rated higher in the eyes of management. If a virus was loose on the network, it meant a Suit had installed forbidden software or opened an electronic message from an untrusted source. Mayhew, the Suit in question, would trust the forged source. Crotty made the note look like it was from his girlfriend. Mayhew would certainly read the message; not many men passed up sex in the middle of the day.

As Crotty was walking back from the lavatory, Mayhew barreled down the narrow hallway toward him, nearly an hour before the Suit's usual lunch break. Mayhew walked like a man who was already late, rubber heels gliding along the floor. With a harried glance, the Suit dodged to the left. Crotty mirrored the move, leaned to the right, and collided into the senior officer. The impact was severe enough that neither could dismiss the accident with silence or a nod. Both men stopped.

Crotty apologized first. "I'm sorry. My fault entirely. "

"It's all right." Mayhew checked his tie, the half Windsor knot perfectly arranged. Satisfied with the spot check, Mayhew stepped away.

"Sir, the Heinz case initiation report is finished," Crotty said.

Mayhew turned back like a man summoned to take out the weekly trash by a nagging spouse. "You can leave it on my desk." The problem dismissed, he began leaving again.

"What's a good time to review the report?" Crotty asked.

"I'll ring you when I'm ready," Mayhew said, a bit rushed.

Crotty loitered at his desk for a minute, pretending to finish another report. First, he called his long-distance carrier. They put him on hold.

A voice, neither recognizably male nor female, announced the wait time was over an hour. Perfect. Muting the handset, he abandoned the receiver and bolted. Since everyone was on assignment or at lunch, he owned the corridor. He had to make it to Mayhew's office before the screen saver locked the terminal; Mayhew had left in too big a hurry to do so manually.

No witness saw Crotty run the shell prompt on Mayhew's terminal. No witness saw Crotty navigate to the directory of interest or search the files created by the keylogger software Mayhew unwittingly installed. No witness saw the software that captured every move, and recorded every keystroke, every user name and password in a text file. No witness saw Crotty log in as Mayhew and run queries against those restricted databases.

The only record: audit trails at the Network Operations Center, the FBI, and the DEA. And all they showed was Mayhew had requested and printed information. Crotty wrote down the user names and passwords for future reference, uninstalled the key-logger, and wiped the local files the program created.

Crotty returned to his assigned desk, still on hold with the long-distance company. He increased the volume. Ads for the telecommunication services over a soundtrack of mangled Mahler crackled on a headset speaker. Scanning the profile, he was intrigued. The Partner was vague about what the background check was for, whether it was in consideration for employment or blackmail. What Crotty read about the target so far, he rather liked.

Line two rang. The display flashed *Mayhew, P.* Crotty still languished on hold on line one with the phone company.

"Where's the report?" asked Mayhew, his voice petulant. Crotty kept the report to preserve his alibi. As far as the official record was concerned, Crotty had been on the phone for over an hour, never in Mayhew's office.

"Sorry," Crotty said. "I've been on hold since we spoke. I'll drop it off now."

Crotty stuffed the findings for the Partner in a self-sealing, legal-size manila envelope. He found the best hiding places were right in front of everyone's eyes. Secure from nosy office mates, he slid the envelope under a pile of other papers on the desk.

His Mike Brody research would have to wait.

11:20:31 AM

Outside the stable, a breeze washed over the morning, and ranch hands paired each guest with a horse.

Horses were Jessica Barrett's first love and a major part of her life. As a child she had owned an older horse named Poco who suffered from degenerative arthritis. When Poco passed on Jessica's thirteenth birthday, it was devastating. Sympathetic to the loss, her father gave her a fantastic Arabian, Majique. And with Majique's help, Jessica got over Poco, and mastered riding.

Majique could be difficult, refused any formal training, and demanded a confident rider. Only Jessica sufficed, only Jessica dared ride bareback. Every summer morning they sailed through the open fields until the sun rose. Winters she dashed off the school bus and rode until an hour before sunset.

Saddling up at the dude ranch that morning on Tic-Tac, her horse for the week, transported her back to Majique. Tic-Tac strongly resembled her beloved companion. The similarity was welcome, yet almost overwhelming. After talking Andy through his mount, she climbed on Tic-Tac from the left side, right hand gripping the cantle. From the instant she eased into the saddle and fed her foot into the stirrups, it all felt right and familiar. Rolling with the feeling, she tested out Tic-Tac. First a stand, then a gentle trot.

"You're a natural," Erich said to Jessica, approaching on horseback.

"Thanks!" she gushed, enough to hear it in her own voice. There it was again, that feeling of self-consciousness and attraction stirring at once. She had been there before, long ago. What she wasn't certain about was if she was ready to go back again. She concentrated on the riding, and tapping a connection so treasured from her past.

"In fact," Erich said, "you are way ahead of this group." A smile revealed a row of capped teeth.

Jessica glanced backward. Behind her, a mishmash of guests struggled, some fighting their animals by climbing up the right side. Even Andy trailed Erich by nearly a dozen lengths.

"Oh." The embarrassment of neglecting Andy in her enthusiasm was too acute to conceal, so she tugged the reins, and looked away as she spoke, avoiding his gaze. "I'll circle back."

"Take your time," Erich said. "I believe you'll find his stride quite powerful when you need it." Erich peeled away and rejoined the group. Jessica turned her focus on Andy.

Jessica suspected Mr. Jones—Andy's ready and willing horse—wanted a rider with more chops, a rider somewhere between novice and intermediate. Andy was not quite intermediate; he was more a novice. Before Pine Woods he had not ridden in a year. She decided that Andy might not be the best rider, but he was right enough for Mr. Jones. While she doubted he was entirely ready, she was willing to take the chance. She would keep an eye on her son.

"Doing great, Andy," Jessica said. "Remember, keep your hands on the reins. Never drop them."

The boy gripped the leather straps tighter, rising from a slump. "Do you think Dad will make it to dinner?" Andy asked.

"When he gets back, he'll be here," she said.

"So by tonight?" Andy said.

This conversation was far too familiar for her taste. The divorce had spared them all the inconveniences of Mike's many unplanned, always inconvenient, absences. Whether he was in Arizona tracking an escaped prisoner or in Palau leading a scuba dive excursion, her ex-husband was out more often than he was present. She had tried everything to resuscitate the marriage. She fought valiantly, but a SWAT team of therapists had failed at helping them resolve their marital issues. Now with their separate residences and lives—it was just normal business—he was gone. This trip was supposed to be different.

Yet there was no convincing Andy that Mike was anything other than a hero. Mindful of that, she tempered her reply. "We'll see." Noticing his disappointment, Jessica fell back on what she could control. "You ready to learn a little bit about riding?"

"Yeah," Andy said, excited, "teach me how to ride like Dad."

Jessica almost said Mike hated riding and only bothered with it because sometimes the tours required it. "How about I show you how to ride like you? Get a feel for it first. We can go from there."

"I guess so," Andy said.

"When you're ready, I promise I'll show you a trick your dad doesn't know."

"Really?" His eyes lit up like a boy presented with a treasured family keepsake, then struggled with the weight of the gift. "But Dad's an expert!"

Suggesting anything to the contrary was futile. Jessica knew this. The boy loved his father as much as the stories that surrounded him. Someday her son would see Mike as a whole person, the balance of strengths and faults. Today was not that day. Today the boy worshiped his father and saw no wrong.

"Sounds crazy," Jessica said, "but I know how to do a few cool things, too."

Andy laughed. "Sure, Mom."

They smiled at each other and then glanced back to the group wrestling with their animals. A man traveling with his wife and son cursed at his Arabian. The insult drew a stern correction from his wife. Some of the guests had struggled long enough to be surrounded by clouds of dust.

A female wrangler, not a trace of dirt on her jeans, helped load the cowpokes onto horses, directing the stragglers in a patient tone. The soil of the riding pen resembled a parking lot on a snowy night after a teenager had turned figure eights in a sports car.

"Take a picture for Dad," said Andy.

Discretely, Jessica clicked two shots. One was a woman with a neglected manicure riding along the rail, as if she might surrender at any time and clutch the posts. The second was a teenager whipping the butt of a horse with an open palm. She suppressed the urge to yell at the teenager. She had enough problems keeping tabs on Andy.

Taking both pictures on the sly, she remained mindful of the surroundings. No one else snapped pictures right then, or even held cameras. The presence of photographic equipment or tape recorders often colored people's responses. Some might be more animated, exaggerating details and experiences, or outright lying.

On the flip side, some people shunned a recorded conversation. In between the gung ho and the shy was the story. A reporter got there by keeping both the extremes and the middle in play. Everyone's point of view mattered.

There was already talk swirling about Jessica and Andy thanks to Mike. Discretely, Jessica sheathed the camera inside her saddle bag, comforted that no one had noticed.

"What do you think Dad's doing now?" Andy asked.

"Whatever it is," Jessica said, "I'm sure he's giving it his all."

11:45:22 AM

Now Mike had to decide whether to fret about Dagget or continue farther into the woods. Dagget was a grown man, a police officer with gear, a man with alleged woods savvy—so Mike had been told. Mike was seriously questioning that assertion lately.

Regardless, finding Sean Jackson was the priority, and hunting for Dagget took time away from that. To Mike, that was unacceptable.

Yet, like it or not, he needed Dagget to some degree, primarily as a conduit to the other searchers. Mike had not proven himself to anyone on the force but Lisbeth, and until then, the others probably would discount his opinion. Should the same words come from Dagget, they might just listen.

Besides, working with Dagget offered other advantages. Two sets of eyes were better than one.

Dagget also had the backpack, which held an extremely important item: epinephrine for Sean. Mike improvised many things in his years, but never a sealed vial of epinephrine. There was no natural equivalent in the wild.

But waiting for Dagget was also unacceptable. Rotting away in limbo hampered the search, provided Dagget even returned. He had only one way for contacting Dagget—no walkie-talkie, no cell number—so he shouted the officer's name a few times. To Mike, the lack of options put both men in a regrettable position.

After ten minutes of shouting and waiting in vain, he pressed forward.

In case Dagget decided he wanted back in the game, Mike marked the trail. Every four hundred feet he placed a reflective marker in the soil. When he turned left or right he set two markers parallel to each other, and staggered them. The higher of the two indicated the direction of the turn. He wasn't certain if Dagget would be able to read the marks, but he knew he had done all he could.

What to do about Lisbeth and her briefings was another matter. Her phone number was on the business card in Mike's back pocket. He still had cell signal. He could call now, tell her the score, or wait. He chose the second.

Technically, his first report was due within the hour. *How's it going with Dagget?* Mike imagined Lisbeth asking. *Just great. He left. Been fantastic ever since.*

Like Dagget himself, Lisbeth's motives for the assignment were baffling. Even given the shortage of resources and the small department, certainly a less surly officer was available. Lisbeth had chosen Dagget anyway. Well, Mike had worked with the police before, and managed various personalities and agendas. He could deal.

Pop psychologists said resistant clients were clients in transition, poised on the cusp of a breakthrough.

His ex-wife was a big fan of psychology, having minored in the subject during college. Mike had been the target of many of her theories. Certainly, Dagget was resistant. Maybe all the officer needed was a nudge to the light of reason. Winning converts to the cause of tracking was less interesting to Mike Brody than results. In the end, everything else—all the discomfort and inconvenience—was only temporary.

His results-based approach was less about the ends justifying the means, and more about the ends. Sidestepping local politics was costly not just in terms of ill will and hurt feelings; it was isolating; it forced Mike into a leadership position. He believed energy served him best when funneled into areas with a chance for clear results. And that area was tracking, not ego stroking. Leaving the situation with Dagget behind at the trees, Mike began following Sean's movements.

Heading west, Sean had stuck to a trail wide enough for two men shoulder to shoulder. The boy's movements were less rushed, though they still belied confusion. Mike pressed on, hiking farther up the path.

These were the moments when time stopped mattering. After hitting his mark, moving across distances required less effort, even great ones. He moved effortlessly. Only the barest details distracted him: a breeze, pine needles brushing against the skin, branches lying on the trail.

Another half hour passed. Sweat beads dribbled down his forehead and neck, chilling his eyebrows and trapezius muscles. Perspiration slithered and stung a cut on his chin. He let the beads roll.

Dryness spread across his lips. He opened the canteen. Just a tiny sip. Water was crucial and grew more important over time. A steady supply of potable water was every hiker's dilemma. Here it was doubly true, since Dagget had the iodine, leaving him no way to purify the water on the move. He must conserve.

When he committed the waypoint into the GPS back at the road, it showed a network of streams within two miles. A sprawling finger pattern covered the screen.

Mike revisited the coordinates. Navigating through the display by clicking a round button on the top of the device, he noted the tributaries. The level of detail was incredible. Roads, streets, lakes, and town names all had been available on these maps for years. Lots of 4x4 trails and lately many hiking trails were visible, though the level of detail varied by region. Heavily traveled areas had the best coverage. And as more backpackers used GPS units to collect and exchange data, the number of uncharted trails shrunk yearly. Now remote, unmapped areas in twenty-first century North America were rare finds indeed.

A stream was within a half mile, perhaps ten minutes on foot. Mike had antibiotics if contaminants had soiled the stream. Virtually all open streams in North America had one of several bacteria that caused uncomfortable stomach issues. With a finite supply of water left, this was the time for awareness and planning. Better consider options now, rather then later when he was tired, Mike reasoned.

He reached for his cell phone just as it started ringing.

11:59:10 AM

Lisbeth called ahead of schedule. That she had the number already was not all that mysterious. Law enforcement officials could obtain information easily.

"Are you ignoring me, Mr. Brody?" Lisbeth said.

"Not at all," Mike said.

"I tried the walkie-talkie."

"I didn't hear it," Mike said. True, Dagget had them.

"And all these years everyone has told me I'm too loud," Lisbeth said.

"More authoritative than loud."

"Let's not get into semantics," Lisbeth said. "Give me your coordinates."

Mike gave them to her, wondering what to say about Dagget.

"So where are we with the search?" Lisbeth asked.

Right to business, no wasting time. "I suspect Sean fixed on something in the distance for navigation," he said. "Once I figure what it is, we can cut a lot of time. It's probably something obvious, but I'm not getting it just yet."

"We head him off?"

"Exactly," Mike said. "Get there before he does, and box him in on as many sides as possible. Then we start pressing."

"I like it."

Sensing the moment was right, Mike tried a question. "Where

are the other searchers in relation to us?" he asked. "I haven't heard much out this way in a while."

"Don't worry about where everyone else is. I'm on top of it. Keep in mind that it's a small but growing search team, spread out across a large area. What matters is that we stay in contact and can converge when we need to."

"And the helicopters?" Mike asked.

"All I get are promises for callbacks," Lisbeth said.

Unfortunate, thought Mike. Helicopters excelled at scanning large areas, especially when combined with thermal-imaging systems. Some imaging systems like FLIR were sensitive enough to capture the heat patterns from an animal's breathing five minutes after it happened. "That guy that owns the ranch, Erich, mentioned something about a Cessna. Maybe he could help."

"I've worked with Erich before," she said. "I can try that. So how is it going with Dagget?"

He had to admit, Lisbeth was sharp. "Uh . . ." Mike stalled. "You know Dagget."

"He didn't answer his cell phone or the walkie. I'm almost positive both are functioning properly. So . . ."

"Right. He's not with me," said Mike, trying to avert the question he expected.

"Where is he? Taking a whiz?"

Lisbeth provided a perfect excuse. "I'm sure at some point that will happen," Mike said, his tone a bit leading. He felt like she would not entirely believe the misdirection.

"Am I smacking into the brotherhood?"

"The brotherhood?" Mike asked.

"Men stick up for each other. Especially if one of them is in trouble with a woman. They never admit to this, of course."

Mike wished such an organization existed; he might still be married.

She continued. "Now, is there anything else you want to tell me about Dagget?"

He's a pain in the ass, he thought. Aloud, he said, "He's Dagget. How much is there to say? You know him better than I do."

"Despite his brusque manners," Lisbeth said, "when push comes to shove, he gets things done. Sometimes he just needs a different kind of convincing to get there."

Right then, Lisbeth reminded him of Jessica. Lisbeth was strong. She was not one who waited around for answers from others. And like his ex-wife, Lisbeth gathered her own information and drew her own conclusions. Even when the hunches missed, he respected that she voiced them.

Lisbeth continued. "That being said, without a search partner, I can't let you continue. So I expect to hear from Dagget within the hour—however you make that happen."

After promising to have Dagget call her back, Mike said good-bye.

Still thinking about Jessica, he called and left a quick voice message for her. As an afterthought he mentioned Lisbeth's helicopter crisis. To another person, it might have seemed odd to mention that tidbit, but if they had spoken she certainly would have asked about the search.

As he hung up, a boot snapped a branch in half two hundred yards behind him.

12:10:24 PM

Though he could not see, Mike heard someone creeping among the pines. He yelled Dagget's name. Awaiting a reply, he called again, more forcefully. Only the snapping of a branch reverberating through the trees returned.

In the woods, *hello* was a word used with caution. Near hillsides, voices echoed off of rocks and ledges, which sometimes mangled the word *hello* into *help*. A wicked trick of acoustics and far from the truth, because Mike Brody wanted no help. He wanted a response and the lack of one unnerved him. Enough that the receptors in the midbrain, the reactive part of the organ responsible for survival decisions, engaged. Racing, his heart compressed several beats into one.

When perceiving stress, he took three quick breaths, exhaling slowly on the third. The rush of oxygen relaxed his taut muscles and calmed his nerves. Saddled with Dagget—his personal penance for abandoning the vacation—he could not relax easily.

And then the footfalls stopped, replaced by the baying of tree frogs in a nearby lake bed. A breeze magnified the scent of pines. His breathing and pulse self-corrected, leveling at forty-three beats per minute.

Dagget appeared, solving one problem.

"Where did you go?" Mike demanded.

With a similar intensity, Dagget countered, "Why didn't you come back to the trail for me?"

"I might ask the same thing," Mike said, unyielding and unrepentant.

"You disappear for twenty minutes and I'm supposed to hang around doing nothing?" Dagget said. "No way. I heard someone, so I checked out a few things on my own."

Mike said this harshly: "I asked you to wait."

"Like you waited?" Dagget asked. The red on his face deepened as he pointed at Mike. "It's a damn good thing you dropped those markers or I'd have no idea where you went. Did it ever occur to you to look for me?"

"I'm not here to track you. I'm here . . . "

Dagget interjected. "I shouldn't be here, either. That body was my find. That's the case I should be on."

Mike thought for a moment. Detectives handled homicide investigations, not street cops like Dagget, and he wondered why Dagget was wishing he could do someone else's job. Then again, the body vanished under his watch.

The officer probably felt a little guilty—and maybe embarrassed—about what went down at the murder scene. "Okay well, we're both here now, so let's move on."

"This is crap. *Mr. Famous* just waltzes into the middle of something . . ." He paused and pointed at Mike. "Something that you have no idea about. I hope you know what you're doing. I'm praying right now that you actually do. Ask yourself something. Is this being run like any other search you've ever seen?"

Mike had to admit it was unusual. But that was not necessarily a bad thing. A search reflected the decisions made by those in charge, and the individuals involved. Each was unique. "There's always confusion at the beginning until everyone gets up to speed. It smooths out over time."

"Very diplomatic of you. That doesn't make Lisbeth less manipulative or answer my question."

Mike had trouble thinking about the situation in the terms Dagget suggested. He had trouble because it meant doubting Lisbeth. "Right. I hear you're frustrated," Mike said. "Let's start moving and we can talk about it. I'll listen."

Dagget sighed and followed Mike. They moved again in silence, save for Dagget's staccato breathing pattern. Air pushed through his sinus cavity and rattled the malformed cartilage of his deviated septum. The net effect: a short, low-pitched whistle when he inhaled. Not every time, but often. Mike had missed it earlier.

"Lisbeth wants you to call," Mike said, at a point which seemed the right moment—in the lull before their conversation started.

"And why am I hearing this from you?" Dagget asked gruffly.

"She said she tried you first," said Mike, shrugging.

"News to me." Holding down the button on the walkie-talkie, Dagget buzzed Lisbeth. A few moments passed before the dialogue started. Lisbeth did most of the speaking.

Dagget peeled off from the trail to have the conversation, turning the volume down, although Mike could still hear both sides of the conversation.

"You disappeared," Lisbeth said.

"I was checking something out."

"You are supposed to be checking things out with Mike. As in together."

"It was just a misunderstanding . . ." Dagget said.

"Work through that," Lisbeth said, "or you're both coming back in. And you don't want that, because there's really nothing much for you to do around here. Unless you like the smell of car exhaust and parking tickets. That clear enough?"

"Yes, Detective." The shock was all over his face.

"Excellent. Next time answer when I buzz you." Her firm statement ended the conversation.

When Dagget jammed the walkie-talkie into the belt holster, the plastic catch almost snapped in half from the force. He scowled. He did not look at Mike for some time. Finally he spoke. "There's a stream a minute from here. I'll go fill the canteens."

• • •

Sean Jackson hardly remembered the sensation of pedaling his arms and legs. That was before the stiffness in his muscles and joints. Sore from sleeping on the hard ground, he was tired. A mild case of dehydration aggravated a pull in his quadriceps. Hunger and thirst made his head throb.

When he found a wide stream, he celebrated by shouting, collapsing on the soil, and dunking half of his head beneath the surface.

The liquid turned his stomach on end and burned his sinuses, but he gulped more. Sean drank greedily without regard for taste or temperature, sucking in so much all at once he nearly choked. His throat was raw and burned as if he had puked. He was so happy, Sean could ignore the stomach acid. At last he had water.

For half of the first day, he denied his predicament. He just rejected it without question. Surely the right trail, the right turn, the right move was around the next stretch. It just *had* to be.

In the beginning, the trees had varied as he crisscrossed through the woods. He remembered that. He had noticed the difference between a beech and a pine. This was no longer true. Fatigue had sharply eroded his cognitive skills.

Now when he noticed the trees at all, they were part of the same blur: massive, knotty trunks, covered with green, pirouetting toward the sun. As daunting as the landscape might be, he stared upwards for long stretches, missing breaths. This lack of oxygen further aggravated his panic receptors, making his steps more unsteady.

His chest was clear and open, and for that he was grateful. Whenever it tightened, he tapped the inhaler and a warm rush washed through his lungs.

What scared Sean about asthma was less the symptoms and more the loss of control. Painful as asthma could be, the physical discomfort only explained a small part of his fear. The real terror was how the attacks struck without warning, and knowing the only thing that might save him was the inhaler. And he was most afraid that someday his chest might constrict so completely that the inhaler would fail, leaving him utterly helpless.

Above him a small bird roosted in a tree. He mistook the finch for a woodpecker. Distracted by the bird, his left sneaker skated across something lodged in the soil. Nearly slipping, he righted himself midstep. Sean glanced downward at the long, thin, almost cylindrical object in the soil. He barely recognized the object at first.

A human thighbone.

12:24:34 PM

The Partner's tone changed midconversation. A shift of inflection at the end of sentences. A slight rise in pitch when asking questions. Subtle cues, and Crotty perceived them. He noticed because he was trained to observe details. The impasse between them gave him plenty of opportunities to sharpen his skills.

For months now, they had handled most business contact remotely. Every request, every discussion, every argument—and there were more disagreements than anything—played out over public telephones and cells. Working from a handset receiver, Crotty mastered the nuances of timbre and tone that made the Partner's voice unique.

Face-to-face contact was too costly. This was true on both an emotional and professional level. Recovering from a meeting took hours.

Neither desired more time in the other's presence than necessary; each considered the other repulsive. Like a marriage forged from convenience, it functioned best in a vacuum where each participant followed their own daily script—separate and equal.

The Partner's limits were the primary source of Crotty's insomnia. He saw tremendous potential where the Partner saw only further complications and risks. Being narrow-minded was no way to make real money. The longer they worked together and clashed, the harder time Crotty had falling asleep, and the less rest he got when he did nod off. Quite often he stared at the ceiling longer than he lay with his eyes closed. Killing David alleviated part of the stress, albeit partially, because now they had new problems and he had new worries. And many of the same old ones. Like the stunted growth. With the new distribution routes, they literally had permission to print hundreds, and still the Partner plotted expansion in nickels and pennies. It was galling to Crotty. When he protested to the Partner it was always *Let's see next quarter* and *"Not sure the numbers justify that purchase just now.*

Not that the Partner flinched when spending the proceeds. Oh, hell no. The Partner planned small, but chewed operating cash by the truckload. Expenses ballooned each quarter, swelling as fast as sales increased. Four million this fiscal year, three million the last, and two point seven five the year before that. If it shined in the light and cost lots of money, the Partner bought it, probably twice to spite Crotty. The bleeding never stopped.

If Crotty were sitting across from the Partner right then, he would have driven the phone straight through the Partner's skull.

"We need to talk about the situation," the Partner said.

"Agreed," said Crotty. "We're going to bleed red ink soon if you don't reel in these costs."

"Not the money. *The situation.*"

"Yeah, yeah, I'm on it." Crotty knew exactly what the Partner meant.

"And what about the searchers?"

"Do you bother to listen to the police-band chatter? They've got nothing," Crotty said, sure of himself. "They never find anything."

"Maybe," the Partner said. "How did the background check come out?"

"Mike Brody might prove useful. Do you want to review the key details now?"

The Partner ignored Crotty. "I can't see how he's going to be an asset. I'm worried."

"God forbid you worry about something," Crotty said, his strong voice dripping with disdain. "Natural selection has been very good to us so far."

"Listen to me, Crotty. It's not like the other times. We're up against someone who has a different deal with nature."

Such claims were blasphemy to Crotty. What had worked before still worked. Nothing had changed. Of course the results would turn out the same.

"They say he's the man you want when the one you love is missing," the Partner said.

Crotty smirked. "Oh, that's just so precious. Just because he has a cute tag line doesn't mean he can find a goddamn thing before it's too late."

"We can't risk it," said the Partner. "Neither of us can."

Crotty shook his head. "Actually, you could do a hell of a lot more. But once again, I guess I'll have to pick up the slack. You know, I really like this Mike Brody guy. Ex-Delta Force. Seven years as an Army Ranger. Smoke jumper. A real adrenaline junkie. I say we use him."

"Everyone says he's incorruptible. Believe me, I listen for the cracks in character."

"Hearing declines with age," Crotty said. "Like your logic."

"Whatever is to be done, it needs to happen quickly," said the Partner. "The sooner the search ends, the better."

Crotty said, "Let's just get to the heart of this. You're less worried about what Mike Brody is looking for than what else he might find."

A long pause, then a concession from the Partner. "Maybe."

Satisfied with the exposed bluff, Crotty continued. "Stop worrying. I'll take care of it."

"How exactly are you going to handle this?"

"The fastest way to anyone is through the people they love."

"Wait a second. What are you going to do?" the Partner asked.

"You mean, *we*."

12:27:55 PM

Andy's rapid progress in the riding pen delighted Jessica. The boy, while not a natural, needed far less instruction than the other guests. Mr. Jones was more horse than Andy could handle, but he grasped the basics. She was proud of her son's ease.

What satisfied Jessica most was that Andy got this trait from her. Mike could not claim it came from him. Watching Andy in the saddle, feet hooked through the stirrups, hands clutching the reins, she saw herself. This was an unusual experience; she welcomed it. One way or another, Jessica had committed herself to learning a little more about Andy on this trip. To Jessica, these were the sort of moments that were only possible on vacation. If Mr. Mike Brody passed on the opportunity, well then that was his loss.

Lunch was homemade chili around the fire pit, just as the Pine Woods brochure outlined. Sizing up the crowd at breakfast, the chef, Chappy, had estimated the number of people who wanted seconds and prepared exactly the right amount for lunch. A biker with a grayed-out ponytail and tattoos peeking past the ends of a long-sleeve shirt—Chappy was a model of food-service efficiency.

The woman ahead of Jessica asked Chappy, "Is this vegetarian?"

Chappy heaped a massive glob into her wooden bowl and said "There's vegetables in it, sure, uh-huh."

Douglas fir pines cast long shadows over the group as they sat cross-legged in a circle; the shade cooled them. Many leaned against the tree trunks for support. The scent of chili powder and leather polish filled the air. The food was delicious, the blend of herbs and spices warm and rich. Serving the last wrangler, Chappy dropped the cast-iron lid into place, snuffed the fire by kicking dirt over the embers, and left.

Erich appeared halfway through the meal. "How's everyone doing?" Bringing his hands together, palms clasped tightly for punctuation. A dramatic gesture from an engaging man.

The crowd concurred that everything was going well. Erich stood at the edge of the circle, closest to Jessica. At least that was how it seemed. She decided his proximity was coincidental, that it meant nothing. Erich just needed a place to stand, she told herself. Yet the glare of his charm was infectious, almost addictive, as was his effect on an audience when he spoke.

"Remember this is just the beginning," Erich said. "Now that everyone has a feel for riding, tomorrow is a half-day excursion. We'll take you down to the base of the lake. We might see a bit of rain, so please bring a jacket with a hood or a hat. Afterward you'll learn a little bit about tending cattle. And don't forget the bonfire tonight!"

Jessica had a question, and hesitated. Her own recalcitrance was surprising. For the third time today, she wondered what was wrong with her.

Killing time between activities, she went back to her room to wash her face and make some phone calls. On the way she got Mike's voice mail and had some ideas for Lisbeth, how she might help the search. Jessica had a lot of contacts and it sounded like they were needed.

Heading toward the room with Andy, she saw a woman with twins in the hallway. Jessica had noticed them at meals, but had not yet been introduced—only caught a mention that the trio lived in Utah. To keep the woman and the face straight in her mind without a name, Jessica dubbed her Utah mom.

"Do you want to play with us?" one of the twins asked Andy.

Andy smiled at the two girls. "Can I, Mom?"

Although she had overlooked Andy's skill at this, he had mastered one of the most crucial concepts in social life already: he was very approachable. The boy genuinely liked people, so people liked him.

"Stay near the main building," Jessica said. As the three tore off, she called after them. "Just for ten minutes. Okay?"

The women sat on the porch—a comfortable space between them on the oak bench—to watch the kids play.

"I'm Cara Isham, by the way."

"Jessica Barrett."

Cara's clothes—so perfect—said designer label, straight from the finest New York stores. Her jeans probably cost more than

Jessica's entire outfit. "I guess our kids are trying to tell us it's time to meet each other," Cara said.

"I think so," Jessica said, with a little laugh.

When the children were out of earshot, Cara said, "I bet you're a reporter. You have that look of someone who likes asking questions."

"Freelance work mostly."

"Oh, that's so exciting. Gosh, I always wanted to write." Vibrations from her cell phone distracted Cara for a second. Checking the caller ID, she ignored the call. Like her wardrobe, the cell phone was top-shelf, so new, it was unavailable to most service providers.

This was cutting-edge gear Cara possessed and Jessica approved.

"Normally," Cara said, "I'd answer that, but I've had enough fights with my partner today. Always harping about my spending habits. Please." Her eyes rolled, the deep brown irises almost lilting. "I'm very sorry for the interruption."

"It's okay." Returning to the subject of writing, Jessica said, "It's amazing what can happen when you allow yourself the time." She indulged those who fantasized about the writing life, rather than betray the truth about the drudgery and isolation the job required. By not dispelling a myth about the trade, she reinforced it. Telling newcomers writing was really work was pointless, anyway. Beginners fixated on the good points. She remembered doing the same herself a dozen years ago. She had not listened when a kind mentor told her hawking one's words was the last profession a sane person should pursue.

"Maybe that's the problem," Cara said. "I just don't have the time. My work keeps me busy. And my kids, of course!"

"What do you do?" Jessica asked.

"I have a minority interest in a few small companies," Cara said. "One makes GPS equipment and other high-tech gear. They hook me up with gadgets."

"Have you been here before?"

Cara explained. "Months ago, I was in the area checking on some investments and there was a black-tie affair at the ranch. It was so much fun, I decided to bring the family back as guests." She paused. "Say, I could help you with your story, even if I can't write. I can proofread. That's almost writing."

"Did I mention a story?" Though surprised—and a little taken aback—at Cara for being so direct, Jessica stuck with her cover. At least for now. She wanted to know if she could trust Cara first.

"Isn't that what the tape recorder and camera are for?" Cara asked, smiling. "I figured you were researching."

Jessica laughed. "Just taking a few notes. For personal reference."

"Taking many notes about Erich?"

"Erich?" Jessica fumbled, and had trouble containing her surprise here. Apparently Cara had no problem sharing blunt observations with strangers.

"Ah, well," said Cara, shaking her head. "I notice. He's been watching you from the word go."

"I'm not absolutely sure about that." Jessica expressed this a bit dubiously, yet leaned closer toward the woman. Hearing that Erich noticed her—someone else was validating what she suspected herself—made Jessica want to hear more from Cara. She could not deny her bias.

"Well, from what I saw today," Cara said, "it's pretty obvious."

In part, she wondered if Cara was teasing. There was a trace of playfulness in her voice, perhaps, but her demeanor was so gentle Jessica did not dismiss her new acquaintance's words as pure jest. Also, Cara smiled a lot, which was disarming.

Minutes spent in conversation passed quickly; the kids played well beyond their allotted time. Then Jessica realized she needed to make a phone call.

Hailing Andy over to the porch, Jessica said, "This has been very pleasant, and I hate to cut this short, but I need to take care of something."

"The kids are having so much fun." Cara stared at the blur of children dashing toward the bench. "If you want, I can watch Andy. I know how exhausting it is being a single mother, trying to juggle everything by yourself. You deserve a little break, right?"

Jessica felt relieved that at last someone understood—even recognized, bless her new cherubic friend—her plight. Thanking Cara, Jessica left and made two phone calls in her room. Both the numbers she needed were inside her planner on the nightstand. First she called Lisbeth, to find out what she could do for the search.

"The one thing I need desperately is a helicopter," Lisbeth said. "Every time I think I have one lined up, somehow it falls through at the last minute."

The second call Jessica made was to a well-placed friend in the National Guard. He and Jessica had traded favors in the past, and he was a good friend of the family. "Briggs," Jessica said, "I need a miracle in Montana."

"I haven't walked on water much lately," Briggs said, "but for you, I'll try."

"There's a search for a missing child in some rough terrain and the local PD can't get any helicopters. Any chance you have a spare one under a rock?"

"How long has the kid been in the wild?" Briggs said.

"Over twenty-four hours."

"That's too long. Give me the search lead's number and I'll work out the details with them. It might not be there until morning, depending on what we have on hand locally."

After Jessica thanked Briggs and hung up, an odd sense tugged her. It took a moment to pinpoint it. The planner on the nightstand. She noticed because she set the planner beside the hospitality basket on the bureau that morning.

Certainly, she did. Right after she wrote down Lisbeth's number. And since she had no need for any information inside the organizer since then, it should have been just where she left it.

Odd, perhaps a bit strange, yet not impossible. Maybe she had a brief lapse of short-term memory, moved it herself, and had forgotten doing so. Nearly any other cause was better than her one great fear of losing the planner. After all, her whole life was available in it at a glance. For reassurance, she flipped through the pages quickly, pausing at a see-through divider. She ran her finger over the plastic sleeve that held pages of photographs. Looking at them almost always lifted her mood. And it worked then, until she hit the third page.

Where there should have been a picture of Andy at a water park this past summer, there was an empty spot.

Jessica rushed back to the porch to find Andy.

12:28:20 PM

Sean discovered more than one thighbone in the soil. Femurs, gray and pallid, littered the trail, each picked clean as if acid had dissolved every ounce of muscle and flesh.

He had zero experience with death. It was different than on television or at the movies. School had failed at preparing him, too. True, there had been a partial skeleton in the junior high biology lab, but that model looked fake, and so he ignored it. These skeletons were real, though, and belonged to real people, who were now really dead.

Two skeletons, or rather a set of rib cages, spines and skulls, terrified him. Exposure to the sun and wind had bleached the bones a pale light gray. The bodies were seated. A nylon line looped through the clavicles and thighs, fastening the slumped torsos to tree trunks.

He wondered who the people were, what killed them, and if they had been lost like him. He also wondered how similar they were to him when they had lived. A whole lot different, hopefully.

And then a rustling came from the trees, and he swore something, something inhuman, was watching him. Shaking, heart pounding, he took a few terrified steps, and once past the bones, he bolted. He only made it a few feet when he smacked his left arm against a tree trunk. The watch cracked, breaking into pieces, and fell off his wrist.

His timepiece lay in the dirt.

The hands stopped.

The tracking conditions were perfect; Mike could not ask for more. The soil, which was firm and responsive to the slightest touch, documented the critical movements of the missing boy. A breeze wicked moisture from his brow. Wind mixed with sweat and chilled him. Even beneath the dense tree cover, the sun lit their path. A classic fall afternoon, it was so serene that under other circumstances he might wish that it would never end. Lastly, there was silence—blessed and uninterrupted. Dagget had been tight-lipped around Mike since the exchange with Lisbeth.

Not that the officer was any more resigned to the situation. In the face of a reprimand, Dagget was an unrepentant son of a bitch. Insults may have stopped streaming from his mouth, but the foul attitude persisted. Mike wondered when the next tantrum might burst. He suspected not very long.

When Dagget ate or drank, he did so alone, sharing none of the provisions. Lagging on several occasions, he nonetheless preserved a two-stride gap between Mike and himself. After Dagget missed the mark for the third time in ten minutes, Mike called back to him, "Do you want me to take the pack for a while?"

"Sure you're ready?" Dagget asked, ostensibly relieved yet trying to save face. Approaching each other, they exchanged gear, the rifle holster for the backpack. Perspiration had coated the straps of the backpack, making the nylon slippery. "A few more hours and I might start to feel it." Dagget said this nonchalantly.

"No doubt," said Mike, with a small smirk.

Dagget pretended not to hear him in an obvious way.

More silence. "Hey," asked Dagget, "when Lisbeth asked where I was, why did you cover for me?"

"What was there to tell her?" Mike asked. "It's not like you quit."

"What if I had, let's say, considered heading back. Strongly considered."

"There's nothing for you back there," Mike said plainly.

"Who says?" Dagget wore a frown that reflected his petulance.

"Whatever you were doing only got you here. Didn't it?"

"All I'm saying is thanks for not mentioning it to Lisbeth."

"Just holding up my end of the brotherhood," said Mike.

Dagget look confused. "What brotherhood?"

"Lisbeth believes men cover for each other when a woman is involved," Mike said. The dubiousness in his voice was obvious. "There's some organization and official decoder ring."

"She believes in a lot of things," Dagget said dismissively at the mention of her name.

"And one of them is you."

Dagget cocked his head slightly as if such a thought had never crossed his mind.

• • •

Crotty planned the initial overture with care. Restraint was the key. Even when one had a trump card, it was better to wait for the right moment—and to make sure it was worth the risk—to play it.

Throwing a trump surrendered all other possibilities before the game even had begun. There was no fun in that. For now every option must remain on the table. And before drafting the list of actions most likely to yield results and selecting the best, he needed additional details.

With phone cards and a cell phone, he tagged a few sources for information. He also dialed the main desk of the local police department. When he posed as an out-of-town sheriff volunteering resources, a local beat cop unwittingly provided him the names of all key players in the investigation.

An Internet search returned a number of articles by Jessica Barrett and a few about Mike Brody. The articles provided texture, and he craved substance. He loathed the little surprises hidden in the fine print. A little voice insisted there was more about Mike Brody to uncover.

So he continued, probing for the vulnerable spot the way a neglected dog in the backyard leans into a chain, certain that the weakest link will eventually snap.

• • •

A candy wrapper fluttered in the soil. Though Dagget had been relieved of the backpack, Mike reached it well ahead of the officer. Mike crouched on his haunches, and turned the paper over with a twig, examining the find.

Dagget groaned. "Why are we stopping for garbage?"

"It might be Sean's," Mike said.

"That could be from anybody," Dagget said. "It's probably been here for years."

"Well, for starters, we're in the middle of nowhere, and he crossed through here within the last twenty-four hours. But secondly, notice the wrapper interior? It's bleached white. This can't have been out here very long, because sunlight reacts with wax and causes yellowing. And it's badly wrinkled, which makes sense, since he ran with it in his pocket."

"The wind and rain could have done that," Dagget said.

"The logo's still intact. The lines are sharp and clear. Exposure bleeds out the graphics, makes them fade."

"Well. . . ," said Dagget. "If he was hungry, and he had this, why didn't he eat earlier?"

"He knew enough to conserve his resources. He's got some skills." To Mike, the real question was why they had found so little refuse up to this point. Trash was a staple on North American trails. Yet these woods were immaculate, as if a private individual had posted all the land, and claimed it all for exclusive use. Mike set another reflective marker in the soil. Then he committed a waypoint in the GPS for Lisbeth. The device could recall the coordinates later more consistently and accurately than he would from memory.

Gripping the wrapper with tweezers, Dagget inserted it inside a small evidence bag. "No sense in littering," he said.

• • •

The investigation continued. As Crotty amassed details, he transcribed the data onto index cards, recording one critical note per card. He grouped and tacked the cards onto a wall-length slab of corkboard in the basement. Fastened at shoulder level were color photographs of each key player. Beneath each picture, the related cards. A literal who's who in the search for Sean Jackson.

Blacked-out windows, the glass caked with a special polymer, absorbed all sonic vibrations on his side, and thwarted eavesdroppers armed with electronic devices. From outside, all an observer might notice about Crotty's basement were four windows wanting for a dust rag. A halogen lamp to the left of the workbench spared the room from complete darkness. The floor was concrete and cold. Even as the coils of a space heater beneath the workbench pumped electric heat, a chill penetrated the soles of his shoes.

The cell phone he used was disposable, the phone cards purchased with cash at a convenience store.

For each call, he used a different phone card. Once activated, the call forever linked the phone used to the card, and by proximity, to the caller. Therefore, using the card again on another phone at a later date was foolhardy. Despite his thriftiness, in four hours he would destroy the phone and the entire series of cards, even if they had a credit balance left on them.

A few hours and a few favors later, he had completed dozens of index cards. Pinning the last note to the corkboard, he stepped back from the wall. The most useful parts of a personal history, all at a glance, all at his fingertips. He drank his gin, hands trembling a bit, and considered the rest of the handiwork.

Next to the pictures, a topographic map. Red Xs marked sensitive regions, blue X's marked the rough position of the searchers. Police scanners were indispensable, fantastic tools that captured radio jabber between the cops. However, the last and very important detail remained unknown.

Grabbing another phone card, he dialed the head of company security—at his company with the Partner. "Mohawk Dry Cleaning," answered the voice.

"Got two jackets in need of martinizing. A double-plus rush job." Martinizing a jacket was a triangulation trace on a cell phone. The trace provided the geographic location of the caller.

"Yes, sir! Do you require pickup and delivery service?"

"Just a pickup," Crotty said.

"Your address is on file, so we just need a current contact phone number."

"555-2323 or 555-5309," Crotty said.

"I'll dispatch a customer service representative to your location immediately."

Crotty finished his gin and stared at the topographic map.

One final detail before the real work began.

07:00:01 PM

A surge of anxiety overwhelmed Jessica like a tide rising above the high-water mark. The source of the distress: the missing photograph. Throughout the afternoon she caught herself straying from the moment, returning just long enough to drift off once again, wondering. The racing thoughts took root during the day's second ride. She was distracted by Erich.

Even Tic-Tac—with whom she mastered when to push and when to pull, what he enjoyed, and what he disliked—did not hold her focus.

It was not the missing picture itself that bothered Jessica; it was replaceable. She kept digital copies in a safe place back home. Twenty minutes with a high-resolution color printer, and she would have a shiny new photograph. What gnawed at Jessica was the thought of someone picking through her belongings, and removing such a specific one.

And she was almost positive that was what had happened. Jessica used the planner constantly. If there was a change, she made it. The picture was in its plastic sleeve earlier. Definitely. She had glanced at it when Mike left that morning.

Maybe Andy had moved the planner and taken the picture without her noticing, but she doubted that. The top of the bureau was taller than he was. Reaching it would have been difficult, and moving it served no real purpose. They had been together almost the entire day, and when he was in the room, she was with him. When she asked him about it, he had no idea what she was talking about.

So she crossed Andy off the list at the start, which left the cleaning service. But the cleaning service seemed a reach, too. Not because she knew them personally, or vouched for their characters, but because they had passed over jewelry, a spare camera, and a laptop—three easy-to-sell items she left in plain sight. A photograph held only sentimental value, but it bothered her tremendously.

The fact that whoever it was let the expensive items be, made the loss harder to process and accept. Having no idea why someone had swiped the picture rattled her far more than the actual crime.

A bit cautious, a bit paranoid—to Jessica, both seemed reasonable given the situation—she checked her other belongings, her son's, and then Mike's. By all appearances the possessions were where they should have been. Just as she remembered them. Good enough for now. Making a big deal out of a minor incident was unnecessary, and would attract unwanted attention.

She turned to her second worry: the bonfire. From a purely social point of view, the event was appealing. Jessica enjoyed parties, especially large ones. A show of hands after lunch seemed to suggest every guest might attend. And the time was right to mingle and make friends.

Very few people had noticed Mike disappear after the orientation, and even less had seen them together in the first place. Whatever apprehension she had felt earlier about flying solo had ended. No one would ask why she was alone. Her real problem with going alone lay deeper.

The event meant a chance for conversation in a relaxed setting. Fine on the surface, but she was out of practice. There was just so little opportunity with a career, a son, and a failed marriage to keep her social skills active. Jessica worried she might be rusty at making connections outside of work.

Guiding a story out of someone over the phone or chatting up sources at junkets was different than making a friend. Journalism meant getting the job done and done quickly. Life in hyperdrive—that was how she lived. Every decision, every contact, every sentence advanced her to the next piece. In contrast, a party was so laid-back, so meandering. With so many opportunities to say the wrong thing. Jessica took a deep, steadying breath.

Jessica spot-checked herself in a square mirror above the bureau.

Carefully, she worked a tortoiseshell brush through her hair, which wet from a shower, grazed the top of her turtleneck sweater.

"Do you think Dad will be at the bonfire?" asked Andy.

The question reminded Jessica that there had been no additional news or messages from Mike. Typical, regrettable Mike Brody behavior. "I don't really know," she said, and plugged her cell phone into a wall charger. She did this even though the cell phone had sufficient charge. The battery level was incidental. If Mike phoned her tonight, he would have to wait for a return call.

Searching for the right pair of shoes, she lingered in the closet. Hiking boots seemed too gauche, sneakers too casual. She decided on black leather boots, the shaft tucked beneath her denim slacks. The boots were sturdy yet stylish, the one-inch heel squared, clog-style. Almost finished, she applied lip gloss.

"If Dad's not coming, who are you dressing up for?" Andy asked.

"Jeans and a sweater is hardly dressing up, honey," Jessica said.

"What about the makeup?"

Jessica pocketed the lip gloss. Sometimes Andy was too perceptive for her liking. Too similar to her, as it were. "My lips are chapped."

A knock at the door ended the explanation. Cara, the mother of the twins Andy had played with earlier, saved the day. "We're leaving in two minutes, so be ready. Okay?" Jessica said to Andy. Then she stepped into the hallway with Cara, and shut the door.

"You look nice!" said Cara, beaming. "I like the lip gloss!"

"Thank you," Jessica said. "And so do you."

"Oh, I'm an old hag," Cara said. "But it's good to hear all the money I spent on plastic surgery paid off."

"I never would have thought you had work done," Jessica said. She meant it. Cara looked like an all-natural, pampered woman.

"The best surgery looks like nothing was done at all," Cara said. "And costs a fortune." Here she giggled.

Shifting gears, Jessica said, "Andy had a good time playing with your girls today."

"My daughters won't stop talking about it," Cara said. "Any time you need me to watch him this week, just holler."

"That's so nice of you!" The invitation surprised Jessica.

"We mothers have to stick together," said Cara. "And that way, you have a shot at some grown-up time with you-know-who."

Jessica stared at her blankly.

"E-R-I-C-H." Cara rolled her eyes.

Jessica was at a loss for a response. Despite avoiding thoughts like this, here the truth found its target. Smacked her right in the face, even.

Erich was a great-looking diversion, but there was no guarantee he actually liked her. He could certainly flirt, and like any good business owner he could charm a client. Erich might be nothing more than a fisherman who strung lines of compliments together like lures. He might not even care which particular net worked, only that one did. And each time she heard his name in conversation, the possibility that he was married or gay grounded her.

Finally Jessica spoke. "I don't think that will be necessary."

"Maybe you're thinking too much."

07:02:58 PM

Very little daylight remained for the searchers. Mike could track through most weather events and conditions, save a blizzard or thunderstorm. But working at night over an area with no clear boundaries—the kind investigators established at crime scenes—greatly increased the odds of a mistake. They would need to stop soon and rest.

Mike mentally took their inventory. A bit of provisions, the core supplies still intact, and they had suffered no injuries. A good start. By Mike's estimates and the GPS waypoints, they had gone close to twelve miles today. If not great navigation skills, the boy had stamina. Signs of their progress abounded, though there were miles still to travel before they slept. Even then, rest meant finding shelter first, a spot up on higher ground that offered a bit of cover.

They hiked for some time with only their footfalls between them.

Out of sight, water pulsed through a streambed, and roared above the background noise. Hearing it at once, both men stopped and glanced through the canopy toward the sound.

"I'm going to check out that running water," Dagget said. "Maybe there's some fish. I'll top off the canteens."

Mike agreed. He wanted to speak with Jessica without Dagget eavesdropping. "Let's meet back here in fifteen minutes," he said. "While you're gone, I'll scout out a potential campsite." So there was no doubt about the rendezvous point, he jammed two reflective markers in the soil, and formed an X beside Dagget's boots.

Jessica's phone rolled calls straight to voice mail. He gave a quick overview of the search, and then wished her and Andy a good night. He hoped they returned the message soon.

Tapping *end* with his thumb, *number unknown* flashed on the screen. He answered.

"Mike Brody," a voice said. "I have a business proposition for you." The electronically altered voice could be male or female. It was nearly monotone, with the identifying inflections removed.

"Actually, I'm on vacation right now," Mike said. "Let me give you my office number and you can speak with Erin Sykes, my associate. Whatever sort of excursion package you're looking for, she can help."

"Ms. Sykes can't help me find a missing boy, can she?"

Mike stopped, suddenly wary.

"Who is this?"

"You have something I want, Mike, and I have something you want. That's much more consequential than introductions."

"I don't understand," Mike said.

"Bad things can happen in the woods, my friend. You know, two men disappeared last spring a few miles from where you're standing right now. They were never found."

"What is it you want?" asked Mike. He had a sinking feeling about what the voice was after.

"For you to do what you were recruited to do. Find the boy," said the voice. "And when you reach him, you let me know first. I'll take it from there."

"First off," Mike said, "tracking is a best-effort situation. I never make any guarantees that I will find anyone. I can't. Only a fool would promise that. Second, if I find Sean before the rest of the searchers, the only place he's going is to a hospital with his parents, not off with some stranger."

"You're more motivated than the others, Mike. This is why you will succeed." A long pause on the other end. "*The Velveteen Rabbit wears a brown skirt* is quite an unusual expression, wouldn't you say? Cryptic, like a code."

The code phrase, Mike thought, clearing his throat. *The key to Andy's trust. How did they get that?* Only three people in the world knew it. And yet somehow this stranger did, too. It was disconcerting.

The voice continued. "When I first heard the expression, I wasn't sure what to make of it without some context. But since it's scribbled on a recent photograph of your son, it probably means something. By the way, Andy is a real cute boy," the voice said. "Now about our deal . . ."

"I haven't agreed to anything," Mike said. "And I don't do business with nameless people who hide in the shadows."

"This can go hard on your family, Mike, or this can go very easy. Take the easy road."

"What does that mean?"

"Don't even think about going to the cops with this, or it's over for them right now." Another beat. "You can call me the Partner. We'll talk again soon."

07:21:37 PM

At the bonfire, tall flames licked the air and lobbed embers into the blackness. Wood crackled. The scent of seasoned wood, domestic beers, and barbecued pork encircled the group. Children played flashlight tag, whooping in the night beyond the clutches of their parents. A full moon drifted westward across the sky. Near the buffet table a horde of people surrounded a cooler the size of a coffin.

Loaded with ice and chilled beverages, the red-sided cooler held more booze than sodas or water. Nearby, Jessica drank from a long-necked bottle and chatted with those who approached. She might have felt anxious, but her actions suggested otherwise. No matter what bothered her inside, Jessica could work a crowd. Her station, so natural looking to the other guests, was deliberate.

She knew precisely where to stand: close to the action without obstructing the beverage line. As people fished through the ice, she matched faces to brands, and committed both to memory.

Once the alcohol took hold of the group, her real work began. Circulating, Jessica met everyone she could, on the hunt for a hook she might use in her article. Many great quotes were accidents, offhand statements from unexpected places. A modern day Lao-tzu probably floundered among the crowd, and awaited discovery; she saw it as her job to unearth that diamond.

Less-experienced drinkers lost coherence by the sip, so she targeted them early. Jessica appeared at the proper moment. Right as a guest finished his beer of choice. And before he drew from a nearly empty bottle, Jessica stepped up with a fresh replacement. No one refused her. With a rapport established, she drew them into a conversation. And though her lead-in questions varied throughout the night, her purpose remained the same: to unravel what a particular guest thought about the Pine Woods Ranch.

Jessica said to a couple from Minnesota, "I'd just love to hear your impressions of the ranch." Simple declarative statements concealed her questions.

"This is the only vacation where it doesn't matter who you are. However important you are out there, for a week in here we all share the same experience," said a man with a suntan that looked like it came from a bottle.

Moments later Jessica asked a couple who said they were from New Jersey, "You've visited many times; what keeps you so interested?"

"What keeps me coming back?" the male half of the couple said. "It's got nothing to do with the office. No one asks about the office. No one even mentions it."

Jessica suspected that, deep down, the man actually wanted to be asked about his job, that he was a workaholic. She fought back the urge to confirm this suspicion.

Moving among the guests revealed a mixture of viewpoints. Some came for the fresh air. Some enjoyed the horseback riding and personal instruction. Others liked the blend of ruggedness and personal amenities.

She checked on Andy. For her sanity, and perhaps her conscience, she had set Andy up with an activity that kept him close: trapping fireflies. The twin girls played too, racing after insects then clamping the metal lids against the mason jars. Jessica checked on the bug-catching crew every few minutes. Periodically she ditched the main party and brought the kids snacks and sodas.

On one pass, she ran into Chappy, who held a plate of food, and a beer. "You're hungry," Chappy said. "I can tell."

"How did you know exactly what I wanted?" she said glibly.

"I got a sense for people's tastes," Chappy said. With a nod, he gave Jessica the plate, and took her empty bottle. After tossing the glass in a recycling container, he returned from the cooler and drank deeply from a bottle of his own.

"So are you enjoying my fire?"

"It's fantastic," Jessica said. "Very nice job."

"I loved starting the bonfires," Chappy said. "Back when this was all mine."

"Really?" A part of her had trouble imagining Chappy as a business man.

"Uh-huh," Chappy said. "Biggest mistake I ever made was losing the ranch. I'm working on the financing to get it back, though."

Several times Jessica caught herself avoiding Cara. Not because Jessica disliked the woman. In fact, Jessica considered Cara engaging. And she really admired Cara's fashion sense. But she avoided Cara because it meant girl chat, and Jessica was unprepared; there was no news. An hour into the bonfire, Erich remained at large—a bit disappointing.

For now, Jessica worked the crowd, watched, and listened. Hearing all those stories, in the words of the speakers, made the evening pass more quickly. The large group thinned a bit; the chatter persisted on in small groups. Jessica moved closer to the fire, holding her arms across her chest for warmth.

Cara appeared, bearing two fresh beers. "We need more drinks!"

"Okay," Jessica said, "but this is my last." Three beers in two hours seemed like a good cutoff point to Jessica. Sensible without being prudish. "I feel so out of touch without my cell phone. I can't believe it."

"Well, I can't believe Erich skipped his own party," Cara said. "You can use my phone if you need to."

"Let's give Erich a chance," Jessica said. "He has a ranch to run."

Cara winked and said, "You'll give him more than one chance, I bet. I would."

The fire cooled. Cara left to check on her twins. With a massive black poker, Chappy rearranged a few logs. Flames rose higher. Embers sparked into the night. Then the fire settled.

Andy raced by with his jar, the girls in tow.

"A fire is like a life, you know," Erich said, behind her. "We burn bright, we burn fast, and someday, we burn out."

She liked the line and would use it somehow. Best of all, it came from someone who arrived at the right moment. She faced Erich.

"I have something for you," Erich said. He held yet another beer. Unlike the others, this was her brand of choice.

"Sorry. I'm at my limit for the evening." A reaction purely of reflex, it was a refusal she regretted instantly.

"I'd say you want one more," Erich said.

"Would I?" She gave him points for confidence, and wondered if it was real or a front. She wanted it to be real. She wanted him to be genuine. "Is that your opinion?"

"I'm quite open with my opinions around you." Erich grinned.

"You know," Jessica said, "sooner or later everyone gets the face they deserve." Her words sounded harsher than she intended. Silently she cursed her clumsiness; she had meant something else entirely. Something flattering. What she said was anything but.

His smile disappeared. Flatly, Erich said, "Never fashioned you for a plagiarist, Jessica."

If there was one charge that rattled a journalist to the core, it was the theft of another's words. Particularly a seasoned reporter like Jessica. "Come again?"

"Henri Cartier-Bresson said that about aging. As you are an avid photographer, I presume you've heard of him," Erich said as a statement of fact, with no trace of condescension.

"Of course." Bresson's photography was brilliant. She enjoyed his work and was a major fan of his black-and-white studies. The actual quote as she recalled it: *after a certain age, you get the face you deserve.* An insightful admonishment, much like the man. More interesting to Jessica was that no one had ever recognized the source of the quote before, much less corrected her oversight. Instead of being offended—like she expected—she was impressed. "Really though, I don't make a habit of non-attributed quotes."

"I understand," Erich said. "So, are you finding everything you're looking for at the Pine Woods Ranch?"

A tight opening line still eluded her, though she was having fun. "I think I can figure out what I need to." This she said a bit coyly.

"I'm sure you can." Erich nodded. "And how about this beer?" He still held the opened bottle in his left hand. Positive there was no wedding band, she checked his ring finger again anyway. All clear. To be safe, she checked the right hand, too. His manicured hands were bare, the skin smooth.

"Normally," Jessica said, "I'd refuse, but since you are so very thoughtful . . ." The bottle was warm from where his hand had gripped the glass.

"Before I go, I have a confession," Erich said.

"There's a dangerous thing to say to a reporter." Jessica sipped.

"I was watching you tonight," Erich said. "What a clever way to meet everyone. I'm impressed."

"I try," Jessica said, modest. Now she wondered how many might have been studying her as she watched the crowd. She had not considered such a thing.

"You do a fair bit more than try. So I've read, anyway."

He started to leave. "One more thing, Erich. I wanted to tell you that something is missing from my room. I don't believe it's lost or misplaced. It's not a big deal, really. Just a picture of myself and Andy, but I thought you should know."

Erich stopped, turning back toward her as if in slow motion. "That is not the sort of thing we take lightly here. Rest assured, I'll take care of it personally."

And at that, he left. He weaved through the crowd, chatting with guests. She wondered what else Erich had heard about her. Watching him through her hair, she bet he would glance back. Jessica realized she was acting liked a schoolgirl, surprised at the intensity of her attraction to a man she hardly knew. Regardless, she waited for the sign all the same. Moments later he glanced back. Delighted, she checked on Andy, and rejoined the party.

At last the fire peaked.

She stepped beyond the perimeter of warmth looking for Andy. A chill surrounded her. It seemed much later than it was, because so many guests had retired for the evening. She took the cue. She locked eyes with Cara across what remained of the flames, and smiled.

Andy held a jar full of tiny flashing lights, looking so very proud of his haul. She waved to him. Suddenly Jessica's knees buckled, and she collapsed. The background noise stopped. What was left of the crowd froze except Cara, who dashed over.

"Jessica! Are you okay?"

And then blackness.

08:13:50 PM

Right after his conversation with the Partner, Mike dialed all the numbers he had for the ranch. The front desk, the nurse's station, the owner—each attempt to reach a live person failed. When he did get through, no one knew anything that could help. He tried Lisbeth—she did not answer. Mike tried every person he had numbers for who might have information. When he exhausted his supply of contacts, he called directory assistance and requested more numbers. And when the new ones tapped out, and he didn't hear from Lisbeth, he called Erin in California and set her loose.

His business associate Erin was a bulldog with details. Better yet, Erin knew when not to ask *why* he asked for what he did, and when to call him on being stupid or paranoid. He knew she took the request seriously and went to work, exploring additional venues, like emergency services or cab companies.

Besides how Jessica and Andy were doing, and whether they were all right, he needed more information: principally, who the Partner was. There were ways to get those details, though none of them were easy in the middle of nowhere and past the close of the business day. For that assignment, he enlisted Shad, the gear guru who set them up that morning. A long shot, and Mike knew it, but he figured the tech was up for the challenge.

"So you want a reverse lookup on all the calls to your number for the last day?" Shad asked.

"Absolutely," Mike said.

Shad hesitated for a moment. "That's a gray area, Mike. Legally speaking."

"But you're law enforcement. What's the problem?"

"I'm a police officer, not a Homeland Security agent. There are privacy laws protecting phone records. Officially, requests like that take subpoenas. And those take a judge."

"I understand. I'm sorry I troubled you so late at night," Mike said. "I'm out of people to try, and I thought of you . . ."

"Were you threatened by one of the callers? That could speed things along."

"I just need a name," Mike said.

"And not one you want Lisbeth catching wind of either, I bet," Shad said.

"Exactly. Can you help?"

"Hey, you need data and not a lot of questions, you need the Shad. I can do this, but it will take time."

"How long?"

"Give me six hours."

While Mike waited for Erin's and Shad's results, he and Dagget began setting up camp.

They settled on a level patch at the peak of a hill. The location was Mike's choice and Dagget followed without griping. Climbing the thirty-five-degree grade, their fingers grappled for holds. Moonlight threw tall shadows from their bodies across the rocks.

Scaling the crag took the tracker moments and Dagget minutes.

Close to the trail, the site provided an unobstructed view down either slope. Mike leaned the backpack against a boulder and sat, bent at the knees. For the first time since breakfast he relaxed. He sipped from the canteen in between bites of a protein bar.

Rifling through the sack, Dagget grumbled. "We're almost out of packaged food?"

"Not quite," said Mike, finishing his protein bar. He folded the wrapper into a square.

"You have food left?" Dagget asked.

"A bit." In Mike's pocket were two protein bars, the final reserve.

"Can I have some?" Dagget said.

"You were down there long enough. I figured you rolled some sushi."

"There were fish. They weren't biting." Dagget rubbed his temple. "I'll get up early and try again." He shook his head. "Christ. It's hard concentrating with my head throbbing like this."

That sounded like carbohydrate withdrawal to Mike. There was no easy fix for addictions. "Suggestion?" Mike said.

"At this point," Dagget said, sounding resigned, "I'll even consider advice from you."

"Let yourself feel the discomfort instead of fighting it."

"What?" Here the officer almost shouted.

"Yield to the pain," Mike said. "I think you'll find it will hurt less."

"That's the stupidest thing I ever heard," Dagget said. "Where did you learn that?"

"Try it and see if it works."

Dagget was silent for a while. "If I don't catch any fish tomorrow morning, and we run out of food, what's the plan?"

"We find some." A simple solution to a complication—just how Mike rolled. Dagget's question begged another question. "What sort of survival training have you had exactly?" Mike asked. "I was led to believe you had skills."

"I do have skills, all right?" Dagget said, exasperated. "But Lisbeth says a lot of things when she wants a yes. Truth is, about three years ago I took a four-day course on search and rescue, and a two day seminar on wilderness survival."

"And have you used any of that training since then?" Mike asked.

Dagget shrugged. "I went hunting once. I really can catch fish. I'm pretty good when I have my rod and reel."

Mike stifled a sigh.

"I've been thinking a lot today." Dagget wiped his brow with his sleeve. "This terrain is pretty rough. Why did Sean wander so far?"

This was a question that Mike had also considered.

"Fear can be a powerful motivator," Mike said. "Something scared him from the clearing. Something else spooked him enough to . . ."

A burst of illumination below and the sound of tires over loose stones preempted his statement.

Heading south, on the opposite side of the hillside, a row of lights raced along the basin floor. Round beams, four pairs. Maybe Humvees, definitely trucks.

Both men watched the action below the ledge from their perch.

"Odd," Dagget said. "We're miles from the nearest road."

Mike fished out his long-range binoculars, zoomed in tight, and watched the vehicles race under the big sky.

One by one, the lights disappeared into the night like snakes beneath a curtain.

09:15:27 PM

Cell service on top of the ridge was sketchy. Signals dropped out without warning, disconnecting calls in progress. After trying a few different spots, Mike climbed down and walked for a minutes, stopping when he locked onto a stronger signal. Cool air whistled against his exposed arms. A call from Erin reached him before he could dial her number. She brought mixed news.

After exhausting the usual channels, she had located Jessica Barrett at Washington Memorial Hospital, a facility about an hour from the ranch. Since Erin was not a family member, the staff would only confirm that Jessica was a patient, and did not release any details about her medical condition. But Erin did convince a nurse to give her the physician's cell number. Mike took down the number, grateful for Dr. McCrane's contact information and Erin's efforts.

If Mike had tried the same moves, he would have left a trail of irritation behind him, and gotten maybe a twentieth of the results. Besides following details to the end, Erin had a way with people over the phone. Something about her voice made people weep and confess their sins. He believed this implicitly, had seen her handiwork up close, though Erin often had disagreed.

Another concern was tougher to address: Andy, and where he was right now. Once again, since she was not a relative, hospital staff had been reluctant to discuss private family business with Erin. Her hope and Mike's was that the boy was resting with Jessica in the hospital. Erin bowed out then, and told Mike if he needed to talk, he could call at any hour.

Before trying to find out how Jessica was, he wondered whether her predicament was connected to the earlier phone threat. His cell phone rang. With the second call from the Partner came the answer.

The Partner said, "I heard Jessica passed out at the bonfire and was rushed to the hospital. That must be unnerving for you."

"Are you saying that's not a coincidence?" Mike asked. His stomach sank. He wanted to throttle the Partner, but kept his cool.

"Thirty-four-year-old woman in perfect health, with no history of fainting, a light social drinker, collapses at a party. A coincidence?" The Partner tsked. "Do you think her doctor can explain how it happened? I'm betting he can't. Not to your satisfaction. He'll say something like Jessica was drunk."

"What did you do to her? Drugs?"

"Let's just say," the Partner said, "she'll recover."

"I don't appreciate your involving my family. They have nothing to do with this." Mike knew enough not to make threats.

He was at a disadvantage and it was too early to even determine how great that obstacle might be. First he needed to get the Partner talking, and figure out what he was dealing with, then find a wedge to drive into the weakest point.

The Partner left him with this advice: "Give Dr. McCrane my best, would you? And rest up, Mike. You've got a lot of work tomorrow."

09:27:34 PM

Mike heard the weariness in Dr. McCrane's voice. "Pending final tests results," Dr. McCrane said, "the initial diagnosis is dehydration, a deficit of electrolytes and sodium, compounded by exhaustion. A few nurses indicated she appeared drunk. Alcohol consumption would certainly aggravate already low hydration levels."

Plausible, but Mike did not entirely believe the doctor. Because of the Partner he could not. He had another reason to doubt the diagnosis.

In all their years together, Mike had only seen Jessica drunk once—at a late summer wedding where everyone got blitzed, including the bridal party and both sets of parents. She drank so responsibly he trusted her to know when she had enough.

For now, according to Dr. McCrane, Jessica languished in room three-twenty-three, still asleep, her vital signs stable. Dr. McCrane anticipated a full recovery after she slept off the effects. Mike asked to speak with Jessica, but the doctor advised rest was paramount.

This development marked uncharted territory for Mike. For the past few years, besides his recurring knee issues, his family had been very fortunate. Normal colds, a light touch of stomach flu, nothing serious. Her last trip to the hospital was for Andy's birth, almost a lifetime ago.

"About my son, Andy," Mike said. "Is he in Jessica's room?"

"Let me think about that for a second," Dr. McCrane said. "I see a lot of patients every night, and I focus on them much more than visitors. It's been awhile since I was up there. When I first treated Jessica, there were three people in the room with her: a man, a woman, and a boy. The boy had red, curly hair and looked about eight or nine. The man introduced himself as Erich Reynard. I didn't catch the woman's name."

To Mike, the description sounded like Andy. "So Andy is with Jessica?" Mike said.

"I think so, but I'm in the middle of rounds on the opposite wing of the hospital," said Dr. McCrane. "I'll send a nurse up there to check and call you back."

The long silence weighed heavily on Mike. He did not want more time to think about forces he could not reason with, much less control. The tense moments were painful, almost more wrenching than the thought of not knowing where his son was. And if anything happened to Andy . . . if the Partner was involved . . . he had the training for most any situation. He doubted he would have the restraint.

Dr. McCrane called. "I just heard from the head nurse on duty. Jessica is still resting comfortably. But . . ." Dr. McCrane trailed off.

"But?" Mike pushed, prompting the doctor.

"Andy's not there. The nurse says Jessica has been in her room alone for the last half hour."

09:47:59 PM

After a lot of dialing, Mike caught a break and reached Erich at the front desk, who explained what happened after the three left the hospital together. Andy had ridden to the hospital with another ranch guest, Cara, in the ambulance. Erich followed—and stayed as long as he was permitted by the guest policy. Partly because Andy was under fourteen, and because it was way past visiting hours, the hospital urged all three to return in the morning. Erich and Cara agreed Andy could stay with her until they heard otherwise from either Mike or Jessica. The real hitch was Andy, who did not want to abandon Jessica, and protested with great fury. Mike knew exactly what kind of fight Erich was talking about. He had taught the boy a number of self-defense maneuvers. Complaints about the ruckus on floor three reached security; they summoned the police.

When Lisbeth caught wind of the radio chatter on the police band, she intervened and vouched for Erich. Instead of starting a case report with a social services agency, the police escorted all three back to the ranch, trailing Erich's sports car.

Unfortunately, Jessica's phone was back in her room, the front office locked, so the only way they had to reach Mike was to return to the ranch and look up the contact information on the computer system or through Lisbeth. "It must have been spotty coverage where she was, because we couldn't reach Lisbeth. And that's why I didn't call you earlier," Erich said. "By the way, I took care of all the financial arrangements at the hospital. It will all be first class. The charges are coming straight to me. And she's in excellent hands. I regret this happened."

"I'd like to thank you properly later, but first I really need to speak with my son."

"Of course," Erich said. "I'll transfer you to Cara's room."

The line beeped twice. Cara answered. "I was waiting for the number from Erich to call you. I'm sorry about Jessica. You must be worried sick. Your son is more than welcome to stay with me and my daughters as long as he needs to. He and my girls get on fabulously."

"I appreciate the offer," Mike said. "Thank you very much. And thank you so much for what you've done so far. At the risk of sounding gruff, may I speak to Andy?"

Footsteps thundered on the other end of the line. "Dad!"

"How's it going, champ?"

"I was so scared about Mom. I didn't want to leave with Mr. Reynard, but the police said it was okay. They didn't have the code phrase. Did I do okay? Am I in trouble?"

"Not in the least," Mike said. "You did great. We never rehearsed this kind of scenario. That's my fault, not yours. But we've got a new code phrase as of right now, all right? I don't want you to go anywhere with anyone who doesn't have it, except Mom."

"Okay," Andy said.

"The new code phrase is *Unchain my heart crazy diamond*. Got it? Don't say it aloud. But do you have it?"

"Got it, Dad."

"Seriously, it's more important than ever before. No exceptions next time. Especially with your Mom being sick right now."

"Are you coming back soon?" Andy asked.

"I'm working on it, champ," said Mike.

"I hope it's soon," Andy said. "It was scary when Mom fell down."

"I'm so proud of you, you know that?" Mike said. "I'm going to make this up to you when this is over. Now this woman Cara you're with, is she all right? Do you feel safe with her?"

"Oh yeah. We're right next to our room. Mr. Reynard brought a cot up for me. It's pretty soft."

"Are you okay staying with her tonight?" Mike said.

"Yeah," Andy said.

"All right, let me talk to your mom's friend again," Mike said. The phone passed back to Cara.

"It's so unfortunate this happened," Cara said. "If only we had a number for you, you would have known all along. But there was no way to reach you. I'd be worried to death if I had no way to call my partner in a crisis."

They agreed to stay in touch, especially if there were any developments about Jessica.

Afterward, his rudeness hit him. He had never thanked Erich properly. When he called back to do so, the line was busy.

11:59:00 PM

In a dark field, Sean rested against a tree. Although he was more fatigued than the previous night and craved rest above everything else, he was too anxious for sleep. His skin was cold, his lips dry and cracked. He had finished the last of his candy, back . . . well, he no longer remembered exactly when, only that he lost the wrapper earlier today. But maybe that happened yesterday. Sean was not sure.

He shuddered. The chill gripped him like a seizure. Deep undulations rippled from the base of his neck to the tip of each limb, and then thrust back up his spine. His muscles, strained from two days of wandering, twisted into tight knots, far beyond the soothing reach of massage or stretching. The soreness was inescapable. Fatigue, though, was just one problem. There were other challenges.

Using a wet book of matches that he had found earlier, he had tried starting a fire. It was too damp to cast sparks. Now the useless nubs and discarded cover stamped NJ TAVERN, lay on top of a bundle of haphazardly arranged sticks. He shouted a collection of the worst expletives he knew, all phrases his father had blasted at his mom. At that instant it was all too much for him. He cursed. Instead of feeling better, he felt drained, so he stopped. Complaints were useless. Yelling at no one: pointless.

Unlike many only children, he never talked to himself. Even if he was desperately lonely, he fought the urge, and bottled the thoughts deep inside his head. This was a conscious choice, as well as a learned behavior.

Many times he was tempted to speak aloud, to express some idea, even a good one that struck him when no one was around to share it with. He dared not. The one time he succumbed to the urge, that would be the moment his dad caught him. That could only lead to disaster.

Dwelling on the possibilities of what might happen next—every last one beyond his influence—touched off his asthma. A tightness enclosed his chest. He took a quick hit off the inhaler; it tasted like plastic and cough medicine. The small canister was almost empty. Another few hits and the medicine would be gone. Yet even in the depths of his frustration there was solace.

The good news was that out in the woods his father was less scary. In fact, everyone's expectations mattered less by the hour. For once he had license to be selfish. Consolations, even poor ones, were welcome. Anything that kept his mind off the hollowness in his stomach was a plus.

His stomach rumbled. Digestive juices gurgled and sloshed at the base of his esophagus. Starved of fuel, the booming within his belly deepened. He felt differently since stumbling into that bone yard earlier and losing his watch.

His nerves had been blown already and although the sight of human remains had frightened him less than being chased by the killer, the image had rocked Sean. Hours afterward, those piles of bones still consumed every thought.

Discouraged by his predicament, he shuddered again. The landmark that he expected would point him back to the ranch, the very one he was so convinced was just around the next bend in the trail, continually betrayed him. Certainly he was closer to that landmark than before, yet not one step closer to the dude ranch. That was the basic state of affairs in Sean's eyes. All day he wandered. Directions were meaningless. All paths seemed wrong. Underdeveloped navigation skills had failed him. Gaps in his education had stranded him. Even his watch had quit on him.

The lost timepiece was an unfortunate turn, and it meant he failed on yet another count. The watch was a test his father had set. They had a deal.

If Sean could keep the second-rate watch in working order for a year, his dad would buy him the one he truly coveted, a waterproof dive watch with cool dials and knobs. But Sean had broken the cheap watch, and lost it no less, and blown the deal. His father would hold him to the terms. He suspected there would be no professional-grade dive watch any time soon. Another father might forgive him, given the circumstances. Not his. He was pretty certain about that.

And without a timepiece, his moments were measured now by sunrise, sunset, and two periods of endlessness on either side.

Day Three

As Mike dreamt, images led him through the dark corners of his psyche like a beacon. Mike knew every step of the journey well. Far too well. Until a year ago, he had relived the same dream sequence four times a week, twenty out of thirty nights, for six months. Before that, it had been every night.

The dream always started with scent dogs . . .

A lean, muscular canine barked. Yanking at his leash, the beast jumped up and down frantically, testing the handler. Reaching the blockade on the country road, Mike waited in his truck while an officer verified his credentials and waved him through.

Next to the parking lot of the supermarket was a grassy field a half-mile wide, bordered on three sides by a thicket of pines. The sheer number of people in the field was a concern.

That would make things harder, maybe a lot harder. Parking near a shopping-cart kiosk, he took a final swig of coffee and hoped this time would be different.

The officer in charge approached. They shook hands and walked toward the field together. A grim and restrained look crossed the officer's face as he shared the details. A seven-year-old boy had been missing for seventy-two hours. The surveillance tapes captured the child's exit from the store with his mother shortly after 8 AM. One hundred searchers had worked around the clock, but the police had little so far.

Besides the boy, Mike was only concerned about two other people at that moment, and he asked if the parents were available. Nodding yes, the officer pointed to a woman near the edge of the field and asked if he wanted to talk with her. Mike said not yet.

There was a small monitor hooked up to a portable player in the back of one of the vans. The black-and-white security footage rolled a few times. Nine seconds long, the capture showed the boy wandering away toward the field, and then moving beyond view. A time-and-date stamp at the top of the picture confirmed the details.

Since the video was grainy, Mike requested a picture that showed the boy's face. From somewhere came a snapshot, which he studied carefully. In the dream, the photo was blurry like the face in the video, the features unclear. Still, seeing the picture, he was certain he knew the face—this boy was not a stranger. Mike returned the photograph to the officer, who told him to keep it, but he refused. He had his reasons for returning it. Mike asked the officer if he could pull back the other searchers. Unmoved, the officer explained that some of the men might not understand what he was trying to do. Maybe he should dive right in, the officer suggested. The officer said a lot more, but Mike cut him off and said he needed thirty minutes and a clear field. This time the officer issued the order. Reluctantly, the searchers retreated toward the inner perimeter of the police tape.

If he found something, experience said their scrutiny would intensify. Not that they wished him failure. They just preferred that they were the ones who succeeded. Mike shared that view because he never wanted these calls. They came anyway.

A single track caught his attention. Crouching, he placed his fingers inside the depression and closed his eyes. In Mike's dreaming mind, he saw things from the missing boy's perspective. The boy had torn away from his mother and dashed toward the field. Reaching out for an adult's hand, the boy clasped it tightly. It was someone the boy knew and loved . . .

Loud crashing sounds jarred Mike awake.

12:19:53 AM

Metal ground into metal, displacing Mike's visions of the grassy field and searchers. Freed of the night terror, his mind rejoined his body atop the hill. Maybe this round the dream had ended before it finished, but the physical consequences were identical. He was covered in sweat, his heart racing.

"That crash sounded bad," Dagget said. "It woke me up, too." He stared at the tracker with an incredulous expression. "You look awful."

Mike drew three quick breaths and then exhaled. A drop of acrid sweat burnt a cut on his cheek. "I'm fine, thanks."

"Serious, man. I just nodded off again. You've been roaring like a beast," Dagget said. "Punched me about a half hour ago, slammed me right in the shoulder. Would've capped you but I saw your eyes twitching. That must have been some nightmare." Dagget crouched against the wall of rock.

Joining Dagget, Mike kept a space of two arm's lengths between them.

Down the basin, a circle of identical Humvees converged near the crash scene. There was just enough light for the binoculars. One vehicle had a busted headlight and lay sideways. The other vehicles were intact, but the angle made it hard to figure out what was going on. Stray bits of conversation reached their hilltop perch. Filtered by the distance and trees, nothing said at the road made any sense to Mike or Dagget.

"Probably seventeen-year-old kids drag racing Daddy's truck," said Dagget.

"We should check it out," Mike said.

"We?" Dagget said with a great deal of disbelief. "No, I'll do it. There might be injuries."

"Another reason for me to tag along," said Mike. *Should bring the Marlin, just in case.* The rifle faced away from them, barrel pointed downward, still wrapped in the holster sling.

"You'll just get in my way," Dagget said gruffly.

"So you can hold the Maglite in your teeth while crawling down the ledge, huh?"

Without conceding, Dagget grappled for the walkie-talkie. Moments later he barked a few expletives into the night. Despite several attempts, there was no answer. Absolute radio silence. Switching to his cell phone, Dagget tapped the screen, then he said, exasperated, "No signal."

"Mine's been cutting in and out up here. This must be a dead zone." By habit and as a precaution, he powered down the device.

"But what if someone tries to reach you?" Dagget asked.

"I'll take the chance. The ringer is loud, even on vibrate. Something about those trucks looks wrong to me. If the situation is legitimate and they need help, I'll turn it back on."

Dagget grunted and shut off his own phone. "Maybe you are good for something."

They brought the first-aid kit and the rifle. With reports of mountain lion sightings burning hot in both men's minds, neither wanted to be caught unarmed. Still, Mike had grave doubts about carrying more than what they needed. Even if a big cat assaulted them, the window for intervention was very short, and sighting a rifle in the dark was difficult. All the same, Mike carried the Marlin in the sling.

Descending the ledge was more time-consuming than the ascent had been, even though the hill down to the road was less severe. Dagget scraped a few of his knuckles raw when he moved too quickly and dragged his hand across a jagged rock. Once they cleared the ledge, the real task beckoned: navigating canopy by moonlight.

At several points the narrow tunnel between the trees forced them to proceed single file. The air was cold, and the thicker overhead cover that surrounded them made it seem even colder

Suspicious of the way distance and terrain distorted conversations, Mike reserved judgment about the noise at the road until a loud, unmistakable insult sliced through the darkness: "Wrekker, you bastard! What were you thinking?"

Advancing closer to the headlight beams with Dagget in tow, Mike strained to match bodies to voices, but the caravan of Humvees concealed all the actors, save for a lone figure—a man near the hood. The headlight beam caught the barrel of a MP5, a fully automatic machine gun, slung across his shoulder. All the rules had changed.

"It was an accident is all," another man answered, also out of view.

"You know how hard it is to flip these vehicles? Please. Tell it to someone who cares." This was the voice of the leader, the man who called the shots. "The rest of you get everything out of the truck and spread the load out. Let's go, ladies!"

Doors slammed as figures extracted sealed boxes from the downed vehicle, feeding them forward assembly-line style. The crew ran a winch between two Humvees and flipped the vehicle back on all four wheels. It made a lot less sound than one might expect. The shocks dissipated the weight as if the truck were merely a quarter bounced against a blanket. Seconds later, the engine of the downed vehicle caught.

"Hit it!" the leader said.

Breaking ranks, the crew piled into the trucks, except for a point man, a lone figure near Mike and Dagget. He alone had remained motionless in front of the hood, squinting into the trees. With his shoulders rounded, his upper body betrayed the direction of his stare. The stance and back lighting overstated the man's height. Gripping the stock of the MP5, his first finger rested along the barrel edge as he raised the weapon. There was a click as the second metacarpal joint in his right hand involuntarily cracked from the suddenness of the movement.

The red point of the laser sight mounted on the MP5 had settled on Dagget.

Grunting, the point man tracked left from the tree trunk to Dagget's forehead. The Marlin, which Mike held, was useless to Dagget. Dagget aimed his handgun back at the point man. One drop of muzzle flash from the MP5 meant he was already dead. Even if Dagget fired first, it might be too late. So he had to shoot now. A dead officer was useless to the public. There was no other option. With his fingers wrapped around the grip, Dagget steadied himself and threw the safety.

His elbows were even, his left arm almost straight and supporting the weight of the firearm. Applying an even pressure to the trigger, he pulled. The hammer lifted away from the firing pin.

Just before the trigger crossed the terminal point, the very instant where inertia would drive the hammer against the firing pin and launch a bullet through the barrel no matter what Dagget wanted, there was a loud whistle. From inside a Humvee came a demand in the unit leader's voice. "What are you doing?"

The point man remained as before. Dagget noticed and held his trigger steady. A 9mm round awaited release from the chamber. Certainly blasting the point man was easy and reasonable. But he waited.

"There's something in the trees," said the point man, eyes locked on the laser-beam point.

From his spot, Mike noticed Dagget's right eye as it twitched.

The point man lowered his MP5, and with it dropped the laser sight.

"It's nothing," he called back to the leader.

"Shag ass back in formation. This night's been long-enough as it is."

When the last Humvee roared out of sight, Dagget uncocked, holstered the gun, and stepped out on the road. Mike was already crouched near the side, staring at the ground and examining debris.

"Those guys were strapped down," Dagget said. "Every last with high-capacity mags. Like a damn army."

"Expensive weapons." Mike's first thought was how lucky Dagget was. How they both were, really. His next thought was something else: *there was only one Army*. In other circumstances, he might have corrected Dagget. He had bigger problems. Maybe outwardly he appeared calm, yet his vitals—heart rate, breathing, blood pressure—were elevated. Sweat covered his face.

He knew the chemical effects of a fight-or-flight experience on the body were inescapable. Facing a threat, higher-level brain functions largely shut down. The midbrain, which lay dormant until called to action, unleashed a wave of adrenaline to boost strength levels. Military exercises reinforced these midbrain reactions. Over the course of several thousand repetitions, one's response to a threat eventually became automatic.

"Our department can only afford two MP5s," Dagget said. "We're no match for these guys. Maybe we should move along before they come back."

"I want to check the debris." Mike hoped the men were negligent in the cleanup, and had left something behind at the accident scene. With his thumb, Mike clicked on the Maglite.

"What do the caravans have to do with Sean?" Dagget wondered out loud.

"Nothing right now," Mike said. "But it might have everything to do with it." *Or the phone threats from the Partner.*

"Five minutes," Dagget said, "and we're out. The caravans are running all night. At least so far they have been."

"Got it," Mike said. "This might take longer, though."

"Do what you need to do. Just get it done in five minutes. I'll try a few more spots and make some calls," said Dagget.

"By the way, Dagget," Mike said, looking up, "thanks for not firing. If you had shot the point man, it would have set everyone off. That would have been a bloodbath. You did the right thing."

"It's Officer Dagget," Dagget said over his shoulder. "And I had him, you know. Could've put two in his chest."

Exhaust from the trucks still hung in the air, even near the ground, where Mike was crouched. The noxious fumes made him cough. He searched the accident scene, moving toward the tree line and the point of impact. Coming up empty-handed, he worked the opposite side of the road. He had hoped for more.

Rising, the bright beam of light bobbed in his hands and caught a bit of metal just ten feet beyond in the grass—a piece of headlight casing. Mike discarded the bent metal and continued.

One minute. Two minutes. Moments ticked past and there was nothing to show for his efforts. He wasn't certain what he expected to find, but he was almost positive a sign awaited discovery.

Ahead of time, Dagget returned. "I spoke with Lisbeth about the caravans. She said she would look into it."

"I might spend a few more minutes here in the morning, all the same."

"What the hell are you looking for that's worth getting machine-gunned over?" Dagget said.

"I'll know it when I see it," Mike said.

If Mike had any doubts about deferring the search, the sound of stones ground beneath approaching tires ended them.

01:19:40 AM

Violence, Crotty decided as he contemplated punching Wrekker, the idiot who had crashed the Humvee, was an unfortunate—yet necessary—behavior modifier. It worked, but the dramatic results came at a price. So when he prepared to slam his fist against Wrekker's cheekbone, he hesitated, because he knew it would amplify his own darkness and self-loathing. Still he wanted to pound

Wrekker once anyway. He had his rationalizations.

To Crotty, the course of a life followed one basic path. Men avoided pain and sought pleasure. The more severe the pain inflicted upon a man, the more effectively that pain altered his behavior. A scared man heard orders. A scarred man followed them. The Partner disagreed with that philosophy.

When employees like Wrekker made mistakes, the Partner chose the passive route. Crotty knew all about the bullshit reasoning. Dangle a carrot on the end of the stick long enough and eventually a rabbit hobbled in the correct direction. Crotty believed that in certain cases a stick served more effectively as a club.

That he could be violent was not to say he delighted in suffering. Really, Crotty abhorred the pain of others, regardless of who decided their fate. There was little joy for him in broken spirits or shattered bones. He was hardly a child who blew up frogs with firecrackers and laughed evilly in the corner. He savored neither the action, nor the process. He merely wanted the outcome, wanted a sign he was understood.

Wrekker sat before him on a chair, looking at Crotty like he expected the worst.

Crotty asked, "What were you doing out there tonight?"

"The job."

"Not quite. You had one task. Transport my property," said Crotty. "You failed. Now I trust this is the only time we need to have this conversation."

"Yes, sir," Wrekker said.

"So we're clear?"

"Absolutely."

"Good." Crotty dealt Wrekker a hard blow, square in the face.

Wrekker slid sideways in the chair from the impact.

"I think we are, too," Crotty said. The point made, Crotty helped Wrekker to his feet and gave him an ice pack.

As Wrekker walked unsteadily, he clutched the ice pack to his already swelling cheek.

01:21:59 AM

Crotty and the unit leader were alone in the room. By custom, the unit leader remained at attention during disciplinary actions. The unit leader spoke now: "Sorry about the error with the convoy, sir. I take full responsibility. My men's failures are my own."

Crotty stifled a smirk. His precepts echoed back at him in another's voice. A reassuring affirmation indeed. "Did anyone see the contents?" Crotty asked. "Some searchers are very close to the area."

"There were no witnesses," the unit leader said. Crotty stared at him for an eternity without speaking. "Then the issue is closed. I have a new task for you. Ready four of your best grunts and bring them to me. I care about only one thing. How much damage they can inflict."

"Perhaps more information might guide the selections?"

Crotty flipped his hand like a wealthy lord dispatching a street urchin blocking his way. "I want your four best."

Alone, Crotty took off his gloves and locked them inside a portable kit. Seamless polymer, designed for assault, the gloves concealed the telltale marks of a fistfight on the wearer's hands. When one must remain presentable for the Suits, scrapes in odd places were bothers he would rather not explain.

He removed the chain of rosary beads from his pocket. He rubbed two of the largest beads together. The smaller plastic spheres clicked as they slipped around in his hand.

His moment of quiet passed too quickly.

The phone rang and Crotty picked it up. "What do you want?" This Crotty snarled.

"We have a problem," said the Partner.

"And why the hell are you telling me about this on this line? This is not how we work." His thumb hovered over the *end* button, ready to kill the call, when the Partner's voice roared back at him.

"This is a nuclear-grade situation! I didn't know what else to do." The unusual show of nerve from the Partner gave Crotty pause. The Partner sounded disoriented, almost spastic with worry.

Crotty regretted not being present to witness the panic.

"Rule number one in problem solving—admit you suck at it and let me handle it," Crotty said. "Now what is the problem?"

"They've got a helicopter." Just hearing the Partner's words, Crotty realized the very serious issue they faced. The Partner added, "It's coming tomorrow morning."

"And what sort?" asked Crotty. "If it has thermal imaging equipment, we've got something beyond a nuclear situation."

"It definitely does," the Partner said. Crotty heard the apprehension.

"And how did a two-bit detective from the middle of nowhere manage that so early in the search?" Crotty asked. "Especially since I got the other requests stopped."

"That reporter Jessica Barrett knew someone high up in the National Guard. She called him before the bonfire."

"This is exactly what comes of being soft on employees," Crotty said. "I've told you before, draw boundaries with them or they think failure is acceptable."

"Enough blame game, right?" the Partner said. "I can't control everyone all the time from where I am. We need a plan."

Crotty thought until a solution appeared. Decisions under fire came more easily when there was no middleman running interference. Unlike at the office, where any notion required a pony show for the Suits, a seven-page report, and twelve meetings—here he was in charge.

He clicked the rosary beads together and thought. "Listen carefully, this is what we're going to do . . ."

05:51:18 AM

The rest of the night, Mike Brody slept badly. Sounds from the caravans running through the basin and racing thoughts kept him awake. Leaning against a stone, one knee bent, the other straight, he observed the caravans. Every twenty-three minutes a crew raced past, as if on a schedule, until the final truck rolled out of earshot at dawn, and the canopy swallowed the last vehicle. By dawn, the count was fifteen passes. Sixteen counting the one he and Dagget had investigated.

The cell phone, which had functioned inconsistently on the ledge before, did not work at all the rest of that night. He checked it a few times anyway, in case the signal improved.

Around 3 AM, Dagget woke up and mumbled about the awkwardness of sleeping on the hard ground. Mike ignored the officer's complaints.

He knew what covering great distances meant—aside from the exhaustion and hunger—and these were discomforts he wished upon neither man nor enemy.

In between the long stretches of quiet, Mike worked with his GPS and maps. Knowing what direction the caravans were headed, their rough speed of travel, how much time elapsed between trips, and allowing for time to unload or load the contents, he estimated the location of a few possible destinations. He stored the coordinates for later. Maybe they would make sense then.

The calculations finished, he repacked the gear and wondered what the trucks were hauling that needed such protection.

Lisbeth had said something earlier at the ranch. When he said *And murder doesn't happen often around here?* Lisbeth had replied, *We see more overdoses than anything else.* At the time the detail seemed irrelevant, forgettable. Now the tidbit seemed important.

Dagget stirred. Mike let him toss for a few minutes before starting a conversation.

"What sort of drug activity do you have in town?" Mike asked.

"I'm the wrong officer to quiz about that," Dagget said, wiping the sleep out off his eyes. "Never worked the narcotics desk. Probably about the same as most. We had a heroin ring a few years back, but the DEA shut that down."

The purest heroin in the United States, and possibly the entire world, flowed from the shores of New Jersey, Mike mused. At the epicenter of the trucking and shipping industry for the entire East Coast, Jersey was the birthplace of several "brands," including Capone, Homicide, and Greyhound. Their purity levels exceeded ninety-seven percent. As shipments traveled westward, the quality of opiates decreased sharply, because dealers cut the product with other chemicals to stretch their supplies. When the same-sized bag of heroin landed in San Francisco, it averaged less than twelve percent pure. A skeleton of what circulated on the streets of Newark or Plainfield.

While not impossible, being this far west, Mike doubted heroin was in the caravan.

"Why do you ask?" Dagget said.

"Lisbeth mentioned a large number of overdoses. I'm just asking some questions without worrying if the answers make sense," Mike said.

"We do have drug issues," Dagget said. "Most towns do, unfortunately. So you're thinking that's what the trucks were carrying?"

"Since we didn't see anything, I'm not forming conclusions," Mike said. "There are a number of possibilities."

Dagget rubbed his eyes again. "I can ask a friend on the narcotics desk and see if he has any ideas." Then Dagget wedged the backpack under his head like a pillow. "I'm grabbing another half hour of sleep."

Mike nodded. "I'll swing back later then. I'm going to stretch out my knee and wash my face."

Sunlight painted the horizon orange and red. Leaving Dagget to rest, Mike climbed down the trail side of the ledge with the rifle and canteen. Another few hours of sleep would've helped, but he had pressed ahead with much less reserves before.

Water lapped against a large boulder in a stream five minutes from the ledge. Mike filled the canteen, dropped an iodine tablet inside, and shook the canister. He drank carefully, collecting every drop from the nozzle. The salty mixture burned and left a purple tint on his tongue. Almost like home. Foul as it might be, it was better than getting diarrhea from a bacterial infection. One bout of Giardiasis kept many a man from drinking from open streams for life.

His phone rang. *Caller unknown*. The Partner.

"I trust you see things my way now," the Partner said.

"What am I supposed to do about Lisbeth?" Mike asked. "She wants coordinates when we recover proof of Sean. Another group could use them and follow us."

"Give her wrong ones and tell her to try searching areas you know are a waste of time," the Partner said. "Every so often, serve up a little detail that checks out and makes her happy. She'll keep you in the game, but with reservations. She has to want to believe you and doubt you at the same time."

Mike said, "I need a number to reach you at. Sometimes the cell coverage is sketchy out here. We might be talking, and all of a sudden the line will go dead. I don't want to miss anything critical."

"I've told you what you need to know," the Partner said. "You don't need my number for that. So keep your cell phone on, in case something changes."

"I meant what I said earlier about leaving my family out of this," Mike said. "They have nothing to do with us."

"But your ex isn't so innocent," the Partner said. "She's interfering with the search, helping secure resources the local authorities could not. And that sort of meddling needs to stop immediately. The helicopter is not appreciated by certain parties."

Mike wasn't surprised Jessica called in a favor for the search. She knew the right people—which was a problem. At times like this he wished she was a bit less remarkable. Mike just wished he could protect her now. Knowing they—Jessica and Andy—remained at the whim of someone else was frustrating. He still hadn't decided what to do about the Partner. He spoke cautiously. "Trying to lead Jessica where she doesn't want to go is like telling the sun not to shine."

"When she comes to, get a bridle on her, Mike. And do it fast. I told you before, do what I tell you, and Jessica and Andy are going to be fine." The Partner paused. "At least for now."

"And then what?" Every second he kept the Partner talking revealed a little bit more about his foe. He needed a lot more information to be effective.

"Then their security is in your hands."

Mike returned to the ledge, and discovered something wrong with the campsite. The backpack was half open. Dagget was gone. Mike checked the equipment inside quickly. At first glance, nothing appeared to be missing. What he cared about were the syringes of epinephrine, and the flares, because both items were irreplaceable. The flares he found. The syringes he did not.

He studied the ledge, probing for signs of someone besides Dagget or himself. Working a stone or concrete site was harder and more time-consuming than tracking in soil. It was possible to follow animal trails—even across substantial distances—over less accommodating surfaces, however.

As he peered down the trail side of the ledge, his phone rang once, then dropped the signal. Lisbeth's number flashed on the display. Shelving the sweep, he climbed down the ledge, and returned her call.

"Heard about Jessica," Lisbeth said. "I'm sorry, Mike. How is she doing?"

"She's supposed to be better by this morning, according to her doctor," Mike said. "I'm going to try her soon."

"I wish her a speedy recovery," Lisbeth said. "The search owes her an enormous debt."

Lisbeth explained about the helicopter, and Jessica's efforts. That his ex-wife volunteered her services was not surprising. She loved breaking stories; it was her nature to spot them early and insert herself into the action. Under normal circumstances, he would have admired her direct action. Here he had to figure out how to make her stop, without making her shut down and close off from him.

"I had two questions for you," Mike said. "When the fracas broke out in the hospital over who Andy was going to stay with and you vouched for Erich with security, why didn't you give someone my number? No one knew how to reach me. I would have liked to be in on the discussion."

"I gave Erich your cell number," Lisbeth said. "And he said he had it already. Maybe in the confusion, he forgot to call."

Buying the reasoning in part, Mike pressed on with his next concern. "Second question: What's happening about the Humvees and the accident last night?"

"Humvees?"

"We went to see if anyone needed help when a caravan crashed near our site, and we almost got shot over it. Some men with MP5's"

"Dagget mentioned nothing about it when we spoke last night."

Mike listed as many of the important details as he recalled.

"I don't know what to say," Lisbeth said, rather politically. "Except that it might be awhile before someone can look into it."

"We can make a quick pass before breaking camp," Mike said. "Just for fifteen minutes. Might turn up something."

"I'd prefer you didn't. We need every pair of eyes on the search, Mike. Your diligence is noted and appreciated, but the best thing you can do is press on. Dagget knows to file a report when he gets back to the office. I'll check into the matter myself when the search wraps up. You have my word on that."

In Mike's mind, her logic was sound, yet it oozed utter bullshit. True, she had few resources to work with. The force was tiny. For a crisis like this one, it was feasible that there were no spare officers. Like before, he trusted her on that. Still, he believed the caravan and the missing boy could be connected. He could not be certain how, but it seemed worth checking out, worth knowing why. Now, on her orders, nobody would ask the question until the answer probably would not matter. And that shortsightedness bothered him. Especially since he could be at the scene in under five minutes.

Lisbeth continued. "You already have one detour planned. Shad took your comments about the syringes to heart and set up a care package for you. Auto-injectors, food, and fully charged batteries for your cell phones. A few other things, too."

He made a note to call Shad next. He owed him big. And maybe Shad had been able to trace the Partner's phone number back to a name. He was less thrilled about taking a detour. As Lisbeth mentioned, each moment counted. Searchers had finite amounts of energy and daylight, diversions must be brief; participants must remain focused.

Dropping out for more supplies meant time away from the cause. However, this discounted the Shad factor, and the fact that the syringes were missing.

Given Shad's expertise, the additional gear would probably justify the time spent retrieving it. Mike believed Shad could deliver. If mission-critical gear lay in reach, then charge for the equipment. Sound enough in practice.

But the phone threats changed all the protocols.

He and Dagget needed the gear. They also needed to stay on point.

"How will the equipment arrive?" Mike asked.

"Smoke-jumper style. We'll drop the pallet with a chute from above," Lisbeth said. "I'll give you coordinates and a time; you get there any time afterward, and keep a watch out for incoming."

"I'd prefer you saved the gas for the search," Mike said. "We can manage with what we have."

"You need these supplies, Mike. And the longer you stay out there, the more you will need them. Besides, we plan sweeps near you today. It's no trouble logistically speaking."

"What about the packing materials and leftovers?" Smoke jumpers carried out whatever equipment they brought into the woods. No exceptions.

"Stuff any refuse with the pallet," Lisbeth said. "We can clean up the mess later. I'll take the heat from Bureau of Land Management, if there is any. Hungry searchers make mistakes. Less regulations, more breakthroughs."

With some reluctance, Mike agreed. Lisbeth read the coordinates for the drop site. Mike skewed them slightly, placing them a bit more west and north than they actually were, though it hardly mattered, because she had a rough idea where they were from their last discussion anyway.

Lisbeth added, "Also, the search is expanding this morning to include some trained volunteers. We've got seventy-five more people, fifteen on horses. And I may have another plane lined up. Other searchers can start checking out your leads today."

They signed off. He pocketed the cell phone, bent down, and

doused his face with cold water from the stream again. Tiny droplets weaved through the day-old stubble on his face. Washing off sweat and sleep, he held his eyelids closed tight. Scouring his cheeks with his hands, the stubble against his fingertips was like sandpaper to wood.

Eyes still shut, he listened to nature. Morning doves cooed from the trees. Water splashed against the boulders and stones in the streambed. Air bubbles rose and popped on the surface.

A voice echoed over water toward him.

06:15:22 AM

Recycled air pumped through the AC unit beneath the window and made the fine, red hair on her arms stand on end. The air conditioner hummed steady like an idling car. A deodorizer stick in the wardrobe covered the scent of eggs and burnt bacon down the hall. In the corner, an unset tile in the suspended ceiling exposed a black crevice above it.

Jessica wanted a glass of water. A headache clawed at the base of her neck. Blinking, she had trouble focusing on objects past the bed.

Moment by moment, the lines of the darkened room became clearer. The primary source of light was the instrumentation surrounding her. After taking in the IV taped above her wrist and the remote control on the nightstand, she noticed a man in blue scrubs.

"Where is Andy?" Jessica croaked, surprised at the weakness in her voice. She leaned up, a bit too eager, and fell back into the pillow.

"You need rest right now." He smiled, and added a good morning. A name tag over his right breast read McCRANE, DONALD, MD.

Recording his observations, he signed his initials with the usual doctor scrawl, unreadable to all but the most senior nursing staff. He threaded the clipboard through a hook at the foot of her bed. "We'll talk when I get back."

The doctor left, his rubber heels clopping down the empty hall.

Even in her private room, she was not yet alone. A figure seated beneath the television rose and crept forward from the shadows. Jessica briefly wondered if it was just a specter of her overactive imagination. Recognizing Erich, she asked, "Why didn't the doctor answer my question?"

"I was really worried," Erich said. "One minute you're charming everyone, next thing, you're here. Thank God you're all right. I feel so responsible for what happened. How are you?"

"Fine," Jessica said. "Where is my son?" Her voice wavered.

Erich stood near the bed, and maintained a healthy, appropriate distance between them, though she wondered if she wanted him to move closer. The heart monitor beeped faster. She shook off the grogginess.

"Andy's staying with Cara Isham," Erich said. "The doctor couldn't answer you because he didn't know that."

Jessica shook her head, grinning. "I keep wanting to call her Utah mom. Don't know why. Maybe that's the painkillers talking."

"One advantage of running a ranch," Erich said, "is that I have an excuse to meet all the guests. I get to know them quite well, actually. After a few days away from the rat race, people really open up. They help each other."

Jessica added, half serious, "Plus you have everyone's name, credit card numbers, e-mail addresses, home phone . . ."

Erich nodded. "Well, my business is the people element. Financial issues are matters for the accounting department. Long as my checks clear, someone in the back office is doing his job. And I'm just fine with that."

"I need to talk to Cara about Andy," Jessica said. "Do you have her number?"

"Actually I do." He thumbed through the contact list on his cell. Finding the right entry, he read it to Jessica, who remembered she had left her phone back in her room. She reached toward the nightstand—a million miles away, it seemed—for a black phone next to the television remote, and missed. Inwardly she cursed her decision to leave her own phone where she couldn't get it. The next outing she would not be so hasty or spiteful.

Erich matched her glance. "Take mine," he said. "Just hit *send*. I'll give you some privacy. Want anything from the vending machines?"

"A bottle of water would be great." Instead of dialing, she called after Erich. "Hey, were you here very long? I'd hate to think I kept you away from the ranch and everyone."

"This is my second visit," Erich said. "I was here last night. But this morning I lucked out. I walked in just before you woke up."

For the second time in as many days, Jessica noticed Erich's uncanny way of appearing at just the right moment.

06:19:34 AM

Opening his eyes, Mike focused on Dagget. The officer dangled two trout from a stick. Young freshwater fish, close to the legal size. There was no point throwing them back for the sake of compliance; they were dead already.

"Man, were they biting up a storm this morning," Dagget said. "I'll finish gutting them if you build a fire."

Mike gathered and arranged the kindling, then lit the wood with his micro-butane torch. Since he knew the right mixture of slender and thicker pieces, it caught fast, and soon burned hot enough for cooking. Fish baking over the flames released a pleasant scent, and the result tasted even better. "Lisbeth didn't have any idea about the Humvee accident," Mike said.

Dagget said, protesting, "I told her everything we saw . . ."

"She says otherwise. Lisbeth doesn't want us checking out the accident scene, either. Any thoughts on why?"

"Probably worried we'll waste time," Dagget said.

Or that we'll find something. One of them, either Dagget or Lisbeth, was lying about the conversation last night. That begged the question: who and why. Lisbeth could have dozens of reasons. Maybe she wanted the search moving forward above everything else. The only certainty in that strategy was by narrowing the gap between the search teams and Sean. *Possible,* Mike thought.

He played an alternative scenario, too. Maybe Lisbeth knew the purpose of the caravans and considered the matter too dangerous for Mike and Dagget to investigate alone. Hard to argue with fully automatic weapons. Regardless, the lie, if it was hers, bothered him because it cast doubts over their whole dialogue. It was not exactly her first omission. After all, his involvement started in all this because of facts she withheld; she only admitted the murder in the clearing when he pressed her about his findings.

Then again, she could be telling the truth and Dagget might be guilty.

As for why Dagget would lie, Mike had some ideas. Least toxic among them: Dagget discussed the accident with someone, just not Lisbeth. Conceivable, and perhaps a little too convenient. Dagget might have been amped up on adrenaline, yet probably not so juiced that he forgot what calls he made, and to whom. So either it was selective amnesia, or he said nothing to Lisbeth, and told Mike he had. As for why, possibly the answer went back to Lisbeth. From their exchange before the search started it was clear she had no qualms about saddling Dagget with assignments he disliked. But she would not order an investigation into a matter she had no knowledge about. Telling her also meant filing a report. Dagget did not strike Mike as a fan of documentation.

Besides, the officer had at least one other good reason for avoiding another close-up at the accident scene: it was he who had stared down the MP5 barrel. Mike could sympathize.

Whoever was lying, Dagget and Lisbeth agreed on one thing: Neither wanted Mike taking a second look at that road in the daylight. Perfect grounds for Mike to do exactly that.

Dagget swallowed hard. "I wasn't exactly straight with you when you asked about the drug problems in town earlier." Dagget cleared his throat. "There have been rumors for the last few years as to why, no matter how many dealers get popped or labs the narc guys raid, the amount on the street never changes. The real supply is obviously coming from someplace else. For that to flow continuously, someone is protecting the traffickers."

"Are you saying Lisbeth might be involved?"

"All I'm saying is she may not want certain questions asked. For whatever reason. It's not like she's been one hundred percent honest with us to this point anyway. Now she's lying about me not reporting the accident."

"And why?"

"How should I know? Look, I'm just saying I told her about the accident. That's all. She may have other motives. Keep that in mind when dealing with her."

"One could say the same about you, Officer Dagget."

"What do you mean?"

"What happened with the syringes?" Mike asked.

"You are on top of everything, huh?" said Dagget, quite sarcastic. "When I sacked out again, and used the pack for a pillow, something blunt was jamming into my neck. Turned out it was the box of syringes. So to keep from crushing them, I took them out."

"And you put them back?" With a flick of his boots, Mike snuffed out the fire, sending dirt straight into its heart. The flames withered.

"Sure. Right next to the flares."

They were quiet for the next few minutes, both focused on their chores. Dagget filled the canteens; Mike ensured the last ember from the fire was dead. Plenty a forest blaze started because a hiker pronounced a fire "extinguished" while it still smoldered, and abandoned camp only for the wind to revive the flames and burn wild. Mike Brody had jumped two fires that started that way.

Up on the ledge, as they broke camp, Mike called out Dagget. "Okay, listen. We need to level with each other, because this can't continue."

On his haunches, Dagget adjusted the straps of the backpack. "What are you talking about?" He rose, a perplexed expression on his face.

Mike walked over to the side of the ledge that overlooked the valley. Reaching into a narrow space between two rock slabs, he extracted the missing box of syringes. After making sure the needles were intact, he shut the case. "No one has been in this site besides us. After I left this morning, you slept for about twenty minutes, then spent five walking around in circles trying to decide where to hide the syringes. You tried a few places." Here Mike pointed out several alcoves and crannies around the ledge. Each location obviously corresponded with a place Dagget had tried hiding the box. Suddenly, Dagget went pale. Mike continued. "You even climbed down the ledge once, looking for an overhang. But this one interested you because the space conceals what you were trying to hide so nicely, and it would take a flashlight and a lot of patience for someone to notice it."

"I wasn't going to leave them here. I was just . . ." Dagget said.

Mike unzipped the pack, and slid the syringe box inside carefully, then zippered it shut. "I don't want these syringes outside of the backpack again unless Sean Jackson needs an injection."

Mike set the backpack on the rocks, faced Dagget, and continued. "What exactly were you trying to do, anyway?"

Dagget looked stunned. "Somehow this got twisted. I wasn't thinking clearly."

"What were you thinking exactly?" Mike kept pushing for an answer. "I'm having trouble understanding your motivations. This stunt could have made our entire effort for nothing."

After a small fumble, Dagget answered, meekly at first, then growing stronger, "I . . . I wanted to see if you could do what the papers say. How much you actually notice, especially when no one prompts you." He paused. "It was foolish."

"Then let's work together starting now. We have a missing boy to find."

07:31:47 AM

Mike wrestled with whether they could afford two detours. Because although they could use the extra gear—the more Mike thought about it, the less he trusted the fragile syringes to work right in an emergency, and besides, his cell battery charge level balanced on the wrong side of halfway—he also wanted a second crack at the road below the ledge. In order to determine whether there was sufficient tolerance for such maneuvers, he needed an estimate of how much time the gear drop would require.

The site Lisbeth described was several miles from the ledge.

Based on Sean's trajectory so far, their route to the gear would parallel the direction the boy traveled, albeit with several miles of space between the respective paths.

If Sean had swung right hard enough, the second detour might even cross his tracks. That was the idea, anyway. Rose-colored spectacles aside, there was a concern.

To reduce odds of a collision from above, Lisbeth had selected an open field bordered in part by rocky hillsides. She had described to Mike a simple, ready-made target for the pilot, easy to spot from the air. But for those arriving by land it was a very different proposition—at least according to the GPS. Hiking across long stretches of uneven rock was hard on the knees, quadriceps and lower back. Not that Mike minded the physical strain. However, he recognized that sort of terrain increased the risk of ankle pulls and fractures. Neither man could afford a real injury in the deep woods. So that meant a slow, controlled hike. At the very least the trip would crimp their pace, maybe significantly. And so he estimated two miles per hour—consistent with the difficulty level of the terrain.

"So two to three hours total?" Dagget asked when Mike explained the new plan.

"Worst-case scenario, yes," Mike said. "And that's end to end. We should be able to cut his tracks, so there'll be no need to come back here. If everything goes our way, one hour."

"Do we really need this gear that badly?" Dagget asked.

"Theoretically, maybe not. Practically, yes. Especially if we are out here another night."

"But are we going to be out here that long? And even if we are, I can fish, you can hunt. We can get by."

"Depends on Sean and his energy levels," Mike said. "There are no signs he stopped moving yet. His brand of determination is rare."

"If you think it's the best course," Dagget said, "then let's go for the gear. I'd just as soon keep on the way we are going, though. Seems to be working."

"Understood." Mike put on the backpack, sliding his arms through the straps. "And thanks for the vote of confidence. Wait here, I'm going to check out the road."

"How long are you going to be?" Dagget said.

"Five up, five down, and then ten to investigate the scene," Mike said. "Twenty minutes, round-trip."

"What am I supposed to do in the meantime?" Dagget asked.

Mike lowered himself past the first stone. "Make some phone calls."

Actually, Mike planned a few calls of his own during the descent, conversations which he did not want Dagget overhearing. First, he tried Jessica's hospital room, but there was no answer. He left a message with the head nurse, requesting a callback, then a duplicate message on Jessica's cell phone. Since Andy slept in late most mornings, he let him rest. Next on the list: Shad.

"Thanks a lot for the care package," Mike said to Shad. "We're going for it soon. Any luck in your quest?"

"Yes. My hacking chops are a bit rusty, and I was going crazy trying to figure out how to trick the phone company into giving me the information, but then I had a moment of clarity in the midst of my bureaucratic retardedness. Why waste police time asking questions the private sector probably answered already? So I called up a friend who works at a data clearinghouse. They'll get me all activity on your cell phone for the past week up until a half hour ago, no questions asked. And no paper trail."

"That's legal these days?" Mike asked.

"Close enough," Shad said. "It's legal for me to have any data purchased through private channels. We can speculate that the company who procured it broke laws. But then the liability is all theirs, not the department. I can just assume that they did not and be covered. Good enough. Think of it like the way repo men work. You miss your auto loan payments, the bank takes your car. Except they don't really.

"The bank calls in your note, and a private firm goes out and actually steals the car for them. Technically the repo man on the street commits grand larceny." Shad laughed. "Mornings like this, I think about why I love this country."

"How much longer will it take?"

"You remember the creed right?"

Mike wasn't sure what that had to do with the question, but he answered anyway. There could be only one. Shad meant the Ranger creed. "Sure."

"Like word for word?"

"Yes. But what does that have to do with . . ."

"Check your e-mail in a few hours," Shad said.

07:45:05 AM

Even before he started searching, Mike had a bad feeling about the accident scene. It had changed. The traces of glass, metal and plastic the Humvee had left when it crashed were no longer strewn across the dirt road. He remembered the uncountable bits that shone in the Maglite beam. Now not a sliver of foreign material was present. And that was not the only oddity. If he had not been a witness, he would have doubted there had been an accident at all.

The tree that the truck hit should have had paint flecks mashed into its wood. He expected to find the marks. But instead, at the point of impact were a series of deep slash marks, probably hacked with a machete blade.

And the dirt road had a manicured look, as if someone had dragged rakes and flat sticks across the surface, further obliterating the tracks. Mop-up work like this he had encountered before, though usually from far less accomplished hands.

When criminals tried thwarting investigations by staging the scene, often their attempts at concealing their presence created additional evidence, and betrayed even more about themselves or their crime. Here the perpetrators had done much better. Their sanitizing efforts were nearly perfect.

Now the tracks told another story besides an accident. In essence, a team had combed over an unremarkable patch in the woods, and sliced pieces out of a tree. He doubted it was the same crew who crashed the Humvee the previous night. Maybe it was the bunch who detailed the murder scene. If so, they had learned a great deal since that day. They had improved on their methods.

So much for Lisbeth's investigation. No point in her bothering now. And that, he suspected, was probably very much their goal.

The phone rang. Jessica dialing from an unfamiliar number. He felt his head lift at the relief of knowing she was back.

"How are you doing? Are you okay?" Mike asked her. "Thanks for returning my call."

"All right, I guess," Jessica said. "The nurse wouldn't let me check out without calling you first. You made quite an impression on her, apparently."

"I try," Mike said, a bit woeful that it had taken yet another crisis to spark a dialogue between them. Bringing them to the same table took extreme measures, it seemed. He wasn't sure how he felt about that. "I'm sorry I put you in this mess."

"You mean about Andy being off with, basically, a complete stranger, because you were out doing your thing, instead of vacationing with us like you promised?"

The analysis stung a little, but he figured he deserved the barb. "Listen, I know this is a mess. I screwed up. I shouldn't have put you two in this position. I should have listened right from the start."

"Hold on a second," Jessica said. "Yes, I'm annoyed that you weren't there for us. It's a perfectly awful feeling waking up in a hospital and not knowing where your only child is. But that's not exactly your fault. It's not like you put me in the hospital. I'm mad because you broke your word."

Mike hesitated. Of all the people in his world, probably the one he could depend on most was Jessica. Even after the divorce. "Listen, Jessica. There's something going on out here, and I'm not sure exactly what, but I think you should pack it in and go home. You're at risk, and Andy may be, too."

"What's going on, Mike?"

He knew it would sound crazy to her. He had no choice. She would pry it out of him eventually, and maybe while forming a grudge, so he might as well get to the point. "I think you were drugged at the bonfire."

"I suspected the same thing. What doesn't make sense is why."

He outlined the phone threats, and his theory on the connection between the murder and Sean. He also explained the deal with Partner. "The Partner, or whoever it was, said something would happen to you, to show me I needed to do what they wanted. And it did. Why else would you pass out like that unless you were drugged?"

"But how did they miss it in my blood work?"

"The tests they conducted on you weren't for chemical agents. They knew you had been drinking, everyone said you were drunk, there was alcohol on your breath, so they likely left it at that. Presumptive diagnosis. Happens a thousand times a day in emergency rooms. We need to figure out who it came from. Do you have any ideas?"

"I'm not sure how this happened," Jessica said. "It's not like wild parents were passing joints around and slamming back Whip-Its in the bathroom stalls."

"Did anyone bring you drinks at the party, maybe? Or did you leave something unattended that you ate or drank later?"

There was a long a pause before she relived the chronology of the previous evening for Mike. "I was doing a lot of serving actually. But three people did bring me beer, and the bottles were already opened. Erich, Cara, the woman from Utah Andy is with now, and Chappy, the chef. Now that I think about it, Chappy brought me a plate of food, too."

"So maybe the Partner is one of the three. It makes some sense. They all have access to you and Andy."

"You're jumping ahead here. Let's just say I was drugged." Jessica paused. "By someone. Even if it is one of them, that doesn't make the person the Partner. My question is, why not hurt me more seriously? This is a pretty low-key attack. Why not kidnap me or Andy if they want real leverage over you?"

"They were sending me a message that they could get to you. And they probably didn't want to raise any more suspicions than necessary."

"Exactly," Jessica said. "And because they're not in a position to do whatever they want without attracting attention. So I'm going back to the ranch and collecting Andy, but we're not going anywhere.

We have to work through this together."

His first instinct was to give in to the frustration. He fought back that reaction. Jessica was impervious once she made up her mind. He tried anyway.

"Please," Mike said. "Can you reconsider for Andy?" He hoped playing to her maternal instinct would work, but was almost certain it would not.

"As much as I dislike this situation," Jessica said, "you need my help. We need to figure out who murdered the guy in the clearing and how it all links together with Sean. You can't do that from where you are. You're going to need information and someone with contacts, and someone who can ask the hardball questions and get away with it. Erin Sykes would lie down in front of a train for you, Mike, but she's a people pleaser. Everyone likes her. She's too nice for this."

In part, Mike saw her logic. Jessica was good at asking the right questions. And Erin—to reframe Jessica's blunt assessment—had a business to run, and enough distractions and problems already. "I don't know," Mike said. "That was part of the warning, too. The Partner mentioned that specifically, in fact. You were to stay out of the search, effective immediately."

"Oh, no problem. I'll stay out of the search," Jessica said. "I want nothing to do with it. That's your area. My role will be to look into the murder. I already have a rapport with Lisbeth established. I'm just taking it to the next level. The only difference is, I'll be far more discrete."

"I don't know if she can be trusted, Jessica. She might be involved." The hospital situation and Dagget's accusations weighed heavy on his mind. He had a concern or two about Dagget, for that matter.

"That's what I'm talking about, Mike. You're out there in the middle of nowhere, carrying this weight all by yourself, and you don't know who to trust. Well, you're going to need to trust me. Trust that I know what I'm doing, that I'm a big girl, and that I can handle Lisbeth. I'll decide if she's honest or not."

He pondered for a long moment. Again, she was right; he could not do this alone. Again her reasoning swayed him. He had one condition that was non-negotiable. "If this thing breaks down and we both agree that it's too dangerous, then will you take Andy and not look back?"

"Mike, if it goes that bad, and I feel that there is no other recourse, yeah. I'll do it. I'll grab Andy and we'll go; I promise. We'll go to the place only you and I know about."

They said their good-byes, and Mike checked the clock. It was time to catch up with Dagget.

A gun fired a single shot in the distance.

Mike faced back toward the ledge. A figure rushed inside the canopy, scattering debris. Branches snapped and broke. Dagget burst through the trees and onto the road, his face red. He glanced at Mike, hooked left, and kept booking along the tree line. The Marlin, wrapped in the sling, bounced with his long strides.

"I tried to call you . . ." Dagget called backwards, between heaves. "We've got trouble."

07:55:23 AM

Before Dagget could get any farther, Mike slid out of the pack and tackled the officer. Dagget fought back with threats and curses. "Get off of me, damn it! What the hell are you doing?" Dagget said, seething. Mike locked Dagget's shoulders up and wedged a knee into the officer's back. Dagget gave up fighting when he realized he was beat. Mike had the advantage of leverage and strength. And most importantly, the tracker had struck first, and caught Dagget by surprise. That edge made the biggest difference.

"You're not thinking," Mike said. "If someone is shooting, you stay low until you figure out where it's coming from. I'm not tearing off after you until I know what the problem is. Now what happened? And take it slow. And breathe."

"Add another citation to the list. Remember, Mike, everyone gets what they deserve."

"I have no problem living with that." Leaning into Dagget a little harder, he said, "Are you going to relax? Can I let you go?"

"Let's get out of the road, at least," Dagget said. "Out of the open."

"Fair enough." He released Dagget, and they tucked in between the trees. They sat with their backs leaning against the trunks, quiet at first, expecting another shot.

Dagget shuddered. He caught his breath, one eye trained on the ledge a thousand yards away. "I was all set to leave, when two guys appeared on the trail side of the ledge. Both dressed in camouflage. They poked around what was left of the fire, and looked around a bit. They were carrying rifles with scopes. Remington rifles from the shape of them."

"Sounds like hunters," Mike said.

"Gee, Davy Crockett! Wonder why I didn't think of that first? Big problem—it's not hunting season for a few more weeks. And these boys were not wearing orange vests. Both of which I was about to bring to their attention, when some giant furry blob leaps out along the base of the ledge, running like a beast of hell. This monster was flying. The men split up when they saw it, and ran in different directions. There was no point calling after them. They get what they deserve."

"A mountain lion?" Mike asked.

"Didn't stick around to find out for certain. A definite maybe, I'd say. It tore off as fast as it appeared. I didn't even have a chance to unsling the rifle and rip off a shot. By the time I started thinking about it, it was already too late. When the reality of this all hit me, and I knew they were gone, I took off."

"No wonder you ran," Mike said. He might have disagreed with Dagget's response in part, but could sympathize with the officer.

Mountain lions were incredible runners, and if a man crossed one on the wrong day, in the wrong manner, that meeting might prove that man's last unlucky break. Defending their considerable territory was a task the big cats took seriously. They were the sort of prey a hunter had to be willing to die for, because mountain lions could kill or maul whole groups of people, even when seriously wounded. These fierce fighters—the most awesome of land-bound carnivores—deserved respect. They had Mike's, for certain.

"I told you before," Dagget said, "I even think there's one around, I'm gone. Any man says he's not scared of mountain lions is a lying bastard. I kinda like them in theory, and would never hurt one. Don't particularly think highly of people who do. But I don't ever want one within a thousand yards of me."

"I can understand that," Mike said. "But why did they only fire once?"

"Christ, who knows?" Dagget said. "They probably wet their pants and froze up. Or they were running too hard to squeeze the trigger."

"That shot wasn't from a big bore rifle," Mike said. "It sounded like a handgun. Maybe a .45, or a 9mm. I hope they weren't trying to bring down a mountain lion with that."

"You might have noticed, this ain't California. People carry whatever sidearms they want to carry. It's all legal here. I know people that hunt with .357s, and they were probably after deer with the rifles. It happens a lot during the fall. Some people are a little too eager for their first buck and want a leg up on the season. They didn't count on running into a mountain lion."

To Mike, the account felt a bit on the sketchy side, though parts he could prove true. Of the following, Mike could verify: Dagget was spooked so he abandoned the ledge; a shot was fired; none of them wanted to be caught in the jaws of a mountain lion. Fortunately, the risk of stumbling into one was low. Thus far he had not encountered any tracks or droppings.

He made a note to watch out for the possible signs of a big cat. The time to pay attention was before they stumbled through a den.

"You know what?" Dagget said. "Now that I think about it, I know one of them. One of those guys was the hunter that called in the dead body two days ago. Same guy I picked up at the murder scene." Dagget shook his head as if the prospect was unthinkable. "Can't believe Lisbeth didn't hold him for questioning for at least forty-eight hours."

"Lisbeth told me he was innocent."

"Mike, everyone is a little dirty."

Just before they left for the drop site, Mike had another thought. Since it came from the gut, he trusted in it. Whoever the Partner was, or worked with, they probably knew his exact location. And he bet he knew how: their cell phones. Tracking people the old-school way was possible—lots of people could do what Mike did—but it was far easier with technology, especially in urban environments. Where the option was available, anyway.

As long as his phone stayed powered up, and in range of a tower, the phone doubled as a homing beacon. That was why the Partner demanded that he leave the phone on; it was not just so Mike could be harassed at whim. The Partner needed an active cell signal to "see" Mike. Leery of advertising their detour, he would have to shut it down to avoid detection.

Unfortunately, for a complete blackout, Dagget must follow suit and turn off his phone, too. Mike had no reason which might sway Dagget. He was not ready to voice his predicament outside the circle of trust yet, so he needed a justification, topped with a large dose of duplicity.

"We should go," Mike said.

"What about the hunters?"

"We can scale the ledge farther down, more west than where we camped. Won't come anywhere near them, hopefully. You said they scattered, so I don't expect we'll see them."

"I think we would be better off pressing ahead like before," Dagget said. "It could be even worse crossing elsewhere. It's your decision, though."

"We need to do this." Mike shut his phone down, while acting like he was doing the opposite. The screen went black. "If you want to save your battery a bit, I'm live for now."

Dagget nodded and turned off his phone. "I really hope Lisbeth delivers what she promised or this side trip will be for nothing."

08:13:10 AM

Crotty glanced at the monitor, marveling at his latest brainchild. Two of the yellow digital dots flickered and then vanished off the screen. He shook his head. He laughed.

Mike Brody was getting cheeky. The tracker probably even thought he was clever. Well, not fucking clever enough.

Crotty loved engineering, as all the males in his family did. For him there was lots to love, starting with the varied branches of study. There were endless directions for a fertile mind to travel. Among the disciplines of engineering, though, computer science he considered his favorite. He savored the precision of a microprocessor, generating the same answers to problems over and over into infinity. Human error and emotion never entered the calculations. He thought that's the way it should always be.

Even more than engineering, he loved the cutting-edge solutions that advanced his vision. He understood that the true cost of a technology project was more than the price of the materials. To save development time, he often used a research partner. It spared him tedium and freed him to concentrate on the design. He had no problems with shortcuts. Where the numbers favored buy versus build, he hesitated not at all and bought. Still, he relished the challenge of an original creation.

Like the device upon his desk, a few inches beneath the monitor.

A next-generation prototype, it extended the key functionality of a frequency-jamming device they had deployed previously with much success many times before. Crotty had known from the beginning that there would be a need for this creation. The only question: when that exact day might arrive. Today, naturally.

This black box was so much more than a frequency jammer. Blocking a signal made a GPS expecting a data stream appear like it was broken. His new tool made a GPS look like it worked perfectly. Only it did not. Instead the device displayed whatever Crotty wanted it to show.

He adjusted a setting on the device with the turn of a knob. A small red indicator light on his magic black box blinked.

. . .

They hiked single file among the trees, pressing toward the drop site at an even, almost aggressive clip. Dotted with the knots of tree roots, the ground was otherwise soft and level. The air, trapped by the foliage above, smelled musky and sweet, like sweat mixed with honey. At points the denseness of the canopy forced them to use a Maglite.

Mike clicked on the flashlight only infrequently. Every fifty steps he cast to the left, to the right, and then straight ahead.

Several minutes in, Mike wondered if something was amiss. He thought they ought to be clear of the trees by now. He tapped the screen of the GPS three times, rattling the back-lit display. The device indicated that they had traveled north long enough. He mentioned nothing to Dagget. They continued for five additional minutes and finally hit a break in the thicket. Closer to what he anticipated, the spot still seemed all wrong.

Mike stopped for a moment. A hill similar to what he had targeted was ahead in the distance; not immediately before them as he expected. Based on the coordinates provided by Lisbeth, they stood moments from the epicenter of the planned drop site. In Mike's eyes, an unfortunate location for the drop, since the chute that slowed the fall might drift considerably in the wind. Lisbeth had been vague about the exact dimensions of the care package. He was expecting a modest-sized box, far less than a pallet's worth of mixed items—the size of a backpack. Now Mike wished he were certain about the specifications.

Like the last gasp of a wick drowning in a pool of wax, helicopter blades died off and then faded. The sound was far away. He thought he was mistaken, though, and the noise was merely wind rippling against the rocks.

. . .

From the moment the Partner had mentioned helicopter sweeps for the boy—which meant unwanted eyes—Crotty had schemed.

The challenge of keeping the searchers at bay was significant. There were many tactics he considered, but a crude show of force was never an option. Downing a helicopter, while within his power, involved investigations. And not just from the local cops. The Federal Aviation Administration and National Transportation Safety Board would intercede, and possibly the FBI too, if the act appeared terroristic. None of this was scrutiny the company needed. The distribution infrastructure depended on open gateways too obscure to attract attention. He had a growing business to run when this ended.

And since the electrical and navigation systems of an Apache were shielded from external interference, the helicopter got a free pass. The bird flew where it liked.

But those on the ground, those that traveled by foot, who depended on data from third-party equipment, like Dagget and Mike, well, they faced another challenge.

For coordinates might be intercepted and altered en route to a GPS device, and the owner would never notice. And if the data was twisted just so, the owner might find himself far and away from where he expected to be.

Crotty twisted the knob again on his magic black box, sending more doctored images and false coordinates to Mike's GPS.

• • •

"Where's the copter?" Dagget asked. "I swear I heard it . . ."

"Don't see it," Mike said. *At least it wasn't all my imagination.* Hunger and stress could affect the senses, but he imagined himself in better shape than that. *Focus on the goal, not the challenges.* The goal was paramount.

Mike had a plan.

A few feet apart, they stood back-to-back. They stepped in tandem, spotted what lay above the horizon, and turned clockwise in slow increments until each man had covered one hundred and eighty degrees of sky. And then they continued, completing a circle, rotating a full three hundred and sixty degrees. Total coverage, Mike hoped.

"Got anything?" Dagget asked.

• • •

"Thank you. Come again," Crotty said so proudly to the screen. He smirked to himself, awash in his own approbations swirling through his head. Being clever was good. Being brilliant was better. "Next time, stay on point, Mr. Brody."

• • •

"Nope," Mike said. "Sorry. Nothing."

"Sure we're in the right place?" asked Dagget.

"I can't see how we're not." As Mike said this, he checked his GPS. In case of a software malfunction, he power-cycled the box, shutting it off and then turning it right back on.

Reinitialized, the main screen with the correct options appeared, and the device reconnected with the network of satellites. Spheres on the display that corresponded to a given spacecraft thousands of miles away darkened—the darker the circle, the stronger the signal. All functions were good. The reboot ate about two minutes, and during this he ignored the screen.

Listening for the helicopter, there were only the sounds of the woods.

08:55:43 AM

Courtesy of a ride from Erich, Jessica made it back to the ranch for the tail end of breakfast. He helped her from the car, through the main lodge and to Cara's room, where Andy awaited her return. She knocked at her neighbor's door; it opened.

At the sight of Jessica, Andy cleared the room in three leaps, moving so fast the toes of his sneakers barely graced the floor. She thought he had impressive agility for an eight-year-old.

Reaching her, Andy cried, "Mom!" and made as if he might dive through Jessica. Protecting her left arm—the IV recently attached to her wrist had left a substantial bruise—she reined him toward her right side for a half bear hug, tight as she could manage.

"I'll see you two at breakfast," Cara said, leaving with her twin girls. "I'm glad you're okay, Jessica. It was a real pleasure to have Andy overnight. He's welcome whenever."

"Thank you so much," Jessica said to Cara. "We'll talk soon, all right?"

"Of course. There'll be no secrets between us now."

Mother and son hugged in the hall.

"God, it's good to see you!" Jessica held Andy to her body, and gripped him like only a mother could. "I missed you so much. I'm so very sorry."

He glanced at his mother with the eyes of a doe. "I'm glad you're better, Mom. I didn't know what was going on."

The hug ended. "Sorry I wasn't there for you last night. It won't happen again. The rest of this trip, I'm Super Mom. Anything you want, just say the word." She flexed, making a muscle with her right arm.

Andy giggled, and clamped her bicep as best he might, surprised at how solid the upper arm was. "You're strong, Mom!" he said. "So, I can have anything?"

"Yep," Jessica said. "This is going to be a real vacation from here on."

"Can you make Dad come back now?" Andy said.

The question was shocking. Now she regretted the absoluteness of her offer—it was impossible to rescind. Jessica asked, "Is that what you want?"

"Yeah! Cause that would make it, like, a super-plus-good vacation."

His suggestion sunk her spirits like a sail collapsing against a mast. Moments like these made her feel like her presence was obligatory in Andy's life, and her love was inconsequential. Like all Andy wanted was a father. His father. Forcing back a sigh, Jessica held him close for a while longer, tussling his hair.

The position hid the tears on her face from Andy.

10:12:35 AM

Mike made the decision to reverse course and resume tracking Sean almost immediately. They would not make a second attempt that day for the provisions; the risk of wasting more time was too great. For Mike, the mishap was clear as it was regrettable. Reviewing the chain of events, something critical had gone askew. Wherever the helicopter dropped its load, the gear landed far out of hiking range. And as much trouble as he had with the idea that maybe Lisbeth botched the coordinates, or that the pilot had dropped the pallet at another location or abandoned the run completely, he could not believe that his own gear had betrayed him.

To this point the GPS had performed like a champ. Flawless. Accurate. Secure. So why the device malfunctioned now was perplexing. Government surplus or secondhand consumer models, well, from those he expected data loss and system crashes.

Mike Brody demanded the best; he bought the best; he worked with the best. Except here, commercial-grade equipment malfunctioned—that shortfall was a big, big problem. He needed accuracy. He needed absolute trust in the coordinates he used.

Aborting the run, Mike left a voice message for Lisbeth and explained his rationale for keeping off his cell phone. And going forward, he decided to keep the cell running until the charge level dipped below ten percent. Open communication lines beat out his anxieties about being pursued by shadowy figures. Besides, if a crew—if the Partner—was tracking him or Dagget via their cell phones, it meant they were on the move. Still in play. When they reached Sean, he would manage the problem then.

The more angles he considered, the more his doubts grew. He became less sure about the real costs of his involvement. Everything had seemed clearer yesterday, before the phone threats and Jessica's collapse. Perhaps minor successes along the way—the items from Sean they recovered—duped him into complacency. Maybe the error was not equipment-related.

Or the error could have been his. He might have misread or

misinterpreted the coordinates. While he disliked the idea, he did realize that he was perfectly fallible. No matter the experiences a tracker brought into the field, mistakes happened.

And in the best cases, with every advantage and skilled people involved, results were not guaranteed. By habit, he avoided speculation with the police or the parents about what value he might add. Fools predicted the unknown, or tried to. At the end of the day, he had no more answers than anyone else. He just knew the signs, and of those, only the signs he allowed himself to see.

Spotting the signs made the difference between hitting or missing a target, and he based decisions on them. About Sean he considered the signs very positive overall.

But what their chances were for finding Sean in time remained out of his control. What he determined was putting himself out there, trusting the signs, and pressing ahead.

Picking up Sean's trail again, about a half mile ahead of where they had left off the previous night, Mike halted.

"Let's take five minutes," Mike said. "Hydrate up. We've been pushing hard. We're not too far behind where we need to be."

"Okay," Dagget said, breathing out his relief. Sweat oozed from his temples. He looked like a man who needed a break. "I'm going to ask Lisbeth what happened to our bird."

Mike drank deeply, then held some water in his mouth without swallowing. He had a few questions for Lisbeth, too. He walked away from Dagget for a minute, and let his shoulders hang, relaxing. At least here, he was back in his element. Tired, and a little worse for the wear, but back in the groove. He was ready.

He was thinking about how much he missed Andy when Dagget stumbled back.

"This is turning into one messed-up day," Dagget said. He sighed, drawing it out, as if he needed the extra seconds to gather momentum.

"What?" Mike asked, a little surprised at Dagget's demeanor.

"Shad Hammer is dead."

10:30:17 AM

Right before the day's first riding session, Jessica and Andy stopped by their room. Andy needed his jacket, and Jessica had a call to make. Reaching Lisbeth took longer than planned, and she sat Andy in front of the television.

By coincidence, the last channel selected was the Discovery Channel. That particular day, that broadcast was about the life of a praying mantis. Andy turned ashen, and he glanced helplessly at his mother. He avoided looking at either the set or the remote control. When a house-cat-sized insect bounced across the screen, Jessica reached around Andy for the remote and clicked over to the History Channel, which was running the exact same program, three minutes behind.

Andy shut the television off himself and played his portable video-game device instead, zapping alien invaders.

She got through to Lisbeth.

"Jessica! How are you feeling?" Lisbeth asked.

"Much better thanks," said Jessica. "I'd like to offer some more help."

"If you're up to it, I'll take whatever I can get for this poor kid. What are you thinking?"

"Mike mentioned there was something else you had him look at before he joined the search. A murder. I think I could be very helpful to you in that area. Did you identify the victim yet?"

"Listen, Jessica, don't take this the wrong way, but I don't discuss open homicide investigations with journalists," Lisbeth said. "If the wrong details find their way in print before a trial, cases get blown out of the water in court by defense attorneys. I keep things civil between myself and the DA's office. Surely you understand the gravity of what you are asking, and why I can't answer your question."

"You do make a valid point. The way I see it, though, we're just two women talking."

"We may be talking as friends," Lisbeth said, "but we both know how we pay the bills."

"I'll make you a deal," Jessica said. "Anything you tell me about the murder investigation stays off the record, period. Privileged information. In exchange, I have connections in every alphabet agency who owe me favors and won't drag their heels getting answers. Whatever information they give, I'll route straight to you. Experts, analysis, information. The best there is."

"I have to admit, I like what I'm hearing. What do you want in return?"

"Anonymity. Any information I provide, you take full credit for. Your investigation, your breakthroughs. As far as everyone else knows, I'm a guest at the ranch, and nothing more. A nameless reporter on vacation."

"So anonymous, she sells pieces to *News Story.*" Lisbeth paused. The sound of a lighter flicking over the phone. "It sounds workable. But why do you want to do this? You're not going to write about it, and you won't get any recognition later."

"Help is a two-way street. If I help you now, maybe someday, when I need help, a little comes my way. Besides, how do you think I got all these connections?"

"This all is for karma, huh? I'm not sure I entirely believe that."

"Can you afford to take that chance? I know the longer murder cases stay open, the harder they are to solve. And with so many people committed to the search, your office is stretched thin. Who knows how long the search might last?"

"Put it like that," Lisbeth said, conceding, "and we pretty much have to work together, now don't we?"

"Exactly." Now that Jessica stood on familiar ground, she started charging. "What do you have on the murder investigation?"

"Not a lot. Besides some tainted blood samples, and a few plaster impressions, we have some pictures taken with a cell phone. But they're a bit grainy, and we haven't had any luck sharpening them."

"I know someone at NASA who does excellent image enhancement and analysis. He's verified several pictures for me. He can correct and adjust for data loss, and sharpen the image."

"If I sent you the file, you could forward it to your contact at

NASA?" Lisbeth asked, a bit incredulous.

"Consider it done."

Every so often, the less-scrupulous journalists in the press corps passed off a digitally altered photo as genuine, especially if there was a bounty on the shot in the tabloid markets.

An imagination, an afternoon with photo-editing software, and an editor-in-chief with irrational expectations nurtured a breeding ground for artificially enhanced pictures. The sort of neverland where the truth got a boost. Pictures even better than the real thing. Jessica knew photography well enough to spot the hack forgeries. But she also knew debunking a more skilled one beyond all doubt required more expertise than hers. That's where her friend at NASA proved invaluable.

After they exchanged e-mail addresses, Lisbeth asked, "You have some kind of relationship with Erich Reynard, correct?"

Jessica presumed Lisbeth meant a working relationship. Strictly platonic and professional. Really, the word relationship was overkill for their situation. The term mutual admiration fit better. Sounded better, too. "Why do you ask?"

"Erich owns a small passenger plane and has volunteered it before. I'd like his help again. If you see him, could you remind him to call me back ASAP?"

Recalling that Erich had offered her a personal flight twice already, Jessica said, "I wonder why he's taking so long to get back to you? After all, his guest is missing. I would think he would be doing everything he could to help."

"That's a very good question," Lisbeth said. "And one I've been asking myself."

10:31:34 AM

Mike turned to Dagget, still grappling with the reality of Shad's death. "How did it happen? How did Shad die?"

"A neighbor heard shots fired and called the police. They found Shad's front door busted open, and his body facedown on a couch. Three shots to the head," Dagget said. "His place is in shambles, and he doesn't live in the greatest neighborhood anyway. There are plenty of addicts and dealers prowling the streets. Might have been a burglary in progress that Shad wandered into and the thug panicked and shot him. Some thug hopped up on who-knows-what who didn't even know where he was."

Mike doubted that version of the facts because he knew details the police did not. He knew Shad was asking questions someone did not want answered. He also knew why Shad was asking them, and who requested that favor.

And now Shad's involvement might have gotten him killed. The drug-related break-in sounded like a textbook cover-up for an assassination. Generally speaking, addicts were lousy with firearms—even when sober. Multiple shots to the head required too much proficiency to be accidental. Killing like that took a steady, practiced hand. Not exactly the top tool in the average druggie's tool chest.

"When?"

"They found him about thirty minutes ago," Dagget said. "The gunpowder was still hanging in the room. Messed up, huh?"

"I need to make a phone call."

He had to reach Jessica immediately. He had to talk her out of investigating the murder. She had to leave with Andy now. Right now.

"The canteens are empty anyway," Dagget said. "I'll fill 'em up. I have people to contact, too. Someone has to tell Shad's father."

Mike dialed. Silently, he prayed Jessica would answer.

10:40:12 AM

Four men stood at attention in a single row. By no coincidence, all were the same height, wore the same hairstyles, boots, and shirts. The consistency gave the line a military look. A generator droned in the distance. An overhead lamp dangled from a chain above and behind them, and the backlight spilled shadows from their brows upon their cheekbones. In the corner, a dehumidifier hummed, strained from months of near-continuous use. Ice encased the top three coils.

Except for the fourth, Crotty approved of the men the unit leader had assembled. A slight mismatch he expected, because the men that served the company were as diverse as their talents. Literally a rainbow of skills.

While the Partner allocated personnel based upon a whimsical set of criteria, that was not Crotty's way. Directives Crotty issued to the unit leader requesting the best men really meant the right men, and the unit leader understood the unspoken order. Crotty was often vague with directions. He omitted details purposely, testing the coping abilities of those around him, while concealing his true goals. Busy trying to figure out what he wanted them to do, his men rarely bothered asking why or what he might gain from their success.

Before an important deployment, he conducted quick interviews, so he might make adjustments in personnel. He kept the questions short. Anything more involved than a few per man was overkill, because he had one advantage at the ready always: a hard drive full of employee dossiers. Embarrassing facts a man never wanted in circulation.

Crotty was relentless. He got the dirt, and spread it where it worked best.

As for the fourth man, well, he bugged Crotty for a different reason: a scapular with thin, brown shoulder tape peeked through his shirt. Crotty had never noticed this about the man before. The oversight bothered Crotty. He disliked mistakes. Especially his own.

"Why don't I like you?" Crotty asked the fourth man. He traced the outline of the scapular in the air, inches from the man's chest. "Would you consider not wearing that for a day?"

The fourth man reached inside and removed the brown thread that joined two pictures of a red and blue cross together and held them over his heart and back. He jammed the two-sided amulet down into his pocket. Crotty rebuked him in a sharp tone. "No. No. Let me see that." The article was worn, though in good repair. The plastic covering the images was lightly frayed at the edges. "The Scapular of the Most Blessed Trinity. It's obvious you've worn this for years."

"Since first grade, sir," said the fourth man.

"But not during recruitment." Surely he had not overlooked something so obvious during screening and induction. Crotty decided he had not.

"I always wore a second undershirt to conceal it."

Crotty raised his brow. "All that trouble and at the simplest prompt you removed a beloved effect. If it's not on your chest, it's not providing you any protection. You know this."

"Yes, sir, because you wanted . . . ," said the fourth man.

Crotty returned the scapular to the fourth man, who was uncertain whether to pocket it, or don it again. Crotty spoke. "I'll tell you what I want, not the other way around. I didn't ask you to remove it; I asked if you would consider taking it off. You either stand up for your beliefs or you don't." A single beat. Then came the final judgment. "Dismissed."

"But, sir," said the fourth man. "I feel I'd be an asset to this . . ."

"You're done here," Crotty said. Walking up and down the line, he said, "This assignment requires a lot more determination and listening skills than that. Whoever is chosen needs an unflinching commitment to the goal and the larger picture. It requires reserve under pressure and the ability to work independently." Pausing at the fourth man, Crotty's eyes reflected back only nothingness. "It's three, ladies."

The fourth man stood, the scapular crumpled in his hands, hesitant and confused, head bowed in shame.

"You're all going to have to work faster and more carefully," Crotty said, "especially since you're down a man. That means less breathing room, more chances for mistakes. Just like the first team did yesterday, you have the coordinates, you know what the markers look like. You know what to do with those last few. Just keep the throttle down and be back here by lunch."

Satisfied they understood, Crotty unleashed them into the morning.

The unit leader appeared with good news. "I confirmed with someone on the base that your briefing packet reached the pilot of the search helicopter an hour before takeoff."

"So the pilot knows what dangers might await her crew on the ground?" Crotty asked. "The details that Lisbeth couldn't tell them."

"According to our source, they expect the worst and have equipped themselves accordingly."

Crotty nodded to himself. "Perfect."

10:43:31 AM

A helicopter crept along the horizon. The blade sliced through the air. The rotor hum sent Sean reeling. He charged down the incline of broad-faced rocks, grass, and dirt. His sneakers served as eyes, his arms a compass.

Instead of landing forward of his heels as a long-distance runner might, his toes struck ground first. Then he pushed off his calves like a fell racer.

Sean learned the hard way about the British sport—because he needed to move like hell down a mountain. Casting aside concern for personal safety, fell racers assailed slopes, often treacherous ones, during the dry season. They wore boots with studs, shorts, and a T-shirt. More recently, many events also required windproof clothing, food, maps, and a whistle. Quite a lot more gear than Sean had.

Whatever equipment a racer packed, the principles remained the same. The key to a successful descent was to keep moving, and never resist the downward trend. Those who fought gravity's effects lost. At least he knew that lesson going into the descent.

Endorphins flooded his nervous system. Neurotransmitters blasted signals toward the proper receptors, and sugar coated the pain. Most of his body parts ached, and a heavy pressure weighed on his chest. Yet he continued. He must.

Sean barreled down the slope, a boy in motion. For all the distance and speed gained, he could reach much farther. Just not right then. Wasted movements—the hidden price of a hapless running style—bogged him down. As his right toe struck earth, his torso swayed to the right. His upper body then recentered itself midstride. Leading with the left foot into the next step, his torso tilted leftward, and drifted less noticeably than when he swayed right. The uneven pendulum knocked his arms off balance, slumped his shoulders forward, and sent his forearms swinging across his chest. Damnable inefficiencies, all of them. He paid the price.

On and on he ran. He wondered how much faster he could go. He had so much farther to go.

This was a time for speed, and he wished he had gleaned more from the cross-country coach about proper form. Often he had ignored the former champion who led the team. He almost regretted that now. He had reasons to block the coach's messages out.

Driving alongside the team, the coach prodded them with a bullhorn. He enforced a pack-style run. A pack that moved as a team, won as a team, he said. The goal was a perfect score—fifteen—which meant putting the first five finishers across the line. Whatever the cost, the team stayed together, always at a brisk pace, and always pressed harder.

If a runner lagged, the leader retreated and circled around, pressuring holdouts back into the main group. Leaders nudged or prodded. It was their job to keep the pack in-line. They employed whatever tactics they wished.

Some leaders used exuberance, chatting up the laggards before charging back to the head of the fold. This made it plain to deadbeats that the leader was in better shape, and had energy to spare. One spewed insults, berating the slowpokes. And sometimes silence cut far deeper wounds.

But there were few greater humiliations for a runner than to be reined in several times during the same practice. Sean had suffered this fate. He had endured all of the tortures. He really did not like running for sport, but his father forced him to train. His father made him do lots of things.

Even things that aggravated his asthma.

Curiously, long-distance runners suffered from asthma more often than sedentary individuals. In fact, it often caused exercise-induced asthma, a medical diagnosis his father ignored. If all Sean was good for was running, then he better learn to deal with it early in life. "Learn to catch a ball." he said when Sean protested.

Outside the hostile environment of sanctioned practices, though, Sean proved far more capable. In winter he jogged hours across the parks, the concrete paths and dirty slush. In spring he ran in hail. In summer he ran in smog and heat. He kept charging.

And now in September, he ran for his life. The time for going full out had arrived. He dropped the hammer. Gaining speed, his stride lengthened. The momentum grew. The grade carried him.

Overhead, the helicopter inched closer, the sound of the blades and rotors rang louder. So much more space to cover, and so little energy on reserve. He had to try and make it.

Here he was the lead runner, way out front. He dictated the pace. For an instant, he visualized the entire squad dragging behind him, the coach at the side of the road with a flat tire. And the goddamn bullhorn, that was broken, just shards of useless plastic and smashed electronics.

His left foot slipped across a few stones, which gave way under the impact. Sean slid. Breaking stride, he whipped his arms out like stabilizers, trying to lessen the mistake. Inertia drove him into the next step. The pendulum swung once again. Still upright. He cranked his legs and righted himself.

The helicopter began a turn, circling slowly around over the trees.

He ran faster toward safety.

10:44:43 AM

To Mike's relief, Jessica had answered his call on the second ring. He sucked in three quick breaths before speaking. An arduous task faced him, and he could not fail at convincing her to leave the ranch immediately.

Her persistence, though, made his task much, much harder. Whenever she believed in what she was doing, she closed out any voices that suggested she quit. Criticism, emotion, or arguments— none of these tactics swayed her when she truly believed in what she was doing. And Mike anticipated facing deep convictions here. Journalism was rarely about the published story or the check for

Jessica. Her motives were less self-serving than attention. No, it was about being involved. Because what she knew best could aid the situation, that made her want to help. She almost had to. She helped by bringing information to people who needed and wanted it.

"Someone involved with the case was murdered this morning," Mike said. "We had talked about the possibility that things might get too dangerous for you and Andy to stick around. I think this makes it that time." He explained that Shad was looking at identifying the caller behind the phone threats, and was dead and paid the price.

"I'm sorry Shad is dead. He was just trying to help. Actually, I was going to call you about him," Jessica said. "I forgot that my laptop is still configured to pull from both of our mail accounts. Sorry, I didn't mean to click on yours. It happened by accident. I didn't even notice till much later. Anyway, you got a message from Shad."

"When?" The time the note arrived seemed critical. E-mail could be faked.

"8:30, according to the date-time stamp."

8:30. Minutes before he died, Mike thought. That detail checked out. Suddenly the chronology hit him at once. Shad barely got the information sent off when the assailant attacked. And he missed the mail on his cell phone because the mail software on Jessica's computer automatically removed messages from the server. There was never a chance to retrieve it.

He had set the option on her laptop years ago; the configuration made sense back then. For a while they had shared a machine. By habit, he checked personal e-mail on rare occasions, and used his business account for most communications. A right-enough arrangement that he left intact, despite their divorce suggesting things were final.

In situations like this one, he realized how cordial their relations were and was thankful they were close. Most separations were final, definite. To Mike, they were more of a divorced couple. Though using the word *couple* in their situation seemed . . . inaccurate. They had an unspoken understanding about many things that often tripped up ex-lovers.

"Permission granted to read my mail in emergencies," Mike said. Divorced or not, he hid very little from her. Ninety-five percent of the messages were unsolicited advertisements and stock tips anyway. "So what did Shad find?"

"Maybe we can figure that out together."

"Is it not in English?"

"It is, but it makes no sense. The message consists of a subject, a short note, and an attachment. It's nonsensical. And when I click the attachment, it asks for a password."

"First off, where is the laptop now?" For Mike, it seemed the most important question he could ask.

"You caught me on a riding break," Jessica said. "After that picture in my planner disappeared, I told Erich and he changed the lock. He also offered me access to a huge safety-deposit box. I locked up the computer, my planner, and a few pieces of jewelry. Should I secure any of your things?"

"Thanks, but that's all right." He could live with a few less material possessions. He didn't want to consider life without Jessica and Andy. "Can you recall what the note said?"

"Give me a second," Jessica said. "I'll remember."

While Jessica reflected, he mulled the latest twist. The file wanted a password. Since e-mail was an insecure medium and subject to interception, one technique to discourage unintended readers was by locking the file, and enforcing authentication before allowing access to the contents. However, the method only slowed down prying eyes, and only for a short period. Brute force attacks compromised passwords in seconds or minutes. In rare cases, cracking a text-based pass phrase took a few hours. Anyone with access to a decent piece of equipment might unravel the secrets inside quickly enough. So really that choice was hardly a choice at all.

Encrypting the message contents was a better method and the preferred one. A complex algorithm might take months or years of computer time. For Shad to have done this, Mike would have needed to send Shad his public encryption key first. Then Shad could have created an encrypted message that only Mike could read. They had never traded keys—they had no opportunity to do so—so the only recourse was to password-protect the file, and hope that when an outsider figured out the password, it no longer mattered if the file contents became public knowledge.

Hopefully a clue in the message hinted at the password.

"The subject was The Creed. The note itself was a single line: Mike, Bet number three you know word for word, Shad."

Like many truths in his life, the answer revealed itself when he gave himself permission to see the answer waiting for him. *Of course. The Creed.* Shad had asked if he remembered it. *Number three out of six.* "Point three of the Ranger Creed," Mike said. "Try this: Never shall I fail my comrades."

"Wait," Jessica said. "Is that one long word, or are there spaces like a regular sentence?"

"Spaces," Mike said. "And make the N in *never* capital, just like the phrase."

"Never shall I fail my comrades," Jessica said. "Got it. We'll be back at the ranch for lunch by twelve. I'll check it ASAP. What's in the file, by the way?"

"It's all the recent activity on my cell phone," Mike said. "Incoming and outgoing. Hopefully it tells us who the Partner is. In any case, even if you get this open, I still want you and Andy to take off."

"Once we have the records, we can go to Lisbeth about the threats. Maybe we'll have a name. We won't need to leave."

"And what if she's the Partner? Or if she's protecting whoever it is?"

"Lisbeth strikes me as pretty much what she says. A small-town detective who needs whatever resources she can get. Now, if she doesn't respond the way I think she will, then I'll call someone else."

"Would you consider leaving, anyway? Given what happened to Shad, I'd feel better . . ."

"Maybe it sounds like the wrong approach," Jessica said, "but something tells me you need us to stay. At least for now."

Mike resigned himself to the fact that she was not leaving with Andy. She was immovable. She would decide when she was ready, not Mike. "Can you forward Shad's message to my business account before you do anything?" he asked. "Because as it stands right now, the only proof we have that the Partner exists is on your laptop."

10:49:33 AM

Mike answered his phone and was greeted to another helping of the hissing voice of the Partner.

"That was a very foolish thing you did earlier. Did you think shutting off your cell phone would keep me from figuring out about your little detour?"

"Maybe."

"Guess again," the Partner said. "Stay on task from now on, or a lot more than your GPS bearings will get messed up."

"Understood," Mike said, "but I need you to leave my gear alone."

"Why? It's more fun this way. And it builds character. Pushes you to use your skills and intuition. You've still got those, right?"

"I can't give Lisbeth the wrong coordinates if I don't know what the right ones are. And I don't need to debug or outguess the equipment. That will slow me down. That's bad for both of us."

"Fine," the Partner said. "We'll consider your transgression a mistake. Don't do it again."

"Why did you kill Shad?" Mike said.

"I'd be more worried about who did that, rather than why. Your buddy picked the wrong data broker. Your ex-wife isn't the only one with contacts in high places."

Keeps saying "we" when he talks about operations, Mike thought. Someone else is involved, or he wants me to believe there is. Mike decided to press for that answer. "Can I speak to the other partner?"

A throat cleared on the other end. "What?"

"There are two of you in this, right?" Mike asked. "I just want to know if I'm talking to the right guy. The one who calls the shots. Put him on now."

"You're talking to the right person," said the Partner.

"I want to talk to whoever killed Shad. And I could be wrong, but it doesn't sound like that's you. And if it's not, it makes me wonder if you're the person to do business with. So are you the boss, or what?"

"I promise when you find the boy, Mike, you'll see who you're dealing with."

10:54:10 AM

Sean gazed at the endpoint. His eyes were strong, healthy, and unworn by monitors and poor lighting.

Out ahead, the route was clear. A long distance separated him from the goal, so much area to travel. This time he would not make the same mistake that had gotten him lost. He began again. His movements choppy, his stride awkward, he was perhaps half as fast as before he started out days ago. And still he ran. Down the hill, and among a patch of black cottonwood. The leaves provided cover. He wondered if this was enough, if the leaves shielded him from view.

The helicopter roared. Banking left, the distance and angle obscured the color scheme and make. It was louder than he believed it would be.

Once he caught a television special on aeronautics, which covered the basic principles of flight. Science was his worst subject, and he retained very few details from that broadcast. One tidbit he remembered, though—barring an attack from below, the main weakness of a helicopter was speed. And so the weakness would be his primary advantage, one he hoped would save him. To Sean, it seemed reasonable that his presence remained unknown so far, because the copter had swung away sharply. Because there was always a chance it might circle back, he continued. He could not falter. He dared not waver.

He would not stop, for the men in the helicopter bay held weapons. Black polymerized rifles with long clips, and laser sights, aimed at the canopy. Maybe even trained on him.

From the first sight of their guns, he knew they had not come to help. The killer sent them. He must have. Holding automatic weapons, they looked ready to shoot anything that moved.

Through the trees, past the stout trunks, and over bits of dead foliage, he pressed on. The noise of the copter blades reverberated through the hills. A reminder of what might happen if his plan failed.

As the bird boomed closer, he reached his destination, an alcove among the rocks. There was something better than he expected within: a pathway to a cavern. A cool breeze from deep inside washed against his face. His heart raced as he dashed into the hole.

Smooth sediment lined the walls. Water trickled somewhere beyond the darkness. A grown man could stand upright once past the narrow aperture. Outside the alcove, the entrance disappeared, lost to shadows and lighting.

Sean bent over, caught his breath, and coughed up some fluid.

The noise of the blades faded.

He was done running from the helicopter.

Here, he was safe.

11:35:01 AM

The air was warm. The sun, ablaze in the sky, burnt the backs of Mike's and Dagget's neck and arms. Free of the dense woods, they reached a new point along the escarpment, miles north of the ledge where they had slept last night.

The ledge stretched for miles in both directions, vast and sweeping as if each tip graced the horizon's end at once. Unlike the escarpment, the various peaks here reached much greater heights. From the trees, the first tier of rock drew up like a wall, with flat, smooth sides and few holds. Contour maps de-emphasized the quick rise, and Mike had underestimated the psychological impact of facing a fifty-foot-high sheet of stone. Yet Sean had managed to cross it.

"Any chance there's a better place farther down?" Dagget said. "Something less steep."

Mike checked the GPS and maps for a break in the ledge. Neither tool provided enough granularity for a better estimate. Instincts mattered more than technology at times.

Either follow the ledge north, hope for an opening, or take their chances right here.

Sean had done the climb without a mantle or belay; they would have to do the same.

While free climbing was hazardous, heading north along the ridge meant an indeterminate amount of time. Which path was faster was impossible to predict with the available information. All that Mike knew was that he could not know for certain. Still, he thought it unwise to abandon a trail just because following it meant being uncomfortable.

He had learned to make and live with his choices in tense situations. Trackers considered a variety of angles, decided on the most reasonable one, and took a shot. Any single decision was rarely the deal breaker, because a search ultimately was a collection of many decisions that searchers and their coordinators made. The real enemy was frustration; it made solving problems more difficult.

"You really think Sean climbed here?" Dagget asked.

Mike nodded. "Nearby."

"We don't even have brain buckets," Dagget said, referring to the open-faced helmets climbers wore as a precaution against collisions and head trauma. "No real equipment."

"Neither did he," Mike said.

A hundred feet to their right, a compromise waited.

Better than a slender break, a deep crevice stretched to the top of the wall. Shaped like an inverted wedge, the narrowest tip faced downward. At its most slender point, the opening was two feet wide. Near the top, the gap varied between three and four feet. Holds were numerous. Another major plus: the height was more manageable, just over thirty feet.

Mike smiled. "We chimney it." Out came the nylon rope from the backpack. "I'll lead."

"Then you pull me up?" Dagget said.

"No, you pull you up," Mike said. "The rope is for hauling up the gear. It's probably not strong enough for your weight."

"I don't like this . . ." Dagget huffed.

With the nylon strand tied in figure eights, he hooked a plastic tie through an eyelet in his pants, which held the rope to his clothing. The rest he wadded up in his pocket. Stepping sideways, Mike wedged into the crevice. He pulled his body upward a few feet, then turned to the opening, facing toward Dagget. Alternating his arms and legs, he inched up the crevice. Rocks pressed into his back.

He reached the top of the crevice, and climbed the last few feet with his fingers alone. Lactic acid seared all three heads of his deltoids. Safe on level ground, the rope unwound as it dropped through the air. The nylon whipped Dagget's face like a cat-tail. "Sorry," Mike said.

Once Dagget tied up the pack, Mike hauled it up the crevice. He untied the backpack and set it on the flat stones.

By the time Dagget reached for the last handhold, pulling mostly with his biceps, sweat covered his body. From his chest, neck, and back, moisture drizzled out of his pores, and matted the hair on his forearms. A sheen coated his palms, like a light rub of olive oil.

Suddenly Dagget's right hand lost its grip. His leg drifted back and caught part, though not all, of the toehold. He slid. "Little help here!"

Mike dropped to his stomach, his torso and legs solidly on the right side of the ledge. His hand probed for Dagget's, almost flailed. Still the officer remained just beyond Mike's reach. Dagget had a crazed look on his face, half fear, and lots of adrenaline. "Hold on!" Mike said.

Mike rolled over on his bottom, locked his soles behind two rises in the ledge, and braced himself. Tossing the free end of the rope—the other still hooked to his pants—down the ledge, Mike called to Dagget, "When you've got a decent grip on it, tug three times and say 'haul away.'"

Twenty seconds later the rope jerked. Once. Twice. Three times. "Haul away."

Mike started pulling the rope, and with it, Dagget. Progress came slowly. "Work with me a bit. You still need to climb."

"I'm trying! These holds are slippery!"

With great effort, Mike yanked Dagget's hands level with his boots, pulling hand over hand. The tip of Dagget's head peered over the ledge.

The rope snapped.

11:40:27 AM

Construction of the twin locations had been underway for months and today he christened the new facilities by himself, to great personal satisfaction. Crotty was not this pleased very often.

The layout and dimensions of one processing plant mirrored the other in every regard. Work had even started and finished on the same date at both plants. All the generators and plumbing were in place, the complex ventilation system functioned, the custom-made machinery was calibrated and tested. Little remained besides adding head count. Here the new facilities were far superior in most regards, and required less human involvement. Which meant fewer chances for mishaps and security breeches—by his design.

For maximum secrecy, Crotty drafted the plans himself, and sought experts only where he hit sticking points. After the groundbreaking came a parade of subcontractors, each charged with a small set of deliverables. Builders received designs for their minor task and nothing more. Upon completion, he dismissed the respective contractors. In this way, only Crotty understood the final layout, and kept the intricacies safe from discovery. A play straight from Egyptian pharaohs, only instead of a pyramid with burial crypts, Crotty built the twin props that would transport his new empire to great heights.

To protect the new drug formulation from discovery, manufacturing activities ceased at the main plant. Even though his men had moved most of the raw materials and equipment to the new facilities—the Partner believed the materials were in storage, because Crotty said as much—the original plant had been shuttered. Unfortunately, the closure of the old plant also snuffed out any outlet for finished products, since deliveries meant firing up the distribution system, which might unwittingly compromise the location. Every second that operations idled cost him money, and there was no way to staunch the loss.

But that problem would not matter much longer. The search would end; the sun would shine again.

At the new facility, with the new gear, and at the beckoning of a new era, he smiled. He could almost see his own excitement, an energy that pulsed through his veins, beating like a tribal drum across the Kalahari. The delays and frustration borne of compromise would end. There would be no room, no need at all, for the Partner. Only his will. Soon.

11:41:39 AM

As the rope holding Dagget from sliding into the crevice broke, Mike twisted sideways, leaned forward, and grabbed Dagget's right hand. Deltoids searing, Mike raised Dagget high enough for the officer to grab hold of the rocks and drag himself clear of the precipe.

"That was close," Dagget said, heaving. "Thanks."

"You're welcome," Mike said. His shoulder pain began when the adrenaline rush subsided.

"Didn't think I was going to make it," Dagget said. "It hasn't really hit me that I'm still here."

Mike wiped of his hands and took a long drink of water. He rubbed the sore tendon in his shoulder. "Are you hurt?" he asked Dagget.

"A little raw. Mostly confused. I don't see how the kid made the climb here."

"It was near here." Mike straightened up, and caught the rest of his wind. A vista loomed in the distance. "We climbed this spot because I had a hunch there was something I needed to see."

"Why didn't you tell me that?" Dagget said, the petulance oozing in his voice.

"Because you needed a reason. The fact that a fourteen-year-old boy managed it was all the convincing you needed."

"What the hell is up with you?" Dagget said. "This whole morning you've been all over the map. First we're going for the gear pallet, then we're not. We're making climbs because you have a hunch, and you're not telling me why? I have to say, yesterday I didn't like you very much, but it was because I didn't know who you were. Now that I have a clearer picture of how you work, these mood swings are scaring me. Do you need a break or something?"

"You're one to lecture about lying," Mike said. He started the gradual ascent toward the top. Something beckoned him toward the hill crest.

"Look, I apologized about the syringes. It was childish. I just wanted to see for myself if you really catch what other people miss. Never in a million years would I have left the medicine there. If we find the kid, he'll need it. And after you showed me what you had, I think we're going to find him." Dagget paused. "Somehow I just needed to know that you could deliver."

"Maybe you're right. I could have told you the truth," Mike said. "I'm real short on people to trust right now."

"That's why you did it?" Dagget asked. "You don't trust me? Why not?"

"This isn't the best time for a heart to heart, is it?" Mike said, hoping a redirect would push the conversation elsewhere. Dagget resisted. Mission thwarted.

"We've come a long way," Dagget said, "and we've got a long way to go, but I think we could be more up front with each other. And something is eating you big time. Ever since you heard Shad was dead, you've been a mess. I don't like working with people who are so on edge."

Dilemma: should he tell Dagget about the phone threats and the Partner, or hold it in longer? The debate raged in Mike's head. Paranoia and self-preservation said sit tight until Jessica sorted through the trace records. Then they would have proof. Instinct said level with Dagget and gauge his reaction. If Dagget knew more than he was supposed to, it would show in the face. Unless the officer was truly pathological. Mike had not ruled that possibility out yet.

The biggest problem was that in this instance, Mike knew Dagget was right. He *had* been a little sloppy since hearing about

Shad's murder. Mistakes happened, but if he kept pushing based on his emotions, rather than logic, things might worsen dramatically. It was a gamble, but he also figured Dagget had the right to know the truth about Shad. And there was a chance it might align Dagget more closely with the cause. Then again, Dagget might just blame Mike for Shad's death. In the end, he chose instinct; he told Dagget why Shad had been murdered.

Dagget responded well. "Shad always did the right thing, and that's how he went out. It's a shame." He shook his head. "So Jessica isn't leaving? A lot of women would bolt for the hills."

"I'm trying to get her to take off. So far she won't," Mike said.

"Yeah," Dagget said, with a nod. "I would imagine someone like her would stay. She's tough like my ex-wife. Once that mind is set, say good night. Her way or the highway."

A reporter's modus operandi Mike knew intimately.

From the crevice, they hiked a narrow grade several hundred yards up toward the true peak of the hill. Sunlight baked their exposed skin. A breeze brushed their faces, and blasted warm air back down their mouths. They breathed through their noses in quick fits.

The conditions harshened by the step. At the top, there was no cover, no shade, no relief. Only rocks and the stench of dried sweat.

"I'm kind of wondering why Lisbeth is in the dark about this," Dagget said.

"The Partner said specifically not to tell the cops," Mike said. "Shad didn't even know why he was looking into this for me. Without proof of who's making the threats, there is no upside in going to Lisbeth."

"While you're waiting, I could ask a buddy at the ranch to keep an eye out for Jessica and Andy. They can be discrete. She would never know they were watching unless something happened." Assistance from Dagget was something that Mike did not expect.

"Let me think about it," Mike said. "I appreciate the offer."

"It's almost ironic that you're getting these phone calls," Dagget said. He stopped. "I've been hiding something, too."

Mike beat Dagget to the punch. "The Partner threatened you too?" he asked when the officer revealed his secret.

Dagget explained. "At first I thought someone was joking with me. My position with the force is a bit tenuous these days, especially with the missing body, so I figured some prick was yanking my chain. I honestly didn't believe the calls were anything but cranks. A jerk with a poor grip on reality. World's filled with them, right? Then when I said I didn't believe him, he said he would show me he was serious." Dagget dipped his head for a second. "Then Shad turned up murdered. That was the proof he promised. He said it would appear like a crackhead went wild during a robbery. And that's exactly what the police report shows. I just regret that I didn't do more to stop it."

"Can I ask who Shad was to you?" Mike asked. "Besides a fellow officer."

"We were buddies. We rode together my first three years on the force. Since my divorce, he's been my only real friend. I don't have any family here. He was it. He was a hell of guy. Didn't deserve this. You're not alone in feeling guilty about this, Mike. I'll carry the sound of his mother crying when I told her about his death forever." He dropped his head briefly, and cleared his throat. He looked very uncomfortable—not really sure where to go next.

"What did the Partner want you to do?" Mike asked.

"The deal was simple. Find the kid, throw up a sign for him, and he would do the rest. If I didn't, he'd kill my parents."

The deal rang like a familiar chord for Mike. "Unfortunately, I know exactly what you're going through."

"The thing is," Dagget said. "I got a really bad feeling that if he's willing to off Shad just for asking questions, what chance do we have even if we do give him what he wants?"

Cars rushed by at seventy-five miles an hour. A few rocketed down the left lane, testing ninety. Fumes from the gas pumps and oil on hot concrete drenched the air. An agent caught and held Crotty's attention.

His agents might be rich, struggling, male or female, athletic, or sloths. From junkies to brokers—some were both, poor creatures—every demographic served up a few. They usually did not know they were being recruited for an important task. Nor did they realize they had no choice in the matter.

They also had a similar and tragic flaw about them. Before Crotty approached them with an offer, they exhibited such a thorough disinterest in their surroundings, they rarely noticed him watching them purposefully. And if they were aware, they continued on as if they were wandering the aisles of a supermarket on a Sunday evening, oblivious.

Case in point that day: Regani, a banker, who parked his Lexus in a handicapped spot when he clearly was not handicapped. How very special Regani must have believed he was. Crotty disliked him for another reason; they had a business relationship.

Crotty had followed Regani's Lexus from the highway, right to this station. Out of range of the surveillance cameras on the building near the bathroom, Crotty lingered in his sedan, patient.

Bounding from the car, Regani moved so fast the toes of his polished shoes thudded against the door. Regani grunted. Crotty saw it for what it was: another Suit in a hurry. How precious. How typical.

A hasp fastened the bathroom door to the frame after seven each evening, when the station closed. At that moment, the hasp wanted for a padlock.

Crotty steadied himself and slithered behind Regani into the restroom.

11:59:37 AM

As she promised, Jessica delivered the news about Shad's report before lunch. "The password worked exactly like you thought, and everything is in here," she said. "Names for almost all the numbers. And there are a bunch of calls to your phone last night and this morning from a number I don't recognize."

"Fantastic. Whose number is it?" Mike asked.

"Let me read you the note from Shad about that: Mike, the reverse lookups don't show a name for the number 555-9937 because there is no name associated with the account. The calls were made on a prepaid disposable cell phone. Phones like these are untraceable if the buyer initially pays in cash and never purchases more minutes."

"That's not good," Mike said. He made no effort to conceal his frustration.

"Hang on," Jessica said. "Shad also says: However, I contacted the manufacturer and found out what store the phone was sold from. The same credit card was used to purchase this phone and a dozen others roughly a week ago in a store in Michigan. They gave me the phone numbers for the other phones, which are also in this file. The name on the corporate Amex is Better Days, LLC."

"Not what I hoped," Mike said, "but it's a start."

"You're not kidding," Jessica said. "A quick search on the Internet shows at least five business with that name in the US. That's going to take some time to run down."

"Can you figure out the right one and get a name?" Mike asked.

"Don't worry," Jessica said. "I can get us there."

12:02:21 PM

Commercial-grade cleaners saturated the room with the scent of disinfectant. A dispenser released the solution on a timer. The floor tiles leading to the urinal were sticky, and Crotty's shoes made a crinkling sound as he stepped across them.

Regani, the banker, occupied the solitary toilet. The stall was handicapped-accessible. Wider than normal, the door opened outward. Above a pair of black socks and below the stall, a sliver of pasty white calves showed—Regani's.

While relieving himself at the urinal, Crotty lingered in silence. Then he spoke. "How's my favorite banker?"

"Why must we meet in places like this?" Regani asked, finally.

"Because you're under surveillance. In fact, that's what I want to talk to you about. The heat is coming down real soon. Be ready."

"Jesus. How far down?" Regani asked.

"All the way," Crotty said. "Serious enough that I can't protect you any longer."

"What? Why now?"

"You ask why now? You are not exactly Mother Theresa, Regani. Your bank is a front for a host of money-laundering operations. The state attorney general investigated you three times, and the Feds are two days from a sealed indictment. This is not news. The newsflash is that the check is due now." Here Crotty banged the stall a few times with a closed fist. "By the way, is this distracting?"

"You were supposed to be on top of this. Heading off the investigations early," Regani said, shifting uncomfortably. "What happened?"

Crotty spoke. "I have. And I am on your side. But you have a lot of my money, and you're about to be indicted. Once that happens, every asset you ever thought of will be frozen. Unfortunately, even if you wanted to, you can no longer return what's mine. Transactions with your name attached mean scrutiny. I can't afford attention like that. So you and I are going to work out a barter."

"Why should I even deal with you anymore?" Regani asked. "You betrayed me! You weren't looking out for my interests like you promised."

"We've already covered that. You would've been in jail four years ago if not for me. Now consider the bigger picture. The future. What are you going to do when this indictment hits? What about your pretty wife and her plastic surgery habit? You like being comfortable? Well prison is not so comfortable. Maybe for some felons there's a nice federal trip with golf courses, but you're from the wrong zip code, Regani. You consorted with people whose last names end in vowels. Your daddy went to a state school, not Yale. Racketeering, money laundering, that's serious business. I know you're hearing me, so listen close. Your only get-out-of-jail-free card is going to be to turn state's evidence. And you're going to pray no one caps you before the Feds sell the attorney general on the witness protection program."

"What do you want me to do?" Regani asked.

"The right thing, of course. Cooperate. And when the Feds raid your place, you'll have one extra box of records in the house." Crotty smiled as he thought of his special box of records behind his bookshelf, the cooked books from the business. As far as Crotty knew, the Partner had no idea about the second set. Crotty needed it that way, too. "Keep it in your garage, to the left of your wife's Jaguar. Throw a sheet over it so it doesn't look obvious. Then act pissed off when it's discovered."

"And what does your business partner think about these revelations?"

"There won't be a partner much longer," Crotty said. "Everything in those records points at them. Before the Partner figures out what happened, they'll be in a cell just like you."

"I have to say, Crotty, you are the coldest excuse for a human being I've ever met."

"I do what needs to be done." He removed a chain of rosary beads from his pocket. Crotty rubbed the two largest beads together. The smaller plastic spheres clicked as they slipped around in his hand.

"What if I say no?" said Regani.

"That's your right," Crotty said. "This is America, after all. Every choice has a price. Keep in mind that an attractive woman like your wife commands a healthy sum on the open market. Four hundred a fuck works for me. Maybe more if she gets that second face-lift she saw her surgeon about last week. See, that way, no matter what happens to you, the debts are paid. Of course, it might take years. Hope she earns out soon. I just might have to enlist your daughters, too, when they're old enough."

Surprise resonated in Regani's voice. Obviously beaten, he asked, "How do I get these records?"

"An associate has already placed the box inside your trunk. In your haste, you left the car unlocked. Forget about pulling over and tossing those files. You're being followed. Drive straight home, and leave the garage open as you unload it."

Regani grumbled about his shabby treatment, but the deal was done.

That was how Crotty did business. On his terms, in his way. Poor Regani never got a pawn on the board.

Everything he had done, including killing David St. John, brought Crotty closer to his dream. He was taking the company to the next level. He was closer to getting away with his girlfriend. Leaving Regani to squirm in the stall, and the Partner poised for jail, the question now was whether Mike Brody was ready.

And Crotty rather hoped Mike was. Crotty had arranged a special offer for him.

12:03:31 PM

Jessica typed briskly in the room so she would not miss lunch. She suspected Andy wanted food much more than he wanted to watch her work. Sensitive to his pleas, she bribed him with a brand-new video game, kept hidden until just such occasions.

As Mike had asked, she forwarded a copy of Shad's call-activity report to his business e-mail account. Calls about Better Days, LLC she tabled until after the meal, before the afternoon ride. She owed Lisbeth a picture analysis first; it would only take a minute.

She saved the photos of the dead man to her hard drive, composing a new message to her contact at NASA, rather than forwarding the existing one. No sense in unintentionally introducing two strangers.

Jessica only mentioned that the work could prove crucial to a developing investigation. She digitally signed the e-mail so the receiver would know it was really her, and sent off the images.

To court and encourage sources, she flattered them in print. People liked looking good. She had no qualms about doing this. However, some sources could not reveal themselves publicly. So where they preferred to remain anonymous, she honored their wishes. But Jessica never concealed sources through ambiguous titles like a "senior administration official" or "an investigator close to the case." Facts and sources went on record or they were reported as rumors and allegations, if at all. She would not be a pawn in some backroom game. Too often inside tips came from people with hidden agendas.

So for those sources that refused to be named, she treated the information as an attorney considered privileged discussions. Details gathered in confidence remained private, and never appeared in print.

A knock at the door. She shut the laptop lid, which suspended all functions and locked the machine. Reviving the computer from its hibernation state took a password.

Chappy waited outside with a handcart, a sealed envelope, and a yellow rose. Two cases of water balanced on the base of the handcart. "Erich said to bring this to you ASAP."

"Thanks. And don't worry," Jessica said, "I won't miss lunch."

Chappy stacked the water cases next to her bureau. "I have to get back to the kitchen. I'll keep a plate warm for you two."

The small card inside the envelope read:

Jessica,
May you never thirst at the Pine Woods Ranch.
Erich

Red roses suggested passion, white ones, purity. Now a yellow rose, that was clever. That said just what she could handle: friendship. Nothing untoward about that sentiment. And the gift of water made her laugh. Erich broke through her defenses without being pushy. For Jessica, such subtlety was a lost art.

At the front desk she requested a slender vase. They did not have one, so she used a water bottle. A quick clip with her pocketknife made the stem the proper length. She added an inch of water and placed the rose at the corner of the makeshift desk.

"Why did he send you flowers anyway?" Andy asked.

"He just wanted to be nice," Jessica said.

"Dad is nice." Andy sounded defensive, almost hostile.

"Ready for lunch?"

Since she planned on tackling the Better Days, LLC situation before the afternoon ride, she decided to leave the laptop in the room instead of walking it back to the main building and storing it in the safe. After all, the machine was useless without her password and she would only be gone thirty minutes.

Jessica locked the door.

She checked it twice.

01:13:26 PM

A man could learn much about survival and self-reliance from a few days in the desert. That's what Mike thought about as he and Dagget trudged to the crest, watching for the sign. Given a choice between warm and cold-weather searches, Mike preferred winter. Tracking was simpler over a layer of fine, fresh snow. White powder made spotting marks easier, and a shallow dusting supported cutting the tracks over great distances. Also, during winter the lines dividing a day became less pronounced. With the right combination of moonlight and snow, searchers might continue from dusk through dawn, uninterrupted by the cycling of the sun. Mike relished rundowns like that.

There were technical advantages to the cold, too. Thermal-imaging equipment, like FLIR, functioned best in searches where gaps between body heat and the temperature of whatever surrounded that body existed. The more pronounced the gap, the more striking the image appeared on the screen, and the easier identifying an out-of-place heat source became.

And he believed in one more advantage of the winter without a doubt: low temperatures boosted his visual acuity. Though he could not prove it, Mike was certain that in the cold, he saw farther, clearer.

Yes, the summer had definite benefits to others: vacations, beaches, and glistening hard bodies in the sun—all pleasures unknown to Mike. The lion's share of his sports-outfitting business landed squarely in the summer. Thanks to a stable North American and Western European customer base, the priciest and most sought-after packages launched in July. While others vacationed, he worked.

A sudden shift in the wind unsettled him.

The choppy breeze hinted of a possible storm. A thin ring around the moon toward the later half of the last evening was another warning. That might have meant nothing at all, but the old superstition about a ringed moon forecasting bad weather was often true. What the phenomena proved to Mike was the existence of ice in the atmosphere. A patch of ice crystals at great elevations refracted the light in a similar way, and produced the illusion of a thin circle around the moon. He was moved neither by the legend nor by the armchair interpretation. Regardless, the shift in the wind held his attention. He decided to keep an eye out for cirrus clouds. The thin and wispy streaks often signaled an approaching storm front.

And maybe the wind was just a freak low-pressure zone, a curious quirk of the topography. Maybe.

He certainly wanted to believe that.

They reached the crest, which overlooked a vista lined with pine trees.

And along the horizon, a much more important object held the tracker's eye. Seeing it, he recognized it at once.

He saw what Sean had been running toward from the beginning.

01:14:50 PM

First Mike and Dagget had crossed the ridge in the same stretch where Mike believed Sean had. Now he stood where Sean had stood. Seeing the expansive view from the crest revealed what Mike had hoped for: a critical break in the search.

Up to that point, the tracks along the ridge had reinforced Mike's notion that Sean had aimed for a very specific destination, right from the clearing near the ranch. Like any person on the run, as the distance he traveled increased, so did his wavering. Dalliances that Mike expected.

And yet each time he strayed, Sean had recentered himself and returned to the path. He chased a beacon; he pressed ahead with discipline and he persevered. That spoke about the strength of his character. The fire in Sean filled Mike with hope, and frustration.

From the beginning Mike had been trying to identify the visual lure that was guiding Sean, and failed miserably; it had eluded him. Still, he grappled with the question, as trackers must. And here, quite by accident, came the answer.

The wind died and then stopped.

Far ahead in the distance, beyond the pines, past several other shallow ridges, two mountain caps thrust above the horizon. A sense of déjà vu floored him, the sensation so powerful, so overwhelming, the weight of the realization made his body shudder. The exact mountains visible from the front porch and from room twenty-three at the Pine Woods Ranch.

The twin mountain caps.

He cursed himself, for he had noted that very mountain range earlier—for days, in fact—from different angles. Yet he had ignored their significance. Each occasion before, he had looked without seeing.

Lisbeth needed the information immediately.

Dialing her, Mike noticed his own rushed breathing. The call seemed as if it might not connect.

"Whatever eyes you've got in the air," Mike said to Lisbeth, "please make sure they scan the south side of the twin mountain caps. The massive ones visible from the ranch." Mike added some very rough headings for her, raw estimates of possible bearings.

"Briars Pitons," Lisbeth said. "You can't have made it that far yet."

"No, we haven't," Mike said. "But that's where he's going."

"Where are you, though?" Her voice rose sharply at the end of the question. An out-of-control inflection, so rare for Lisbeth.

"What makes you ask that?" Mike said.

"Because of all the searchers we deployed on horses," Lisbeth said, "no one who used your coordinates recovered any evidence of you two or Sean. Not a scrap. I have to think that most of them are competent and can use the gear. I don't want to believe the screw-up is yours, but I can't believe so many people made the same mistake."

He could speculate, but was not ready to. "I can't explain why the coordinates didn't work out," Mike said. If subsequent teams never found proof of Sean, or the many reflective markers Mike had pressed diligently into the soil indicating their location, he had an even bigger problem than the Partner's phone threats. Besides the brief lapse when the Partner toyed with him earlier and blotted the GPS signals, and the one instance he skewed the coordinates slightly, he trusted the numbers provided to Lisbeth. There was nothing wrong with the GPS. No, there was a more ominous explanation.

Someone removed the markers before the searchers could recover them.

"Hey." Dagget interrupted the phone conversation. "Ask her what happened to our pallet."

Mike nodded and returned to the original conversation with Lisbeth. "I should have listened to Shad and taken his offer of a new GPS. Mine must be broken."

"I hope that is all that's wrong," said Lisbeth. "But you can understand why I'm a little concerned. Every resource is important, and I can't afford to squander what I have on wild-goose chases. I bet big on your findings. Everything looked great on the surface, but now I don't know. Maybe it's like you say: your GPS is busted. In which case, I don't know what we should do. Can we collaborate like that? You won't know where you are really . . . which means I don't know where you are either with any certainty. No one does. That's a massive risk to sanction in terrain like this. Especially given Sean's condition."

"I'll reset the device," Mike said. "Maybe a full reinitialize will do the trick."

"Look, Mike, I'm just concerned." She paused long enough to drag on a cigarette, though Mike was almost positive Lisbeth wasn't smoking then. He had a feeling, anyway.

"Understood." He could see her point. "I wanted to ask you about the gear drop earlier. We had some trouble recovering the pallet."

"If your GPS is busted, that makes sense."

"Well, I just wanted to check it was dropped as planned. And second, if it was, I was wondering how much drift the pilot accounted for? Because it was windy earlier and if they pitched it from a high ceiling, you'd be surprised how far something wanders before touching down."

"I assure you, the gear was deployed on schedule. I can ask the pilot about how much drift she accounted for." Lisbeth sighed at the present state of affairs. "Let's just hope things get better."

Lisbeth hung up.

In the corner of his eye, a swatch of a maple stirred, nearly five hundred yards out. Mike zeroed in on it. *Odd. That doesn't look right.*

Wind patterns could change without notice, at the whim of pressure systems. He doubted this was an isolated dip or swell in the barometer.

The rustling stopped. Lingering atop the ridge for a moment, he hesitated. While he doubted Dagget occasionally, now suddenly Mike doubted himself.

However well his senses functioned normally, under duress, they might deceive him. Compromised senses could make a tiny animal sound larger. Or they might suggest that an object appeared out of place, even though all was in order. Proving there was anything out there was very difficult, because at that angle, at that range, the outermost layer of canopy blocked a direct view. Mike peered through his binoculars for a long time. He held the high-powered specs fixed to his face, and the viewing area pressed a circular groove in the skin around his eyes.

"What's wrong?" Dagget prompted the tracker, finally breaching the stillness.

Mike tightened the focus, sharpening the image.

In the sights, a figure clad in camouflage and a face mask stared back at him through binoculars.

01:19:55 PM

Rumors about Sean's disappearance spread among the guests like a fire built from over-seasoned wood. A lack of details stunted the spread of flames at first; the hounds of gossip worked hard to light the initial log, hoping for a spark. Once the first flame caught, rumors consumed the next log rapidly, and the next faster still. By lunch each guest knew, or claimed to know, about the case. As word spread among the guests, the tone turned speculative.

Jessica pieced the real chronology together by talking with Erich, Lisbeth, and Cara.

Like a good urban legend, nearly all the chatter traced back to a single person. A woman had noticed a double-parked sedan in the parking lot the night before, and a man hollering at a woman as he threw a notepad into the backseat of a rental car. They drove off in a rush. Not recognizing the couple from any ranch activities, this guest asked the girl at the front desk the following morning, who gave a vague response.

Others guests would have dropped the questions then, but the nosy guest happened to be Cara Isham. As she told Jessica later, she did not let anyone give her the runaround when she wanted a straight answer.

So over breakfast the following morning, while Jessica rode back from the hospital, Cara asked another ranch staffer about the vanishing couple. He explained there was a situation, the police were involved, and the ranch trusted the authorities to resolve the problem. Instead of ending there, the vague comments piqued her interest further.

Later that day, the same car returned to the ranch. Again it double-parked in the lot. A woman waited in the passenger seat, her face red, sobbing. Cara went over and asked what was wrong. The three words the woman in the car uttered had Cara's full attention. *My son disappeared*. And that was all the woman managed before she broke down in a heave of shudders.

Later, Cara cornered Erich and asked about the couple. Unlike his staffers, she found him surprisingly forthcoming. Sean's father,

Gerald, tired of the lack of progress and of being denied the chance to look for his son, took matters into his own hands. Without disclosing his plans to Faith, he sneaked into the woods and began searching for Sean. He started at the clearing where it all began. Fourteen hours later, he made a panicked call to Lisbeth. Gerald Jackson had slipped down an embankment and broken his wrist. He had not packed enough water or food, and had no idea where he was. Lisbeth squandered four hours worth of time and resources trying to extract him. More seriously, Gerald had also tainted the murder scene, to the point that no additional evidence uncovered there would be admissible. In response to these mishaps, Lisbeth had ordered the Jacksons off the Pine Woods Dude Ranch and out of her way.

Erich had arranged lodging for the Jacksons at Chariot's, a local hotel, opened a tab for them at the Little Gem Diner, and leased a Lincoln Town Car so they could go where they wanted, whenever they wanted.

The Jacksons remained near the action, a five to seven minute drive from the ranch, but no longer had access to the operations center. What they heard about the case now came only through Lisbeth. An officer stationed at the front gates would notify her if the Jacksons appeared unannounced.

Now, what missing kernels guests lacked but craved, they guessed, and twisted the news like a publicist with an incoming press release. And when those theories failed to satisfy their need for sordid content, they invented details, and added information that would make the story fit the mold they wanted to believe.

Snippets of conversations like these swirled near Jessica and Andy in the dining hall:

". . . the FBI may look into it . . ."

". . . they refused volunteers . . ."

". . . they want volunteers . . ."

". . . are you going to offer to help . . . ?"

". . . foul play might be involved . . ."

". . . as long as there is no sign of foul play, I'll volunteer . . ."

". . .what a shame for the parents . . ."

". . .such nice people . . ."

No one commented on Jessica's reappearance, or questioned her absence. The missing boy held center stage. Several guests noted her return; however, they said nothing more invasive than *hope you're feeling better*. Their odd stares emoted far more than they expressed verbally.

Though she knew the truth, Jessica allowed the wild tales about the missing boy to circulate undisputed. She had kept secrets before. If she quashed the stories, challenged the outrageous rumors, it would only redirect attention to her.

People would ask Jessica questions; people would suspect she had an agenda. Generally, she loved asking questions; she disliked answering them.

As Jessica savored tiny bites of bison and rice pilaf, Cara appeared.

"I can't believe my daughter left the sink running," Cara said. "Good thing she told me in time so I could stop the bathroom from flooding. Hey, maybe we could go shopping after the afternoon ride? There are some kitsch stores on the main drag. I feel like spending money. You want a pair of authentic cowboy boots?"

"Not sure about the boots, but I could be in the mood for some shopping," Jessica said enthusiastically.

"That's what I'm talking about!"

Walking back to the lodge after lunch with Andy, Jessica ran into Erich outside the building.

"Thanks very much for the rose," Jessica said. "And the water. That was very nice."

"Not too much, I hope?" Erich said.

"It was perfect." Feeling herself gush, she cleared her throat, and reminded herself of the question she had for Erich. "Funny I ran into you. I was talking to someone and your name came up. Detective Lisbeth McCarthy mentioned she contacted you about using your plane for the search, and hadn't heard back yet."

"Detective Lisbeth McCarthy?" Erich asked. He sounded surprised. "Oh yes, I remember now. One of my mechanics found a part that needed to be replaced. The problem is there's a tight supply of that part, so we're grounded until it arrives. Once the part is installed, I do a test run, then the plane is hers."

To Jessica, his story seemed reasonable. "I imagine your days are very busy."

"That's true, but I have no excuse for not calling her back. Don't worry, I'll let her know what I told you." Erich paused. "So are you helping with her investigations?"

"Just talking. Mike is still out there, so we chat a bit about it. You probably know more than I do about the search, being from around here."

Erich mentioned he had business commitments and excused himself.

Reaching her room, Jessica turned the key halfway around and then suddenly stopped.

The door was already unlocked.

01:31:47 PM

The question Dagget posed to Mike was what to do about their stalkers.

Mike wasn't worried about why they were being trailed. His real concern was how to get as far from them as soon as possible. And as far as Mike could see, they had one good option.

The ridge base and the edge of maple trees created a natural, and narrow, enclosure alongside the rocks. The enclosure minimized Sean's wanderings, and led him generally north. For a boy being chased, the wall also doubled as a shield. If anyone stormed over the ridge, a thicket of trees at his left provided an escape route. His strategy could work for them as well.

Wiping the sweat off his brow, Mike finally answered. "We keep moving. If by some stroke of luck they are legitimate searchers, we have no worries. If they're hunters, we make sure we don't move like deer. If they're working for the Partner, then we should be all right as long as we press ahead."

"But what if they are out gunning for us?" Dagget asked.

"That doesn't change the fact that we have to keep moving."

"I don't like it," Dagget said.

"Before you start belting out the swan songs," Mike said, "listen for a second. I said we had to keep moving; I didn't say which direction or how. We'll take a route through the woods that will give us additional cover. Every so often, we touch base with his tracks to make sure we're on course. And the cell phones stay off for the next ninety minutes. That should put a little space between us and whoever is in the trees."

"What if the Partner balks about not being able to make contact?" Dagget asked.

"We say we're out of the coverage area," Mike said. He powered down his phone. "It's conceivable that we crossed a dead zone. I don't see any cell towers. Do you?"

Dagget agreed, though the commitment sounded halfhearted.

"Exactly. Out of area. That's our story."

"It makes sense," Dagget said. "But I just know the Partner is going to be pissed about this."

01:32:46 PM

Jessica removed the key, her face ashen, and hoped no one was waiting for her inside.

A few doors down, a maid listened to an iPod while tidying up another room, the volume cranked up. A cart full of cleaning supplies and freshly laundered towels blocked the hallway.

"Did you just clean my room?" Jessica asked the maid. With her back to Jessica, the maid was oblivious, lost in her music. Repeating the question, Jessica raised her voice, and still got no answer. She touched the maid's shoulder gently.

Removing one earbud, the other still wedged against her tympanic membrane, the maid spun around. Vintage Pink Floyd pierced the air. The maid smiled. "Hello." Her hello sounded like *ha-low*. Jessica tagged the maid as Swiss, closer to Geneva than Zürich—a much heavier French influence than German. "You need clean towels?"

"I can wait on the towels, thanks. Right now I just need an answer. Did you just clean my room?" It sounded harsh. Jessica didn't particularly care what she sounded like at that moment.

"Well I start at room twenty-four," the maid said, "and work to room one. Twenty-three is next. But if you need clean towels or linens right now, help yourself to some off the cart." She fidgeted with the earbud, spinning the plastic between her fingers.

"Did you see anyone come in or out of my room?" Jessica said.

"The only thing I see is a huge mess in twenty-four. Hello."

Jessica relented. She pushed open her door. The thick slab of oak swung into the room, and bounced against a rubber stop. At least she didn't need to worry about Andy right then. All children at the ranch were participating in a ninety-minute craft workshop on building fly-fishing lures. Jessica had time to sort this out.

Inside room twenty-three, her possessions appeared in order. She checked her camera and jewelry. Valuables present and accounted for. Everything looked the same, save one item: the laptop. The lid was halfway open, instead of clicked shut. By habit, Jessica always shut the case to send the machine into hibernation, locking the session, and preserving the battery charge.

With the screen display locked, she brought up the login prompt, typed her credentials, and searched for recently modified or accessed files on the hard drive. The file most recently changed bore a time stamp from twenty-seven minutes ago. In theory that was her doing.

The new mail indicator rose above the task bar. A message from her contact at NASA read:

> *Jessica,*
>
> *Perfect timing. Yesterday we rolled out a new software package for image correction that's more robust than the last version, and you caught me working through lunch again. If you need it clearer, it will take another hour. Who was this poor soul anyway?*
>
> *Regards, KF*

Attached to the message were the corrected pictures. The image processing had made a tremendous difference. What had been grainy and coarse now looked sharp and crisp. Jessica enlarged until the picture filled the entire screen. Who was this, indeed. She had not a clue.

Cara rushed inside the room, ebullient. "Good idea! This is a good time for a break."

"You about ready for the next ride?" Cara hovered near Jessica. Peering at the screen, Cara gasped. "Oh, my God!" Her eyes were locked on the picture of the dead man stretched across the screen. Reaching for the bureau, Cara steadied herself.

"Sorry," Jessica said. "That wasn't meant for you to see. It is a little disturbing. I'll shut this down."

Cara shuddered and squinted at the screen. "No, wait. I want to be sure." After studying the pixilated image for a moment, she said, "I can't believe it. That is definitely him."

01:36:02 PM

Surprised, Jessica asked, "You know him?" Inwardly, Jessica leaped at the possibility that Cara knew the victim in the photograph, but she buried her excitement beneath the surface. A friend in need came before the story.

"My God. David St. John," Cara said. She shuddered. "I can't believe he's dead."

"Were you two close?" Jessica said.

"I've known him for years. We fell out of touch very recently. He was a science aficionado," Cara said, "always hanging out in the lab doing research after hours back in school. Very, very bright. Kinda geeky, but endearing all the same.

"He was the sort of person you can have lunch with every five years and not feel like a day passed. As much as he fit in the science lab, he didn't fit in so well in social situations. Still, I can't imagine why anyone would murder him."

Jessica said, "I'm very sorry that you found out this way. Obviously, I had no idea."

"How could you know? I really hope they catch the killer." Here Cara looked away from the screen and right at Jessica. "You don't see someone for a little while, and look what happens." She paused.

"Where did you get this picture? How did you get this picture?"

If there was a good explanation that kept the truth under the covers, Jessica missed it. Instead she fumbled, trying to mask a sheepish tone. "I know it looks odd."

"Does it!" Cara said, astonished. "If I was a more suspicious person . . . I might think crazy thoughts."

"I understand and I'm very sorry about your friend. And I don't want things to be weird between us, so I will tell you that I'm helping the police with a case. But please, you can't let anyone know you saw this picture. People's safety could be in serious jeopardy."

Cara crossed herself and nodded in a way that said she understood Jessica's instructions. "One thing I wonder about you, Jessica. You get huffy about Mike when he picks adventure over time with his family, but you have no trouble working your way right inside the action?"

03:40:11 PM

For the remainder of the afternoon, moderate weather aided the search effort. The sun burnt off a trail of wispy clouds, leaving behind a swath of clear, blue sky. The wind, which had blown like a fury that morning, had slowed to a gentle breeze.

While he and Dagget eluded those who followed them, working through the canopy in silence, growing the distance between the stalkers and themselves, Mike was thankful for their one advantage. He knew as long as they stayed out of sight and kept the cell phones off, their exact location would remain unknown.

Despite the temporary reprieve, Mike remained both leery and aware of darker possibilities. Traces of foul weather beckoned in the distance; when his energy levels flagged, he pressed Dagget harder.

Mike noticed that the officer struggled to keep pace, gasping at points. But until they exhausted the ninety-minute limit there was no respite, no peace, no other choice. If Dagget balked, he did so on the inside.

As they hiked, signs of the approaching storm grew. A rise in humidity, backing winds that changed direction several times—it implied a maelstrom ahead. But again and again, the possibility of bad weather nudged them forward. They must make it as far as they could. The image of the masked face burned fresh in Mike's mind.

Finally Dagget heaved and stopped. "We've gone more than ninety minutes, man," Dagget said, wheezing. "I call time out."

Mike relented. Certainly they had come farther than he expected. And he wanted a closer look at the tracks; that last turn Sean took had Mike thinking.

As Dagget walked away, Mike said, "If you're making any calls, be brief and shut it off as soon as you finish. The longer we stay off the grid, the less chances they have to tag our location."

03:41:57 PM

Crotty didn't wait for an opening. He had no time for social graces. "So tell me, what does Ms. Jessica Barrett's laptop say she knows?"

"Just talked with my eyes on the scene," the Partner said. "Your program worked perfectly. I heard it took longer to restart her machine than to bypass the password and scan the contents. And it changed the time stamp on the accessed files. Jessica will never know anyone snooped."

"Didn't I tell you?" Crotty said. "But again I find myself asking, why am I asking you about details that I should already have?"

"Because they won't ever be in your hands, unless my contact gets a second chance at the room. There was just enough time to realize it was gold, but not enough time to dig it up and copy the files. The maid almost walked in."

"Lovely." Crotty was seething. "Wait a second, where are you calling from?"

"Goddamnit. You know exactly where I am."

And Crotty did know. He asked anyway, because pressing people to answer questions he already knew the response to was a habit he enjoyed. If he knew the answer in advance, he also knew if someone was lying. He learned it by watching lawyers. "So what do we allegedly know?"

"At the very least," the Partner said, "Jessica has all of Mike's recent cell phone records, a crystal clear picture of our old friend, and a charge record linking a company to a certain disposable phone. There could be more."

"He was never my friend," Crotty said. "And he wasn't yours, either. As for the phone being traced back to its owner, let them. I planned for that possibility. The phone only dials out, so there's no way they can touch you." Crotty was proud of that particular rewiring and programming job. It could send whatever it liked, but it could never receive. "Right after this call ends, take out the battery. Then wipe the phone down for prints, and ditch it in a moving stream so it drifts far away."

"And Jessica Barrett?"

"Sounds like if she has enough time, she'll figure out the rest. Or enough to be dangerous. We need to slow her down." More forcefully, he added, "Maybe we can stop her and teach Mike a lesson at the same time. His cell phone has been dark for well over an hour and a half."

"How are you going to stop her?"

"There's one person Jessica Barrett will drop everything for." Crotty detailed his sly plot with great vigor.

"Now just a minute," the Partner said. "That's unnecessary and I don't want any part of it."

"I expected you to have a problem with this," Crotty said matter-of-factly, "so I made sure it was taken care of. It's already in motion."

"I can't let that happen, Crotty. It's too risky. Too many variables."

"Risky is thinking for yourself. Besides, there's nothing you can do about it."

03:42:22 PM

Just beyond the riding stable, Jessica helped Andy slide his foot into the stirrup. Then with a tiny push, Andy propelled his body over Mr. Jones. His bottom thudded against leather as he fell onto the saddle. Proud that he had mounted the horse unassisted, he smiled at his mother. Jessica smiled, too. The boy recalled her earlier instructions. To be safe, Jessica reminded Andy anyway. "Never drop the reins."

She caressed Mr. Jones' neck. Satisfied Andy was ready, she climbed on Tic-Tac.

There was much to love about riding horses: fresh air, speed, the escape. But of all the benefits, she most relished the chance to view things from a new perspective. To her, riding had no equal. She was at home on a saddle.

Jessica and Andy nearly led the entire pack, goading the staff leader from her spot a length behind. The pace varied; Mr. Jones broke stride at points and Jessica talked Andy through several bumpy spots. Despite Andy's improvement the past few days, she maintained reservations about the continued pairing of Andy and Mr. Jones. She sensed the horse wanted a more experienced rider on his back. But she trusted her skills, and believed in her son's willingness to listen and follow directions. Andy's patience helped assuage her concerns; while Mr. Jones might not be the ideal choice, he was not entirely the wrong one either.

Early afternoon. At a vista edge, the group paused. The scenery stretched beneath them, overwhelming and awing the crowd. The wraparound landscape was picturesque. Right before the lead rider, a hawk circled, dove, and spiraled down the valley. Sensing a photo opportunity, Jessica ripped a few shots off with her digital camera and panoramic lens. Other guests did the same.

From the vista, they traveled single file on a trail wide enough for two horses. A half-mile from the head, the path ended at a sprawling lake. Pine needles layered on the lake bottom made the water appear reddish brown. Riders dismounted and stretched their legs. Gathering at the bank, a pack of horses drank heartily.

Jessica snapped a few more pictures, this time of the horses lapping water, though the shots also captured a few people nearby. Cameras often inspired one of two feelings from people: excessive interest or aversion. They had to be photographed; they hated being photographed. Neither extreme produced a very interesting shot, and forced photographers on a tightrope between the two extremes.

How a photographer dealt with someone that did not want his

picture taken varied, but Jessica had a simple answer. She was there to document, not sell. She wanted the right subject more than the best-looking one, and the right person revealed himself through his actions.

Perhaps the first one that caught her eye was perfect; but many times it was not. Appealing qualities often lurked beneath the surface of a shyer person. Someone typically overlooked by most, who hung back, who disappeared in crowds. More reserved, he rarely considered himself photogenic. To encourage the reluctant, she introduced the camera early, listened, and waited.

Knowing that people who anticipated a picture posed, looking forced and uncomfortable, Jessica never counted or announced when photographing people. Her approach encouraged people to reveal themselves. Jessica needed only be there at the right time and capture the results. If she waited until she became aware of the shot in the viewfinder, it was too late. The moment was gone forever.

Not wanting to lose herself behind the lens, Jessica ruffled Andy's hair. A horrified look spread across his face. He patted his unkempt locks down and checked for witnesses to his indignity. The braver of the two twins laughed at Andy. Andy grinned first, and then glared at them. Both girls ran.

In the spirit of childlike play, Andy chased off after the girls. All three children tore away from their respective parents, and dashed for the trail head. Squeaky childish voices echoed back to group.

Jessica watched them go.

Moments later, with an authoritative tone, the staff leader announced the end of the break. By then, Andy and the twins had veered out of sight. Jessica called out Andy's name clearly, her tone steady. Cara stood beside her, hollering for her own girls. Her twins appeared. "Hide-and-seek," the braver one explained. "Andy's it."

Jessica thanked the girls and yelled for her son, making it clear the game had ended. Andy didn't answer. Jessica called again, and this time her voice shook.

He didn't answer a third time.

Jessica corralled the twins. "Show me exactly where you saw him last." Reluctant, the girls looked at their mother for guidance. Cara nodded approvingly.

The braver one clasped Jessica's hand, and led her fifty paces up the trail. Cara lingered with her more timorous daughter back near the group.

The twin pointed to a maple that curved inwards to the trail. "He closed his eyes there and counted to ten. Is Andy in trouble?"

"Not at all," Jessica said.

"Cause he is not real good with numbers." The girl grinned, nervous.

Jessica almost said that she understood that about her son very well.

She heard Cara scream.

03:46:04 PM

Sean's route twisted back and forth like a vagabond wandering, and fed toward them without warning. Mike noticed the change. Fresh evidence of the boy's fatigue: patches of low-hanging branches Sean had mashed underfoot. Branches Sean might have stepped around or over easily. Noting the shift in Sean's behavior, Mike stopped cutting the tracks. The chance the boy might suddenly detour again seemed high. There was more going on here than an unanticipated turn. Some stressor impacted Sean's emotional state. Mike wanted a handle on that before advancing.

There was something different troubling Sean. Anxiety was Mike's first guess. A few feet later, Sean veered off and emptied his bowels. The fecal matter beside a tree appeared firm, maybe ten to twelve hours old.

Inexperienced campers on long excursions had to relearn a basic instinct their predecessors knew practically from birth. On average, people battled constipation in the wild for four to seven days before they stopped fighting nature and allowed themselves to do what humans did freely before outhouses and John Harington's indoor flush toilet. Now there were bestselling books on how to shit in the woods—as if the idea were revolutionary.

Stepping downwind from the recent discovery, Mike massaged his left hamstring. The dense muscles in his rear thigh were taut. Easing the tension required a series of prolonged, hanging stretches. Unusual cramping in the legs suggested two possibilities. Low calcium levels, or worse, dehydration. One had symptoms that could be checked out easily enough.

Wiping his finger on his jeans first, he dabbed his lips. Raw and dry. Beneath the slightest pressure of his fingertips, a thin crack threatened to break. The tiny strip of flesh would tear soon, and blood would trickle and dry upon his chin. It sounded much worse than it looked. Even at a range of two feet, only a trained eye might notice.

His ears buzzed. Normally, his hearing, like his sight, verged on perfect, though his ears rang at odd intervals. Inexplicably the problem had begun eight years ago. An otolaryngologist studied the condition, fully expecting tinnitus. Convinced of it, in fact. The presumptive diagnosis made by the ear, nose, and throat specialist proved inconclusive. Successive auditory tests and examinations did not explain the anomaly. Mike, however, believed there was a reason; it was a warning. Like a mother wolf that could sense her young were in danger, so could he. Now whenever his ears rang, he knew Andy was in serious trouble.

He powered on the cell phone. Before he could dial Jessica, the Partner called again.

"What did I tell you about keeping your phone on?"

"You never mentioned sending goons to shadow us," Mike said.

"We had a deal," the Partner said. "And you broke part of it, and now there are consequences. For Christ's sake, manage the ex! She's endangering everyone. Get her out of the picture."

"What if I can't?"

"Just do it! There are others in the organization less reasonable than me. I'm trying to do what I can to head them off. Remember what I said!"

And the Partner was gone. Mike dialed the Partner's number, which Shad had died for. He wanted answers. He wanted an explanation. He got something else: a recorded voice:

This call cannot be completed because the number is not in service.

03:47:19 PM

Cara Isham's scream did what many editors had believed impossible: badly rattle Jessica.

Accounts of Jessica's reserve were legendary among the press corps. Work tested her often, hardened her at the edges. Now a crisis, even one charged with emotion, seldom affected her in the moment. Her secret was a tough reporter face, and an even tougher disposition. She needed the protection.

That stoicism allowed her to walk among tragedy victims without absorbing their negative energy; it kept her from internalizing their pain. She respected the people affected by disasters. She sympathized. She saw what happened. But she did not become overwhelmed by their emotions. Instead, she observed, recorded, and produced. On time, every time.

But the scream from Cara, Jessica heard differently. It touched her personally. She wrestled for the right word, and suddenly, diction became irrelevant. No description she could muster then would do the scream justice. What followed the sound enveloped her, seized everything inside, and choked off the other thoughts. All that remained, all there was: a scream. A scream that jabbed her eardrums like an ice pick to a block of steel. Whatever Cara actually said did not matter. Her words—if the wail earned that title—defied recognition.

Hooves clattered against the soil.

A second scream answered the thunderous footfalls.

Jessica grabbed Cara's daughter, clasped her around the torso, and yanked the small girl clear of the trail. Together, they danced backwards and dipped between the trees. Jessica scraped her right elbow on bark. She drove both arms tight against her body. Her chest heaved. She shielded the girl from harm.

A horse thundered up the trail, in full gallop. Mr. Jones. Andy's horse. Before this, the horse had acted docile. Maybe a trace cantankerous, and definitely a bit under challenged, but normal. Absolutely normal. That was then, though. Now he had changed.

Now the animal appeared every inch a madman. His eyes, solid spheres of black, reflected only darkness. If animals communicated emotion through facial expressions, Mr. Jones spoke the language of a street fighter. Beneath the leather reins and bit, a snarl dripped off his mouth. His powerful legs flexed, pumping out massive strides. He was a runaway train carving his own tracks.

And the conductor inside Mr. Jones spurred him faster, faster still. Mr. Jones fired ahead, and thrashed his way over the exact spot Jessica and the girl had stood. As he advanced on their hideaway, Jessica understood what Cara actually meant with her yell: demon on the loose.

Aboard Mr. Jones, Andy gripped the cantle, both feet out of the stirrup irons. The reins dangled, out of his reach, useless. For each stride, the boy rose off the rippling body, until gravity slammed him back against the pommel. Bobbing up and down, at points he rode a cushion of air inches above the saddle.

His right leg slid, his ankle nearly snaring the beast's legs.

03:49:37 PM

With the young girl lagging, Jessica stormed the group, gunning for her own horse, yelling "Hang on, Andy. I'm coming!"

Those who witnessed the next part agreed on one fact. Somehow, Jessica vaulted over Tic-Tac, and lodged her feet in the stirrups. Yet, no one ever noticed her knees bend, or her legs swing over either side of the saddle. She was simply on the horse just as an instant before she was not.

Leaning forward, her head hung near Tic-Tac's. "Go!" She spared him the sting of boot heels against his sides, and in return, Tic-Tac responded, knowing exactly what to do. He launched them both off into the woods, a case study in earthbound flight.

Jessica sensed Tic-Tac could get her where she needed to be. A fortunate trait within the Arabian bloodline was speed. Tic-Tac was a fine example; he had loads of it. Genetics endowed him with so much power; in fact, she suspected very few riders—or perhaps none, even—had realized his full potential. Fewer still probably considered him manageable. In Jessica's mind, this assessment was one-hundred percent correct: he was not for every guest. So the typical rider probably passed up Tic-Tac for a kinder, gentler horse. Maybe now and again, someone with actual chops climbed aboard Tic-Tac, yearning for a more responsive and capable horse. Maybe an experienced rider like her. But even among those infrequent pairings, she bet they still had overlooked the raw power smoldering within Tic-Tac. They had underestimated him, because it was quite easy to do so. After all, he looked quite ordinary on the outside. But she had seen past the surface and made the connection. Her Tic-Tac was special.

And there was another reason for her fondness of the Arabian.

To Jessica, he had very much picked her. Kindred spirits in manner, she saw him for his excellence, his incredible strength. Now for Andy's sake, Jessica needed Tic-Tac's magic.

And Tic-Tac delivered.

They charged down the trail. Images at the edges of her vision merged together from the speed. The leaves, a wall of greenish hues. She scarcely noticed the blurring effect. Squinting, her eyes settled on Mr. Jones.

"Mom!" Andy wailed.

"Hang on!"

For endless moments the distance between the horses remained constant, unforgiving. As if both animals churned in place, chained on opposite sides of a great divide.

The gap narrowed slightly, though a sea of openness still kept her from Andy—the space between them enormous and overwhelming. An inch was too much. She focused on breathing as best she could while jouncing on horseback.

And she worried how much more steam Mr. Jones had left before exhaustion flattened him. Of what might happen to Andy if his horse collapsed. Well, she wasn't going there.

"Come on, Tic-Tac!" she pleaded. "Do it! Do it now!"

Tic-Tac did it. Rocketing ahead, the gap halved, then halved again. They gained more ground. Her head ached from the rush.

With a fresh surge, Tic-Tac drew within five lengths of Mr. Jones. The boy turned briefly toward her. Andy's features were clear, his terrified expression seized her heart. Their faces mirrored each other; the fear was evident on both.

She drew closer still. With a tap of the reins, another booster rocket engaged beneath her legs. Incredible. She sensed even more juice awaited her commands. Right there, Jessica struck a mental bargain about Tic-Tac. If Andy escaped unharmed, she would purchase the horse, whatever the cost. Tic-Tac could live out his days in a field of sugar plums and carrots, enjoying daily massages. Whatever her horse—the hero—wanted, would be done. She would promise him that.

Five seconds, three lengths, and twenty feet—these were the obstacles between her and Andy. The trail ended, emptying into a sprawling field of dried-out grass. Bordered on the left by woods, on the right by a stream, and straight ahead, by a cliff, the scene made her heart sink. And just as the scene became almost too much, at her right shoulder, a strong, sturdy voice said: "Right behind you!"

Jessica turned; Jessica blinked; Jessica squinted. Erich Reynard remained. Never had she been a woman who believed in miracles. She thought she might start believing.

"I'll try the reins. You take the right!" Erich yelled the directions over the thunder of hoof falls. Jessica nodded in agreement.

Side by side, they pulled even with Mr. Jones' hindquarters, each on opposite ends of his rump.

It seemed to Jessica that Tic-Tac found his cruising speed first, then Erich's horse. Three horses barreled as one, dashing toward the vacant sky like painters fixated on their work, oblivious to concerns beyond the canvas edge.

"Mom! Help me!" Andy screamed. Like a rehearsed dance, Jessica leaned leftwards, her arm extended. Her well-toned limb shook from the motion, exhausted by the stress. She steadied herself. Reaching as far as she could toward Andy, she yelled, "Give me your hand!"

Andy flailed, struggling for his mother. His body swayed with

Mr. Jones' movements. The nails of his left hand dug harder into the cantle. Thrusting his right arm out, he clutched at the waiting hand. He missed, two inches shy of deliverance. Andy grappled once more, harder, reaching farther, but Mr. Jones drifted, whisking him along.

"I . . . I can't . . ." Andy said, terrified and choking. Tears ran down his face.

Five hundred yards left to the void.

"You can!" Jessica implored. "Keep trying!"

"Steady boy . . ." said Erich in a commanding voice to Mr. Jones. Erich's own horse idled just beneath Mr. Jones' line of vision. An out-of-control animal was bad enough, one spooked by the sight of approaching horses could become completely unmanageable.

With a desperate lunge, Andy turned and pushed away from Mr. Jones. The boy reached for Jessica, hands thrashing. The soft parts of their hands brushed one another.

"Almost! Try once more!" Her voice rang out achingly. Jessica held back the tears swelling inside.

The next hundred yards melted faster than the last. For Jessica, the world went silent. Her heart rattled like a train through a concrete tunnel.

Three hundred yards left, and closing fast.

Instead of going for Andy's hand, she eased Tic-Tac back, and slackened the charge. She stood in the stirrups, tilted toward Mr. Jones, and hooked Andy around the waist. She yanked. He held firm to the horse, petrified, unable to unclench his fingers.

"Let go! I've got you!" Jessica commanded.

Andy could not, or would not, relax his grip. He cried.

"Let go!"

". . . my. . . hands . . . numb ... so scared." Leftover tears stained his face red and purple. Sobs slurred his words.

Two hundred yards.

"Andy! Let go! Right now!"

Jessica saw Andy's grip on the cantle did not relax. Not a bit.

Forcefully Erich seized Mr. Jones' reins. With a thumb and a finger, he wadded one end of the loop into his fist. Erich glanced across at Jessica. A nod acknowledged his readiness.

Primed to heel Mr. Jones, Erich hesitated. With Andy still in the saddle, and Tic-Tac in kicking range, braking without sufficient room meant a terrible risk.

When they breached the hundred-yard mark, Jessica decided the best way through his primary fear of falling from Mr. Jones was by playing to a deeper, darker fear. A deceitful avenue. A final opportunity.

In a moment of genius inspiration, she shouted. "Andy, there's a praying mantis on your arm!"

"Get it off!" he screamed, swatting wildly at himself, spastic. Faced with a more terrifying possibility, Andy's grip finally loosened. With a whoop of glee, Jessica scooped him clear of Mr. Jones, and nestled her son onto the English-style saddle.

Andy kept kicking at phantom insects for a while until he finally stopped fighting. He trembled. She held him close, squeezed him tightly against her bosom. Under her control, Tic-Tac slowed and veered for the stream.

Erich wrestled with Mr. Jones as long as possible, trying commands and then pleas that might assuage the unruly beast. But Mr. Jones did not yield. He did not stand down, or respond. He raged on.

With less than a dozen yards of solid earth left, Erich surrendered, and halted his own horse.

And Mr. Jones vanished beneath the horizon.

03:53:22 PM

Suddenly Mike stopped worrying about concealing his movements from observation or his calls from interception. He only cared about reaching Jessica on the phone and making sure Andy was all right. Though he moved away from the trail, it was pacing, and releasing nervous energy, rather than putting distance between himself and his last discovery.

"I was just going to call you," Jessica said.

"Tell me you and Andy are all right." Mike said, his heart

hammering. "I had a bad sense something was wrong."

"Unfortunately," Jessica said, "you're right. We're on our way to the hospital just to make sure these bruises and cuts aren't hiding something more serious, but I'm pretty sure we're both fine. Crazy accident. The horse Andy was riding went berserk, and dragged Andy along for quite a ride. It's a good thing Erich came when he did. He really helped. I've never seen a well-cared for animal behave like that. Given what happened, Andy is doing great."

"Thank God he's okay." Then he added grimly, "Maybe it wasn't an accident."

"What do you mean?"

"I believe it was the Partner. They were trying to send another message. Please listen for a second. I think it's best if you and Andy pack up and leave after you get checked out at the hospital. You know where to go." Back in the days before they were married, they camped at a cabin at the basin of a five-hundred-acre lake most every autumn. Long nights, and a perfect view of the stars. He loved the place.

"Did the Partner call you again? Did they say it was connected? Like before?"

"Yes, though they didn't give out too many specifics. It was a quick call. They just said they were trying to head it off."

"I don't know, Mike. I don't know what to think anymore. Maybe you were right. Something is happening here. It might be too risky for us to stay on," Jessica said. "To be fair though, Mr. Jones was a bit more animal than Andy was ready for. I should have gotten him another horse."

"I don't think it's your fault. You just said you've never seen an animal act like that."

"Right," Jessica said. "So what are you thinking?"

"Someone drugged Mr. Jones."

"How?"

"Whatever it was, the delivery mechanism was probably on a time-release, so it took awhile to affect him. If he was acting crazy at the beginning, you wouldn't have let Andy on him."

"Maybe you're right, Mike. I don't know." There was a pause and then she snapped her fingers. "I almost forgot that someone was in my room around lunch. It might have just been the cleaning woman, but I'm not sure."

"Was anything missing?" Mike asked.

"Not at first glance. Someone played around with my laptop, though. The screen was up and I always close it."

"Was the session locked?" Even if she took that step, it hardly mattered much. A tech savvy enough to interfere with cell and GPS signals could have easily beaten her security measures.

"Definitely it was," Jessica said. "If we leave, what are you going to do?"

"I don't know yet," Mike said. "I'll figure something out. I've been in worse situations. The Partner said you need to go *now*. And they were very specific that something would happen."

"We can't skip out yet. We're too close, Mike. A name for the missing body fell in my lap. All I need is to fill in a few blanks. Then once we unravel who owns Better Days, LLC, we got the Partner. And once we have that, it's just about Sean . . ."

"Jessica, it's just too dangerous for you and Andy to stay on at the ranch. Research can be done anywhere there's a telephone and the Internet. Can't it?"

"Why don't you call this what it is, huh? You feel out of control. And that scares the hell out of you."

"Maybe," Mike said.

"Is there more?" Jessica said.

"Only that I feel like I really messed up getting involved in this one. I didn't count on it . . . I didn't want it to affect you and Andy like this."

"Mike, your work always affected us. It didn't end when the case wrapped up, either. Whether we were directly involved in the case, like now, or you just pushed all the emotions down in those dark places you carry with you everywhere and never spoke a word about it, it impacted us. But that's who you are. At least, that's who you are right now. It doesn't have to be that way, though."

Lost in thought, Mike fell silent. He thought a lot about what she said. Eventually, he mustered enough resolve to continue. "Are you going to leave with Andy?"

"Not yet," Jessica said. "Because that's who I am."

03:58:55 PM

The Partner almost crowed into the phone, "So I hear your little plan backfired."

"My, we're getting cheeky," Crotty said. "Didn't I tell you to ditch this phone? And it wasn't entirely a wash. I'm sure the message got through."

"Whatever you like," the Partner said. "Point is, I know what you're up to."

"What's that?" Crotty asked.

"Regani just called. The banker spilled his guts. Don't think for a second you're leaving me to take the fall while you walk into the sunset with the cash. The Feds will never see those records as they are now."

"Are you threatening me?"

"As far as I'm concerned," the Partner said, "what tatters remain of this partnership will evaporate the second the boy surfaces. We go our separate ways. I'm working for me now."

Crotty chuckled at the Partner. The mere thought of it was ridiculous, and a bit ironic. The Partner breaking it off. Such an unthinkable image. He didn't know how to start visualizing it. And yet, here after all these years, the first hint of nerve showed its face. Too bad there wasn't more of that will present at the beginning. If only the Partner had showed that resolve—even a trace of it— before, then there might have been a chance for a future. A chance for a stronger company. But alas, there was no blue sky waiting on that horizon. It had come to this separation. It must be this way. "Sure," Crotty said. "And good luck with that. The way you spend money, you'll be tapped in three months."

"You're not the only one who can read a ledger."

"True," Crotty said. "But, sadly, you are not one of those people who can add the columns up properly. Now since you have all the answers, I have a question. Did Regani run to you because I made a mistake, or because I wanted him to?"

When it was obvious the Partner had no idea what to say, Crotty snorted. "Always pick your enemies like your life depends on it. It just might."

03:54:05 PM

Mike was not ready to admit defeat, but he knew Jessica meant every word. She and Andy would stay. The only recourse was to trust her judgment that she would know when, and if, the time came to flee for safer ground. He admired the firmness of her convictions amidst the chaos. She would not be deterred. She would not be shaken. Above all, Jessica was her own person, with her own approaches, needs, and wants. Faced against Mike's concerns, her views won out.

That was not to suggest that he liked her decision—on any level. In fact, he abhorred it. But he had no choice. He had to accept what he could not change, move on, and concentrate his energies where they might make a difference. With dozens of miles between his family and himself, he could do little else.

A bit of metal flashed in the sun. It glimmered twice more. Mike crouched, opened the binoculars, and concentrated on the burst of light. He waited.

Flickering again across the grass and trees, it disappeared. A thin patch of clouds blocked the sun from striking the metal at the right angle.

But Mike had isolated the reflection source already. A Humvee sat parked two hundred yards away, the bumper facing him. One with a cracked head lamp.

The Humvee. The same one from the accident the previous night.

03:54:45 PM

Mike investigated. He turned off his cell phone to avoid any mistakes, and crept closer. He drew close, weaving through the trees in a deliberate fashion. His purpose was to disturb the surroundings as little as he could manage.

It was not an easy task. After days of moving as he pleased, now he contained his movements—a complete reversal of his former approach. Being quiet mattered and meant he could not walk in the most efficient way. Instead of quick, direct movements, he took slow ones. Stealth was the principle that propelled him through the trees.

The training and conditioning came back to him and soon enough he reached the narrow path and the Humvee. He hesitated, making sure he was alone. He sensed he was not.

He also wondered why the truck was idling right here. There had to be someone nearby. Or maybe inside the truck. Tinted glass made the windows into dark shadows. Exhaust fumes saturated the air.

His gut said wait where he crouched, so he did. Footfalls wound through trees, toward the truck. Two different sets. Voices followed the steps.

"He's still pissed at me," one said.

"Be happy he didn't drop-kick you through the door, Wrekker." *Wrekker.* The name from the accident scene.

"I'll never understand," Wrekker said, coming into view, one side of his face swollen and bruised, "why we had to carry materials in and out like this. It's a cutting-edge facility, yet we had to walk the last quarter mile."

"It decreases the chance that the path appears like a road on satellite or helicopter sweeps," said the other man. "Same reason we vary the routes to the entrance constantly. Less wear means less attention. We haven't used this one in at least six months."

"Maybe before that was a threat, but what difference does it make now? I didn't appreciate hoisting all that crap inside today. Especially not those chemicals."

"Don't be such a whiner. They were in a stable form. You know what I don't understand?" the other man said. "How come I pulled grunt patrol with you. It's not like *I* wrecked a Humvee. Hell, why am I even here? If you hadn't smacked up the truck in the first place, and cost us all that time, we would have finishedby now."

Wrekker hoisted a cardboard box near the rear of the truck. The other man watched Wrekker struggle with the heavy load. Black block print on the label peeked above Wrekker's forearms.

Drain cleaner, Mike thought. *If gallons of that stuff came out, what did they bring in?*

Inside the truck were a lot more boxes with the same print, stacked up to the seat backs. "That's the last of it," Wrekker said. He slammed the truck-bed door closed.

"Great," the other man said. "Let's get out of the way so the next team can finish their work. Cause I definitely don't want to be around for that. Stable or not."

With the other man at the wheel, the Humvee tore off, kicking up a light dust cloud.

Mike rose, crawled out of the observation point, and looked down the winding road in the direction Wrekker had traveled from previously. He consulted maps on his GPS. Another road his navigation gear claimed did not exist. Pulling up the coordinates he saved the night of the accident, he checked out the possible destinations for the caravans against his current location.

Of the possibilities he plotted, two were miles and miles off from where he stood. Those coordinates he filed away again temporarily. But one estimated location lay within a half-mile. Roughly. If his present bearings were correct, at least. Still stinging from the Partner's broadcast interventions, he couldn't be certain about them, unless he conducted reconnaissance and took another detour. Not worth considering unless it took him closer to Sean. Right now, he did not believe it would do so. There was no evidence of Sean here or at the other end.

The temptation to investigate further was tremendous, though. A quarter-mile—that was Wrekker's claim—would only take him five minutes. Maybe less.

But he sensed he and Dagget should stay the course. They had a goal, and a shrinking window of time to deliver on it and recover Sean, thanks to the weather. A few dark clouds loomed at the horizon. Other signs of an approaching storm mounted. Mike feared there were not many hours left before the weather turned foul. He pocketed the GPS and stared down a path that faded into a swath of trees. He wanted to uncover what lay at the other end of that quarter-mile.

To his right, Dagget peered through the trees and said, "And you'd be doing what, exactly?" He sounded younger and Irish.

"Nice accent, there. I wouldn't have thought that was you," Mike said. "And I'm thinking."

"Cut that out," Dagget said. "'I've been trying to call. I found something huge."

03:59:34 PM

Intrigued, Mike followed Dagget away from the road. Along the way was more evidence of Sean. In the broken branches at knee-, shoulder-, and ankle level. In the deep, heel-to-toe strikes in the soil. And in the frenetic pace he must have traveled while leaving those signs. The terrain cropped his gait, so the space between his steps shrank dramatically.

As for so many miles before, the new tracks reaffirmed Sean's almost unrelenting determination. Predictable and very rigid. Almost like an automaton, Sean had stamped each track into the earth, instead of like a frightened kid on the run. He gave Sean a lot of credit; the boy had incredible stamina. Consistency among his tracks made spotting the next one easier.

Mike hoped that endurance held as long as Sean needed it.

"Can you believe this?" Dagget said, motioning ahead of them with a broad stroke of his hand. "Probably not related to Sean, but it's something isn't it?"

Before them was a clearing with the two skeletons. Both men paused, studying the same scene Sean had discovered. Dagget broke the ice. "Bones are picked clean."

Crouched beside the skeleton that was fastened to a tree, Mike said, "Chained up and left to die. Might have been alive when they were eaten."

"Nasty way to go. A pack of wolves?"

Already Mike had seen enough to know the culprit. "A single

animal did this," Mike said. "Wolves hunt in packs. A crew of them would have spread bones everywhere. Mountain lions hunt alone and leave the carcass behind. They might cover the kill sometimes, try and keep it cool. The trees provided a natural shade, so a big cat could leave it here without worrying."

Spotting a broken watch near a tree trunk, Mike stopped. He turned on his cell phone. With the camera in the phone he took a picture and emailed it to Lisbeth. Then he marked his find in the soil, recorded the coordinates, and tucked the watch carefully into the backpack.

"It's all related," Mike said. "This is Sean's watch. I recognize the band." He shifted gears and asked, "What made you come over here?"

"I was just waiting for you and I thought I saw something out of the corner of my eye. So I checked it out. I'm going to call Lisbeth and let her know about the skeletons. Maybe they can be identified. They might be important people."

Mike nodded his approval. "Well, good work."

"Oh," Dagget said, dialing, "plenty of people would be surprised by what I can do."

03:59:56 PM

With his stomach on the cave floor, Sean listened for the helicopter. It buzzed overhead then retreated, returning later for another pass. There seemed a deliberate pattern to the runs, consistent enough to set a watch by. Sean wished he had one.

At first, he noted every second between passes. Unraveling the pattern seemed urgent, possibly critical for his salvation, and he measured time between them as best he could. Numbers whirred constantly in his head and soon got to him. So he switched to counting off in five second blocks instead. When that became too tedious, he switched to minute intervals, and then every other minute. An hour tapped out like that in his mind. Maybe a little more. Maybe a lot less.

During one pass, the copter hovered at one hundred feet. When he realized how close the flying machine was—the peril it implied—he withdrew from the entrance. He burrowed like a mole shunning light. And he remained so still, so breathless, so terrified.

Waiting in suspension for ten seconds, paralyzed, was harder on him than an hour of exertion in the open air. Long-distance runners loved motion; they craved constant movement.

He might be many things: young, nearsighted, an average student, and asthmatic. Collectively, to Sean, the items read like a list of downers. But being a runner was a plus. He knew the lifestyle well. Lonely, driven souls who arose in darkness to trade a warm bed for damp air and sweat. He loved running purely, wholly, the way a boy loves before he discovers girls. And as a runner, many times before he had trained for races he had no shot at winning. Kind of like his predicament now. He knew what other runners felt like when they struggled in the back of the pack.

The most organized competitions with finish line tape and chronographs could not be settled by merely separating packs of runners into one winner and lots of losers. Races were more complex than that. In large events, each of the top ten placers revealed themselves as a possible champion early on, often within the first minute. At a certain point in the race—it varied by the participant—the others accepted their position in the pack. They might gain dozens or even hundreds of places, but their gold waited for another day. Yet they continued, knowing they would not win.

Sean knew why they kept on in spite of the odds. Win or lose, the journey offered its own reward. Runners ran for the feeling of getting somewhere on their own steam. It tempted every soul who strapped on a pair of trainers and muscled their way inside a pack. The more consistent the supply of endorphins, the better.

Now he lay, jagged rocks cutting into his stomach, petrified of breathing too loudly. He knew it was a ludicrous fear; there was no way people in the helicopter could hear him breathing. He was still scared, and as far as he imagined from chasing endorphins.

He was done chasing this afternoon. Probably for this evening, too. Instead, he was being chased. He was the prey. He wanted to do more to save himself. And he wanted to go home.

Stretches of idle time made his skin itch. He clawed at his forearms. Wild swipes with his nails caught a few insect bites. Irritated, the bites turned red.

The helicopter approached again. Outside the alcove, it drew very close, nearer than ever before. Rotors sliced at the atmosphere; a long, black horizontal propeller generated lift, raising or lowering the bird. Shock waves rattled the treetops and tore leaves and branches. Aviation gas, exhaust, and sweat merged into a sweet fragrance. All around Sean the valley rumbled like a dam bursting.

Sean's chest tightened from the stress. He waited and watched, half expecting a landing near the cave opening. A breath forced its way into his sinus cavity. The inhaler stayed in his back pocket because the medicine inside was too precious for anything but a genuine attack. He cycled another breath, this one by breathing through his nose.

Several times over the last two days he could have sworn the thin canister of asthma medicine was tapped. Then an attack would strike. He inhaled. Relief arrived. Rationing conserved supplies but could not replenish an empty canister. He wondered how long the lucky streak might last. He was too old to believe in forever anymore. He only hoped for as long as he needed it.

He still had an important objective: finding a way he could break out of the cave. To Sean, the timing absolutely depended on the helicopter.

He noticed the shift in pitch as it banked leftward. He exhaled, as slowly as he could.

He wanted to scream at the goddamn thing. Tell the pilot to go harass someone else. He thought about throwing rocks at the copter.

A tiny bit of damage might force them back to the hangar for repairs. That would buy him an opening. Maybe a big enough one. He could run then.

The more moments he spent penned in like a convict, the better the notion of lashing out seemed. Once, he even scooped up a flat-sided rock, ideal for lobbing great distances. He almost pitched the rock at the metal underbelly.

Then reality hit.

First, his upper-body strength paled in comparison to his legs. Throwing anything a few hundred feet exceeded his abilities. Even if could he lob a stone that far, his poor sense of aim ensured, at best, a near hit. Third, and more likely, the crew inside would spot him. He did not want to be seen. Attacking from below virtually announced his location. So he waited.

The helicopter reversed course. The mountain swallowed the noise. With the threat past, the stress engulfed his body. All the symptoms of an asthma attack pounded him at once.

His heart rate doubled. His breathing became faint. His chest and throat tightened. He rose, or tried to. Weakness rode him right back onto the cave floor. Fumbling for the inhaler, he crammed the plastic nozzle into his mouth and squeezed, hands trembling, fingers cold. A trickle came out, maybe a quarter shot. Enough to ease his breathing, but not nearly enough to stop the attack. Frantic, he shook the device a few times, and listened for the familiar rattle inside the canister.

This time the inhaler was empty.

04:13:08 PM

Somewhere in the string of moments that shaped a day, fall began. Mike had sensed this earlier at breakfast, when a chill nipped at his exposed skin. He had tucked the observation away then, almost nonchalantly. Viewing the same landscape now, Mike regretted his haste. He remembered his yard in California; he remembered the great scenery he had missed back home.

Above the sprawling landscape of mountains and forests, the turn of season was more obvious, and showed in the leaves. Longer nights slowed the production of chlorophyll, a component that made foliage appear green. Once chlorophyll production stopped, two other chemicals, arotenoids and anthocyanins, were released, and their bold pigments ignited and revealed themselves. From green, the leaves turned shades of yellow, orange, and red.

When he had left for this trip, the transformation was localized, striking patches of trees, but not all. Four, five, six at a time turned, surrounded by green slopes. Now the patches of sharp colors would be more apparent.

"You ready to move ahead?" Dagget asked.

The prompt shook Mike out of his daze. "Maybe," Mike said. "I saw our Humvee a few minutes ago."

"No way."

"Busted headlight and all. A few men were loading it up with boxes of drain cleaner."

"And you want to investigate?" Dagget asked.

"I almost did. They were coming from somewhere nearby. At least that's what I picked up from their conversation."

"So that's why you kept your cell phone off," Dagget said.

"Well it's staying on from now on. That's what the Partner wanted," Mike said.

"They warned me about the same thing. Any luck with Jessica?"

"Jessica never quits easily."

"Maybe she'll come around."

"I'm hoping." Mike said. "What are your thoughts on another detour?"

"Did you notice what time it is?"

"4:14 PM." The day was vanishing, and Mike felt it.

"And you realize how long that poor kid has been out here? Even presuming we're very close, he's gotta be running on vapors with his meds. It's about him, remember? You told me that. We don't need to know where a Humvee went to bring home the gold. Besides, the cell phones are on full time, and they can figure out where we are."

Dagget's explanation was hard for Mike to accept, but he knew the officer was right. His selfish reasons were not compelling enough justification for another detour.

So they pressed on.

05:00:00 PM

Feet upon the desk, reclining in a chair, Crotty dialed Detective Lisbeth McCarthy's direct line.

"We have a mutual interest in the Sean Jackson case," Crotty said seriously. "I have information about the missing boy."

"I'd love to hear all about it," Lisbeth said. "But I usually don't handle tips myself. We have a hotline for that. So why don't we start with who you are, and go from there."

"There are a few things I need before I tell you where he is, Detective."

"I like to know who I'm talking to. How about a name?"

Crotty heard a lighter flick over the phone.

"Check the number on caller ID," he said. "Homeland Security."

After that, it was a whole different conversation. "So what do you know, and how can it help my search?"

"The boy stumbled very close to a place of interest in a deep-cover investigation," Crotty said. "He turned up on our video surveillance today. The men involved with this place of interest—to say that they are killers is putting it mildly. So far the boy has stayed under their radar, but I can't make any promises that continues. Now I hate to make decisions like this, play King Solomon and all, but more than a year went into this investigation. Since your helicopter sweeps, they've already quieted their operations considerably. If we go charging in for the boy right now, they'll ditch the whole facility and move on. Then again, if we don't . . ."

"What are you proposing?" Her voice betrayed she was considering the proposal.

"An arrangement that works for both of us, partner."

05:10:05 PM

The helicopter patrols stopped. Mike noticed the exact moment the whirring in the background disappeared. At first he thought it had circled back for refueling, and another would take its place. After an hour of silence, Mike questioned whether one was still circling anywhere.

Mike went to fill the canteens; it was his turn. After he plopped the iodine tablets in the untreated water, he left a message for Lisbeth asking why the helicopter sweeps ended, then called Jessica.

"I've found our guy," Jessica said, excited. He could hear her broad smile echoing down the phone line. "I think you'll find his story interesting."

"The Partner?"

"No, on that one I need a little more time. I mean the missing body, David St. John. Or more precisely, the dead chemist. My contacts delivered the information I requested about and then some. A whole dossier. Clippings about David, pictures from high school and college, a credit check, DMV records, and more."

"Sounds like you've got the who nailed," Mike said. "Now why did someone kill David?"

"If I may be so bold," Jessica said, "the answer is also in the folder, and it explains the who. Just listen for a second; it's worth it. David's story up to a certain point reads like a prodigy. Perfect college admission scores. Undergraduate work at BYU, graduate work at Duke, doctoral work at Harvard. Two-year postdoctoral fellowship in Stockholm, Sweden, working with one of the greatest minds in advanced pharmaceutical research. Everything about his credentials says, *Nobel Prize–bound. He's going to be somebody.*

"Then his life takes a different turn. David applies for a teaching position in the Ivy Leagues. He applies . . . and waits. Six months after throwing his hat in, he's got nothing but a stack of rejection letters. For twenty-four years of academic life, he's never tasted failure. Not for a moment. Nine months go by; every school he wanted said no, save one. Harvard, his first choice, holds out.

"David panics. Nine months is a long time waiting around for a gig. Desperate, he canvases the tier-two institutions. Then they reject him, week after week. These schools do it quickly, instead of dragging it out over months. Ninety days later, the only course left is tier three. At last he gets some bites. He interviews for a university smack in the middle of one of the roughest neighborhoods in America: Trinity. They sign an agreement and he relocates. He moves his wife, now pregnant, with him to a small apartment near campus. A very bumpy start but everything is at least moving in a forward direction.

"Weeks after settling in, his pregnant wife is stabbed walking home from the grocery store. Two junkies. Creeps get forty bucks and her keys. He's barely mourned her when a letter comes. A year after his application, he gets the job at Harvard. The dream research position. If the letter arrived two weeks earlier he'd be miles away with his family, and he'd definitely have a better job. He contacts Harvard to accept the position. They ignore his calls. Another message arrives via post. Because he's affiliated with another university already, Harvard retracts the offer."

"His personal life destroyed, his professional life set back decades over a late letter," Mike said. "Unfortunate."

"Heaven help a rejected man, right?" Jessica said. "According to people who knew him, David took the whole thing personally. He drops out of the game. Landlord comes knocking for the rent one day, and all David's belongings are still inside. No one on the straight and narrow sees or hears from him again. He ceases to exist. Except to one person . . ."

"Who?" asked Mike.

"About two years ago his mother was diagnosed with terminal cancer. She's old, alone, and in danger of losing her house as she struggles to keep up with the hospital bills. Then, as if by magic, her money problems disappear. The mortgage is paid off in full and financial arrangements are made with the hospital ensuring her the very best care for the rest of her days."

"David came back for his mother," Mike said. "That's quite touching."

"Almost. Officially the arrangements come through a third party. All I could pry loose was the name of the company. Better Days, LLC."

"The same Better Days, LLC that bought the disposable cell phone the Partner is using?" Mike said.

"I can't prove that yet," Jessica said, "and Mom isn't talking. She's in a coma. The hospital won't divulge any more payment details."

Something bothered Mike. "This is all good journalism, Jess, but why is David St. John dead?"

"Oh, sorry," Jessica said. "I got totally caught up in my story.

Here we go. This guy was trained to design cutting-edge drugs, and I think that's exactly what he did. He's a trained chemist through with playing things straight. There are plenty of smart guys on the wrong side of that business."

"Designer drugs," Mike said. "Now that makes sense. Explains the caravan security."

"Or making existing drugs more potent. Or even converting legal components into illegal ones," Jessica said. "Walk in the park for a man with his credentials."

"That still leaves the why. Maybe he brewed up a bad batch for the wrong crowd," Mike said, thinking out loud.

"Well, I imagine a bigger course for David," Jessica said. "Science types like him get bored unless they tackle a real challenge. What if he stumbled upon something groundbreaking? His own legacy. A discovery that could have propelled whoever controlled the formula to number one. Maybe it was too risky to take a chance letting that formula leak onto the Internet. They killed him so he couldn't defect or talk."

Drugs. The theory was working for Mike. "Here's something that may be unrelated. Earlier I saw the same truck that wrecked into a tree last night. The only thing inside were boxes of drain cleaner. What do you think?"

"Hmm," said Jessica. "Drain cleaner can be used in the manufacture of methamphetamine. They still need ephedrine, and some other components, but that's easy enough to get."

Mike took a deep breath. "I don't like where this is heading."

Jessica said, "I want to get back to the research."

"Does Lisbeth know all this?" Mike asked.

"Just got done telling her before you called. She was so happy about ID'ing David, she agreed to investigate the Better Days, LLC connection immediately."

"You told her about the phone threats?" he asked sharply. "What if she's the Partner? Or working with them?"

"There's always a possibility, but I think it's unlikely. She just doesn't strike me that way. Besides, she needed a reason to poke around. At the very least, the phone threats connect the caller to

Shad's and David's murders, and maybe a whole lot more."

"It could be her."

"Lisbeth is not the Partner, Mike."

"Maybe not. But she hasn't been entirely straight with us, either. Remember she didn't even tell me there was a murder? She left that for me to figure out. Why? And how about the missing gear? And I don't understand why the helicopter patrols stopped."

"All that you'll have to ask Lisbeth."

"I will," Mike said. "If she ever returns my calls. I suppose there must be an explanation for what she did. Check your e-mail when you get a chance. There's a message with some coordinates. When the Humvee caravans were cruising back and forth, I worked out some possible destinations. If anything happens to me, take them to someone in narcotics who you trust and tell him to check out those spots."

"What do you think is going to happen?" Jessica asked.

"I really don't know at this point. Just be ready to get out of there with Andy."

"I will. You be careful, too."

An idea touched off inside him then. "Erich could be the Partner."

"Erich as the Partner? Come on, that's even more ridiculous! He wouldn't hurt anyone."

"Just because he's helping you with a story," Mike said, "doesn't eliminate him as a suspect."

"You're talking crazy," Jessica said.

"I just find it curious that every time something happened to you or Andy, he showed his face at the perfect moment. And he's got keys to everything, plus knows the schedules, and what time he can pop into a room without running into a guest."

"That key part makes some sense. He certainly has time and opportunity. But most everyone at the ranch was around me when those other things happened—including Erich. And a lot of staff have keys to guest rooms for maintenance and cleaning. Plus, if it was him, why did he save Andy?"

"The Partner said they would try and stop whatever was going to happen. They had issues with those decisions."

She stifled a sigh. "I'm just having trouble buying it, Mike. I understand you're worried. I'm worried about you, too."

"Maybe I am a little raw," Mike said. "But I never heard or saw his Cessna do any flybys. I would think he'd do everything possible to get a missing guest back."

06:35:57 PM

In the dining hall, of all the food Chappy had prepared so far, dinner that night was the best. That was Jessica's opinion and that of many of those around her. Meaty, choice cuts of sirloin grilled to taste, asparagus spears dipped in real butter, fresh-baked sourdough, and slow-roasted garlic and herb-encrusted potatoes—each item cooked and served with an expert touch.

An elegant presentation accented the fare. Colorful wedges of carrots, oranges, and yellow squash sprinkled with dill covered the plate brim. This balanced out the colors, and as Jessica discovered, tasted mighty fine. And there were other touches.

Golden tablecloths and fabric napkins instead of paper. Vases filled with fresh-cut Gerber daises. China replaced the usual ceramic dinnerware, sterling silver instead of stainless steel flatware.

Jessica made certain the chef heard her praises, and cornered him in the kitchen. His response was expectedly humble: "Good folks, good times, good meal, uh-huh." Again he declined an invitation to join the guests. Bad karma or something like that, he claimed.

Erich rose for the announcement like a more humble man might make a toast. Rectangular tables lined the edges of the room, leaving an opening in the center. He spoke from that point, his stage. "Everyone get enough to eat?" he asked. Voices chorused from the crowd:

". . . absolutely . . ."

". . . best meal yet . . ."

". . . fantastic!. . ."

"Excellent, excellent," said Erich. "I want to put a few rumors to rest. Something very unfortunate happened today on the afternoon ride. There was an accident with one of our most-seasoned and loved horses."

He paused, giving the impression that what he must say next was a heavy weight upon his back. "No one was hurt, and I'm incredibly indebted to the quick thinking and expert riding skills of one guest." Here Erich stared squarely at Jessica. "I want to stress that as much fun as we want everyone to have, we also want guests to be safe. Right now, two vets from different animal hospitals are carefully examining every horse in the stable. Any horse that receives less than a one hundred percent clean bill of health will no longer be made available for riding. If anyone has any doubts about their animal tomorrow, please let a staff member know. We'll find you a replacement. Any questions?"

"Would it be okay if I sat out tomorrow morning?" Cara asked.

"Certainly," said Erich. "Though I do hope you change your mind."

"Oh, I'm not worried about the horses," Cara said. "But I'm having a bit of . . . monthly pain. So I might do a little work and kick back some chocolate. Will those cramps away."

Mostly, people got the joke and laughed with Cara; it was hard not to. Jessica liked that Cara had a way of being naughty, yet funny at the same time.

Erich concluded by saying, "If you'll excuse me, I have some work to do. Have a good night, everyone!" He crossed the room in big, confident strides, and stopped before Jessica's table.

Cara leaned in real close, grinning, hoping to catch the details. Erich glanced at Cara, who kept staring at him. Her lips pursed, opened slightly.

"Could we speak outside?" Erich asked Jessica. "Just for two minutes."

"I'll watch Andy," Cara said, smiling.

Outside, sunlight caught a wispy trail of clouds rising off the horizon. Cumulus clouds. Rain clouds. Jessica recognized them. Sunset was approaching.

Erich said to Jessica, "I'm so sorry about today. Can I do anything else for you or Andy?"

"You've done everything possible," Jessica said genuinely.

"Thank you. I've tried my best."

In the distance, the dissonant tones of a siren rang.

"Can I ask you a question?" Jessica said.

Erich nodded.

"Did those parts come in for your plane?"

"Yes, they did. Unfortunately, there's a storm coming, and I can't join the search until it clears. Forecasted to be pretty nasty. Shame. It would have been a great night for you and I on *Destiny*." His eyes dropped for a second. Then he added, almost as if becoming uncomfortable with his oversight, "And Andy."

"Maybe another time," Jessica said, a bit hurried. "I think I'll get back to dinner and help clean up."

"Jessica, wait," Erich said, setting his hand on her shoulder. "What did you think about your dinner? It was all for you, you know."

"What do you mean?"

The siren drew closer.

Erich looked into her eyes. "I wanted to invite you to dine with me at a restaurant in town, but I thought you might find being singled out from the other guests awkward. Plus, I have to make appearances during the day, so I couldn't break off for that long. So I brought the restaurant to you." A beat passed. "To us."

"It was a great meal, thanks. You didn't have to . . ."

Erich stopped, turned, and leaned toward Jessica. His face was smooth, fresh-shaven. Erich raised his palms to her face. His thumbs grazed her cheekbones gently. He leaned closer. Closer again.

Regardless of what his body said, she could not. It was a difficult decision. Part of Jessica wanted to welcome his warm lips. She drew back with a small step. "I can't," she said with regret. "I'm sorry."

"But why are you sorry?" Erich said, visibly uncertain, almost confused. "Did I misread you?"

Jessica voiced her apprehension. "That's not the problem. This isn't the right time for me."

"Are you afraid of what might happen?" He stroked her cheek; she withdrew slightly.

"Yes. Maybe. I . . ." Jessica collected her thoughts, bolstering her reserves. Hold the line, she told herself. "I only know that now is not the best night to open these doors."

"There are many doors in life," Erich said. "It'd be a shame to shut them all this early."

"I agree, but . . ." Feeling his stare, she stopped.

Erich took a long look into her eyes. It was as if his gaze transported both of them elsewhere briefly and then returned them to the moment with a new insight. His expression dramatically shifted afterwards.

"I was foolish not to notice earlier." His arms hung, slumped at the shoulders, as he realized the truth. Despite every outward sign to the contrary, her heart wanted the same person it had for years.

Three police cruisers burst through the main gate and tore across the parking lot to the dining hall. Red and blue lights blazed and flashed. Stones flew up in the wake of the cars. A crowd gathered at the windows and watched the action through the picture windows. Lisbeth stepped out of the lead car. Four officers appeared at once near her, ready to assist. Together they rushed onto the porch.

"Erich Reynard," Lisbeth said gravely, "you're under arrest for the murder of Officer Shad Hammer and conspiracy to murder David St. John."

06:46:24 PM

Erich protested like the only man caught speeding in the fast lane—shocked and indignant. "I don't even know who those people are."

"Fascinating." Lisbeth blunted the sarcasm enough to maintain a professional tone, yet not so much that a passerby could not tell what she felt about the situation. "Then why were you the last person to call Shad with a disposable cell phone purchased with your credit card? The same phone used to threaten Mike Brody. The charge card statements and phone records say it all. You are the principal of Better Days, LLC, incorporated in the state of Delaware."

"Better Days is a community service-focused organization! We help all kinds of people. My company purchases hundreds of disposable cell phones each year," Erich said. "We donate them to women's shelters. They distribute them to women in abusive situations so they have a way to call for support without their spouses finding out. Please tell me I'm not being harassed because one person misused them."

Metal clicked as the officer closed handcuffs tightly around Erich's wrists.

Lisbeth continued, "You're under arrest because a murder weapon surfaced near the scene tonight. The serial number matches a handgun registered in your name. If I were you, I'd quit talking now, because anything you say can be used by the prosecution. And besides, scenes like these are bad for business, aren't they? Especially for a man who cares so much about public relations."

It all clicked for Jessica. "There was never anything wrong with your plane, was there?" Jessica asked Erich. "You just wanted to slow down the search for Sean."

"No!" Erich said. "It wasn't like that. All I wanted was a chance to fly with you. I knew once I got involved, I wouldn't see you at all. It was selfish of me, but nothing more."

"Shameful," Jessica said. "Just shameful. And what about your 'rescues'? Appearing at just the right moment. You knew just when to appear, didn't you?"

The police led Erich to a squad car.

Looking back at Jessica, Erich spoke with enormous anguish, "He doesn't deserve you. Are you even going to tell Mike that you still love him?"

Lisbeth slammed the car door shut, with a disgusted look on her face.

07:31:06 PM

Dark clouds accumulated slowly and enveloped the valley. Electric bolts supercharged by collisions between pressure zones awaited release. The air smelled of raw almonds. When the sun went down, a stiff gust roared to life. Wind rushed them from every corner, whistling in their eardrums. Thunder groaned in a distant valley.

Although Mike hoped the storm would pass over, he knew better. They needed shelter. Right now. The time for establishing camp was before the sky went black and heavy rains forced their hand; the will of men was nothing against a storm's fury.

The line between a minor rain event and full-scale riot were questions of fate. Nature did whatever she pleased. And once a melee broke out, the safest course for those left behind was to get out of the way.

Unnerved by the approaching weather, Mike wanted more time, wanted to press ahead, and present conditions made that impossible. Already he had pushed farther than yesterday, much farther than was logical, given the impending storm. He had waited too long to quit for the day. They could have stopped a half hour ago and found shelter. Despite this, he had continued. No effort they had made so far seemed good enough; there was more they must do to find Sean.

And then the storm materialized like a roadblock. The obstacle was maddening, because he sensed they were close to Sean. He wanted to believe they were so very close. He had to believe.

At the base of the twin mountain caps, he made two executive decisions: find shelter, and contact Lisbeth. He needed cover and answers, starting with what happened to the helicopter. The Apache sweeps had stopped hours ago. If she had received his messages requesting an explanation, she ignored them.

Should the clouds peel away after the storm and before daybreak, he would urge Dagget to press ahead, with or without contact from Lisbeth. He planned to continue as soon as possible—even in the blackness of night across sloppy terrain. This decision contradicted his normal protocol. Tracking in the dark increased the chances for mistakes, so by habit he stopped working after dusk, then waited out dawn, resting. But the searches he aided rarely stretched across multiple days. This situation was one where Mike was willing to bend his own rules, because of his experiences.

Often a common thread connected successful cases. Those recovered alive often wanted to be found more than their actions had hinted initially. While they evaded searchers, or deliberately hid from them, they left behind evidence, signs that betrayed their location. Sean wanted to be found or he would have been more careful. He just did not know whom he could trust.

Tracking meant spotting tiny truths like that from the false statements. Parents lied out of love. Cops lied by omission. The press lied to sell papers. But tracks did not lie to Mike Brody.

Beyond the mountain caps, a thunderbolt cracked and lit up the mountainside.

Dagget topped off the canteens and scurried ahead. "It's looking like the end of the world, man. Where are we going?"

"I'm working on it," Mike said.

Four minutes away on foot, peeking out from behind a swatch of trees, a sheet of yellow and white nylon rose off the ground. The wind caught the fabric and buoyed the edges. Something restrained the nylon; it rose and fell with the wind, fixed to the same spot.

A second bolt crackled. The deafening howl rang long after the bolt touched down on a tree. The tip struck a quaking aspen near them and seared a black streak down the trunk. Sections of the tree shattered. Wood flew through the air.

Unnerved by the explosion, Dagget dropped a canteen, which bounced off his thigh. Water seeped out the half-tightened cap.

The flapping nylon had to wait, Mike decided. Finding safer ground came first.

"This is crazy!" Dagget said. He cradled the dripping container. He pointed towards the base of a mountain. "I'm going for cover!"

Rocks made poor conductors. In an electric storm, he and Dagget would fare better under sediment than beneath trees or in the open. The base sported many nooks and crannies. A square-shaped breach within spitting distance met all their requirements. Large enough for both men, a wide roof shielded against run-off. The entrance was high enough to protect them from rising water.

Mike led them to the hill. Tagging behind Mike at first, the officer stayed back until he spied the opening. Then Dagget raced past Mike as if a bear chased them.

Both men ducked inside as the storm unleashed hell.

Rain dropped in sheets. It was a merciless tempest. For hours, the torrent ravaged the valley like a flood tide. Winds raged. Thunder boomed. Bolts shaped like jagged knives lit up the sky. The water swallowed a bit more land with each new advance. Primal instincts guided some animals to high ground, some into crags, some down caves.

Inside Mike and Dagget's shelter, the men wrestled with a different problem. The rocky overhang they retreated beneath had proved a facade. It was terribly cramped. Low, shallow, awkward, the quarters forced both men into a hunch. The tight space cramped up their neck and shoulder muscles, restricting upper body motion.

Flecks of rain splashed their clothes. Moisture chilled them.

Fortunately, a bright bolt revealed a hole in the mountain that looked like a better shelter. When the lightning passed, Mike beamed the foot of the opening with his Maglite. Thirty feet ahead, the narrow tunnel twisted into the unknown. Certain of more beyond the turn, Mike seized the chance.

"Where are you going?" Dagget asked petulantly.

"Inside," Mike said, as civilly as he could.

Dagget chortled. "Rocks. Rocks and mold. That's all that's in there."

Standing within the aperture, Mike extended to his full height. The relief was immediate. "Enjoy squatting until the rain lets up," he called back to Dagget, creeping into the tunnel.

07:47:28 PM

Still Dagget hesitated at the entrance. Lightning crashed overhead. Thunder echoed off the rocks. "Maybe it's worth a quick check," Dagget said.

Uneven layers of rock lined the tunnel walls. Some were quite jagged, and the same barb caught both men across the left arm. At its end, the tunnel opened into a chamber.

Once, someone had made a home here, Mike observed, though now the chamber stood barren. Whoever had selected the chamber made a wise choice, because the spot had many natural advantages. Beyond the reach of a floodplain, the floors and walls stayed dry. A draft spilled through the wall from the left side, delivering healthy supplies of clean, fresh air. The room was sturdy and durable; no event less than a major earthquake could damage the structure.

And since light never penetrated the walls and the room was partially underground, the chamber maintained an average temperature of fifty-two degrees Fahrenheit throughout the year. In case that proved too cold, occupants could burn wood in a massive fire pit.

The quarters were spacious. It was wide and deep, with a high ceiling that made it feel even larger. A virtual palace for a camper of humble means. Or two exhausted men.

Inside was a small stool with four legs—the solitary furnishing. Below the seat, tattered from years of use, was a blanket rolled in a tight cylinder. Against one wall stood an arrangement of empty tin cans with the labels removed, forming a pyramid.

The fire ring—a circular arrangement of stones on the floor that corralled flames—was loaded with gray ash. Carbon deposits from the most recent fire stained the inner rim. Intense heat had split many of the stones. Safe from the reach of embers rising from the flames, a half cord of dry, seasoned timber leaned against the wall.

Finished surveying the aesthetics, Dagget spoke. "There's been chatter about a recluse out this way for years." With a casual dip, he claimed the stool, grunting as his bottom touched the seat. "It was said he lived on the outskirts of town, holed up in the woods. Every once in a while a trespass call came in about a short, bearded guy with long coal-black hair and blue eyes. He Dumpster-dove behind a few of the supermarkets or restaurants. We'd cruise in, check it out, but he always slipped out ahead of us. The creep was mobile, didn't stay in one spot very long. Wasn't much point chasing after him. He never hurt anyone.

"One time, though, things turned real sour. Damn madman blew up half a construction site with homemade explosives. To stop a mall development, the papers said. That brought the Feds knocking. He disappeared right after that. They say he burrowed deep into the woods. Hasn't been a sighting since. Papers made the thing into a bigger deal than it really was."

"Reporters are good at that." Mike Brody knew the struggle. How some in the media twisted a minor happening into the event of the century. Oddly though, he had heard tales of a similar man fitting a similar profile, The Ridge Runner. Jessica had published a story about a fugitive in Northern California several years ago. She had coined the unusual nickname based on his habit of skirting across difficult rock ledges without climbing equipment. From Dagget's description, Mike wondered if the two legends were the same man. He hoped not. Nearly five years ago he had chased the Ridge Runner—Oswald Lecher was his real name—through the deep reaches of a remote Northern California forest for nine days. Worst rundown of Mike's life. The Ridge Runner was an expert at evasion, though Mike prevailed. Barely. These days the Ridge Runner was serving hard time at Sheridan on terrorism charges.

Mike gathered an armful of logs from the pile, and bent down to arrange the wood inside the fire pit. A fire that burned high above the ring worked best—it meant less crouching for warmth, brighter light, and better ventilation—so he propped the ends of three logs against each other, forming a tripod. With a knife he carved off slivers and bark. The kindling he placed underneath the logs.

A bright flame from his butane torch set off the kindling. Monitoring the fire's progress for fifteen minutes, he stayed until two of the medium-sized logs caught. When he rose, his right knee cracked. He winced, though not from the sound.

Dagget removed his boots and set them upon the ring. The black laces dangled down the shafts, tips below the soles, but above the flames. He rubbed his hands, chattering.

Mike swept the room for more proof of life. In the space between the woodpile and the wall, a draft flowed openly.

A compartment the size of a large breadbox stowed four cans of pork and beans and a can of mixed vegetables in the wall, all sheathed in a wad of dark plastic. The freshness date on the canned goods showed that they had expired last month.

"Oh sweet Jesus, tell me we have a can opener," Dagget said.

"Those boots of yours are real close to the fire," said Mike.

"Yeah, yeah." Dagget dismissed the observation as if it were the ludicrous raving of a village drunk. "So we got a can opener?"

"Not exactly."

After Dagget's face collapsed, Mike opened an ice pick-styled blade from his multipurpose knife. To kill bacteria, he held the blade to the fire until the steel glowed red. Then he jabbed dozens of perforations into the lid, and around the lip of one of the cans. Stabbing downward, with each plunge a new perforation nearly overlapped the edges of the previous. Can by can, he sawed off the lids. Then he lined them around the ring to cook in the warmth of the fire.

After dinner, Dagget appeared more relaxed. "That was the best-tasting canned food ever."

Mike warmed his hands by the fire.

"I never thought we'd be out here so long," Dagget said.

"It's been a trek." Fires drew conversations out of people. Mike suspected Dagget had more to say.

"It's a good thing, is what I mean." Suddenly Dagget changed gears midstream. "My wife and I used to sit around our fireplace like this." He sighed. "Before the divorce."

"How long has it been?"

"A couple of months." Dagget dipped his head for a second, apparently still ashamed of his predicament.

"Same for me," said Mike. "In a year, we'll compare notes."

"You and Jessica seem very cordial," Dagget said wistfully.

"Looks are deceiving. A lot of people thought we had a great marriage. We even believed we did. It looked good on the outside."

"Well, you managed a trip together," said Dagget. "I'd be happy if my ex stopped hanging up on me in the middle of a phone call."

"Sorry to hear that. I know how hard a breakup can be." During the legal proceedings, a physician had warned Mike that a divorce stressed the body as seriously as a cardiac arrest. Mike believed it.

"Did yours run off with another woman?" Dagget said. "Think I got you beat there."

"Was it a surprise," Mike said, "or were there warnings?"

"I knew it was coming," said Dagget, "but didn't want to admit it. We had problems. She was unhappy. When Rita told me about Sheryl, though, here's the messed up thing: I forgave her. I blamed myself. Worked too many hours, too many days in a row. Sooner or later, people look elsewhere for what they're missing."

"Healing takes time," Mike said. "Don't beat yourself up."

"I'll get there eventually," Dagget said. "It's just messy. Rita's dad is the Chief of Police. He's one hundred percent in her corner, which I understand. She's his daughter, why wouldn't he be? The sticky thing is he's important in the community, and he and I have butted heads since the breakup. It was like someone threw a switch. One day we were hunting buddies, the next minute I was a stranger. What I can't understand is why he blames me for her being gay. Like I had any control over her sexuality. Hell, like I had any control over her at all. She's a woman. She does what she wants."

"What makes you say that the Chief has it in for you?"

Dagget almost convulsed when he responded, excited, and a bit enraged. "Because somehow everyone on the force knows the intimate details of my busted marriage. I'm not talking public knowledge like her sexual identity. I mean intimate stuff. Tons of it. Details you never discussed with your closest friends, because only one other person knew. And they weren't hearing these things from me, because I kept my home situation as quiet as I could.

"Just walking past my colleagues is a land-mine dodge. It's like this ugly, open secret, only worse because this one people gab about around every corner. The next cheap shot is only as far away as the water cooler or the locker room. I don't bother to ask who heard what anymore. They've heard everything.

"Believe it or not, once I had a stellar reputation. I was a model cop. I exceeded my quotas, and earned yearly citations for excellence. I was on the detective track. I aced the exam. Virtually a done deal. Then this business with Rita happened. Suddenly, I get passed over, not once, but twice, and officers less qualified and younger got promoted instead. The first time, I sucked it up. But when it happened again, I took it personally. Before I drew good assignments, ones that might lead somewhere. Now I get drafted into cleanup work and Hail Marys."

"What about Lisbeth? Does she side with the Chief?"

"I can't be certain, but the information and directives are coming from somewhere. And the missing body is another black mark to hold against me. At this rate, I'll be lucky to have a job next week."

"A man against the ropes," said Mike, with conviction, "is a man who has a chance for a comeback. When the real test of courage comes, I think you'll surprise yourself."

"I just want a chance to prove I deserve a chance," Dagget said.

"Opportunities are everywhere," Mike said. "You just have to let yourself see them."

After much consideration, Dagget said, "I never thought about it like that. The new girlfriend is good, at least. I've got high hopes for that situation."

"Things will get better when you're ready for them to," Mike said. "You'll get your shot."

08:34:51 PM

At the cave's entrance, Mike phoned Jessica. Dialing, he sat cross-legged as water pounded the terrain. Drops beaded on his knees, and seeped into the fabric quickly. Because of the rocks and weather, the call took three tries to connect.

"You were right." Her voice came plaintively through the sounds of the storm. "It looks like Erich was the Partner. Lisbeth just arrested him with everyone looking on."

"That had to be a scene."

"Yeah. And you were right about something else. I guess he was more interested than I wanted to admit. Erich made a pass at me."

"And then what happened?" It was as close as Mike could get to asking her if she had returned Erich's advances. He stared at his bare third finger, where the titanium band had once been. These days, the ring sat in a drawer fifteen hundred miles away, wrapped with tissue paper, arranged inside a tiny box with a clasp. If Jessica even had her ring still, he wondered where she kept it.

"Two officers tossed him in the back of a patrol car," Jessica said. "Erich is being charged with murder and conspiracy to commit murder."

"How did he look?" Mike said.

"Shocked."

"I could be wrong," Mike said, incisive, "but I doubt Erich murdered anyone."

"Make up your mind! An hour ago you were certain he was the Partner." She sounded exasperated by his dissent.

"He might be the Partner." Mike spoke this slowly, conceding the point with much reluctance. "I'm just saying I don't think the Partner is a killer. The name implies there's a cohort. Or a few cohorts. And when I pressed the Partner about wanting to talk to the real boss, whoever they are got very agitated that I suggested they weren't calling the shots."

"Did you ever consider that the two might be one and the same?" Jessica said. "Perfectly normal-looking people can create double lives, and invent personalities to compensate for their weaknesses and cover up their neuroses."

"That's a pretty rare condition. And this isn't *Fight Club*." The reference he meant as a compliment. He loved Chuck Palahniuk's work; he just took issue with her applying the split-personality theory to Erich.

"Since Erich was arrested, you haven't gotten any calls lately, have you?"

"Silence does not equal guilt," Mike said.

A slap. The sound of fumbling. "Wait a second . . ." Jessica set down the phone. "Sorry, I just dropped a bottle of water I was about to open. Gross. There's some kind of soapy film in the top."

Mike had a few ideas about what might cause clear liquid to turn soapy when shaken. One popular date rape drug reacted that way. It might be many things, though most likely it indicated the presence of a chemical besides water. "Where did that come from? I don't remember buying water on the way," he asked.

"Erich. I can't believe he tried to get me again! I'm shipping two of these bottles out in the morning. One's going to Lisbeth. The other's going to a friend in the DEA. If this is what it looks like, he's going down even harder."

After that, Jessica put Andy on for a few moments. Mike wished his son a good night, told him he would do his best to get home soon, and excused himself before the emotion took over his voice.

Then he tried Lisbeth one last time, finally getting through.

"It seemed like the helicopters stopped flybys well in advance of the storm," Mike said.

"This weather," Lisbeth explained, "is causing enormous problems. Basically, the search is on hiatus. I can't send people out in this. I do have some good news about Sean, though."

"That's just why I called," Mike said. "I really think we're in striking range."

Lisbeth took a deep breath. "About that, Mike, there have been some complications on your front besides the storm. Once again, all the coordinates you provided me bombed out. I had them double-checked, by two separate teams. Nothing turned up. Not a single scrap of what you described."

The ski-mask crew after us is keeping busy, apparently. "What about the skeletons?"

"Couldn't check yet," Lisbeth said. "Honestly, we may not have the means until the search ends."

"I understand." Though he disliked it, he understood how it appeared to an investigator when evidence promised never materialized.

"Do you?" She paused. "I'm not certain where I stand on the discussion right now myself. We gave tracking the college try. A couple hours ago a tip from a reliable source came in about Sean's location. A very specific one. Problem is, it's miles and miles from where you and Dagget are. Or say you are."

"I hope they're right, but I'm staying with the search."

"Sean's been out in the wild for three days now, Mike, and we've only gotten, at best, partial confirmation of your work. I think the odds of you finding something are so unlikely where you are that the best move for you guys is to pack it in. Tomorrow a copter will pick you up. Call me first, give me your best shot at your present location, then fire off a flare."

Mike said, "I'd rather keep on until Sean is found."

"I can't stop you," Lisbeth said. "But I think more of the same is a waste of our time."

"Can you assign an officer to check on Jessica until I get back?"

"I will see about doing that. But Erich isn't threatening anyone now or anytime soon. And with the evidence on file, he's not making bail. So don't sweat it. Why didn't you tell me about these threats in the first place? I would have looked into the matter."

"They said not to," Mike said. *And I thought it was you making them,* he thought.

"I guess if I was in a strange town and didn't know who to trust, I might keep something like that quiet, too. I never doubted your ability to get things done, by the way. I still don't. It just seems like your bearings are off on this one. Maybe it's the terrain, or the weather, or the distractions. There's no gain without some risk, but I'd take a chance with you again. Tonight I'm just taking a little off the table."

The few words of praise softening her no-confidence vote echoed in his ears. Cold comfort for a man who wanted only to help. Enough, he decided. Enough doubts, enough fear and loathing. Second guessing had to wait. Before descending an even darker chasm, he hung up.

Mike walked the tunnel back to the chamber.

Tufts of black smoke oozed from the entrance. An acrid scent trailed the dark mist.

08:45:43 PM

Mike called out for Dagget. He crouched at the chamber entrance below the fumes. A raspy, unsteady cough echoed through the haze. The smoke cut visibility, forcing Mike to inch forward, cautious, hollering for signs of life from Dagget. Mike was a quarter of the way inside the chamber before spotting the problem.

Standing next to the fire pit, Dagget lashed at the ground with a blanket. His boots lay sideways on the rocks. A short flame crawled up the boot shaft. He stamped out the flame, leaving behind the awful stench of burnt rubber.

"Never saw that coming," said Mike, not couching his sarcasm.

"Whatever." Smoke and embarrassment turned Dagget's face red. Otherwise, he looked fine.

The flames extinguished, a draft expelled the gray cloud. Luckily, the veil of smoke dissipated quickly. But the smell of singed rubber lingered, potent as if the boots still burned. With the blanket Mike scooped up the boots. They were in a sorry state.

Of the two, the right bore the real beating. In poor condition, the boot was almost useless because of tread damage. Extreme temperatures had melted the knobby grooves into a smooth, frictionless surface. Above the rubber, the laces were a fraction of what they used to be. Flames had eaten more than half their length. Barely enough left for tying.

The left boot endured only superficial damage. Wide scorch marks covered the exterior. The lace was intact, though badly charred.

Mike abandoned the boots and blanket at the main entrance, so they would not have to smell the scorched rubber all night.

Back in the chamber, Mike added another log to the fire and joined Dagget near the flames.

"That's too bad," Mike said. "Those are quality boots. Merrill makes great stuff."

"I've got two more pairs. Are these salvageable?"

"They'll take you as far as we need to go," Mike said. "I might be able to rig up some laces. After that, ditch them."

"So what's going on with Lisbeth? Did she say why the helicopter runs stopped?" asked Dagget.

Mike relayed the short version, and the more Mike detailed of decisions about the search, the more defeated Dagget looked.

"We're on our own now?" said Dagget.

"It seems that way," Mike said.

"She doesn't think we can do it."

"It sounds like she's not the only one." said Mike

"What does she think we're doing out here? Doesn't she understand how close we are?"

"Your commitment is admirable, Officer. Welcome to the minority of two."

"Look, Mike, I may not understand how you do what you do. But I know what I've seen in the past forty-eight hours. We've been finding signs of that kid from the clearing. That must count for something. The watch. The campfire. The skeletons. Come on, now."

Just like Jessica said, results are not enough. "For the record, I don't entirely agree with Lisbeth on this point. She said there's a lead that needs following. I have to believe she has information we don't." Mike explained the problem with the coordinates they sent Lisbeth and how the searchers failed to recover anything. Again.

"Damn stalkers," Dagget said. "Can't they mess up someone else's investigation?"

"I guess we're special."

"Hey," Dagget said, "does anyone we trust know where we really are?"

"Afraid not." Leaning back from the flames, Mike added, "We've been out here awhile. Things appear differently after a few days in the open air." The botched coordinates infuriated him, even if there was an explanation. There was nothing more frustrating than doing a job, trying diligently, holding nothing back, and have some invisible hand wreck all the work.

"Lisbeth didn't tell you this, but almost from the beginning we believed there was a connection between Sean and the missing body."

"Why would she lie about that?" Mike said.

Dagget cleared his throat. "It's real bad business. Dead man found outside a major tourist site, then the body vanishes. Plus a missing guest. It's the kind of thing that draws bad press. Your wife is a reporter. Don't take this the wrong way, but Lisbeth realized who Jessica was way before your name ever came up. This county doesn't need any more negative attention. There are enough rumors."

"What are you saying?" asked Mike, cautious.

"I wasn't exactly square with you earlier when you asked about the drug issues around here," Dagget paused, gathering steam. "We've got the same problems most towns have, Mike. We get a lot of methamphetamine traffic. We see tons of overdoses and crime. I know guys on the narcotics squad, and they're raiding labs constantly. Three a week at least. They're good cops, fighting the real fight, and not holding back. And no matter how many labs they crack, the supply on the street never shrinks. Which means the ones they nail aren't even distributing around here and a heavy producer runs the show."

"How does this tie into the rumors Lisbeth was worried about?" asked Mike.

"That goes back to the never-ending supply," said Dagget. "If the narcotics team intercepts that many shipments, and never slam-dunks the big guys, then either someone must be protecting them or it's really coming from someplace else."

"Lisbeth?" Mike didn't entertain that prospect with any seriousness. He asked only to solicit Dagget's comment.

The officer shook his head. "Absolutely not. She's got her issues, yes. Lisbeth makes questionable decisions. But malice like this demands a lot more calculation."

"Too bad we weren't talking straight with each other from the beginning," Mike said.

"Would you have believed me then?" Dagget said. "I'm not sure you would have heard me. You had one thing on your mind. Finding Sean your way."

For a moment Mike didn't know what he believed about the case. While Dagget had a point, Mike remembered Dagget's tremendous amount of resistance to his methods at the onset of their collaboration.

Dagget continued. "Every cop figured that the murder was drug-related, and that Sean just might have stumbled into something. But no one asked those questions aloud. With the body gone, all we had to work with was a poor missing kid."

09:20:03 PM

The dream returned, building on the images from the previous night, drawing Mike inside the action . . .

Near the field alongside the supermarket, a group of officers watched. The mother of the missing boy yelled at someone. She was behind him. He didn't look back. He couldn't see her, didn't want to see her.

A single set of boot prints with a vertical stripe led to the woods. In his mind, the field vanished, as did all the officers. There was no need for the tracks anymore; he knew right where they went by instinct. A knot tightened in his stomach, constricting further with each step, as if a vise was squeezing his intestines. He walked among the fifty-foot-tall pines.

He followed no defined trail, blazed no new path. Prints left by the man with vertical-striped boots showed the way.

A quarter mile from the field, the tracks T-boned with a narrow dirt trail, then veered back into the woods. Two hundred yards from there, a broad rectangular area of recently disturbed soil next to a maple awaited his discovery. Someone had smoothed out the dirt, scattered sticks and leaves on top, and tamped the soil with the flat side of a shovel.

When the cop asked why they had stopped, Mike asked him to notify the officer in charge and to bring a long pole.

Mike showed the team of diggers the right area. Using the pole, the lead probed the loose topsoil. Two feet down, the wooden post struck an object. Glancing among themselves they all suspected what it probably meant.

He stepped aside, and the officers dug carefully. They used their hands and wore thick latex rubber gloves. Soon enough they hit a layer of plastic.

Every fiber of Mike hoped that he was one hundred percent wrong. But another part knew he was right. Mike told the cocksure part to shut the hell up even though the tracks said this was the spot.

Let me be wrong, he thought. Let me be embarrassed and wrong.

Powerful flashbulbs fired again and again. Photographers documented the scene. A crowd gathered. Mike swung wide of the fray.

The dirt cleared; an investigator carefully cut the bag along the seams. Whatever was inside had been sealed in several more layers. It took an eternity to get through it all.

A round-faced investigator in latex gloves peeled back the last sheet . . .

And then Mike Brody woke up, disoriented and groggy. Heart palpitations, increased blood pressure, and shortness of breath—all the usual symptoms of a night terror.

Dagget sat nearby, his back to the fire ring, legs facing Mike like a blockade. The flames had burned themselves out. The chamber was cold and damp.

"Rough dream?" Dagget asked.

"It's nothing," said Mike.

"You were talking in your sleep again. Throwing punches."

"It's not on purpose," Mike said, more to reassure himself. His heart rate was elevated. "Sorry if I hit you."

"Oh no, not this time; I caught it early and backed off." Another share from Dagget. He tilted his head slightly, as if curious. "Ever talk to anyone about these nightmares?"

"Are you volunteering?" Mike asked dubiously.

"Just seems like something is eating away at you. Something dark." Clearly the prospect unsettled Dagget as much as it intrigued him.

"Everyone has issues," Mike said. "Things better left unsaid."

"Yeah, but most people don't wake up in the middle of the night looking like they had a heart attack." A pause. "Why do you track people?"

Mike almost answered Dagget when the most welcome sound beckoned like a clarion: absolute quiet. The rains had stopped, the storm—over. Mike brushed loose stones off his legs and torso. Upright, he said, "I'm going to check outside."

Beyond the main entrance, a new wrinkle beckoned. The storm may have ended, but puddles now covered large swatches of earth. Overhead, clouds blotted out the moon and stars, permitting only enough light to deliver the landscape from pitch-blackness. Before the foot search could resume, more water would have to drain off the surface.

Mike returned and said, "There's water everywhere. We'll give it until dawn. Then we make the best of it."

Dagget said, "You didn't answer my question. Why do you track?"

"That's a long story," Mike said.

"We got a long night."

"It's just something I do," Mike said, not quite dismissively, but hoping to end the conversation.

"I figure a guy does this for one of two reasons," Dagget said, leaning forward. "First reason is by choice. Something about tracking interested you. Maybe you read something, or heard about it and the more you learned, the more you wanted to learn. The other cause is situational. Something bad happened to you as a kid and made you what you are."

"You certainly have given this a lot of thought, Dagget," Mike said. He was impressed, yet repelled, at the astuteness of Dagget's reasoning. Explaining the truth meant opening some wounds. Mike wasn't ready. "So which do you think it is?"

"I'm going with number two. Something awful in your childhood. Am I close?"

"You really want to know?" Mike asked.

"Yeah," said Dagget, finally all the bluster gone from his voice.

Mike sat cross-legged, relaxed. The flames warmed his face as he decided whether he wanted this conversation now, here with Dagget. Usually Mike avoided discussions like these. He had his reasons.

"We find Sean," Mike said, "and then I'll tell you the story."

Day Four

04:59:43 AM

Convinced the inhaler had given up its last hit of relief, Sean let it fall to the rocks beside him. He slumped against the wall, hands on his knees. Lying down aggravated the attacks, so he forced himself upright.

There was one way through a mild attack without medication: remain relaxed, and concentrate on controlled exhales. He did so, metering out the breaths cautiously. A whistling sound accented each fall of his chest. Every twenty beats, he held onto the air a few extra seconds. Taking in less oxygen slowed his heart rate.

Focusing on a task—even one this basic—distracted him from the dryness in his mouth. After so many days without food, the sensation of being hungry had faded to the background like a white noise.

Occasionally he thought of eating, fantasizing about his favorite meals, but the brunt of the cravings had softened now, and let him be. The thirst, however, would not be so easily ignored.

There were many symptoms of dehydration: a raspy whine in the throat, dizziness, lips that cracked and bled. The fact that he cowered mere yards from more water than one might drink in a hundred lifetimes roiled him. Until his wind returned, though, a short dash out and back was too much strain. Sean needed water. He needed air more.

His senses degraded in phases. First disorientation—a loss of focus. Then the realization that his senses were failing. He understood the process as clearly as he knew any fact, until he crossed the point where he could no longer realize how serious his predicament was.

His sense of positioning—the notion of where his body was relative to its surroundings—changed, too. He wondered where he really was. He was not in the woods. He knew that. Yet he was not inside, either. Not what he considered inside, anyway.

Moisture weighed down the air. When the rain stopped, animals stirred. A few even scurried near him. Of these events, all that got through to Sean were varied shades of gray. The tunnel and the alcove beyond was black. Within the low-light conditions, shadows flickered across the rock walls. Which of the images taunting him were real and which he imagined, he was unsure.

As unannounced as its appearance, the attack eased; his heart rate stabilized. Mucus still congested the air passages, but more oxygen reached his lungs. He heard the difference. Waiting a few minutes to be certain, he was grateful. Although another attack might strike at any time, this one was through.

Now that he could breathe, he thought about drinking. He wanted to stay hydrated and supplies of water were plentiful. What he needed was a means to gather and cache water for later use. If the helicopter patrols resumed before daybreak, he wanted to wait until nightfall before breaking for it. He fumbled around in the darkness, half expecting a bucket to appear. Nothing of the sort materialized.

Then he remembered another lesson from cross-country. Ancient marathoners who traveled incredible distances, running for days, subsisting on just a mouthful of water. So long as they held that water in their mouths without swallowing, it reduced the amount of moisture lost through sweat, and suppressed the sense of thirst. The difficulty would be keeping his mouth closed for a long period. Asthma made it hard to breathe through his nose, so he would crack his mouth open slightly. He would have to. Should an attack take him down, all bets were off. How he wished he had recalled that kernel two days earlier. Panic did terrible things to a boy on the run.

Shaken, he slipped out of the alcove and into the trees. The temperature difference between the cave and outside stung. And it was the darkest night he had ever seen. Somehow Sean knew he would be stuck in the cave until dawn.

Beyond the alcove, water ran off the rocks and formed a super-sized puddle. Large, clear drops collected above, rolled down the ledge, and splashed the pool. Hoping the stream's movement filtered out the impurities, he sipped some. So far he had been very lucky finding clean water, sticking with fast-moving streams.

When he had his fill, he stretched out his legs until the muscles loosened. He shook his head from side to side. Ready, he took one last swig of water, and swished it around his mouth. Instead of swallowing, he held it. Keeping his jaw clamped down was far more awkward than he expected. Swallowing was a natural response. Not doing so required a great effort. He tipped his head forward so the liquid settled against his lips, and he let gravity do the work.

An hour passed, then another. The method worked. He never believed something so simple, so small, could reap such great benefits. At least he learned something from his mistakes.

Coughing, he let his throat claim the water and swallowed. Laying on his side, he used his arm for a pillow and slept—a fitless rest. His mind drifted in and out of consciousness till dawn.

Six hours later, daylight lapped the alcove walls. He woke up, wheezing. Very little air made it to his lungs. He sat against the wall, and tried his usual tricks, but his heart throbbed faster. He could not control it.

A paralytic shock ripped through him.

His fingernails turned a dusky blue, matching his lips.

05:35:48 AM

Morning broke. Mike stood at the main entrance, facing the trees. The sounds and smells of a new day roused him. He almost felt human. Most of the standing water from the storm had dissipated, though rain still covered the lower-lying areas, and slicked the rocks.

Bleary-eyed, he swapped the laces in Dagget's burnt boots with a few feet of sliced-off rope. The grommets were large and accommodated the thicker nylon strands, although a few eyelets on the shaft had to be widened with a knife. He also scraped some of the carbon off with the blade. "That'll get you there," Mike said. "More or less."

Dagget was appreciative. Having a pair of boots, even scorched ones, beat walking barefoot over rocks. He tested them out over a few steps. Satisfied, he said, "Thanks."

"Just be careful walking," Mike said. "You could trip yourself."

"Do you really think Sean made it miles more from here without being spotted?"

"With enough time, anything is possible," Mike said. "He would have been very careful, and maybe walked through the night. I don't think Sean traveled after dark, though. The tracks seem steadier than that."

Dagget nodded. "When you checked the crime scene before we left, I watched you pretty closely. You kinda trance when you work. Anyway, you said something in the clearing to Lisbeth . . . 'I found the second most important track.' What does that mean?"

Mike said, "The first track. It's my baseline. I build a picture of the subject in my mind—how he moves, what he feels, what he might do next—it all flows from the first track. At a scene, most of my up-front time is spent isolating that from any interference."

"So what's the most important one?" Dagget asked.

"The last track."

05:50:52 AM

Drug raids had never been Lisbeth's forte, and the plan for Sean's rescue meant launching one. She enlisted the narcotics desk who supplied both technical expertise and weaponry. They lacked the budget for much personnel, but they had gear: M4 carbines capable of semiautomatic or three-round bursts, a dozen AR-15 clone rifles, a battering ram, and two large utility vehicles. Exercising a collaborative agreement between four local counties, she rallied a few more bodies, bringing the total head count to nine, including herself. There was not enough time to get the Montana State Highway Patrol involved, though they offered air support.

Gathering at 5 AM, they met inside the local office, dressed for the raid. Lisbeth and the narcotics investigator split the management duties, leaving six officers for the entrance and one for additional exits.

"Listen up," Lisbeth said. The other officers gathered around her. "We've got intel on the target." She spread the schematic across a whiteboard, tapping out their route. "Another agency will meet us near the scene for support. Our primary interest is a missing boy named Sean Jackson. You all have a picture of him. The support group's interest is the other occupants at the facility. Anyone detained, they have first crack at questioning, so hold the collateral damage as close to zero as possible. Questions?"

There were none, so everyone piled into the utility vehicles with dark-tinted windows and rolled off as the sun rose over the mountains.

• • •

Sean lost feeling in his hands and feet. This had more to do with the rocks pressed into his sciatic nerve than asthma. Electricity pulsed down his spine, the signals bound for his extremities that missed the proper receptors. He gasped, wheezed, desperate for one full breath.

Trembling, he accidentally rapped his head against the wall.

The color drained out of his face, leaving his cheeks ashen.

• • •

Halfway into position, Lisbeth and her team waited for the promised support group. And they waited. A quarter past six, the grumblings started. The officers gathered around the utility vehicles, wanting directions.

"They're late," said one to Lisbeth.

Lisbeth checked the time on her cell phone. This was unexpected. She dialed her contact number, and got a busy signal.

"Now?" another asked Lisbeth.

Lisbeth surveyed the target—the entrance to the manufacturing facility—through high-powered binoculars. She missed it at first, even with proper bearings. Easily overlooked, it blended into the rocks. Actually, the entrance was *in* the mountain, perfectly concealed from overhead view. The entrance was large enough for a truck, though no vehicles were in sight.

A series of vents to the left of the entrance were the same color as the rocks. She only noticed the well-formed circles carved through the mountain because she knew of them from images faxed to her office. "Not a creature stirring," Lisbeth said.

"Yeah, kinda spooky," said a lanky cop.

• • •

Trying to inhale, Sean gasped. Mucus tickled the back of his throat. He hacked fluid up reflexively. Bile seared his esophagus on the way out.

He thrashed his legs, trying to stir his feet back awake.

• • •

Lisbeth held the binoculars, her eyes lost in the digital imagery. She scanned the areas of interest, diligent as she worked in manageable increments. Tilting an inch to the left or right through the specs translated into dozens of feet. She chanted in her mind, right one . . . steady one . . . look one . . . look two . . . steady one. She kept counting. She kept straining. She kept searching for signs of Sean. "Gimme something," she practically begged the equipment. "Anything."

The spotter mentioned he had the same issue—nothing to report. "Negative so far, Detective," he said.

Lisbeth stopped. She started again, beginning with a crag further to the left of the entrance. She had not moved this wide before. An inlet of some sort. Within the inlet, a tiny movement. Might have been an animal.

She zoomed in tighter.

• • •

To Sean, everything looked smaller, including his own body. Though his eyes were wide open, images assumed a foggy edge.

His chest constricted as if a massive weight balanced on his chest.

Panic took over, fueling the desperation. Before that morning, he had never believed he would die. Now that single thought overloaded his brain. Now the incredibly awful impossibility seemed so very possible. Only once had an attack been this severe, and it had ended with a 2 AM hospital visit. He still had nightmares about the syringe the doctor had used. The needle felt worse penetrating his leg than it looked, and it was the scariest needle he had ever seen.

The closest hospital was forty-five minutes away by car.

His eyes closed themselves.

• • •

"Double-check something for me, please," Lisbeth said to the spotter. She read out the coordinates. The spotter rattled them back and zeroed in on that point. "Do you see it?" Lisbeth asked.

The spotter nodded. "It could be human."

"Is it moving?" asked Lisbeth.

"Maybe," said the spotter.

Lisbeth thought through her options. The promised support was nowhere. She had only what resources she had—which were fewer than she needed. The risks of storming a meth laboratory, particularly an active facility, were numerous. For starters, the chemicals used in processing methamphetamine were hazardous. The manufacture of one pound of meth generated five to six pounds of toxic waste. The super lab inside the cave allegedly pumped out twenty pounds of product per day. Methamphetamine production endangered the public in general through distribution and consumption, and anyone who came in contact with the raw materials in particular. Its grip on users was near absolute.

Even low-level handlers risked addiction. A single dose could hook someone. For that reason, the officers strapped on black bio-hazard suits and oxygen tanks.

Withdrawal from a high-intensity addiction was a vicious beast, and rolled psychosis, anxiety, and depression into a forty-eight-hour nightmare. But that was only the beginning of the journey back to normalcy. A full physical recovery took two years, if an addict quit. Ninety-four percent of meth addicts did not. They could not.

And there was the security factor Lisbeth must consider. Operators rarely left a lab unguarded. The contents were too valuable to trust to the whim of strangers, or the predatory nature of competitors. Intelligence provided by Crotty indicated a permanent force of at least four, armed with fully automatic weapons. Nine against four. Lousy odds, and she didn't like them.

Her team was all competent, seasoned officers, highly regarded men. Their main weakness—they were untested as a unit. Lisbeth patted the pocket where her cigarette pack was. Later, she promised herself, later she could smoke.

The one thought she kept stumbling over: she was no widow maker. She had never issued orders that led to a fellow officer's death—a record she wanted intact. She checked her watch. Thirty minutes was enough delay.

"Hard to tell from this range," said the spotter. "Maybe it's Sean."

"Are you sure?" Lisbeth asked.

"Not one hundred percent . . . the angle is bad," he said, turning toward the entrance.

"We have to be certain," said Lisbeth, deliberately.

A bit of metal glistened near the facility entrance, then disappeared. Lisbeth suspected they had been spotted. The sails of hesitation listed; they had to act before the situation acted upon them. There could be anything inside the facility, but if they waited too long they sacrificed the element of surprise. And that got people killed.

"All right. Holst, head for Sean, and keep him out of the way. The rest of you, this is it! Let's go!"

• • •

Sean's eyes opened in small slits as he wheezed. He barely made a sound. He wanted to tell his mom he was sorry for storming out three days ago, and being so stubborn. This was all his fault. If only he had stayed closer to the ranch. If only he had been brave enough to stick to the road, and not wander through the trees because he was scared of the killer. Honestly, he had tried to make it back to the ranch. He really had.

Mom would worry, as mothers did. He wanted to tell her he was sorry for screwing up.

Even Dad, for all his hassles and tantrums, had fathered him the best he could.

Sean squinted, gasping.

The alcove slipped away . . .

• • •

An explosion blasted red and yellow flames out of the entrance of the old production facility. The fireball spread up and out, scattering materials. Black smoke swirled. A shockwave slammed through the morning air. Debris and shrapnel battered the utility vehicles. The immediate area smelled like fertilizer and heavy metals. The sound was deafening.

Both vehicles braked hard, and the riders twisted and ducked, dodging broken glass. The windshield and hoods absorbed the initial impact. Heat scorched the paint, causing bubbles and cracks.

The officers disbursed efficiently, evacuating as if they had practiced a hundred times. Glass shattered and cracked beneath Magnum Stealth boots. Using the truck bodies as a shield, cops crouched along the steel frame. All present and accounted for, though eight of the nine officers had cuts and abrasions, mostly mild. Lisbeth assessed her condition: she had a contusion. A piece of shrapnel was wedged in her left shoulder. Pain throbbed through her upper body.

"What a mess," Lisbeth said of the explosion. To Holst, she said, "How you feeling?"

The officer hustled over to her. "Aight," Holst said.

"Go check out that spot in the rocks," she said. "We may not have a second chance."

"I'm on it." Holst swung out in a wide arc of the trucks, bolting for the spot.

Behind the utility vehicles, a caravan of three black Suburbans approached from the same direction the police had driven. They all halted, seemingly as one. The front passenger door of the lead vehicle opened. A man kicked his legs out, one foot landing on the step.

"Perfect timing," said Lisbeth.

He was tall, distinguished-looking, and thrust off the balls of his feet. White letters on the back of his blue jacket read, DHS. "Peter Mayhew, Department of Homeland Security." Crotty's day-job boss. "What's your business here?" Mayhew demanded.

"Checking to see if there's a missing boy anywhere near this mess, and picking glass out of our wounds. Where were *you?*" Lisbeth said unkindly.

Mayhew stared at her like a man billed for services he never ordered. "What are you talking about?"

Lisbeth yanked some of the faxes off the seat, and thrust the folder at him. Mayhew glanced at the pages. "You called me yesterday, set this whole thing up," Lisbeth said, glaring. "You faxed over all these specs. I thought this was a joint effort. You showed up late. This was not our deal."

Mayhew shut the file, tucked the folder under his arm, and said, "The fax number is mine. But if you talked to someone in my office, it wasn't me, because I was out of the office yesterday."

06:30:12 AM

Aftershocks spread across the mountain. Ripples from the blast echoed against the ridge. Distant perhaps, though it was still a disturbing sound early in the morning. Mike and Dagget continued.

Picking up at the last confirmed track was priority number one. An oversight the previous night made the job harder than it might have been, had he taken more time. In the rush for cover, Mike had ditched the trail without placing reflective markers. He regretted this decision as a possible endgame mistake. Once again, he cursed waiting so long to find shelter. If he had allowed a more generous window, he might have remembered to set tags in the soil. Whether the markers could have survived the driving rains and rising waters, or the shadowy figures that followed them, he would never know. Right now, the lack of markers was a big problem.

The storm the previous night had eroded the bulk of Sean's tracks. Worse, it had covered them in pools of water, or rinsed them from the earth entirely, leaving behind a murky, filthy mess. Given the conditions and a lack of visual confirmation, he reverted to instincts. He needed a track from Sean. It must be well-formed, and unscathed. While a partial might work, the more complete, the more emotional energy it stored, the sharper a picture he could visualize.

What he had plenty of were impressions left by Dagget and

himself. Mike traced those back to the woods. Among the trees, he found the point where they had strayed, and faint proof of Sean. Unfortunately, a wide dip in forest floor trapped a standing pool of water. There Sean's trail disappeared, caked over in a layer of mud. He checked either side for signs of the boy.

Before the temporary reservoir, he found one near a maple trunk. The boy's foot had slid under a root, which trapped him for a second, and almost toppled him. Left behind in the soil was a smeared track, the indent fainter at the heel than the toe. Extended longer than a normal print, the streak offered the best available impression.

Mike placed a hand inside the track and shut his eyes. An image flashed: the woods from a point above the canopy. His perspective shifted, as if he hovered above the trees. Looking down, he spied himself, and Dagget watching on. Through the mud and water, new tracks appeared, one by one. A phosphorescent glow lit the outline of the prints, drawing his eyes down their path. The arc of his visions were finite, the range very limited. Only a small grouping—a set of a fifty, perhaps—revealed themselves. But it was much more than he had before, at least. He absorbed the details, burning the image into his long-term memory by noting nearby objects.

A trunk seared by lightning, a felled tree with no branches or leaves—these landmarks were anchors for him to hook into.

Rising, his knee cracked. His joints cried for ice and a handful of anti-inflammatories. Maybe a shot of cortisone, too. Usually by the time the doctor gave him injections for pain, he needed surgery. He had been warned repeatedly; the knee could survive only a few more operations. *Just hold up a little longer,* he thought.

Mike opened his eyes. Dagget was looking at him with great curiosity, as if he had spoken in a demonic tongue.

"Whatever you just did, your eyes were twitching up a storm. It was like you were dreaming. What do you see when that happens?" asked Dagget.

"Enough to get us closer," Mike said.

"What if it doesn't?" Dagget said, dubious.

"I have to trust that it does."

• • •

Lisbeth suspected that Mayhew was holding back a lot more than he shared. "We're looking for somebody," Mayhew said. "The information led us here, so we came to check it out," he said. "Instead it's explosions."

Black smoke seeped out the mountain as the fire burned through the chemicals.

"Who did you expect to find in the lab?" Lisbeth asked.

"The owners," said Mayhew. "We've known about them for a few months. Their distribution center serves nationwide suppliers. We had groomed a confidential source of information that led us here. A scientist. Unfortunately, all contact with that source broke off a few days ago."

Lisbeth saw her chance and took it. "A chemist named David St. John, with red hair and a ponytail?" His brow rose, etching lines on his forehead. Mayhew's expression verified this was the right bet.

"How did you . . . ?"

"My department found David's body a few days back. Murdered," she said. "At the scene there were tracks from a boy who was missing from a nearby ranch. We figured there was a connection, that the boy witnessed the murder. We've been looking for him ever since. We got a call last night from your office that said the boy was here, so here we are." She kept pressing. "Six to one, the person who called me from your office is probably the one you're after. How about a name?"

Mayhew cleared his throat, uncomfortable. "I'm not at liberty to disclose that information."

Denials were confirmation enough for Lisbeth.

A voice crackled over the radio headset. Holst, the officer checking for Sean, said: "Detective, our target in the rocks is David St. John. Or what's left of him. Something chewed him up nasty like. He's chained in place. Repeat. Acquired target is David St. John."

"Hold up, there's something approaching . . ." Holst said, his voice wavering. "Mountain lion!" A burst of gunfire followed.

• • •

The tracks fishtailed toward a mountain base a half mile from their enclave. A deep awareness rushed through Mike, a gut-level feeling that told him the end of the search was near.

Fresh tracks from the boy, made after the storm, pointed towards an alcove.

Mike glanced back at Dagget. Something about the officer's face said he understood this was it, too.

Mike clicked on his Maglite and stepped into the alcove.

Inside, Sean lay, breathless, crumpled against the rock walls. His face was white as ivory.

They raced for the boy at the same time. "Hang in there, Sean!" Dagget said. "You're going to make it, kid!"

Mike held two fingers to Sean's neck. There was a timid pulse, so faint it might as well be his own blood circulating. He leaned in near Sean. The breaths came from miles away, rather than inches from his eardrums.

"He's in shock," said Mike.

Fumbling with the backpack, Dagget removed a syringe and two vials of epinephrine.

Mike unclasped a knife. He sliced into the denim, sheared the fabric of one pant leg halfway up the thigh, then sliced clockwise, and ripped with both hands. The fabric tore away under his grip, exposing part of Sean's leg.

Dipping a cotton swab into alcohol, Dagget sterilized a quarter-sized area on Sean's outer thigh.

"You got the injection or you want me to do it?" asked Mike.

"I got it," said Dagget. He ripped open the syringe packet. On revealing the contents, Dagget yelled, "Aw, no way!"

The needle had sheared in half, and the remaining stub was too shallow to pierce the vial of medication.

Dagget swore, "Damn. It must have broken when we were running into the chamber last night. I bumped against the rocks pretty hard."

"There should be another." Mike remembered that from the beginning, when Shad gave them the tactical bag with equipment: two syringes, two vials.

Dagget found the second syringe. Cradling the package, he peeled away the wrapper. The second needle point had cracked; the busted pieces rolled around in his palm—another useless injector.

Mike missed every syllable of Dagget's curses. His mind was on the problem, not the frustration. The way out of tight spots came by working the angles. There were always options, and sometimes a lack of ones to choose from made spotting the right one easier.

One option was off the table. He hadn't spent three days searching for Sean to watch him die. Especially not over an equipment glitch.

Epinephrine had to be administered via injection. Taken orally, it did nothing. Without it, Sean would not last much longer. He knew even with the medicine, Sean might not make it.

Mike handed Dagget his cell phone, and dashed out of the alcove. Over his shoulder, Mike said, "You stay here and try both of the phones, call for anyone that you think might help. You know the drill."

"Wait!" Dagget asked, panicked. "Where are you going?"

"Looking for something," Mike said.

"What!?"

"I'll know it when I see it."

When he ran, Mike focused on two things. First, using the muscles in his legs, rather than the knees to run. Shifting the impact to the quadriceps protected the weakened joints from further damage. The more abuse his quads shouldered, the less his knees absorbed, the further and faster he pushed. He lunged, dodging mud and standing water.

The second focal point for Mike: a brief image from the previous night. Right before they dove for cover, he had seen a large piece of yellow nylon flapping in the wind near their cave. He had not thought much of the oddity then, and in the morning, he had been so obsessed over the marker business, he never considered what the nylon might be. Now he did. From the dimensions, and the way the wind lifted the fabric, there was only one thing it could be.

A parachute.

Since the chute withstood the gale instead of skating across the valley, it must be fastened to a stationary object, and likely a heavy one.

The best-case scenario was the scenario Mike banked upon—that reinforced ties fastened the chute to a pallet, and kept the parachute from tearing off into the canopy. And reaching the chute, his hopes were confirmed: tied to the pallet was the waylaid gear.

And it held everything they needed.

Sealed in plastic were boxes of food, water, batteries, walkie-talkies, flares and ammunition for the rifle and handgun. Better still, two of their very own disposable cell phones. Mike sliced deeper, burrowing into the stack. In the center, a first-aid kit holding an Auto-injector, preloaded with 1.0 mg of epinephrine. A single shot. A single chance.

He grabbed the cell phones, walkie-talkies, a flare, an energy bar and a bottle of water, distributing them across his available pockets. He tucked the Auto-injector into the kit, clutched the pack, and ran hard for the alcove.

A half mile stood between him and Sean's last chance. Before his knee injury, he once cranked out a five-minute mile. That was on open land, over a trail of loose pebbles and steep ascents, with a twenty-pound load on his back. He had one chance to qualify, but the only penalty for failure that day was humiliation. Now he faced half the distance, and a consequence far harder to forgive.

No holding back; he gave it all he had.

His right knee held until the last ten yards. The buckling beneath his thigh rippled up his quadriceps, and ended at his groin, sending Mike stumbling, sliding, skidding. He yelled for Dagget, who darted out of the alcove.

Dagget gunned for the tracker and the kit in Mike's hands.

Surrendering, Mike's knee resigned, and took his body down. He lobbed the medical kit at Dagget. It spiraled toward the officer, turning end over end through the air.

06:44:37 AM

Mike hit the rocks hard, palms first. He tore the flesh on his hands and scraped a hole through his cargo pants. He hauled himself up. Rattled, shaken, but otherwise okay. Walking was cumbersome. The damaged knee could handle weight-bearing pressures, though not much, and not for very long. He used the walls when necessary for balance.

Dagget caught the kit, the contents intact, ready for use. "You do it," he said. "I don't want to jinx it."

Mike nodded. He arranged Sean in the recovery position. Then with a push on the plunger, he injected 1.0 mg of epinephrine into the boy's thigh muscle. Synthesized adrenaline jolted through Sean's bloodstream.

The boy's physical response to the shot was slower than either man could tolerate. Epinephrine worked best when used early in an attack, and Sean was well into a severe episode, so neither of them deluded themselves that his improvement was guaranteed. Even with treatment the condition could be fatal.

"We're taking you home, Sean," Mike said through clenched teeth. "Come on. Talk to us."

"Breathe, kid," Dagget said. "This ain't your day to die."

Tortured, they counted the moments, anxious and hopeful.

Finally, Sean stirred. His eyes fluttered open, and he hacked, his voice raspy.

"Sweet Jesus, you scared us," Dagget said.

Mike checked Sean's vitals: breathing steadied; heart rate elevated; pulse improved. Regardless, Sean required medical attention, and soon. The epinephrine bought him anywhere from thirty to one hundred and fifty minutes. Beyond that point, he was in severe danger of a secondary attack.

"Any luck calling for help?" Mike asked Dagget. "We need a hospital transport now!"

"Negative. Can't get anyone on either phone," Dagget said. "Batteries are tapped on both."

"Okay, I've got clean phones and batteries for the old ones," Mike said, emptying his pockets. "Also walkie-talkies, and a flare. We need to throw up a call for help. Try Lisbeth first. Use the disposables. Whatever you do, keep your old phone off. Anything comes up, hit me on the walkie-talkie. We can't move Sean yet, and my knee isn't good for much more running."

"So that leaves me . . ." said Dagget, beaming. Mike knew then all Dagget ever wanted was a chance to shine.

Mike loaded a fresh battery into his cell phone, and Dagget did the same, but they kept them both off. Then they tested the walkie-talkies, and switched them to the same channel. Mike enabled the speakerphone setting on the walkie-talkie, and tucked it into a pocket.

"Ready to be a hero?" Mike asked.

Dagget nodded, and racked a bullet into his handgun. "It's about fucking time."

• • •

Firefighters in hazard suits blasted high-powered water streams at the abandoned meth lab. Everything stank of chemicals, metal, and singed powders. Besides the explosives, the lab was empty.

A fire investigator uncovered how the blaze started. An igniter set off a container packed with C-4, courtesy of Crotty's men. Heat from the fire caught a row of pressurized containers filled with nitrous, which exploded. To Lisbeth, the curiosity was that a cell phone triggered the initial blast.

Cell phones were such effective remote triggers—so easy to conceal—that the United States Secret Service blocked service for an undisclosed number of city blocks when the President of the United States appeared in urban centers like New York, Chicago, or Los Angeles. Still, the explosives and the high-tech mechanism seemed unnecessary.

Meth labs were filled with highly unstable chemicals and could explode on their own. If it was an active lab, anyway. There was little need to accelerate what nature made happen for free. Unless, that was, the lab no longer existed at the location and the raw chemicals and equipment had been removed ahead of the demolition.

The officer charged with Erich's overnight interrogation called Lisbeth. "Your suspect is relentless. Stuck to his story like a champion all night. Claims someone stole a few of the disposable phones and planted the weapon near the scene."

"He's lying," Lisbeth said.

"Right, that's what I thought. I almost woke up believing that, too. Swears he's been framed, but has no ideas who did it. Then out of nowhere, dude says that he did have some issues with his cook, Chappy. Apparently, Chappy used to own the place and has been trying to buy it back. The negotiations haven't been going well. Erich refused an offer he made a few weeks ago, and since then, there's been a series of odd incidents. Guests reporting things missing from their rooms, room doors found open, petty cash shortages, and the like. Erich suspected Chappy, but never had enough to prove it."

"Interesting, but it's pretty thin . . ." Lisbeth lit a cigarette.

"Definitely. Until I checked out Chappy. He did a five-year stretch years back. Second degree murder. Put two shots to someone's head with a handgun in a staged break-in. Sound familiar?"

"That's all circumstantial so far."

"But it's not circumstantial that the handgun we found near Shad's place was reported stolen by Erich months ago. He filed an official report."

"Then why is there no record with the county clerk?" Lisbeth said.

"That's a very good question. Because we found a copy of the report at the ranch in Erich's safe. It's legit. Verified it with the clerk and issuing officer. They both remembered him filling it out. But they checked both the paper records and the system, and while there's paperwork for the sequential number matching the one before and after Erich's, his is nowhere to be found. The report just doesn't exist."

"Bring in Chappy, then," Lisbeth said.

"Don't worry; he's in custody. Chappy said Erich had nothing to do with Shad or David St. John. Chappy's working for someone else, trying to get a stake to buy back the ranch. He admitted to injecting Andy's horse with a drug, and dosing Jessica's food. He wouldn't say who the Partner is, but he sang like a little girl about some guy named Crotty. A rogue Homeland Security agent."

All at once, Lisbeth realized who Mayhew was really looking for, and where he was headed.

She reached for her phone to warn Mike.

• • •

Mike offered Sean the water bottle. Next to Sean, the Marlin was propped against a cave wall. Weakened, his face pale, Sean mustered enough strength to drink unassisted. His outward disposition improved further when offered an energy bar. The glucose boost added a little color into his face.

"And this is yours, too." Mike pulled out Sean's watch from the backpack and gave it to the boy, whose eyes popped wide as he bore a huge smile. "Hang tight, Sean," Mike said. "I'll be right back."

"Don't leave me," Sean said in a raspy voice.

"No way. I'm not going anywhere without you."

Since there was no signal in the cave, Mike stepped into the alcove to call Jessica. She needed to get out with Andy immediately.

"I didn't recognize your number." Jessica beat back a yawn. "Are you okay?"

"We're good. We've got Sean. If we can get him a doctor soon, he'll be fine. Take Andy and get the hell out of there. Don't look back. I'm serious this time, Jessica. You know where to go."

"You really did it?" She rather sounded like she didn't believe it, but desperately wanted to. "Is Lisbeth coming with the cavalry?"

"Dagget is in charge of that one."

"You want me to call her just in case? Maybe she needs to hear it more than once?"

"Only if you can do that from the road."

"We're halfway there already," Jessica said. "I promise."

Footsteps approached. Mike loaded the Marlin and walked toward them, staying in the shadows.

The man stood with the sun at his back, the bright light concealing his features. He held a chain of rosary beads. He rubbed the two largest beads together. The smaller plastic spheres clicked as they slipped around in his hand.

"Mike Brody?" the man asked.

06:59:13 AM

Sighting the Marlin, Mike lingered in the shadows. He could rip off a clear shot at any time. "Who's asking?"

"No need to shoot." The man presented a badge in a leather case: R.P. Crotty, Department of Homeland Security. "We heard from Officer Dagget that you found Sean. Nice work! Where is the boy now?"

"Resting inside. He needs medical attention."

"Of course," said Crotty to Mike. Into a walkie-talkie, Crotty said, "Got' em. We're going to need a Medivac, and let the ER doctors at Washington Memorial know it's urgent." Finished with the walkie, he clipped it back to his belt, and offered his hand to Mike. "I am impressed. Who would have thought that one man could find a lost boy in the middle of nowhere? But you pulled it off. Just between you and me, I've been rooting for you since I heard you were involved. You led me right to him."

Mike lowered the rifle, but kept it ready. He did not shake Crotty's hand. "I had lots of help."

"Don't be so modest," said Crotty. "And put the gun away already. How much assistance did you really have, when it came down to it? Officer Dagget doesn't strike me as a very able individual. And there were all kinds of obstacles you tackled, I'm sure. Yet you persevered. Not everyone could do what you did."

"What exactly is Homeland Security's interest in a missing person case?"

"As you probably guessed," Crotty said, "Sean witnessed a murder. The victim is a person of great importance to us, and we're anxious to hear what Sean might have to say about that." He stepped closer to Mike. "I'd like a statement from him before the airlift arrives."

Mike stepped aside. In passing, Crotty glanced at Mike.

But Mike was looking elsewhere.

Glancing over Crotty's shoulder, Mike noticed a track in the soil, one that belonged to neither Sean nor Dagget nor himself. Recognizing the pattern, it shocked him. The tracks from the clearing. The same tracks as the killer. With that realization came responsibility.

"Agent Crotty?" said Mike, his voice casual. Turning to Mike, Crotty paused as if inconvenienced. "I was just wondering if you had any suspects in the murder?"

"I need a statement from Sean first. Government business, you understand." Crotty took another step down the alcove, closer to the cave.

Mike placed a hand on Crotty's shoulder. "Maybe we can talk now."

Crotty reached for his Glock 17, still facing away from Mike. With a clenched fist, Mike rammed the base of Crotty's neck, sending him to his knees. The Glock 17 fell to the ground closer to Mike than Crotty. Crotty rolled, jumped up, and spun around so he faced Mike.

The handgun remained on the rocks.

Crotty punched Mike twice—the first Mike slipped, the second slammed home. Mike relaxed his jaw and turned with the punch as Crotty's fist connected, blunting the shock. Pulling back, Mike sucked in three quick breaths. He was too close to fire the Marlin, he needed more room to raise the gun to his shoulder and absorb the recoil. Crotty rushed him, driving his body against the wall, then tried pinning Mike's upper body. The impact knocked the Marlin from Mike's hands; the rifle smacked against the rocks. Mike broke loose, and knocked Crotty off balance.

Crotty slithered off, too far from either gun. He struggled to his feet. Rising, he said, "Do you think saving Sean will make the faces go away?"

"What faces?"

"The faces you found that day, buried in the woods behind the supermarket. When you called for the excavators and the long poles, everyone expected a body," Crotty said.

Mike remembered . . .

Beneath the last layer of plastic had been a wooden crate. Inside, had been twenty-seven pictures of children—all aged ten—the photos taken by a school photographer. Each had been abducted by the same man over a nine-year period. None had ever seen their family again, except for one. The seventeenth victim escaped from the hideaway, navigated by the stars, and ran more than eleven miles to the interstate. A trucker with a goatee discovered him on the road, and drove him to the police. The papers marveled at the boy's survival skills, though he never discussed the experience with anyone, including the authorities. Widely believed dead by the media, officially the perpetrator remained at large. Mike knew what had happened to the boy; he knew everything that happened, because Mike Brody was the seventeenth victim—the only known survivor.

"I have an offer for you," said Crotty.

"You have nothing to offer me." Mike still pushed the long-repressed images away.

"Maybe I do, Mike. We're not so different, you and I. We were both orphaned at three."

"Congratulations. You want the I-have-abandonment-issues jacket?"

"I know where your abductor is," Crotty said. "You remember him, right? Kendrick Purcell. He kidnapped all those boys. Kidnapped and killed your brother. It was too bad that by the time you led police back to Kendrick's deep-woods lair it was too late for Tommy."

"You're lying," Mike said. "He's dead."

"No, I can assure you, Kendrick Purcell is alive. It may be unfair, but it's true. I can give you all the information you need to find him and a free pass from prosecution. You can do as you see fit to settle the score. Whatever happens is between you and Kendrick."

"If you know where he is," Mike said, "then someone is protecting him."

"That I can't confirm officially," Crotty said. "And trust me, you don't want to know. Let's get to what I want. I could use a man like you, Mike. You've traveled. And you've walked tours right through some very strategic places and gotten out unharmed. My business and supply routes are growing. I need a face for my contacts in Baja to interface with. You meet a few people, shake some hands, and pass some communications along. You wouldn't carry any money or handle any product. Hell, you're doing that ambassador type of stuff already. I just need you to do it for me now and again."

"I'm not passing notes for scum like you," Mike said.

"That's unfortunate. Tell me, does it keep you up at night that you didn't make it back in time to save Tommy?" Crotty said, sneering.

Enraged, Mike used his fist like a hammer and slammed Crotty in the face so hard cartilage cracked.

Crotty's broken nose opened up, gushing blood down his neck. Crotty stumbled for a second, and recovered. He faked high, then kicked at Mike's bad knee.

Mike blocked the assault, partially. Crotty tried again, this time hitting the joint. And that's when the real pain started. Mike slipped. A boot heel found the kneecap and Mike crumpled.

Crotty scooped up the handgun, and aimed it at Mike. "You should have taken my offer . . ."

"Stay down, Mike!" Dagget yelled from the opposite end of the alcove. He centered his semiautomatic USP at Crotty, his hands steady, his Weaver stance perfect.

Before Crotty could turn, Dagget pulled the trigger, firing three shots. The bullets pierced Crotty's heart, and he fell sideways. The only shot Crotty managed bounced harmlessly off the wall above Mike. Stepping up, Dagget kicked the Glock 17 out of Crotty's hands, out of reach. Entry wounds from the bullets showed two-inch groupings, just as Dagget claimed he could manage.

"He's alone, I hope," said Mike.

"Lisbeth scooped up three heavily armed guys not far from here a few minutes ago. Good thing you left that walkie-talkie on in your pocket," explained Dagget. "Or I wouldn't have known what was going on. She tried calling us, but our phones were off . . ."

"Lisbeth is coming?" Mike asked.

"She picked up the flare I fired, so it's her and everyone else. State Police, DEA, the press, you name it," Dagget said. "Apparently Jessica called some people, too. There's a press conference later. Let's get Sean and go. I want to sleep in a real bed tonight."

Dagget helped Mike to his feet for the second time that day. As they passed Crotty, he gasped, and reached for Dagget. "The . . . Partner . . ." Crotty said. Blood gurgled out of his throat. Crotty collapsed on the rocks. The combined shock of the wounds was fatal. A chain of rosary beads lay broken next to his body.

"So you're not going to arrest me, Dagget?" Mike asked.

"Oh, we'll get you out of here and your knee fixed up. Then I cite you." This time Dagget said it clearly tongue in cheek. "The good kind. You know, signed by the mayor."

Tired and broken, Mike Brody stepped into the last flickers of a sunrise as a helicopter flew over the mountain.

Often Mike Brody said he would know what he was looking for when he found it. This time it had been Sean Jackson. Even on this search, he was seeking more than a lost child. He was looking for a mission to heal his childhood wounds. And he knew that whatever happened to him, whatever the consequences or risks, he would never stop searching for the missing. Mike could never stop searching, even if the next time was the time he was too late.

Two weeks later

Dagget called Mike Brody at the tracker's home in California. The men had not spoken to each other since the morning they emerged from the woods with Sean and faced the hordes of press and law-enforcement officials. The crowd was a zoo, the likes of which only someone with Jessica's extensive contacts could summon on short notice. Mike left Dagget to deal with it, drifting past the reporters who held cameras and microphones toward them like jousting sticks.

"How's the knee?" Dagget asked.

"Better." Since the surgery Mike hobbled intermittently, and used a crutch when the painkillers wore off. He faced five more weeks of physical therapy, strength training, and aerobics. He had been down this road before, and knew he would recover, though the process would take a lot longer than he wanted. It was the nature of knee injuries—an instant to tear badly, months to heal.

"I wanted to thank you again for saving my life on that cliff," Dagget said.

"You saved mine, too," Mike said. "Thanks for that. Hey, I owe you an explanation still. I promised if we found Sean, I'd tell you why I track."

"We're even," Dagget said. "If you want to tell me someday, you will. Anyway, I'm sorry I didn't call earlier, but an investigation I'm running took all my time. I was calling to thank you for something else." He said this thoughtfully. "It was very humble of you to let Lisbeth and I take all the credit in the papers."

"No problem. You looked distinguished in those pictures, by the way," Mike said.

"They all wanted to know who you were," Dagget said, "and you just walked away with a wink and a nod and rode to the hospital with your family. The coverage has done a ton of good for the department. Lisbeth managed to get more funding and personnel."

"That's good. You said you were running an investigation . . ."

"Yeah," Dagget said. "The chief is making me a detective—second-grade."

"Congratulations!" Mike said.

"The announcement surprised Lisbeth a bit, but as she might say, what the chief decrees, don't dispute, though feel free to doubt under your breath. Can I ask you a personal question?"

"Anything."

"How are things with you and Jessica these days?"

"We've been talking more, and laughing together. In fact, we have a dinner date tonight. She's coming over in a few minutes."

"Oh," Dagget said, with a barely perceptible sigh.

"I don't mean to cut you off. Is there something else?"

"Let's just say, things are better than ever with the girlfriend. But, speaking of Jessica, I guess Lisbeth shut her out of a pretty good article."

"No worries. She wrote another piece." Jessica had sold a review of dude ranches to an adventure magazine. A real light piece for middle-aged suburbanites. "It worked out for everyone, I think."

"You're one hundred percent right. Everyone got what he deserved. This guy Crotty was a lot dirtier than anyone suspected. He was running an empire behind the scenes. The DEA is still trying to sort through it all."

"Heard anything about Sean?" Mike asked.

"The kid is doing great. Lisbeth saw those bruises on Faith Jackson's arms and called out Sean's dad on it. He's going to anger-management counseling, and all three are also going to family therapy."

Mike was pleased to hear that. "I hope it works for them. Did anything ever come of the skeletons you found?"

"Yes, in fact," Dagget said. "Their discovery closed out two missing persons reports that have been open for two years. We ID'd them through dental records. Looks like they both had dealings with Crotty."

"Did my coordinates for the potential facility pan out?"

"Direct hit. Lisbeth will probably call you about that. She raided a plant a few days ago. All that state-of-the-art equipment is scheduled for destruction. Didn't find any personnel, but they got the chemicals and a weapons cache."

"One thing that bothers me," Mike said. "These meth labs are usually tiny. How did they get such large quantities of the raw materials like pseudoephedrine? There are a lot of laws restricting its purchase at the retail and wholesale level."

"Went right to the source. They stole truckloads of it en route to manufacturing plants. Mostly in the US, but also in Mexico and Canada. Thanks to NAFTA, it doesn't take much to get a truck past the borders. Every so often they lose a load, but it keeps on coming. You know, I'm sure glad Crotty is dead. He was dangerous and insane. Inside his apartment they found journal after journal, stuffed in a safe. And you know what was on the pages? Four words, scrawled over and over, sixteen thousand times. Exactly the same way. *The Partner must die.*"

"I still wonder about Erich being the Partner . . ."

"Erich is a good front, charming, and no one suspected he would do something like that for money. Plus he's a pilot, which helps when you need materials moved around. And clearly Crotty needed help like that, because the records show the company was too big for a single person to manage. Crotty handled back-office operations, got rid of witnesses and threats to the company, while someone else ran the business day to day. Crotty didn't care for personnel issues, so that fell on Erich. Or the Partner, as I should say."

"What about Chappy? Didn't he claim the Partner was somebody else?"

"What he said was Crotty killed David St. John, and not Erich. And Chappy is not saying anything these days. A guard found him hanging in his cell, dangling from his belt last week. Besides, consider the source. Chappy committed at least one homicide, and ultimately all roads end at Erich. Especially since there's even more evidence than before. The FBI raided a guy named Regani's house and a box of records turned up details about the financial intricacies of the partnership. The auditors are still working to sort them out, but everything on those pages demonstrates a collusion between Crotty and Erich."

Mike remembered another detail. "Did you make out what Crotty said about the Partner? Right before he died?"

"Ah, dying men can say anything. They rarely make sense."

Downstairs, there was a knock at the front door. Jessica must be early for their dinner date. A bit ahead of schedule, but he could deal with the last-minute change of plans.

"I should get that," Mike said.

"Okay," Dagget said. "I feel like I keep forgetting to tell you something . . ."

There was another knock at the door.

"Before you go," Dagget said, "I just remembered what I wanted to tell you. The results just came back for that water bottle Jessica sent us. First, there was a small perforation in the top of the bottle, exactly the size of a hypodermic needle. Second, there was a chemical agent inside the liquid. Someone certainly dosed the water."

"With what?" Mike wondered if it happened that day when Jessica found the room open and the maid down the hall.

"That's the scary part. It's unprecedented. It's odorless, clear, and has no taste. It's virtually impossible to detect in the bloodstream. We figure it's one of David St. John's creations. That's probably why Crotty killed David. To keep his secret formula safe. The lab has no idea what exactly the substance is or its chemical structure, other than it affects the nervous system in all sorts of disturbing ways. In small amounts, it causes a pronounced sense of euphoria. In large amounts, dehydration, violent outbursts, blackouts, even death. It could be mixed or added to anything. Food, drink, hand soap, whatever, and the person who came in contact with it would never notice. Good thing we got this stuff out of circulation before it hit the street."

Another knock—this one three quick taps.

"I'm out, Detective Dagget. Congratulations again. We should catch up some time."

"Absolutely. Say hi to Jessica for me. And good luck to you both. And if you think of anything that might help, give me a call."

Mike reached for the brass knob, the metal cool to the touch, and turned it slowly.

The oak door opened under Mike's grip. He smiled at the beautiful woman on the other side of the frame.

"I didn't expect you this early," Mike said to Jessica. "Come on in."

"Before I do, I want to ask you something." She looked a bit vulnerable, which was familiar to Mike, but almost forgotten for the tough times.

"Sure."

"Is us being apart working for you?" For once Jessica Barrett asked a question that sounded like one to Mike Brody.

Mike cleared his throat. "No."

She breathed deeply. "Why doesn't it work when we're together?"

"I want it to work," Mike said. "I always wanted us to work."

"Could it?" Jessica asked.

Mike hesitated at first, moving slowly, unsure if she would reciprocate, until their lips connected.

Jessica stepped inside the house, and shut the oak door.

Seconds later . . .

When he finished his call with Mike, Dagget ripped the battery out of the phone and tossed both into the cold water flowing at the base of a mountain. The disposable phone drifted in the frothy current. It followed a few others. Destination: far, far downstream. He kept the voice scrambler Crotty built, though; the device was invaluable at disguising one's identity.

He was glad that things ended well for Mike and Jessica. He never wanted them to get hurt again. They had suffered enough over the case. He would have preferred they had never been involved at all. But he never had control over that. And unfortunately, accidents happened at the worst of times. Or seemed to, at least. After all, one day Chappy started blabbing he wanted to make a full confession and never woke up again.

It cost a lot of money to convince the coroner to overlook the blunt-head trauma and rule the death a suicide. Shame of it was that Chappy was a great inside man. He hated to lose him. He paid the coroner off anyway.

The real coup was swapping out Crotty's journals at his apartment. Crotty had explicitly named the Partner dozens of times within the pages, as well as detailing an entirely new operations guide for running the company. Replacing the original journals with ones filled with a single line ad infinitum completed the profile of Crotty the obsessive killer. Better yet, the new playbooks he inherited were filled with some great ideas for expanding the business. He could use them. There was other information within the pages, too. Unexpected revelations he must confront.

Dagget stepped into a sedan, fell into the deep bench seat, and relaxed. He adjusted the mirror, smiling at the reflection. He was a good-looking man if he did say so, and he decided right then and there to let the tight-cropped hair grow out a bit. Get enough length on top so he could part his hair. That sort of style was more befitting a detective. He could hardly wait for his former father-in-law to pin that silver shield to his uniform. Not that they were even; he still had a few scores to settle with the old man. In due time.

In the passenger seat, the Partner drank champagne. Dagget

watched her take a modest sip. The bottle looked good in Cara's perfectly manicured hands. Like it belonged.

Now it was time for celebrating.

Things had been going great since the search wrapped. Fresh news clippings from around the world about him covered his new office walls. Sure, a few nagging questions lingered in the rumor mill, but Dagget could head those off easily enough. He was making enough money to deal with most any irritant.

Yes, the second facility Crotty built on the sly—the twin plant that Lisbeth never knew about—paid off handsomely. Just for Dagget instead of Crotty. It proved more efficient than he could ever have imagined, pumped out more product than he believed, and generated more revenue than he could spend. Thanks to David St. John's magnum opus formulation, the one Chappy dosed Jessica with, he had a lock on a whole new market from the top-down, and no competition.

Keeping employees happy always boiled down to a question of loyalty. Crotty never understood that. Everyone was expendable, Crotty always claimed. That was Crotty's mistake.

Dagget would not be so shortsighted. He could not afford to be. In the end, it was only people that mattered. He would take care of his employees; his employees would take care of him. Because, like Dagget said to Mike, everyone got what he deserved.

"So it's done," Cara asked.

"Isn't it always when you let me handle things?"

"Well then, champagne?"

Dagget took a hearty swig from the bottle. He leaned back in the seat, one hand on the Cristal, the other over Cara's shoulder and neck. She kissed him. "That was good," Dagget said.

"Which? The champagne or the kiss."

"It's all good, Mrs. Regani," Dagget said.

"Not for much longer." Cara seemed to groan this more than she said it. "The divorce papers are already filed. And legally, I never was Mrs. Regani. I didn't take his last name for a reason, you know. Never felt right. I told you that before."

"Do you miss him?" Dagget asked.

"My husband? That, as they say, obviously didn't work out."

"I mean Crotty. Your boyfriend."

Cara took a deep breath. "How did you know?"

"It was all in the journals Crotty kept," Dagget said. "He wanted to go away with you and start a new life."

"Obviously, he didn't know me very well," Cara said. "And at the end of the day, Crotty was a cheap bastard. That's why I'm with you. You understand my needs."

"Crotty did love money above everything." Dagget paused. "When we get married, will you take my last name?"

Cara pulled in close, as if she might kiss Dagget again. Instead she traced the profile of his face with her first two fingers. She stopped at his chin. Pulling her hand back, she almost smiled. "You do know you're still working for me, right?"

Acknowledgments

To co-opt a maxim from my grandfather's day: behind every man with an idea is a better woman. In my case, it's more like several dozen women and some men. And they stand, or rather have stood, beside me through the years. The list below is by no means exhaustive, but every name represents a real person who made a fundamental difference in my journey; they made me a better writer and person.

First, my mother fed my reading habit from the very beginning. Some mothers give out milk and cookies. Mine served *A Wrinkle in Time* and *Fahrenheit 451*.

In school, several teachers encouraged me more than the rest: Brenda Bigelow and Dr. Mary Balkun, though I was a mediocre student to your considerable talents as instructors. Sorry I was young and stupid. Fortunately you both forgave my insecurities and nudged me in positive ways.

A crew of readers guided the various drafts with their feedback and suggestions. Matt De Vries for his weapons expertise and unflinching ability to call me out for a weak draft; Lt. John A. Dunay (Ret.) for insights on police procedures and gun handling; a few confidential sources who must remain anonymous; Oriana Leckert—tight edits and solid suggestions; Katie Boyer, master of the intricacies of male and female psyches—you were always concise; Jen and Jaysen Lesage, good friends, good ideas; Sheryl Chisholm—I'll build a leaf fort with you any time; Spike Grobstein, a fellow tech who asked the hard questions at the right moments and always got what I was trying to do, even when it wasn't on the page; Erin Amanda Grambling, an eagle-eyed editor if there ever was one; Jacki Meinert, my favorite hippie; Kerry Johnson, a divine editor—how I hated your electronic markup notes, especially when they hit the mark; Kayla Selans, Internet Hosting Goddess—your instant messages kept me going on the long nights; Jake Freedman, of Freedman Tire and Auto on Route 27 in Edison, NJ, you are the greatest mechanic a used car owner could know. Thanks for keeping my old vehicles humming like new all these years.

Elynn Cohen crafted an awesome cover; I love her work.

When a student is ready, the master appears. Many individuals taught my psyche lessons I could receive only from them. Gene Mitelman taught me about quality control, the value of persistence, and to accept only my very best effort; Bill and Susan Schoonover taught me that a good relationship takes the hardest work of all and nets the greatest rewards—with any luck I'll get that right someday; Dr. David Potter DC taught me that pain is an aberration, rather than a normal condition of existence.

A number of people offered friendship and support during this project: Todd Ellis, Susan Busfield, Michelle DeVries, Mario and Jamee Guerra, Ron Picone, Elena Bogan, Jim Biglan—the best boss on the planet, hands down, Ayanna Hill-Gill, Joan Del Negro, Justin Saporito, Jamie Cooper, Gwen Burleigh, George Schneider, Fran Sonneborn, Don Chisholm, Leslie Burns Patient, Steve "Comedy Madman" Patient, Jason "Pain Bringer" Gibson. Steve gets an extra shout-out for the book trailer. Speaking of the trailer, Jason Gibson earns another mention for the fight choreography and the months of martial arts instruction. Extra special thanks for not killing me.

I would be remiss to exclude Ian Rogers, who has quite a few great novels and stories in him, and the lovely Kathryn Verhulst-Rogers, so I shall mention them twice. Thanks, Ian and Kathryn.

When I stopped trying to meet women, inexplicably the right one appeared. Lisa Sisler, thanks for your strength, courage and love. May your considerable writing talents and commitment to the craft yield all the rewards you deserve. You had me at Hemingway, DB.

Still others helped in a different way. Whenever I felt low about prospects for *The Last Track*, encouragement arrived from unlikely sources, often phrased in the form of a rejection letter. I kept the kind notes and shredded the rest.

Over and over again, the story itself provided all the reasons I needed to persevere. Ultimately, I continued for Mike Brody's sake as much as my own. In a strange way, we believe in each other and always will. He'll never stop searching and I'll never stop writing. No matter how long the odds.

About the Author

S am lives outside of NYC with his girlfriend and an army of
four cats—one feline under the legal limit. Working at an all-
girls boarding school, he knows world-class drama firsthand. It's
also the reason he studies Krav Maga and Tai Chi.

Reading Guide available for download at:
www.buddhapussink.com

To schedule Sam to speak with your Book Group,
contact: Marketing@buddhapussink.com

Web site: http://samhilliard.com
Facebook: http://facebook.com/thelasttrack
Twitter: http://twitter.com/samhilliard

Sam Hilliard
c/o Buddhapuss Ink LLC
518-7 Old Post Road #323
Edison, NJ 08817

Made in the USA
Charleston, SC
04 February 2010